TOPAZ DREAMS

CRYSTAL MAGIC #2

PATRICIA RICE

Book View
Café

Topaz Dreams
Patricia Rice

Copyright © 2018 Patricia Rice
Book View Cafe, May 2018
First Publication: 2018

This is a work of fiction. Any references to historical events, real people, or real locales are used fictitiously. Other names, characters, places, and incidents are the product of the author's imagination, and any resemblance to actual events or locales or persons, living or dead, is entirely coincidental.

Published by Rice Enterprises, Dana Point, CA, an affiliate of Book View Café Publishing Cooperative
Cover design by Kim Killion
Map design by Melissa Stevens, The Illustrated Author
Book View Café Publishing Cooperative
P.O. Box 1624, Cedar Crest, NM 87008-1624
http://bookviewcafe.com

ISBN ebook: 9781611387315
ISBN print: 9781611387322

～

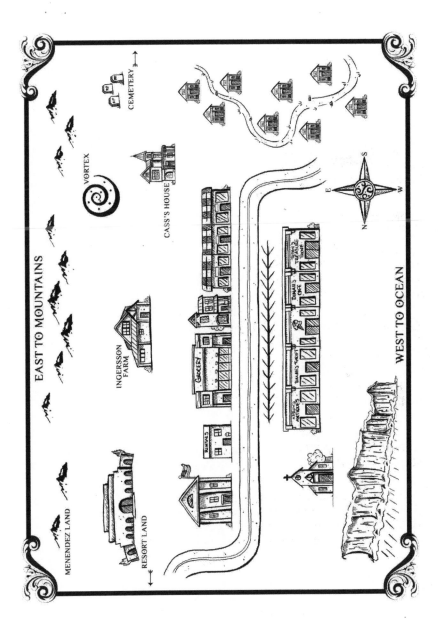

ONE

"WHAT A DUMP!" QUOTING OLD MOVIES RATHER THAN POLLUTE THE MINDS of innocents, Theodosia Devine-Baker gaped at the faded gray clapboard shop her parents and grandparents had once called home—the safe haven they still owned, and she'd hoped to occupy.

She didn't need her weird empathy to warn that her happy childhood home was not only a wreck but haunted. It had Stephen King's signature written all over the rotting window frames.

In their desperate flight up to this California mountain-town, she'd recognized the town's welcome sign of HILLVALE, SPIRITUAL HOME OF 325 LIVES AND COUNTLESS GHOSTS with glee and relief.

She hadn't realized the sign was literal.

"Gotta pee, Aunt T!" the four-year-old Goth in the back of the aging van cried.

Maybe she could become a cartoonist. There was definitely a comic panel in the scene of the battered and peeling sixties-era van parked in front of an ancient hippie crystal shop in a town the world had left behind half a century ago.

Her family had lived above the shop until she was six or seven, and she hadn't been back since, so her memories were obviously rose-colored. Would the plumbing still work? Hadn't the rental agency done *anything* in twenty-plus years?

The kids, and what they claimed was a dog, had been cooped up in the van for hours on the drive here. She couldn't hide them any longer. Taking a deep breath and winging a prayer to any Omnipotence passing by, Teddy beat at the van door handle until it opened, then kicked the door wide. The sheepdog-labradoodle mutt whined until she cranked open the back door so the creature could fall out. The animal was ancient. Teddy suspected it was more sheep than dog.

She hoped there weren't any cops watching. The rolling wreck the kids climbed out of didn't have child restraints. It barely had seats. That reason alone had been excuse enough to buy it—to hide her niece and nephew on the floorboards. It wasn't as if the van could reach speeds of more than fifty, and she'd stayed off the freeways as much as possible. Her sister hadn't given her more than a few days to plan this escapade.

It was a relief to have reached safety—or what she had *imagined* would be a safe harbor for the next few months. Her imagination had always been overactive.

With trepidation, she glanced up at the burned-out swathe of mountain above the town. There were varying degrees of safety, even here. That fire had been recent and a close call. It might mean mudslides this winter, but that wasn't her immediate concern.

Digging the ancient key out of her jeans pocket, she crossed the rickety boardwalk and inserted it in a door that hadn't been painted since Noah sailed the ark. She vaguely remembered it as having once been a magical periwinkle blue.

The key didn't fit. She glared at a relatively new doorknob. *Fu. . . Frigging heck.* Teddy glanced down at the six- and four-year-old following her every word and move.

It was like being watched by Pugsley and Wednesday from the Addams Family. Teddy had dyed their beautiful red curls black, used a straightener on them, and then cut bangs so they no longer resembled their strawberry-blond mother. Teddy's hair was a more fiery auburn-red and hadn't taken the dye well. She hadn't been able to bear straightening and cutting it, so she was wearing her tangled mop in a braid pinned tightly and hidden under a knit cap. She probably looked like a jewel thief instead of a jeweler.

Jeb danced from foot to foot, holding the front of his pants like any good, red-blooded male.

Her usual humor dampened by circumstances, Teddy stomped her heeled ankle boots down the boardwalk to the sagging alley gate. It, at least, opened. Glancing over her shoulder to see who might be watching, she gestured kids and dog inside.

Hillvale was much smaller than she remembered. Despite the brave gaiety of painted planters spilling with multi-colored blossoms lining the boardwalk, the line of structures on either side of the barely-paved road showed little sign of improvement since she'd lived here. Cracked and faded adobe buildings sat side-by-side with the teetering remnants of what could have been frontier storefronts like hers. Once upon a time, all the shop owners had lived above their shops, if they were so fortunate as to have one of the larger structures. It didn't look as if anyone lived here now. She hoped the diner was still down the street because the kids would be starving soon.

A few customers lingered in front of a grocery across the highway dividing the town. They watched with curiosity, but that was any small town. Teddy didn't know if anyone would remember her. She was hoping it wouldn't matter out of the city and out of sight.

The back doorknob had been changed too. *Darnation.* She wondered if editing epithets constituted good nurturing. Since Jeb was already urinating on a pear cactus, she figured Sydony hadn't reared him any better than Teddy was doing.

Sullen silent Mia clung to her sheep-dog's collar and looked around in disdain—worldly cynicism from a six-year-old.

The dirt yard was buried in a layer of gray ash and sported a few straggling weeds and rocks. The tree stump she'd used as a tea table when she was a kid had rotted and developed mushrooms. Pines overhung the fence from the steep downside of the mountain behind the house. There would be cabins beyond the fence, hidden among the evergreens, scattered down the mountainside. She could just barely see the roof of one below.

She studied the dirty windows of the kitchen and second story. Breaking and entering wouldn't be a good example for the kids.

Producing the backpack she'd learned to carry when she was with her niece and nephew, Teddy set it on the stump. "I need to hunt down the keys, kids. Feed the fairies with your snacks and keep Prince Hairy company until I get back, okay?"

Her sister had named the dog when she'd rescued it, back when Mia was a baby. Teddy was pretty certain her niece didn't recognize the reference.

Clothed all in black, her little Goths dug into the backpack in a manner as uncivilized as the original barbarians. She knew Prince Hairy wouldn't go anywhere. His main advantage was that he was big and had protruding fangs ferocious enough to scare strangers.

Teddy checked her cellphone for messages as she closed the gate and returned to the street. No bars. *Frigging darn heck.* How would she know if Syd was all right?

First things first. They needed a roof over their heads. She had used a library computer to e-mail the rental company named in the contract from their parents' lockbox, told them she would be arriving and to not let the house out this summer. But this business of sneaking around and covering her trail didn't come naturally. She hadn't been certain if she should call to confirm.

And now she couldn't even check her phone to see if another e-mail had arrived. Passing a few window-shoppers, she clunked down the warped boardwalk, hunting signs for the rental agency. Her house was at the entrance to town. The two-story town hall was on the far end, across the street. Thankfully, the diner was still a few doors down from her parents' old shop, with CAFÉ on the plate glass window in chipped gold letters. It looked busy, so that was a good sign.

She was actually feeling a little better about Hillvale after passing a consignment clothing store with an upscale cross-dressing mannequin in the window and an antique store displaying genuine Victorian garnets. She didn't need walk-in customers, but if these stores drew broad-minded clientele with deep pockets, she might actually find a new market for her designs. That would give her the breathing room she needed to experiment with the gift she'd just discovered and push her business in a different direction that wouldn't require so much travel.

The rental agency had a business sign in the downstairs window and curtains upstairs. At least this door was painted. She pushed it open onto a sparse office with a desk, a couple of faded chairs, and a paper calendar with a silvery fish photo on the wall. An older man with thinning gray hair, sagging jowls, and a tailored navy blazer looked up. The name plaque on his desk said Xavier Black.

"Hi, I'm Teddy Baker." She'd dressed the part of harried aunt in jeans and plaid cowboy shirt, so she figured she didn't come across as one of the wealthy tourists that occupied the resort above the town. "I e-mailed you about the Baker property?"

Mr. Black stood, looming over her as most people did. "Miss Baker, a pleasure. We haven't had any Bakers here in over twenty years, if I remember correctly."

"Well, my mother's cousin stayed here after we left, but she was married to a Thompson. I understand after she moved out that our parents turned the property over to you to rent?"

He looked exceedingly uncomfortable. *Uh-oh.* He gestured at one of the chairs. "There seems to be a misunderstanding. Won't you take a seat?"

She had strong nerves, but she'd never been responsible for kids before. Her world had turned violent and ugly these last months. She needed a safe new one. Teddy's insides knotted, and she had to deliberately refrain from clutching her fingers into fists.

She perched on the edge of the vinyl-upholstered chair. "What misunderstanding? I have a key." *One that didn't work.* "I have a deed. I have the rental contract. I let you know I was coming."

He laced his fingers together on the desk. "I had to look up the property. It hasn't been listed in your father's name in decades. The Kennedy Corporation purchased it from the Thompsons when they moved out."

Teddy sat stunned. All their plans for escape. . . She couldn't let Sydony down like this. She shook her head until the stupid cap almost came off, rummaged in the messenger bag she carried on her shoulder, and produced the documents from the lockbox. "My parents *own* that property. I have the deed. The Thompsons never bought it from us. They merely took care of it until they could buy their own place. I even have letters from my mother's cousin Thalia with the date she planned to move out, plus the rental contract with your agency."

Their parents were in Malaysia, but they'd left the keys and documents with their lawyer to be used as needed. Surely they wouldn't have left a deed to a house they no longer owned.

Mr. Black looked worried as he perused her documents. "I will have to call Mr. Kennedy and ask for his paperwork. I can call the property tax office, but I've been handling the expenses, and I know he's been paying the taxes and maintenance."

"Maintenance," she snorted. "The place doesn't look as if it's been lived in since California became a state."

"Well," he looked even more uneasy. "It's been a difficult property to rent. Let me call Mr. Kennedy."

Seething, Teddy stood. "You do that. I'll be at the café."

She would not lose her temper. She would not get flustered. She would be calm and patient and not rip the graying hair off an old man's head. She marched out and back to the house, where she gathered up Goth One and Goth Two and paraded them over to the café. His Hairy Royal Majesty was quite happy to remain in his sunlit bed in the yard.

Teddy took the kids to the restroom to wash their hands, then came out to find a sturdy waitress with a lovely black braid adorned in beads waiting with plastic menus.

Teddy wanted to wash the dye out of her hair right now. Her pale skin would never look as natural against black as this bronzed local's.

"I'm Mariah," the waitress said, steering them to an open booth. "Can I bring you anything to drink?"

"Coke!" both Goths piped up.

"Lemonade," Teddy corrected. "And unless you have whiskey straight up, I'll just take water, please."

"Mama lets us have Coke," Mia protested, sliding down in the booth in a sulk that suited her black bangs and sinister black t-shirt with a frowning emoticon. Mia had chosen that one herself. Teddy could scarcely blame her. Her niece's world had been torn in two, then ripped again.

Jeb lay his black hair on the table and sucked his thumb—probably not a good sign.

"We saw you over at the old Thompson place," a plump, cuddly woman not much older than Teddy said from her stool at the counter.

Her auburn hair had a more orange cast than Teddy's natural red, and she wore enough bangles to ring like a wind chime. "I tried setting up shop there when I first arrived, but the apparition refused to share."

Teddy wasn't certain how to respond to that. She was accustomed to sensing strong energies that others didn't, but she was not used to other people blatantly stating weird stuff she thought only she knew.

Unfazed by Teddy's silence, the chatty woman continued, "I'm Amber. That's my shop across the street." She nodded at the window.

The shops visible from this perspective were the grocery and a tarot reader. *Oh goody.* That explained a lot. Teddy smiled in anticipation.

"Happy to meet you, Amber. I'm Teddy Baker." She and Sydony had decided their father's last name was common enough that it wouldn't be easily traced while she was traveling, and gave the added benefit of matching Teddy's ID, if not her professional or full name. Now that they were in Hillvale, there would be no concealing who she was, but there was no reason for Assbutt aka Butthead to know about Hillvale.

"This is Goth One and Goth Two," she pointed her fingers at the sulking kids.

Mia glared. "My name is Mia. My mama used to live here."

Oh well, it didn't take long to take that cat out of the bag. She'd known it wouldn't be easy. Mariah merely swung her beaded braid and departed in search of drinks—not exactly the chatty waitress stereotype.

When she returned with lemonade, Teddy ordered sweet potato fries and veggie burgers for all. Mia demanded a hot dog. Jeb drooled. Before Teddy's patience frayed, Mariah waved a pencil like a magic wand. "Dinah will fix just what you need, wait and see."

"Dinah is magic," Amber said, standing up from her stool. "She always knows what we need, although we don't get kids in here a lot. If you're planning on living in the Thompson place, we can try smudging it again. We're more powerful now that Mariah and Sam are here. Just let Dinah know, and we'll be right over."

As Amber departed, Teddy clicked her boot heels under the table and whispered in delight, "We're not in Kansas anymore, Toto."

She was just exactly where she needed to be while the outside world took care of itself. When their meal arrived, Dinah's fabulous sweet potato pie and crunchy green bean fries improved her outlook. The kids happily dug into vegetables disguised as junk, and Teddy almost felt as if she might conquer this motherhood thing—eventually.

The mysterious Dinah did not appear. Mariah took Teddy's cash at an old-fashioned register. With her decorated braid, the waitress looked like a Disney version of a Native American princess. Teddy was relieved to note that flannel and jeans were the correct attire for blending in, so far as it was possible to blend in a place that ghosts called home.

She took the kids back to the restroom, then carried a sleepy Jeb back to the house, with Mia trailing along, clinging to her shirttail. They'd been through a lot these last few days, so a little clinging was well deserved.

It was cool enough up here on the foggy mountain to feel safe cranking down the van windows and leaving the kids in their bedrolls to nap. She allowed them to run back and fetch Prince Hairy and load him up. Jeb liked to sleep with the dog. Mia would play with her Nintendo or read instead of sleeping. Either way, she was out of the way of confrontation.

Because Teddy wasn't feeling good about the housing situation at all.

Even as she emerged from tucking in the kids, she saw Mr. Black strolling across the parking lot with a broad-shouldered exec in a stiff tie and tailored business suit. This must be the Mr. Kennedy who thought he owned her house.

Her Inner Monitor wasn't reliable and often painful, so she'd quit using it long ago. Recent events had taught her the hard way that was a serious mistake. With the kids to protect, she needed all the extra help she could summon. She reluctantly tuned in as the pair approached.

She slammed into a sensation akin to hitting a stone bluff at a hundred miles an hour. She froze, trying to assess the experience. Instead of radiating energy, the exec was like a powerful magnet—who *buried his power*. Did that make sense? Hastily shutting down her inner senses, she studied him warily, expecting a demon beneath the sophisticated attire.

The tailored civilization of a suit barely disguised the muscular grace of an athlete. Thick-lashed brown eyes matched styled hair burnished to the color of rich mahogany. With his deep tan and stubborn jaw, he appeared only a few years older than she, and definitely not demon material. She'd categorize him with any wealthy man who got his own way too often, except there were tired lines around his eyes and mouth that said life wasn't treating him as well as expected.

"Miss Baker?" he said, holding out a manicured hand as he joined her on the boardwalk. "Kurt Kennedy. Xavier says we have a problem?"

The electrical zap of their joined hands should have warned her.

TWO

JUNE 25: AFTERNOON

PRIMED TO COMBAT AN ANGRY AMAZON WITH THE SUAVE ASSURANCES
that worked so well on the resort's guests, Kurt Kennedy froze at sight
of a flannel-clad, knit-capped butterfly in boots. Why did he have this
vision of her with sunset curls and fairy wings? He mentally smacked
himself and tried to concentrate on his annoyance, but he couldn't stop
trying to puzzle out conflicting appearances.

Teddy Baker, even garbed in men's clothing, was vibrantly female.
Her miniature size came in a luscious package of curves that she
emphasized with heeled boots and stretch denim. He couldn't shake
the image of a fiery redhead even though her lashes and brows were
artfully painted in black. And a black widow's peak peered out from
beneath her ridiculous cap. Her size said she ought to be frail and
feminine, but her attitude. . . was pure spitting dragon. He swore he
saw sparks.

"I would like the key to my property," she said in a purring tone
that belied the flashing fire of golden-brown eyes.

The disaster of this past week had drilled a hole in his soul. A
month ago, he wouldn't have even bothered to listen to her spurious

claim on his dream. Now. . . everything he knew was wrong. His hope of preventing the resort and all its employees from sliding into bankruptcy was down to replacing the crumbling structures of Hillvale before they fell off the mountain. This dilapidated ruin should have been bulldozed a decade ago—and he was the one who knew how to rebuild it.

Fatalistically, he handed her the folder he'd located in his files, instead of whacking her with it. So, they were both suppressing rage. He was generally reluctant to explain himself, but this had to be done. "I'm sorry, Miss Baker. I have the deed of sale here, properly recorded in the clerk's office over ten years ago. We will be happy to rent the property to you, if you choose to stay, but the Kennedy Corporation owns most of Hillvale. The town wouldn't be standing otherwise."

That was the truth as he knew it. If he were to believe the town witches led by his Aunt Cass, he was an ignorant Null with no clue. It had been easier maintaining the distance he needed to make decisions about the town's future by running the lodge and leaving the rental property to Xavier. His damned brother was supposed to be the liaison with the people, but as mayor, Monty walked a fine line between their family's interests and Hillvale's. Kurt had to respect his brother's difficulty in dealing with a town where half the inhabitants hated Kennedys.

The artful butterfly glanced at the deed, flipped through his file, returned it, and produced the same documents Xavier had said she'd showed him.

"My parents inherited that house, lock, stock, and barrel, no mortgage attached. They allowed my mother's cousin and her husband to live in it after we moved out. They never, at any time, sold it to them. I fear your family was duped if they claim anything else. I understand the spouse spent time in jail, so it's possible that Lonnie was not an honest man. Not that I've met many honest men," she added cynically.

And not that Hillvale was filled to the brim with honest men, Kurt mentally added. There were days he almost believed the witches when they claimed that evil ate men's souls here. But the law was basic and conclusive.

"We have maintained the property for over ten years. You will have to hire a lawyer to prove our deed is fraudulent. Your family effectively abandoned the property, so your standing is not as sound as ours. I'm sorry, Miss Baker, facts are facts."

A line formed in the faint freckles over her upturned nose. "I have two children in that van who need a home, Mr. Kennedy. I have a business I need to run. I can't wait for lawyers to fight it out. I'm not poor, and I *will* fight. But right now, they need beds to sleep in. I'll rent the place, with the understanding that the money will be returned once the court rules in our favor."

He felt guilty taking her money for that deathtrap. For her own good, he needed to disillusion her about living here. "This is prime vacation rental season, Miss Baker. We normally charge fifteen hundred a week, six thousand a month."

Her neatly outlined eyebrows shot up. "I doubt my grandparents paid six thousand to *buy* the place. I'll give you a thousand a month, provided utilities are functioning and included."

"For my company to bring the property up to standard would *cost* more than six thousand," he retorted. "You're better off going down the mountain and looking for an apartment."

"I can't run my business in an apartment. And I can't watch the children all summer unless they stay where I work." Her fancy boot heels clicked as she paced back and forth on the boardwalk.

Shoppers didn't normally come to this empty end of town, but Kurt was aware of the locals watching from behind curtains and shopfronts. His spine itched. Monty was better at dealing with people, but his brother was in the county seat, arranging to hire a police chief to prevent any more dangerous situations like the one that had burned the mountain.

Kurt refused to give up on saving his career, the family fortune, and the people who relied on it. The condo project that had died with the fire left rebuilding the town as his main hope of financial freedom. This town was *his*. And this vacant house was his first step toward turning the economy around.

Tapping her document file on her wrist, she swung back to face him. "I'll pay fifteen hundred a *month* and update everything as needed, if you'll handle electricity and plumbing.

"You won't last out the week," he countered curtly. "No one does."

"Why should they? You claim to have been maintaining the property, but I haven't seen much evidence of it yet." She gestured at the peeling door.

"We can't properly maintain a unit that makes no money." As soon as he had the financing in place, he'd put an end to that bad situation. The place was headed for the scrap heap.

Not knowing his plans, she raised her expressive eyebrows and said reasonably enough, "Then fifteen hundred is better than nothing. Surely you have electricians and plumbers working for you who can handle any utility problems. Open it up and let me see if the place is still habitable."

Preferring to avoid public confrontation, Kurt nodded at Xavier, who kept the keys. He'd warned her. If she didn't mean to listen, it wasn't his fault. "For long-term rentals, we require two months' deposit, plus a month's rent in advance," he said, knowing that was mean even as he said it. But she'd insisted, and he was doing his best to discourage her from throwing away her money.

If she wouldn't back down and ultimately fled in terror as all the other tenants had, he'd be forty-five hundred ahead of the game. She'd said she had money—although a guilty glance at the wheeled junk heap she'd arrived in gave evidence otherwise.

His rental agent unlocked the front door. The filthy front window and peeling paint were a disgrace, and Kurt knew he ought to feel ashamed, but other than a few days here and there, the shop had been empty for as long as he and Monty had been in charge of it. He'd never been inside. His commitment had always been to keeping his paying lodge guests happy.

With the mountain currently no more than scarred trees and ash, he had to put their other assets to work. Finally being able to employ his architectural skills to make that happen had him anticipating the moment the bulldozer razed this block.

"Mr. Black, the children are napping in the van. Would you be so kind as to wait by the door and keep an eye on it? Mia might come out looking for me." The butterfly lady graced his agent with a beatific smile that left the old man dazed.

Damn, but she was good. She'd have every man in Hillvale under her thumb before they knew what hit them. Having a little more experience with manipulative women, Kurt merely caught her elbow and steered her into the empty cave of the storefront.

Except it wasn't entirely empty. Shelves, glass cases, and an oak table remained—probably one of the reasons he couldn't rent it as a vacation home. "I should charge extra for store furnishings," he told her.

She snorted and marched toward the back as if knowing exactly what to expect. "My parents installed them. They're mine. I should charge you for their use."

Oh yeah, right, she'd said she lived here, what? Twenty years ago, before the Thompsons had moved in? He started searching his memory, but he'd led a sheltered life as a child.

She swirled around in the middle of the dusty kitchen. "This crap was old when my parents lived here! It's like walking into a museum —*tiled counters*! When was the last time anyone installed white tile counters—half a century ago? Look at the black appliances!" She yanked open the refrigerator, but no light came on.

Odd, they usually kept the utilities hooked up.

"You were expecting granite and stainless steel?" Kurt asked, hiding his annoyance by leaning over to test the refrigerator's light bulb. Had the place been rentable, he would have upgraded by now.

She opened a cabinet door. "Not even good oak cabinets, but plywood with oak frames, are you kidding me? This one is likely to fall off the wall any minute. This is *maintenance*? You better have good lawyers."

"The house has barely been occupied since your cousin moved out. The kitchen is still as functional as she left it." Giving up on the bulb, Kurt rocked back on his heels and studied the outdated kitchen. He didn't see spider webs. Some of Mariah's damned *ghost*-catchers hung above the cabinets, so she'd been in here. Knotted webs of string, beads, and feathers, they looked like the fake dream-catchers sold in gift shops.

He didn't know why Monty allowed a certifiable nutcase to run loose, other than that Mariah was usually harmless. He gestured at the dismal kitchen. "No grease, no stains, everything in good condition."

She opened the oven, and apparently appeased, clacked across the linoleum floor to the staircase. "We left all our furniture. Is it still there?"

Hell if he knew. She didn't wait for an answer. He tried a light switch, but the utilities were definitely off. He reluctantly followed her up the dark, enclosed staircase to the bedrooms. The place even gave him the heebie-jeebies.

"No!" she shouted, abruptly halting. She grabbed the wall like a butterfly snatched by a spiderweb and turned around. "Go back!"

Before Kurt could blink in surprise, a force plowed into his midsection, hurling him backward down the stairs.

TEDDY SHRIEKED AS HER GREEDY-BUT-GORGEOUS LANDLORD HIT THE kitchen floor, cracking his head on the hard wood. Mr. Black instantly appeared, followed by a tribe of people she didn't know.

The spirit who had shoved him had been angry, but that's all she'd been able to tell before it struck. *Damn,* but she should have heeded the warnings and made him stay outside. She'd never met a spirit this strong—or this furious—before. She could feel her even without opening her Monitor.

A tall woman with a lion's mane of white-blond hair, wearing an apron from the café, kneeled beside Mr. Kennedy, checking under his eyelids. "Unconscious and his pupils are dilated. We need to call Brenda. Do we dare move him?"

A man who looked like a university professor with a closely-cut goatee and well-barbered thick chestnut hair crouched down to check his pulse. Kennedy stirred. "He's coming around. Give him space."

Looking worried, Amber of the amber rings and plentiful bangles peered in the front door. "Is it safe?"

A tall, elegantly dressed black woman towered over the tarot reader. She shoved open the door, shaking her head until her gold earrings swung. "Baaaad juju," she admonished.

"Smudging needed," Teddy called from the stairs, agreeing with this assessment. "I don't feel her anymore, but there's definitely an entity inhabiting the upstairs."

Amazingly, no one seemed to question her declaration of the paranormal. She loved these people already. Mr. Black went a little pale, but he pragmatically produced a long shelf from the front room and laid it beside his unconscious employer to use as a stretcher.

"Tullah, you have a landline. Call Monty, ask if Kurt has a physician who can advise us." The professor stood up and glanced at Teddy. "I'm Aaron Townsend, from the antique store. I think he'll be all right, but we need to take him back to the lodge. Is there room in your van for him to lie down?"

"If you can work around a fifty-pound dog, two small kids, and a heap of suitcases. Although the dog will be perfectly happy in the yard if he's fed and watered, I suppose." Teddy dubiously eyed the long length of suited male sprawled on her floor. "It might be better to empty out the suitcases, but I don't think we can live with an angry spirit."

"We can take the suitcases in my truck," Townsend offered, accepting her assessment. "Xavier, can you help lift him or should we look for Harvey?"

"No one's lifting me anywhere," the man on the floor muttered. "Back off. Give me a minute to see if all my bones are in place."

A small, wiry woman pushed her way in and knelt beside him. "Hey, Mr. K, it's just me, Brenda. Open your eyes so I can see if you shattered your brain."

He scowled but opened his eyes. "Brenda, you setting up office here now?"

"I should," she said pertly. "But you won't rent me a building." She studied his pupils and held up two fingers. "How many?"

"Fourteen. We all know you're a witch and hide the extra digits." He pushed up on one elbow, rubbing his head. "What the hell happened?"

"Angry manifestation," Aaron Townsend said. "Probably the last tenant who died homeless after you threw them out."

"They all left of their own accord." Apparently accustomed to sarcasm, Mr. Kennedy sat up, then sent Teddy a glare.

She waited for the accusations and condemnation.

Instead, he just looked weary. "No further discussion of staying here until I have the staircase examined."

"Bullshit." She sauntered down. "We'll take you up to the lodge where you will generously offer us a room for the night while the uninvited guest is dispelled. Any broken bones?"

"Just my skull." He pressed fingers to the back of his head and winced. When Brenda descended on him, he gestured for her to back off. "I played rugby. I know concussions. No TV, no computer, just rest. I don't see any body parts flopping uselessly, so I'm guessing all the bones are in place. Just help me up."

"Rugby, of course." Teddy stood to one side as the tall lion-haired woman in the apron and Aaron Townsend took their patient's arm and helped him stumble to his feet.

Kennedy swayed but didn't topple. Instead of leaving, he gazed up the staircase. "There must be a loose board up there."

"Right, or a dead body. Come along, Mr. Landlord, let's get you home. The lodge, I take it?" Teddy glanced at the others for confirmation.

"I'll look after your dog," the blond waitress said. "I'm Samantha Moon, Kurt's niece. I work over at the café and live up by the cemetery. I can start making arrangements for whatever the Lucys need for removing your ghost."

Lucys? Now was not the time to question. Or ask how a full-grown woman could be a niece or why she worked in a café when her uncle owned half the town.

"Good to meet you, Samantha Moon, and thank you." Teddy turned to Kennedy. "The kids are napping, but there's a front seat, if you think you can sit up. If not, I'll scoot them over."

He looked as if he were about to protest, but the wiry little nurse poked her finger in his chest. "You will not drive for twenty-four hours, absolute minimum. You know that."

He grimaced and, holding his head as if to keep it upright, staggered for the front door.

Teddy gestured at Mr. Black. "Give the ladies a key so they can do whatever they need to do."

Kennedy didn't even protest. Neither did Mr. Black. Would wonders never cease?

"Don't tell me you really believe in loose stairs," she said as they stepped outside. She recalled how Kennedy had officiously taken her arm earlier and steered her as if she were too helpless to walk on her own. She was small and men liked to believe she was weak. In return, she liked to catch them unaware and cut them off at the knees. She had a feeling that ploy wouldn't work here.

"That, or I have a brain tumor that causes me to lose balance," he said grimly, attempting to open the driver's side back door of the van for her.

"Right," she snorted in disbelief, stepping around him to grip the rusted metal. "Handle doesn't work right." She slammed it open. "The other side is easier."

She couldn't read the look he sent her, but it rumbled down her spine and settled in lower parts that often led her astray.

She grabbed Hairy's leash and helped him hop down, handing him over to the tall waitress, who immediately stooped down to rub his fluffy ears. Teddy figured the dog was in good hands.

Holding onto the car, her landlord groped his way to the passenger side and let himself in. "Why the van, Miss Baker? It doesn't look like your sort of vehicle."

Because it hid the kids, offered a place to sleep so they didn't have to check into hotels. Because she bought it for cash in a transaction even cops couldn't trace. Not that this uptight grunt needed to know that.

She leaned over to check on the kids in the back. Even Mia had fallen asleep. Teddy removed the book from her little chest and tucked it into a backpack. Only then did she reply. "Sentimental reasons, Mr. Kennedy. My parents owned one. And please call me Teddy." She rather liked that he assumed a rolling wreck wasn't her style.

"Then call me Kurt. I can't promise those stairs will be fixed or that the utilities will work by tomorrow. Let me have my secretary look for an apartment, or Xavier can work out the details for one of the empty storefronts." He leaned back against the seat and closed his eyes.

"We'll camp in the house, if necessary, *Kurt*. It's mine, and I mean to turn it into a destination that will bring tourists flocking." Teddy was pretty sure she'd said that just to antagonize.

It worked. He groaned.

SAMANTHA

SAMANTHA MOON CHECKED THAT PRINCE HAIRY'S WATER BOWL AND FOOD were filled. The lazy creature wagged his tail in appreciation but didn't move from the late afternoon shade in the fenced backyard. She scratched his head, then reluctantly rejoined the others inside the house.

As instructed, she held a feather duster while her Aunt Cass and the other Lucys chanted and lit their bundles of sage and sweet grass at a candle on the kitchen counter. As they swept the room, she wafted the smoke toward the east first, then counterclockwise.

She supposed the nickname for the Lucent Ladies—the Victorian spiritual society that had spawned Hillvale—was a better name than *witch*. But her scientific education had a hard time buying smoke as a defense against a force strong enough to shove a man downstairs.

"I still think we need an engineer to determine if the house's foundation hasn't shifted," she murmured to Aaron Townsend, who watched but didn't participate. He looked enough like the university professors she was used to that she felt safe in offering her non-Lucy opinion.

The antique dealer shrugged his broad shoulders and ran his palm over the kitchen walls and counter. The Lucys claimed he practiced psychometry—feeling emotions or events on objects. He wasn't very forthcoming on what he found.

"This is an old building, so it wouldn't hurt," he agreed. "Who knows what slippage may have occurred over the years?"

They'd smudged the shop area earlier. Sam almost had the routine down. She continued waving her feathers in the proper direction, concentrating on corners. She would feel ridiculous except the scent did clean the musty air, and she could knock out a few spiderwebs while she was at it.

Mariah climbed up on a stepstool to replace the tattered ghost-catchers in the corners with new ones. The beads and crystals shimmered and shook in the candlelight.

"There may even have been minor quakes," Mariah suggested, tuning into their discussion.

Sam never quite knew how much of Lucy superstition Mariah believed, but she assumed it was like the differences in religion. Mariah believed her intricate nets caught ghosts. The Lucys thought smudging would chase them away. Earthquakes might fit into both belief systems.

Dousing her burning bundle in a bucket of sand, Sam's Aunt Cass shook her head. "No earthquakes in the last forty years that I'm aware of." She started up the staircase toward the building's living quarters, carrying the sand.

Sam's aunt was built much as she was—tall, slender, with thin bones. Except Cass was nearly seventy and would break into a dozen pieces if a ghost shoved her. Or the earth slipped.

Aaron apparently had the same thought. He stationed his much more muscular frame at the bottom of the stairs to catch Cass if she fell. Younger and leaner than the antique dealer, Harvey, the musician, emerged from the front room to push past Aaron and take Cass's back. Cass might be on the weird side of rational, but she commanded respect for her knowledge of Hillvale and its eccentricities.

Everyone carried the carved walking sticks Harvey had created. The wood in Sam's stick vibrated nervously. Or she did. She hadn't decided if ideomotion or the supernatural or just weird energy caused the odd dowsing rods to activate. She anxiously watched her aunt and Harvey as they climbed the narrow steps.

"She's definitely angry," Cass called back. "If she didn't knock the Baker woman down, I'll assume we're safe. It appears she objects to Kennedys."

"She didn't like me when I moved in," Amber reminded her, lingering at the bottom of the stairs with her smoking bundle. "She may have just worn out her energy."

Since Amber believed in tarot cards, Sam could have dismissed them all as superstitious eccentrics—if she hadn't felt the weird energy forces around Hillvale herself. Even now, her staff was swinging back and forth, quite of its own accord. But Amber was right—Cass was showing her prejudice against the Kennedys by blaming the incident on Kurt's presence.

The bad history between Cass and her half-brother's family dated back half a century, like any good small-town family feud. Sam didn't try to understand it.

Once Cass and Harvey reached the top of the stairs, Amber and Tullah followed, swinging their smudge sticks along the walls. Grimacing, Sam climbed after them, using her duster to spread the smoke. Mariah sprinkled herbs and salt. Aaron took up the rear until they were all stationed upstairs.

"It's not much to look at," Cass said with a sniff, setting up the candle and bucket at the top of the stairs. "I have some old curtains I can bring over, freshen up the bedrooms a little better. Sam, you need to tell your tightwad uncle to bring over fresh bedding from the lodge. More than ectoplasm can be in those beds."

Cass and the Kennedys didn't speak to each other. Sam had only been in Hillvale for a few weeks, but if she meant to stay here, she was determined to open communication between the warring sides of her family.

One of the reasons she meant to stay in Hillvale shouted from the shop, "Do I need to call the fire brigade?"

"My very favorite Null," Sam yelled back. "You're interrupting a smudging. Be quiet and stay down there until we're done."

Chen Ling Walker appeared at the bottom of the stairs. Tall and lanky, with surprisingly hard muscles hidden beneath his loose denim shirt, her deputy boyfriend frowned, not necessarily in disapproval. His Chinese mother had superstitions similar to the Lucys, which made him more accepting of their oddities than the other non-believers in town, like her Kennedy uncles.

But Walker's detective instincts belonged entirely to his Irish father. He'd want explanations.

Sam waved her duster at him, then dutifully followed her aunt and her cronies. Aaron and Harvey weren't actually participating in the ceremony so much as doing their own things. She didn't know Aaron well enough to know how real or strong his gift was, but he was frowning in puzzlement as he ran his hands over the walls. Walker had claimed the antique dealer was well known in high-end antique circles and was often called to authenticate valuable pieces, which could indicate some talent for either research or *reading* what he was looking at.

Wearing his usual black t-shirt and jeans, with his dark hair pulled back in a short ponytail, Harvey played guitar, wrote songs, and crafted walking sticks that weirdly behaved as dowsing rods for the energy forms that haunted the town. So far, Sam had learned the sticks could trace people, negativity, and water. She didn't really want to believe they might also track ghosts, but Harvey's stick was bouncing like crazy.

As the Lucys returned to the sand bucket to extinguish their smoking bundles and murmur their final chants, Sam gestured for Walker to come up.

"A ghost pushed Kurt down the stairs," she whispered when he reached her. "Although I think the newcomer who was with him probably wished she could have done it. Word is, he was being particularly obnoxious."

Walker kissed her forehead. They'd only been together a few weeks, and the thrill was even stronger as time passed. She leaned into him for the reassurance he always provided.

"Is that a way of saying I should talk to the new arrival? Where is she?" He wrapped his arm around her waist and watched with interest as Mariah attached the final ghostcatcher at the top of the stairs.

"Are you our new sheriff?" Harvey asked, emerging from the smaller bedroom. He'd tucked his staff under his arm so it no longer vibrated.

Everyone turned in anticipation. Hillvale had been paying the county sheriff for a part-time patrol, but the deputy job had turned into a full-time one recently. Walker had only taken the deputy job to locate his long-missing father. Now that he had the answers he'd been seeking, he had an investigative agency in Los Angeles to return to.

Sam held her breath, waiting for Walker's answer. He'd said he was interested in staying here, with her. But a man like Walker needed intellectual challenges. A small town law enforcement job would keep his talents occupied, but still allow him to run his company as needed.

"Monty and the sheriff have pounded out an agreement, yes," Walker said, squeezing her tighter. "But there can only be one sheriff in a county. I'd have to be Hillvale's chief of police. Bureaucracy now comes into play while they negotiate. But I'm still the law around here, so if I need to talk with our newcomer, I will."

"Talk to Kurt," Cass said with a sniff, stabbing her walking stick against the wooden floor and pushing her way back to the stairs. "The girl claims she owns this building and has deeds to prove it. Kurt's threatening to charge her insane rent for this dump. I don't blame the ghost for shoving him downstairs."

Walker stepped aside so she could pass. Aaron pushed past first, preceding Cass down the stairs. . . just in case.

Walker sent Sam a questioning look, and she shook her head. "Later," she whispered. She was theoretically an environmental scientist, but recently, she felt as if she should have majored in communication.

"Aaron, did you pick up any information on our poltergeist?" Cass asked as they all trooped to the front shop area.

Outside the plate glass window dark had descended and the lone street lamp in the parking lot had come on. Sam couldn't see Dinah's café further down the block, but across the street, on the other end of town, she saw a light in the mayor's office.

"It's an old building. I picked up echoes of children and happiness and love, but they were faded almost to nothingness." Aaron ran his fingers over the counter and an old oak table as if unable to stop himself. "The good is overwritten by rage, fear, great pain—and evil. We probably ought to look into former tenants. I feel violence, but it's. . . I'm not sure how to explain. The violent *spirit* permeated the wood, but the wood was not directly involved."

"Nothing here was used as a murder weapon, and no one knocked their brains out on the counter," Walker translated for him.

Aaron gave him a grateful nod. "I didn't think you believed in our gifts, deputy."

"I can believe in some kind of force called God and an energy my mother calls *chi* without having to see or experience them," Walker said. "Or maybe I should say, I can't *not* believe in them because there is no conclusive evidence of their existence, one way or another."

"You'll fit right in here, young man," Cass said in approval. "I'm glad the mayor is smart enough to see that. Tullah, you're silent. What are you experiencing?"

Sam wasn't entirely certain what Tullah's abilities were. Owner of the thrift store, she often acted as a medium in Lucy séances, so she had some psychic connection to spirits.

"Old haunts," Tullah replied thoughtfully. "I'm not as gifted as Cass, but there's one very strong entity. I don't think smudging and catchers will help. And I agree that evil has inhabited the place. If we investigate former tenants, we may find one worked at the lodge."

"And so we're back to my evil uncles," Samantha said in amusement. "We just sent Miss Baker to stay there. Would she be safer here?"

"Kurt and Monty aren't corrupt, yet," Cass conceded, opening the door. "But if we don't find the source of the negative energy, they're likely to turn into their father. I'm not certain we can recommend that Miss Baker stay in either place."

"Especially with children," Amber said, rubbing her bracelets thoughtfully. "They're adorable and not at all what they seem. I think Miss Baker is hiding up here. She won't leave."

No one disagreed.

THREE

USING THE LODGE'S BUSINESS OFFICE, TEDDY SENT HER SISTER AN E-MAIL through the convoluted network they'd set up—just in case Butthead had figured out Sydony's computer password. If the law had any sense, they'd have kept him locked up. Instead, he was probably holed up in Syd's apartment now that she'd been forced to abandon it. But Butthead was a cop, and they protected their own.

Teddy really wasn't accustomed to hiding. As head of Theodosia Devine Designs, her job required that she hit the road and work public appearances. Only she was so fatigued and nervous, that a shadow passing in the lodge's hall almost caused her to duck.

She relaxed when the lodge owner entered the computer room. "You look worse for wear," she told him, too tired to be polite. Kennedy had left off his suit coat and tie and his hair was rumpled, as if he had just woken from a nap. His five o'clock shadow accented his carved jaw, however, giving him a movie star sexy look. She liked that he didn't tower over her by a foot.

He gave her a disgruntled look. "What did you do with the kids?"

"They fell asleep in front of the TV. You have a marvelous staff.

When I asked the maid if there was a babysitting service, she called her niece. Do they all live around here?"

He shrugged and parked his rather attractive posterior on the corner of a desk. "It's a long drive down the mountain at night. We offer lodging for those who want it. The ones with families live elsewhere and only work days. You probably talked to Maria and hired Serena. They're both single and live here."

"Rotten social life." Teddy cleared out the computer cache, hoping she was wiping any trace of her activity.

"That's why I encourage you to settle elsewhere," he said dryly. "This is a great place to visit, or was, before half the mountain burned."

"I saw that. Lightning?" She got up and confronted his aggressively male posture. She'd had enough real world experience to face down men who wanted to tell her what to do.

"No, one of the crazies set fire to a cross." He stood up and opened the door.

"One of? How many do you have?"

"Half the town, at least," he said with grim humor. "Usually, though, they don't set fires. Tensions have been escalating, unfortunately. How long has it been since your family lived here?"

Half a town of crazies? With escalating tension? She hid her unease and accepted the easier question. "I was almost seven when we moved, so a little over twenty years." She eased past him, aiming for the lounge. "Walking into your lobby reminded me of your birthday parties. I wasn't allowed to go until I turned six, and I was absolutely thrilled to my childish bones to finally attend one."

He fell in step with her. "My mother wanted us to have normal childhoods. She seemed to think normal meant inviting every child related to the town or lodge to an enormous event that left them all hyper and crying by the time they went home."

Teddy laughed. "I didn't cry. I loved it. I got brand new sparkly socks and shoes and a bouncy dress and helped my father make gifts for you and your brother. I took home balloons and candy that I was never allowed to have otherwise and thought it fair trade. And I got to see you wear my sword in your belt as if it were a pirate sword."

Which might be why she felt so at home with this man she ought to consider as the enemy. He'd been a lonely little boy once, and she'd made him happy.

Kurt placed a hand at her back and steered her into a quiet corner of the lounge. He almost smiled. "I remember that sword! It was the only gift I can remember being allowed to keep. All the rest were given to charity, but my mother didn't think a handmade sword was appropriate. I still use it as a letter opener. You were a talented six-year old."

"I'm still talented," she countered, but her mood had improved at the notion of him keeping one of her first efforts. "And if you have a concussion, you shouldn't be drinking."

"I don't drink on the job, and I'm always on the job. Harry knows to bring me seltzer. Chardonnay for you?"

"A small glass, to help me unwind. It's been a long day or I'd go down and see how the Lucys are faring at the shop. I'm starting to remember some of the local slang. They called you a Null. How did people ever come up with that sobriquet?"

He placed their order and settled on the stool beside her. "It's been around longer than I have. I always just assumed Null and Void was the opposite of Lucent Lucy. I'm sure someone had a sense of humor in years past."

"Null, as in you have no extra-sensory gifts?" she asked, relishing this break from her recent routine of worry.

He raised an eyebrow. "You believe in ESP?"

"I'm one of them, yep," Teddy agreed, enjoying the heck out of this conversation and feeling safe enough to open her Inner Monitor and test him. As before, he blocked her, but she could read his facial expression well enough. "You're shocked, disgusted, and just a little intrigued."

He snorted and sipped his seltzer. "That's an obvious conclusion. So you turned to warn me on the stairs, not push me, because you felt a ghost?"

"Or maybe I wanted to push you, and the ghost did it for me," she said with a laugh. "I see what the Lucys do around here for entertainment. Teasing Nulls is fun."

"Now I need another painkiller," he grumbled. "You aren't going to give up, are you? You're probably planning on establishing a rapport with the ghost and selling tickets."

"I've never met a ghost before." She sipped her chardonnay and thought about it. "I'm pretty sure there wasn't one when I lived there. But I'm sensitive to emotional energy, and whatever's in there packs an angry wallop. I'll have to see how it feels in the morning."

"I had a man go down and check the utilities," he said, a little too casually.

Teddy regarded him with suspicion. "And?"

"They're turned on, as they always are for our rental properties. He saw no reason for the electricity not to work, except maybe your ghost doesn't want it on."

She muttered a foul word and took another drink.

FOUR

THE NEXT MORNING, KURT SAT BACK IN HIS DESK CHAIR, STILL FEELING satisfied that he'd zinged the smug Miss Baker with news that her precious *ghost* had blocked her electricity. His headache had dissipated, and despite ringing telephones and a mountain of paper he needed to plow down, he was prepared for Xavier's call.

Xavier had been the crazy who'd burned the cross. Monty had insisted that it had been a drug-induced incident instigated by the criminal Xavier had called friend, and they should give the lawyer a second chance. But Kurt now examined everything his agent said or did, so he had the file on hand.

"The Lucys are asking who rented the shop after the Thompsons left," Xavier said. "Think it's all right to tell them?"

"I've already looked." Kurt flipped open the file. "The Thompsons were never our tenants. They're the ones who sold us the property ten years ago. We've had a few weekly rentals since then, but after we fixed up the place that first year, we received a lot of complaints and no long term guests. So if the Thompsons are Miss Baker's relations, she might want to see who they were murdering."

It felt good to say that. After learning Deputy Walker's father had been killed on the resort by a lodge contractor, half the town considered the Kennedys accomplices simply for living here.

Kurt's father had been dead and Kurt had been only twelve when Teddy's parents moved away. He and Monty had been at school in the city most of the time the Thompsons lived there. The Lucys couldn't blame his family this time.

Although the family corporation *had* acquired the property. Kurt kneaded his temple.

"I'll let them know," Xavier said in relief.

His agent had been through a lot these past few weeks, Kurt knew, but oddly, the older man had become more. . . lucid. . . lately.

"And the utilities are working again, so I'm drawing up the contract you told me," Xavier continued.

"Have the crew go over the lines thoroughly. We don't want an electric short burning the place down overnight."

After the fire that had almost taken the resort, that prospect made Kurt super-uneasy. Unable to concentrate on the paperwork that consumed his life, he grabbed his keys, told his secretary he'd be back later, and set out for Hillvale.

He convinced himself he was going down to check on the property's safety—not to see how Teddy Baker was faring—but he was disillusioned of that notion the moment he walked in the shop's front door.

He'd tried not to notice her too much last night in the dark bar, but in full sunlight Teddy Baker was a knockout. She stood on a stepladder, checking overhead lights, wearing a plunging skin-tight top and jeans that revealed every luscious curve. A figure like that would stop traffic and ought to be illegal.

Her curly hair tumbled down her back this morning. Uncovered by the ugly cap she'd worn yesterday and unfettered by last night's braid, it formed a dark waterfall that shifted and swayed with every move.

He'd spent the night recalling the mesmerizing fairy who had haunted his lonely childhood dreams. At the time, he'd thought fairy tales had been written for her.

"Your hair wasn't black when you were little," he said in accusation.

She gazed down at him from her lofty perch. "Shhh. The world doesn't need to know that I'm artificially enhanced."

"Black is not an enhancement." That was a mean thing to say but it balanced out his insta-lust. She stuck out her tongue and crossed her eyes at him and insta-lust skyrocketed. He countered it with snark. "I take it no one has been pushed down the stairs this morning?"

Children shouted and a dog barked outside. She wrinkled her petite nose and started down the ladder. "I think the smudging soothed the spirit's ire somewhat. Or she's gathering her energy. If I'm temporarily agreeing to rent at your outrageous terms, we'll need new bedding."

"What would you have done if you owned the place and didn't have a landlord handy? I remember our agreement including only utilities." He resisted the urge to help her down by shoving his hands in his pockets.

"If I didn't have a landlord, I'd have forty-five hundred bucks to furnish the place," she retorted. "If I'm renting, fully furnished, it should be furnished."

He might have argued if he hadn't been confronted by a rhinestone-studded t-shirt displaying her many assets, including cleavage that begged. . . His childhood fairy had grown up. Kurt brought his eyes back to her face. Even at this hour, she wore black mascara. The lady was definitely hiding in full sight. "Have you talked to your mother's cousin since she lived here?"

She blinked those long, full lashes in surprise, and he allowed himself another score.

"I suppose my parents have. We used to exchange Christmas cards, but no one does that anymore." She frowned, tilted her head, then headed for the kitchen. "The kids are too quiet."

"They weren't quiet a minute ago. Don't they get a break?"

She didn't respond but aimed for the back door. He really had better things to do than follow swaying hips through an antiquated kitchen.

Or maybe he didn't. Now that business had dropped off drastically after the fire, he didn't have as many guests to pacify. The condos he had hoped to build above the town were supposed to have taken care of his spare time, but thanks to the Lucys, the lawyers had tied his hands. So maybe he ought to spend time in town, learning what deviousness his aunt and niece, and their friends, conspired on now.

The kitchen was blessedly free of meddlers, but the dusty strip of backyard was occupied. With alarm Kurt noted the two black-haired children swaying on the rickety wooden fence. The kids seemed unconcerned about their precarious position, but Samantha looked alarmed. Why was she out here?

He hadn't quite adjusted to knowing that his father had a child out of wedlock that no one had told him about—until Sam had showed up, practically on his doorstep, the fully grown daughter of a half-brother he'd never known. His newly acquired niece had made no demands on him, but she was the reason the condos were tied up in litigation right now—through no fault of her own. Family secrets tended to be ugly.

Sam stood with shovel in hand, biting her bottom lip, studying the situation, just as he was.

Only the dynamo with lungs forged ahead, shouting, "Mia, you cannot climb the tree. I told you that."

Tree? Kurt glanced behind the fence where there was, indeed, a pine tree just begging to be climbed. Why did she think that was their goal?

The petite temptress stormed the fence, hauled the sturdy younger child down, dropped him on the ground, and grabbed the older. "If you can't behave for Miss Samantha, I'll have to tie you up like Prince Hairy."

At the sound of his name, the fanged beast flapped its hairy tail but didn't move more.

"We want to see the ocean," the child addressed as Mia protested. "Can we go up on the roof?"

"Jeb does *not* want to see the ocean. He just wants to do what you do, and he's too little. Do you want to kill your little brother?"

Kurt thought this might be where he parted ways and found a better task, but Teddy threw him a piercing look that meant *stay*, and Sam smirked. What was he missing?

The boy plopped down on the dog as if it were a large cushion and produced a crumpled snack bar from his shorts. He fed part of it to the dog, then ate the rest, unfazed by his sister's protests or his aunt's shouts.

It was the defiant little girl clinging to Teddy's neck who wept, not the supposedly terrified little boy.

"But Mommy said we should watch out, and the tree is the best place," Mia cried. "How can we watch out when we're so little?"

At that, Sam set down her shovel, caught Kurt's arm, and steered him inside the house.

"What are they watching out for?" he asked.

"You'll have to ask Teddy. She'll tell us when she's ready. But look at them—she knows exactly what those children need," Sam whispered. "I've never seen anything like it. It's as if she has eyes in the back of her head and a direct link to their brains."

"That's ridiculous," he protested, casting a glance over his shoulder at the tableau, feeling a tug of. . . softness. "The kids got quiet and she went to see, just like any mother would." Not that his mother ever had, which explained his soft spot for maternal behavior.

"She's *not* their mother. She has no kids of her own. But this isn't the first time today that she's arrived just in the nick of time. I'm right there, and I don't notice. She does."

He shot her a look of disgust. "So they've brainwashed you too? You see magic where there's nothing more than hypervigilance?"

His niece was nearly tall enough to look him in the eye. She patted his coat sleeve and shook her head. "You'll have to see for yourself. I won't waste my breath. The azaleas at the lodge are getting leggy and overgrown. Do you mind if I dig one or two to plant here? I'll trim up the rest and feed them so they'll look good as new next spring."

With a scowl, Kurt nodded. He had little idea what azaleas were, but Sam had a green thumb, so he believed she'd do what she said, even if she was wasting her time. The town would be rubble by next spring.

Out of Teddy Baker's compelling presence, Kurt again considered leaving. As if she knew exactly what he was thinking, the female in question kicked open the back door, still carrying a child much too big for her and trailing a now crumb-smeared boy.

"That fence needs replacing," she announced without preamble, glaring right at him. "I'll take the cost out of the first months' rent."

Damn, but she was good. Kurt almost laughed as she pushed past him, a galleon in full sail skirting around him as if he were in an insignificant buoy.

He couldn't remember the last time an eligible female had treated him like a piece of furniture.

∾

"It's okay, Mia, honey." Teddy soothed her niece, rocking her in the chair she remembered her mother using. Apparently her mother's cousin had left the old furnishings intact, for the most part. "I'm here to watch for you, okay? And there's a whole town full of people who will watch too." She hoped. It had been one of the reasons for coming here. "Your job is to keep an eye on Jeb and make sure he doesn't eat any rocks or lizards."

The child hiccupped, rubbed her runny nose on Teddy's shirt, and nodded. "Mama says he'd eat the house if someone cut it up for him."

Teddy laughed. "We'll have to teach him proper dining. Can the two of you stay up here quietly if I put a DVD in the computer?"

Thank goodness she'd brought supplies. No cell phone coverage put a serious dent in her ability to download movies. She'd have to inquire about cable.

"Okay. Can I have *Little Mermaid*?" Mia hopped down.

After cleaning up Jeb and settling the kids on the floor in front of her laptop, Teddy figured her landlord had fled. It was a pity. He was the one good-looking thing around this dump. She'd far rather spar over contracts with him than dithering Mr. Black, maybe over a candlelit, wine-soaked dinner. She may have given up on relationships, but she wasn't quite ready to give up on sex.

To her surprise, she found the businessman stripped of his tailored coat, with his shirt sleeves rolled up, prying at a speaker in the shop wall with a pocket knife.

"What are you doing?" she asked with curiosity. He was a handsome hunk after all, and she was always a sucker for a handyman. Not that she believed for one second that wealthy Kurt Kennedy had ever lifted a hammer in his life. The Dashing Prince of her childhood had been pretty but hadn't known how to make swords. That had made sense to her enamored six-year-old self.

"Looking to see if this is how you produce ghost wails," he said, popping off the ring and inspecting the interior. "Where does this connect?"

"I've heard no wailing ghosts, and as far as I'm aware, that's an ancient speaker system my father installed. He liked piping in music. It's a wonder it's not playing the Grateful Dead."

He sent her a look that made her laugh. Okay, so that had been a poor choice of bands.

She contemplated the layout of the old shop. The shelves attached to the walls needed a good coat of paint. The counter glass just needed cleaning but the base. . . stain or paint?

"Even the Dead could produce better tunes than static," Kennedy said, climbing down the stepstool. "The other sounds the same." He pointed his knife at the speaker over the window, then looked around at the empty shelves. "What did your father sell in here?"

"Keeping in mind that they were young, and twenty years ago, Hillvale still had a hippie vibe, they sold candles, wind chimes, the ever-popular medieval sword, crystals, anything tourists might buy." She studied the speaker over her head. It did seem to be producing a noise. "They inherited the building free and clear, but they had to put food on the table while they were finding themselves. I'm not entirely certain they ever found reality, but they're career missionaries these days."

"Lucys," he said in disgust, examining the ceiling and walls. "What tripe do they sell to the natives? Bibles?"

Teddy understood his attitude and didn't call him on it. She returned to the staircase and followed where the wires had to run. "Healthcare. They teach how to purify water, set up camps for vaccinations, build latrines, glamorous things like that. They're probably spies and subversives as well, but I've quit worrying about them. What happened to the attic door?"

"What attic? Is it okay if I go up there?" He tapped the wall with his knife, still looking for wires.

"There used to be a pull-down staircase from the attic, where my father kept the Christmas decorations." She led the way up, nearly breaking her neck studying the ceiling above where she distinctly remembered a rectangular door. It wasn't there now.

In their room, the kids were still hypnotized by the movie. They didn't even look up as Teddy and Kurt examined the staircase wall adjoined to the ceiling. "If the attic is still there," she said, "then I would think the wires ran up to equipment. There's no room on this level for it. I never paid much attention as a kid."

"Well, there's your ghost then," he said with a shrug. "When the electricity came on, the equipment was activated. You'll need to find the switch or cut off the wires to the speakers."

"My ghost isn't in speakers. That's the faulty wiring. I hope your electricians are good." Teddy crossed to the bedroom window. "There's one out there now fiddling with the box. That's probably the cause of the static. He found a dead fuse."

Looking over her shoulder, Kurt towered over her by a head since she was wearing ballet flats instead of boots this morning. He troubled her in more ways than one. She knew she ought to practice her seldom used Inner Monitor, but she didn't need it to sense his lust. His intellectual curiosity wasn't an emotion—more an instinct, she guessed. But almost everything else about him was repressed, trapped behind a steel wall. Not knowing if he was angry or sad or bored put her off balance.

"We need to hammer out a contract so I can start deliveries," she announced, turning quickly and deliberately forcing *him* off balance. She didn't want to be the only one in sexual torment. Creating a new, more secure home took effort, but there was no reason she couldn't play a little as well.

He backed off, studying the ancient iron bed and solid chest of drawers adorning the bedroom.

Before he could comment, a woman called from below, "Yoo-hoo, anyone home?"

A blast of cold air dropped the temperature to freezing. Teddy shivered. Kurt tested the window frame.

"Down in a sec," she called, before returning to examine the window. "The panes are old and leaky, but it's summer. We won't freeze." Although they'd just been outside and it hadn't been this cold in the sun.

"You don't believe we're being visited by a spiritual entity blocking out the heat?" he asked dryly, following her to the stairs.

"I read people, not ghosts, not usually. I think the one here had just built up a lot of steam waiting for someone to walk in, and you got the worst of it. I'd feel better if we laid her to rest though."

"Or found out why she's here?" he countered.

"Yeah, that too. That's why the Lucys are gathering. Want to join the séance?"

"Will you be putting up a tarot reading sign too?" he asked in disgust as they reached the bottom and found the shop filling with women.

"No, I sell high-end jewelry, but I'll start with crystals, geodes, and local crafts and see what the market bears—as soon as you get me that contract." Arriving in the shop, she greeted Amber, the tarot reader, and Tullah, the owner of the upscale thrift store. Several women she hadn't met milled around, studying the ceiling where the static had become more pronounced.

"Xavier is working on the contract. I'll leave you to your entertainment." Kurt's tone was dry, but his curiosity was high, Teddy noticed.

"The ghost is trying to reach us," one of the ladies said worriedly, studying the speaker Kurt had discombobulated.

"We'd better ask Aaron and Harvey to join us," Tullah agreed, with a similar frown of concern. "The entity has proved powerful recently."

"Not just recently," Amber corrected. "She was a full-blown poltergeist while I was here."

"Why do you refer to her as a *she*?" Kurt asked, heading for the door. "Can't ghosts be male?"

"Because whoever she is thinks of herself as female," Tullah said with dignity. The tall African-American shop owner dressed as regally as she spoke, although her fashions tended toward the slim ones from half a century ago, ones that emphasized her curves. She wasn't a small woman, by any means, but a statuesque goddess.

Before Kurt could respond, the speakers whispered, *"Kill him."*

FIVE

KURT WOULD HAVE WALKED OUT THE MOMENT THE SPEAKERS PRODUCED the ludicrous whisper, except a crash reverberated through the old walls—and his electrician yelled. *Screamed*, actually. Screaming was never good. He raced for the back door shouting, "Stay here," at the women.

Of course, the women did no such thing. Half followed him. Half headed straight for the stairs, probably to look for the ghost.

The worker had been on a ladder to the second story. The ladder lay now on top of the newly-crumpled fence, with the upper branches of the downhill pine tree holding it up. The electrician dangled from a rung, desperately trying to find a safe purchase, but the fence was on the brink of collapse, and pine branches were too far away—and too weak to hold the ladder for long.

Kurt scrambled up on the unstable fence to grab the electrician's dangling ankles, but his precarious perch couldn't stabilize him. They'd both tumble down the steep hillside shortly. "The ladder is going to give," he called to the women. "Get some help out here."

Teddy had run upstairs to the children first, which was a relief of sorts. They didn't need to watch this, especially if the fence sent them crashing into the cottage roof below.

The tallest of the women, Tullah grabbed rungs and tried to steady them. "Will the stepstool in the front room reach?"

"If it doesn't, I can at least climb it and hold the ladder up," Kurt said. "If you order your friends to bring it out here, will they listen?"

She cocked her stately head and gave him the evil eye but nodded. Unaccustomed to communicating with the weird women who seemed to run this town, he was relieved that she acknowledged his request.

Before Tullah could go in and ask the women to do as suggested, Teddy appeared with the stepstool in hand, as if she'd heard them.

The long ladder tilted. Kurt hung on to the bravely silent worker while the women uttered muffled gasps of horror. After opening the stepstool near him, Teddy sat down on the bottom rung of the longer one to steady it from tilting more. Kurt shifted his weight from the shaky fence to the more stable stool and climbed higher to catch more of the electrician's weight.

He couldn't see how they could possibly coordinate this effort, but by the time Walker and Monty arrived, he'd walked the electrician down from rung to rung until he could almost reach the tall stepstool. Kurt had never been so glad to see his slow-walking, slow-talking jock brother in his life. The deputy was a bonus. One held the long ladder, the other climbed up to shoulder the weight of the dazed worker. Between the three of them, they maneuvered him to solid ground.

"Drinks all around, boys, I'm buying!" Teddy cried.

"I think that's my call," Kurt said, shaking the electrician's hand while steadying him at the same time. The surge of adrenaline required release, regardless of the time of day. "Drinks are on me. What the hell happened?"

The man shook his head. "No idea. I was double checking the line into the house when it was like a big wind caught me and blew me backward. I held onto the ladder, and you saw the rest."

"The window upstairs was open," Teddy said soberly. "I'm pretty sure we left it closed."

The window they'd looked out to watch the electrician work? The window with the cold draft? Kurt gritted his molars and fought down irritation. "I refuse to believe in ghostly killers. There's a rational explanation."

Deputy Walker brought down the long ladder and heaved it across the back yard. "Better keep the kids and dog out of here until the fence is repaired."

Since the hairy monster was lying lazily in a sunny spot, tail wagging, Kurt had the notion the animal wouldn't willingly go anywhere of its own accord. But Teddy caught it by the collar and led it inside. He'd feel ten thousand times better if she stayed at the lodge instead of this disaster-prone flophouse. Looking anxious, the Lucys returned inside with her.

While the electrician took a seat on the ground and buried his head in his hands to steady himself, Walker and Monty lingered in the yard to examine the wreckage.

"The place isn't safe," Kurt insisted, which was why he'd chosen this structure for the first knock-down. "Don't we have a law condemning dangerous housing?"

"Nope," Monty said, mayor hat on. "Since we made ourselves a town, people can live in houses without roofs around here if they're so inclined."

"Then pass a law. Even if their aunt is crazy enough to stay, those kids need to be protected." Still flying high on an adrenaline overload, Kurt paced the decrepit yard.

Monty snorted. "Control issues, much?" he asked.

From the house, the voices of women rose in excitement. Walker helped the electrician to his feet. "Sound like they're going anywhere?" the deputy asked.

Kurt rubbed his head where the ache was returning. "They're arranging a séance."

"Then let's leave through the alley. No way am I getting caught in that gaggle of hens." Monty led the way to the side yard.

Kurt hung back. He couldn't help feeling the house wasn't safe, and he didn't want to risk another disaster that might end more tragically than this one. If he hadn't been here. . . Imagining the electrician tumbling through tree branches, screaming, he shuddered.

He let the others go without him. Monty could ply the electrician with drinks, if needed.

In the kitchen, the refrigerator hummed normally. Kurt stopped to look inside while he listened to the chatter in the front room. The light functioned. Maybe he should go upstairs, check on the kids, and stay out of it. He was so far out of his element that he was treading water and in danger of going down.

But for the first time in years, he felt as if he were alive and not a cardboard stick figure. How had it come to this?

The static from the speaker escalated to an electronic shriek.

TEDDY YANKED OUT THE WIRES ON THE SPEAKER KURT HAD LOOSENED, BUT the racket continued from the one in the ceiling. *Damn.* She needed to get into the attic, but that wasn't happening until she demolished the ceiling.

"Perhaps the speaker will give the spirit voice," the dignified older lady who'd been introduced as Cass Tolliver said, taking a seat at the old oak dining table. With her gray hair pulled back in a severe bun, emphasizing her starkly angular bone structure, Cass was another one who looked like she ought to be teaching at a university. Weren't psychics supposed to dress in Gypsy garb and wear turbans?

Teddy hung out behind the counter, but Tullah gestured for her to join them at the table. "You have already made contact with the spirit. Since this is your house, you may have some connection that will help us."

There were only chairs for six. Amber—who *did* resemble a Gypsy in long skirts, amber rings and bangles, and flowing lace top—spread a garishly embroidered cloth over the old wood. An older woman to whom Teddy hadn't been introduced settled a crystal ball in the center. Samantha and Mariah joined them at the table, only because Cass pointed at the chairs and silently commanded it. There was only one chair available after Amber and Tullah took seats, so Mariah remained standing.

Teddy tuned in to the children, but they'd fallen asleep in front of the laptop with Prince Hairy on guard duty. These past weeks had been stressful. She was glad the adult disturbances hadn't penetrated their world here as it had done in the city. She sent up a prayer to the Great Whoever for Syd's safety.

Someone had hung black-out drapes over the shop window. Black-braided Mariah closed them at Cass's nod. Tullah lit candles. The women sprinkled herbs and chanted. Teddy had to make herself tune in to all the differing wavelengths. She'd tried this sort of thing in college, but her Inner Monitor had seen through the falsity of the perpetrators too easily for it to be interesting. This time, she only felt a reassuringly consistent belief in the women around her.

The instant they all clasped hands, the anger of the unknown entity sliced through Teddy's empathy. *Crap damn.* It was bad enough being battered by the emotions of live humans. She didn't need to be assaulted by dead people.

She shut off her monitor when Cass began speaking in an irate voice not her own.

"It's in the triptych! Find my art. You'll see!" The last words emanated from Cass's throat as a cry of frustration.

Teddy fought a shudder at the eeriness. Was Cass faking it or could there possibly be a spirit strong enough to speak? This really wasn't her sort of thing.

"Where do we find the art?" Tullah asked in a deep, somber voice.

A wail emerged from the speaker, one so grieved and furious that it shivered down Teddy's spine. She glanced around, and the others seemed as uneasy as she did. Cass had sunk into a deep trance. Her head had been upright when she spoke a moment ago, but it slumped now.

"He hid me," the speaker hissed.

"Who, who hid you?" Teddy demanded, needing more than airy warnings.

"Lucinda knows all," the speaker whispered, before even the static died.

Tullah led another chant, then released the circle of hands. "She is strong, that one."

Sam rubbed her aunt's bony hand while Cass came around, muttering under her breath and looking weary. Mariah produced a bottle of wine from her bag.

Teddy entered the kitchen in search of glasses, nearly running into a frowning Kurt as she did so. "Why are you still here?"

"You expected me to leave while the wiring screeches and those witches are plotting revolution?" He raised his eyebrows and sipped from a water bottle, looking darkly handsome and self-assured while she was shaking in her shoes.

At least he didn't ask if she believed any of that crap. Teddy had no idea what she believed right now. "We don't seem to be in any danger, and I see no revolution. You could leave through the back the way the others did."

"I know when I'm not wanted." He set down his bottle. "But I think we need to look into opening that attic you claim is up there."

Teddy nodded in relief. "I agree, and the sooner, the better." Although she wasn't certain she was prepared to find what had been concealed.

Picking up his discarded suit coat and tie, her landlord saluted her like a boy scout and ambled out. She wished he didn't have to be so damned attractive. Or that she wasn't feeling so weak as to be attracted to his heroics in saving the electrician. She had feared she'd swoon watching the muscles in his arms bulge under the strain. Men in suits shouldn't look like jocks.

She gathered up the collection of eccentric glassware that had accumulated in the kitchen and carried it back to the shop.

"Do we ask Dinah to send over lunch or just get quietly drunk?" Sam asked, accepting her glass and studying it with interest. It appeared to be a jam jar.

"Did you get in touch with the art dealer you said knew Lucinda Malcolm?" Mariah asked, sitting cross-legged on the floor as if it were her natural position.

Teddy had decided Mariah had to have Native American genes, but now she wondered if they didn't include a healthy dose from India as well. With those big, heavily-lashed brown eyes, Mariah would look good in either sari or buckskin.

Sam cautiously tasted the wine, as if unaccustomed to it, then nodded. "Elaine has promised to be up this week to look at Dinah's mural and the artwork at the lodge. But the ghost never said where to find the art."

"She said *he hid me*, in response," Mariah said, frowning. "Not helpful unless the spirit is a work of art."

"Kurt said he'll open up the attic. Aren't ghosts supposed to hang about where they died?" Instead of sitting down, Teddy studied the dangling speaker wires in the wall. She had about a million questions, but she didn't want to appear completely ignorant.

"Not always," Mariah answered, surprisingly. "Unless we want to believe a whole lot of people died at the lodge. It's ectoplasmic heaven over there. I have no way of testing my theory, but I think the spirits might be following the vortex energy and simply get caught somehow."

"The vortex is near the cemetery, so it's more likely the dead are being swept up in the energy and thrown out at the lodge," Tullah suggested.

"But I understood this vortex acts in reverse, drawing *down* instead of lifting up. I think it's just the energy in this place that holds onto whatever ghosts consist of—ectoplasm, spiritual forces. . ." Sam shrugged.

"Emotion," Teddy offered. "I sense them as emotion, which might be why we think of ghosts as people who left things undone or people who died violently."

"It's all the same, dears," Cass said, sipping her wine and frowning. "We are our emotions, our spirits, our energy, our souls, however you wish to color your word choice. But I really do want to look into whoever lived here before. Someone had time to seal the attic, if there was a stairway, as you say."

Mariah wandered around, inspecting her ghost catchers. "I'm not seeing any remnants of other spirits. And this one certainly isn't ready to move on. Are you going to stay here?"

"I want to," Teddy said, setting her jaw. "I need my own place, and the kids need normal. So far, she's only attacked men. Do you think it's safe?"

"We've done all we can," Amber said worriedly. "She mostly threw things when I was here. She never attacked me personally. But she shattered my best crystal ball, and I got tired of picking up my tarot decks."

As if in response, Sam's wine glass went flying, knocked by an invisible hand.

SIX

KURT WANDERED AROUND THE NARROW FRONT ROOM OF HILLVALE'S TOWN hall, studying the artwork strewn haphazardly across the dirty walls. It had been forty or fifty years since the world-famous art commune on Samantha's land had known notoriety. Could any of these pieces be worth anything?

Looking like a surfer with his overlong hair hanging over his bronzed brow, Monty emerged from his office to join him. "What now?"

"The Lucys are up in arms about art for some reason." He wasn't about to say *ghosts* were complaining about art. He figured Cass had some bee in her bonnet and was about to let the whole hive loose. The Lucys were impractical tree-huggers who had been complaining about the resort since it was built. They'd staged sit-ins over clearing the land, the logs used in building, and currently, Kurt's desire to upgrade the area from shanties to condos. Cass was almost always behind the protests.

"The whole town is littered with paintings," Monty said, bending over to peer at a canvas half-hidden in shadow behind the pamphlet case in the reception area. "I figure the artists in the commune used them as cash to pay for services rendered."

"Probably. Think any of them are valuable?" Kurt lifted a canvas from the wall and carried it to the room's front window. "We have it all over the lodge as well, although I assumed most of it was Uncle Lance's."

"We could call an art dealer. I wouldn't have the foggiest." Monty shrugged at the one Kurt was holding. "Those same figures turn up pretty often, I've noticed. I think they used each other as subjects, although there don't seem to be any faces on that one. There's a big mural at Dinah's behind the counter with the same people. You really think the Lucys are on to something?"

"I can't imagine what. I assume without documentation, the art is owned by whoever possesses it, so the town and the lodge stand to profit most." Kurt returned the painting to the wall. He wasn't much of an art critic. It was a pleasant painting, unfortunately hung, nothing more.

"If you haven't noticed, profit is not what concerns the Lucys. It will be some mystical magical reason they're looking into. If you really want to know what they're up to, you need to hang out at Dinah's more. Want to go get a burger?"

"I won't get ptomaine?" Kurt asked, checking his watch. It was well past noon. "I ought to be back at the office."

"Doing what? Looking at bills we can't pay? C'mon, let's eat." Monty headed for the door.

Admittedly, it was much more interesting to play with money when there was money for playing. Deciding which bill to pay was monotonous. So maybe it was time to take a closer look at the town he meant to overhaul.

Kurt followed his younger brother across the street. The lunch crowd of locals and guests from the resort filled most of the seats inside the café. At Walker's wave, they joined the deputy in a booth.

"Sam working?" Monty asked, sliding in across from the lawman.

"Yup. When her shift is over, we're moving my stuff into the Ghost House. I am seriously uncomfortable with the nesting process, so if you have a more valuable use for my time, I'd appreciate it." The half-Chinese deputy deliberately lowered his eyelids in his best enigmatic expression and watched the women chattering at the counter. Samantha was in the middle of it. Despite Walker's attempt at inscrutability, Kurt thought he looked like a man in over his head and falling fast.

"Ghost House?" Kurt asked, rather than comment on the women.

"Yeah, Sam says the ghost of the former owner lives there and keeps up the gardens. It's pretty spooky how the yard seems to tend itself even though no one has lived there in a year. I figured the locals were doing it in the dearly-departed's honor." Walker sipped his coffee and studied Kurt over the brim.

"Is it one of our houses? With the exception of the lodge grounds, we usually just plant drought tolerant landscaping and leave the yards alone. It costs too much to maintain anything else." Kurt studied the menu the tall female with the beaded black braid handed him. He recognized the waitress from around town, but other than her name, he didn't really know her.

She and Monty entered into a discussion of the day's specials. As mayor, his brother knew everyone. Kurt wondered if he should learn more names and faces. Managing the lodge had never been his long-term career goal, but he could handle it, and he didn't know anyone else who understood the eccentricities of a family-owned resort. So, if he was never getting back to the city, it might behoove him to learn more about the town.

But he wasn't much of a people person. He placed his order without questioning the waitress. Only when Teddy and the kids entered did he look up.

"Nah, we're renting the place from the ghost's heirs," Walker answered his earlier question. "I'm even getting used to talking about ghosts. This place gets to you."

If he didn't have to worry about yard maintenance, Kurt wasn't interested in Walker's domestic situation. He watched Teddy settle her niece and nephew on stools. He wondered if their hair was dyed too —and why.

The tough-looking but diminutive transgender cook brought out plates she set in front of the kids without anyone ordering. Kurt was focused more on Teddy's hair. That black simply didn't suit her.

"What would it take to have you investigate everyone who has rented the old Thompson place since Teddy's parents moved out?" Kurt asked, unexpectedly. He'd been ready to dismiss the ridiculous notion that the place was haunted, but investigating wouldn't hurt anything, and he thought Teddy might appreciate the gesture.

Although he wasn't entirely certain why he wanted her appreciation.

"Including the Thompsons?" Walker asked in surprise.

"Yeah, I think so. If it turns out that he illegally sold the place to the corporation, then I'd like to sue his pants off." That was explanation enough to satisfy Walker.

"Until you're ready to file fraud charges, I can't do anything on the sheriff's dollar," Walker warned. "I'll have to employ my own investigators. They're not cheap." Walker owned a corporate investigation firm in LA.

Kurt looked at Monty. Along with their mother, they constituted the property's owners.

Monty nodded agreement. "I think it will make the Lucys happy, and if we have some chance of getting our money back, why not?"

"I doubt the result will justify the expense," Walker warned. "Real estate prices were pretty low back then."

Samantha brought over their orders. "Teddy wants to know what it will cost to investigate previous tenants in her house."

"It's not her house," Kurt automatically responded. And then he realized he'd just agreed to spending more than the house was worth for the same information. *Head-desk.*

Walker chuckled and Sam raised her eyebrows in inquiry. With a shrug, Kurt added, "Tell her we'll add the investigation to our contract and see who ends up paying for it."

He would drive Xavier back around the bend with contract amendments like that one.

As hoped, Teddy left the kids at the counter and came over to the booth. The sway of her hips called up musical refrains he hadn't heard since college days, when he'd been shacking up with a music major and still thinking he would design houses. Bad, bad sign.

"Thanks, I think," she told him. "But it still doesn't tell me how much money we're talking. I'm not a bottomless vault."

"I'll give you the friends and family discount," Walker said, leaning back in the booth to look at her. "Give me a budget."

"What can you do for the forty-five hundred she's going to lose when she moves out?" Kurt asked, trying to keep that barrier up.

"We left our resident poltergeist flinging glasses," Teddy said, expressionless. "I'm not about to be defeated by a frustrated ghost."

"I can find your Thompsons," Walker said, answering her question. "Maybe locate the next few tenants. Depending on how easy that is, we can dig deeper if you ask. Well under forty-five hundred is probably a safe number. Unless you discover one of the tenants is a mass murderer, I don't think investigating former tenants will help find a ghost though."

"I can send messages to my parents to ask about her cousins, but I don't know when they'll check e-mail or if they'll have any answers. So yeah, go ahead, please," Teddy said. "I'm just worried that Mom's cousin may still be in the attic. If her husband sold our house without owning it, he's not exactly good citizen material."

"Gruesome." Monty munched his fries, leaving the financial dealings to Kurt, as usual.

"I'm more interested in knowing why the attic was sealed off. There could be rodents up there gnawing through electric wires. I'll call my carpenter and have him saw through the ceiling. It will be a mess. Are you sure you don't want another place that would be less maintenance?" Kurt couldn't very well look away from Teddy as they spoke, but watching the fire in her eyes was hard on his libido.

He had to recall that he meant to tear down that place this winter, so they could start building in spring. With any luck, Teddy would be gone by then.

"Harvey has already told me he can fix the fence if you can provide the posts. I'm not leaving." She swung on her heel and marched off.

Walker whistled. "Want me to investigate her too? My mother would call her a dragon lady who knows what she wants and goes after it."

The lady breathed fire, for certain, which perversely stirred his lust.

"I already know who she is," Kurt said, reaching for his water and wishing for a beer. "What I want to know is why she's hiding up here."

The makers of magical swords couldn't hide easily.

～

AFTER LUNCH, TEDDY TOOK THE KIDS TO TULLAH'S THRIFT STORE, WHERE anything anyone could want was available at far less than half the price. She found the perfect set of plastic dishes and glassware and bought the kids old-fashioned board games.

"You have a gift for knowing what people need," Teddy told Tullah in admiration as she paid for her purchases in cash.

"E-Bay is my friend," Tullah stated solemnly. "I have boots and a jacket arriving tomorrow you might want to look at, and I'm scouting children's clothes as we speak. They don't really dress in black all the time, do they?" She nodded at Goth One and Two pushing a wooden toy train.

"We haven't unpacked yet. What I really need is a laundromat. I suppose I have to go down the mountain for that?"

"Or ask Kurt to use the lodge's," Tullah said in amusement. "You've got more action out of the man than anyone else has for as long as I've been here. But if you don't want to tackle the Nulls, I have machines in back you can use. I like my inventory to be clean."

"Kurt doesn't seem to be a bad sort, but he does seem to be exceptionally stressed. Maybe we should be nicer to him." Teddy gathered up her purchases.

"Wait until you meet his mother. I don't think there is anything we can do to relieve his stress."

Teddy had a hard time believing a tough businessman like Kurt could be stressed by his *mother*, but she remembered a few offhand remarks about Mrs. Kennedy's volatility. If she owned part of the family corporation, Teddy supposed confrontation was inevitable.

After dragging the kids away from the toy train, depositing her purchases at the house, and letting the Prince out on a leash, Teddy braved the grocery. She'd never cooked for kids before. Judging by their eating habits, she probably ought to cruise the frozen food aisle. It wasn't as if she existed on more than salads and take-out.

Pasquale's Grocers wasn't busy in the middle of a week day. Tourists in shorts bought snacks and pharmacy supplies. Those would be her potential customers, so she sized them up as she strolled the aisles. Teddy smiled at a few locals she'd seen in the café and almost relaxed at the normality of small town coziness. If Buttass showed up here, she'd know about it instantly. Not that he had any idea that the children were with her or where she might be or even care. Old One-Track Mind would still be hunting Syd.

Letting Mia and Jeb tote their favorite cereals and snacks, Teddy carried her groceries down the street to her old home. She'd paint the door in the morning, she decided, then get busy having her inventory shipped up here.

Oops, she'd need cable for internet, and there was just the person she could ask. Kurt was directing men carrying posts down the alley. The bastard already had her front door open. She might have to change the locks.

Rather than yell at him, she went after what she wanted first. "Is cable installed?" she asked, shifting a sack to Kurt's arms when he offered. "It should be part of the utilities."

He snorted. "What world do you live in that cable is included in rent?"

"An expensive one," she admitted.

She frowned as they entered and she heard men talking on the floor above. "Permission to invade my property would be nice," she admonished, heading back to the kitchen.

"I'm not comfortable with you and the children living here until I'm assured it's safe. A bad ceiling job could fall on your head. If the wiring in those speakers is faulty, the house could catch fire." He deposited grocery sacks on the tile counter.

Jeb sat down on the worn wood floor and opened his cereal box. Lying in a sun spot from the kitchen window—it faced west, making the kitchen too warm—Prince Hairy looked up eagerly at the rattle of plastic packaging. Teddy thought she ought to have a word with her sister about the care and feeding of children and animals.

Focusing on tasks, she put her anger on simmer and the groceries in the refrigerator. She needed to clean and spray the cabinets before adding food to them. "We need to set a few boundaries here, Kennedy.

I am an adult. Given my parents' non-parental sensibilities, I have been taking care of myself pretty much most of my life. I do not need a caretaker at this late date."

"As long as this house is my responsibility, I have to take care of it and its occupants," he retorted, washing out one of the new plastic glasses and pouring milk at Mia's request. "What happened to the glasses you were using earlier?"

"I told you, our resident specter took objection to them. Have you considered turning the town into a year-long spook house? You know, the way some places sell Christmas all year?" she asked sarcastically, taking the rest of the dishes from him and filling the sink with soapy water. "You could sell Halloween Hillvale."

He actually looked serious at her suggestion. "I'm afraid the road up here wouldn't sustain sufficient traffic. I'm having enough difficulty convincing the highway department that it will sustain a residential development."

"A development?" she asked in incredulity, over the noise of saws cutting up her ceiling. "Unless you pay your employees extraordinarily well, who in their right mind would buy houses up here? There isn't even a school! It must be a bear to get kids into Baskerville in winter."

"I'm thinking a vacation condo situation and a ski lift—short-term rentals." He leaned against the counter and crossed his shirt-sleeved arms, but he couldn't hide his passion for his plans. She regarded him skeptically as he continued. "The town would have high end boutiques like Vail. San Francisco is so densely packed these days, the rich will pay anything for a little space and quiet."

He was testing her, she sensed. This must be a touchy subject—with the Lucys? Yeah, she could see that. It was nice having this private enclave of weird people, but it definitely wasn't profitable.

"Speaking as a shop owner, I could work with rich customers," she agreed, sounding out her plans for her new direction. She reached down to take the cereal box from Jeb before Prince Hairy ate tomorrow's breakfast. She couldn't send the kids upstairs with carpenters, or out in the yard with no fence. She cut up a plate of apples and led them to the table in the front room.

Kurt miraculously retrieved the board games from where she'd dumped them and followed without being told. The man had some uses.

"Hillvale could actually start charging a sales tax and cover improvements," he said. "We could have parking fees to pay Walker's salary, property taxes so we might have schools someday."

"People can have boutiques and schools anywhere," she pointed out. "You just want them here because you own the land and want to make money. I have no objection to money, but I can make it anywhere. I cannot find what Hillvale offers anyplace else. You have yourself an existential dilemma."

"Nothing existential about it." He raised his voice over the pounding of hammers. A cloud of plaster dust filtered down. "People hate change, but progress has to be made or we stagnate."

Mia apparently already knew how the board game worked. Ignoring the argument over her head, she bossily explained her version of the rules to Jeb, who was more interested in the plastic figures than rules.

Teddy eased toward the steps, straining to see what was happening upstairs. The carpenters had covered the top of the stairs with plastic to catch the plaster, and she couldn't see anything. "Are they safe up there? Will that plastic hold if someone falls?"

Kurt stood in the doorway with her. His proximity wracked her already rattled nerves. Painful experience had trained her long ago not to use her Inner Monitor. That neglect had cost her dearly. After the unfortunate episode with her thieving ex, she was determined to learn the uses of her odd talent. Still, she only dared open herself for brief amounts of time. Should she open it just to test for the ghost? She didn't think she could warn the carpenters from down here even if she knew the spirit meant to strike. Learning how and when to use her woo-woo ability was part of the process. This time, she opted for less painful ignorance.

"There are different types of change," she reminded Kurt. "You could fix up the town, hide quaint bungalows in the woods, even set up campgrounds. Poor people need a getaway as much as the rich."

"Would you be satisfied with the income from poor people?" he asked in scorn.

Actually, that had been her intention for this shop. She didn't have the chance to say so.

The dog emitted an ear-piercing howl. Alarmed, the kids looked up from their board game.

And plaster crashed into the plastic barrier, accompanied by an unearthly shriek, a cloud of dust, and screams of terror.

SEVEN

KURT PRACTICALLY FLUNG TEDDY BACKWARD AND OUT OF THE WAY OF precipitating plaster. Coughing, he covered his face with his sleeve and ran through his mental checklist of emergency procedures. With no cell coverage, he couldn't call for help. He didn't know if the shop had a land line. If it had been the lodge, his next step after calling 911 would be to send trained employees with emergency kits to see if his contractors were injured.

With no employees to call on, it looked like it was on him to see what had happened. Leaving Teddy rushing the children outside and shouting for help in the street, Kurt held his sleeve over his nose to keep out the worst of the dust. He eased his way up the treads, stepping carefully around the torn plastic barrier. Remembering his last experience in this stairwell, he pressed his back to the wall—just in case. This was what happened if he left his orderly office—Hillvale was chaos.

"Bud?" he called over the dog's howls. "Bill?"

"Here, boss," a rough voice on the left answered, coughing. "Sorry about the mess. The ladder fell."

Cursing from the second worker on the right didn't sound as reassuring.

"Bill?" Kurt tried to see into the dusty gloom above, but the electricity had gone off again, and sunlight didn't reach this hall.

"That effin' ladder was pushed," Bill growled from the vicinity of the bigger room on the left. "I damned near broke my tailbone."

"There was no one here to push it," Bud called from the kids' room. "You didn't fix the crossbar tight."

Another stream of curses followed. Kurt didn't bother following their obvious direction and conclusion. Or ask about unearthly shrieks. For all he knew, the damned dog could hit high notes. Peeling back the remaining plastic, he emerged on the second floor to survey the debris.

From below, Walker shouted, "Need a hand? An ambulance? Or a dump truck?"

"A ghostbuster?" Kurt suggested, finally locating Bud inside the kids' room, past the fallen ladder. Thank all that was holy, the dog had stopped howling. "Can you stand or do we need to call for help?" He offered his hand.

A heavy, big-bellied man, Bud accepted his aid and hauled himself up with a groan. He rubbed at the back of his head. "Whacked myself good but nothin's broke that I can tell."

"He couldn't tell if his head broke or not," Bill called from the other side of the stairs, emerging from the thinning dust and rubbing his bruised posterior. "I'd better take him down to the doc."

"I recommend you both get looked at. Insurance covers it, and you'll receive your full day's wages." Kurt leaned down to see Walker coming up. "You might want to haul these two down the mountain for a look-see."

"At this rate, you'll need to set Brenda up with that office she wants. A nurse practitioner would be handy." Walker emerged from the dust to study the damage.

Teddy followed up right behind him. "I just sent the kids and dog with Amber. Mariah is fetching Brenda. A nurse will have a better idea if anyone needs the ER." She studied the plaster dust, the fallen ladder, and glanced up at the ceiling overhead. "Looks like you've uncovered the attic stairs."

The falling false ceiling had revealed a rectangular, white-painted wooden trap door.

"Bad plaster job," Bill grumbled. "The whole mess came down at once. Look, the old rope is still there."

Kurt grabbed Teddy's hand before she could reach for the twisted rope. He wasn't certain why. Bad vibes maybe. Besides, the rope had been cut off and was too high to reach without a stepstool. "Let's get this cleaned up and think about it before we tug that rope. It could be rotted. The stairs could be dangerous, and that could be the reason they covered them."

"Unhinged stairs," Teddy muttered in annoyance. "I'll fetch the broom and see if anyone has a vacuum."

"We've got one in the van," Bud offered.

"Unload it downstairs, and then take the day off," Kurt advised. "But let Brenda have a look at you first."

By the time the workmen had departed, Teddy was eyeing him with one raised eyebrow.

"You look like a demented leprechaun when you do that," he told her. "I still see your hair as red."

That appeared to jar her back to normal. She ran her hand through her hair with a rueful grimace. "I should have whacked it off. I'll start washing it out now that we're here and staying."

"You shouldn't be staying," he warned, wondering why she'd had to hide her hair but refusing to show interest. "This place is dangerous. I'd put you up at the lodge for a while, but we're booked weekends. You can still stay the night."

"Not owing you more, mister," she countered. "I'm ridding this place of demented ghosts. This place is *mine*, and no one, corporeal or not, is taking it away."

That was *not* what he wanted to hear. He'd been bulldozing this place and rebuilding it in his mind for so long that he thought of it as *his*, even though it belonged to the family corporation. He set his jaw and didn't respond to provocation. A woman accustomed to luxury wouldn't last in the dump for long.

Walker came up carrying the vacuum cleaner. "Why do I feel as if we need to just burn this place down and start over?"

Validated, Kurt pointed at him. "See? Even Walker agrees with me."

Teddy grabbed the heavy-duty canister and hunted for a wall plug. In that tight t-shirt and jeans, she looked like a pocket-sized rock star. When she straightened and glared at him, the impact went straight to his groin. Kurt grabbed the machine handle, flipped the switch, and began sucking dust rather than speak.

"His cleaning crew has taught him a thing or two," Walker said with appreciation.

"What do we have to do to test the safety of those stairs?" Teddy studied the wooden frame overhead.

"Any windows in the attic we could try to climb in first?" Kurt asked above the roar of the machine.

"Not that I remember," Teddy admitted. "It was just a black hole for Christmas decorations. I sneaked up to explore whenever Dad had the stairs down."

Samantha appeared at the bottom of the stairs and called up, "Amber can't work and take care of kids for long. Should I take them and the dog somewhere safe while you decide who's killing himself?"

"Is there anywhere safe?" Teddy called down, sounding dubious.

"Brenda said she could take them to her place. She has a fenced yard and her grandkids' playroom. And she says Bill and Bud are fine, and if someone would buy Dinah a beer license, they'd be even better."

"Tell Monty to call the lodge bar and open a tab," Kurt said, turning off the vacuum. "I don't think we have the cable hooked up in here so I can't call him."

"So I don't even have a *phone*?" Teddy asked, glaring at him over the dustpan she was using for the larger chunks of plaster.

"I'll get you a phone and internet since the place is in the corporation's name. But I'm raising your rent to cover them." Kurt held a trash bag for her to dump the plaster in. "We need face masks for this work."

She handed him the dust pan. "Let me check on the kids and talk to this Brenda person. I'd make a lousy mother, but I try to be a good aunt." She dashed down the stairs.

"So we go up now?" Walker suggested, his body language showing interest even if his stoic cop demeanor gave away nothing.

"Only if we can do so by not standing under it. Looks like it opens toward the bathroom and not the stairs." Kurt looked for the stepladder that he'd seen earlier. Finding it, he set it up in the bathroom doorway.

"You're not doing anything up there without me," Teddy called from below. "I can practically hear your wheels turning. Give me a minute."

"She's kinda spooky," Walker said, peering down at the shop area. "The women are gathering down there, nattering like birds. How can she hear us?"

"She probably has the place bugged," Kurt said, only half jesting. He scanned the walls and ceiling looking for wires, but they'd already done that. If there were wires, they were in the walls.

Feeling like a voyeur snooping around, Kurt looked for anything that he could use to knot on the stair rope—until he heard steps on the stairs and couldn't resist watching Teddy.

"This won't help if the rope is rotten, but it's all I've got." Teddy emerged from the stairwell carrying a bungee cord for securing suitcases.

"Good score." Kurt would admire her mind-reading ability if he wasn't so irritated at her interference. But she was living here, and he wasn't her boss, so he had no authority. He hated that.

As he took the cord from her, she muttered "Control freak," apparently reading his mind again.

Kurt ignored the complaint and climbed up to see if he could fasten the cord directly to the stairs. But the rope went through a hole and the ladder wasn't tall enough. Walker sensibly stood to one side as Kurt knotted the two cords together. Teddy stood at the bottom of the stepladder, watching.

"If the ghost shoves me, I'll land on you," he said in frustration, testing his knot.

"Just making sure you're a good Boy Scout and can handle that knot," she said cheerfully, stepping aside to lean against the wall of the tiny bathroom.

She was relentlessly cheerful, even when covered in plaster dust. Kurt wanted to add that to his list of complaints but knew he was being unreasonable. Her defiance was just getting under his skin.

"If there's any chance of a crime scene, maybe I should go up first," Walker suggested.

"So you can sue me when this ladder gives out or the door falls on your head?" Kurt asked. "I'm thinking we ought to turn the place into a Halloween spook house."

"The whole town," Teddy reminded him of her suggestion.

"We're blamed lucky Valdis isn't here, howling about evil spirits." Walker glanced down the stairs as the noise level rose below.

"Valdis?" Teddy raised those evocative painted-black eyebrows.

"Our resident death goddess, Sam's aunt. The fact that she's not around says we don't have to worry about dead bodies," Walker explained.

"Or that she's busy cooking up trouble on the Ingersson land and isn't here to howl," Kurt corrected, still resentful that his condo development was stalled until the court decided whether he or Valdis and Sam owned the farm. His father's fraud and subsequent death had left a lot of screwed up property. "She and Daisy have been up there all week sending smoke signals."

Impatiently, Teddy stood at the bottom of the ladder. "There is no crime scene in my house. Quit stalling. Want me to go first? She doesn't mind me."

"There is no *she* to it. I'm here, it's *my* house." Kurt knew he was growling like a dog with a bone, but he was fighting a lot of inner demons, the condo snafu being only one of them. This damned door was *his*. He tested the knot with a yank, watched in satisfaction as the cord tightened. He tugged a little harder. The door didn't budge.

"Would they have nailed it shut?" Teddy asked with worry.

"It's wood. Wood dries out or wicks moisture and warps. We may need a jig saw to shave off the edges." Kurt wrapped the rope around his hand and applied steady pressure.

"The man knows his tools," Walker crowed.

"A man of many facets," Teddy agreed. "Let me help pull. I don't mind if your butt lands on my face."

Kurt's mind instantly landed in the gutter. "So you can bite me?" he countered, keeping his cool.

With the rope wrapped around both fists, he increased the amount of weight he put into the tug by stepping down a rung of the stool. He wanted to feel any give and have time to shout a warning.

"How's it going up here?" Samantha joined Walker at the top of the stairs. "The ladies are smudging the shop again. They say the spirits are restless, and I think I hear Valdis wailing in the hills."

"No howls, no wails, no shoves," Teddy called to her from around Kurt.

The attic stairs plunged down without warning.

Kurt released the rope as he fell backward past the last step. He shoved Teddy into the bathroom, out of reach of the wooden rails falling down. A dark hole gaped above—from which a cloud of red and blue sparkles billowed.

Shock engulfed them as they watched the air turn purple and twinkle like pixie dust.

"Evil!" Teddy and Sam shouted in unison.

Kurt slammed the bathroom door on the weird dust, trapping him in with Teddy in the small area. Outside, he heard the other bedroom door bang shut as Walker did the same with Sam.

In the faint light from the small window, he could make out Teddy hastily running water in the sink. She handed him soap. "Scrub," she demanded. "That stuff feels lethal."

"Fetching toxic clean-up," Walker shouted, evidently daring pixie dust to open his door. "Don't leave that room. I think you caught the worst of it. I want to test this stuff."

"It's probably hallucinogens," Sam called, sounding almost gleeful. "Can we have an orgy while waiting for clean-up?"

Teddy didn't chuckle at the byplay from the hall. Kurt stuck his hands in the running water and accepted the soap. "Evil?" he asked in a low voice while more voices seeped through the thin panel.

"Bad vibrations," she muttered without explanation. "Pretty though." She admired the pattern of red and blue on her shirt.

"I doubt there's any manual for cleaning up *evil*, but I have basic protective gear in my car," Walker called through the panel. "We're going to try to clean up as much of this dust out here as we can without tracking it downstairs, just in case there are toxins involved. Most of it flew toward you."

"Like a whirlwind," Sam added. "You sucked it right in. I think our poltergeist doesn't like you Uncle Kurt."

"Quit calling me uncle," Kurt grumbled. "You make me feel a hundred years old. And we'll all feel like fools if this is just Christmas decoration dust."

A vacuum roared on the other side.

"It's not glitter," Teddy said, looking more grim than he'd ever seen her. "This is more like glass or crystal."

"And you should know why?" Kurt had put two and two together and figured he knew, but he wanted to see how long she would keep up the disguise.

"You're rich enough to know my designs," she said, piercing him with a glare. "You know my name. Work it out."

"Theodosia Devine Designs," he said in satisfaction. "I bought my fiancée one of your bracelets after she insisted no one can live without one."

"Let me guess." She dashed soap from her face and wiped it with a towel as she spoke. "She left you right after that."

Shocked, Kurt turned off the faucet with his elbow. "What, you jinx your jewelry?"

She shrugged. "Not exactly. But the crystals I use have power. They tend to bring out true character or open eyes to illusions or act as a kind of truth serum. They're disruptive."

Hands dripping, Kurt stared rather than take the towel she offered. Before he could find an adequate response, a new voice carried through the door—Cassandra.

"The dust is embedded with. . . negativity," Cass called through the door.

"She means evil," Teddy whispered. "She's trying to spare our delicate sensibilities."

Kurt reached for the door, fed up with the nonsense after that last low blow. *Truth serum?* Give him a break. Teddy grasped his hand and shook her head. Her touch cooled his temper a few degrees.

"We can't let the dust on your clothes spread," Cass said from the other side. "We're gathering fresh ones. We'll give them to you in a plastic bag you can use to deposit the dirty ones in. If the shower works, I'd advise you to use it to scrub your hair."

"I can't believe you said that," Teddy called back. "You want me to shower with *Kurt*?"

"We all make sacrifices," Cass said dryly.

"What's Walker doing about the attic?" Kurt demanded, trying hard not to think about Teddy naked in the shower.

"I have Monty calling in clean-up for possible toxins," Walker responded. "I want all the dust upstairs and down vacuumed out professionally before anyone tries those stairs."

"I told him we'd all turn into purple unicorns if he isn't careful," Sam called.

"You don't believe that crap. You're just making Cass happy," Walker argued.

Kurt tuned out the lovers' spat in the hall to concentrate on Teddy, who was studying her purple-dusted hair in the mirror rather than look at him.

"I don't believe in that crystal power stuff," Kurt asserted. "Kylie left me because I'm non-communicative and taciturn, and I didn't pay enough attention to her."

"Women don't leave men who buy them expensive jewelry. Just putting her up in a pricey house is attention enough," she pointed out. "And I'd bet good money you did that too. The crystal made her realize money isn't enough. She wanted love."

Even lower blow.

"All San Francisco real estate is expensive. She wasn't poor." Kurt thought back to that painful time. Had Kylie actually seemed to regret breaking up with him? Nah, that was just Teddy turning his head around backwards. Women could do that to a man if he wasn't careful. Kylie had just wanted a man on her arm every time she went out, and he didn't spend enough time in the city to be there for her. He knew his faults.

Teddy shrugged. "Have it your way. But the crystals I mix with my gems come from a supply my parents accumulated up here. It took me a long time before I realized they had any effect, so I don't expect you to get it."

"Truth-telling doesn't sound evil." Kurt relaxed a little now that she was showing sense.

"My fiancé emptied my bank account and took my box of precious stones after I made our engagement rings using embedded crystals. A high price to pay to learn the truth about him." She said it matter-of-factly, as if men stealing from her was just another day on the planet.

Kurt wasn't certain how to handle that underhanded emotional lob. He focused on the financial end, the only part that made sense. "Bet that set you back a while."

She shot him another one of those fiery topaz glares. "In more ways than one."

Ouch. He could feel that shot—she wasn't trusting anyone, particularly of the male variety. Kurt felt the same about women, so that made them even, in a stone-cold way.

She took off her shoes and pulled aside the shower curtain just as someone knocked on the door.

"Laundry delivery," Walker announced. "Sam and I get the next round. Cass won't allow us downstairs."

Kurt opened the door a crack and took the laundry bag handed to him. "You realize this is all a ridiculous waste of time?"

"Better safe than sorry." Walker closed the door.

Teddy emptied the bag, sorting their clothes and fresh towels on the closed commode. "Any more truths you want to hear?"

When he didn't reply, she stepped barefoot into the shower, pulled the curtain, and began dropping dusty clothes outside the tub.

Kurt watched in stunned silence as she casually stripped that curvaceous figure on the other side of a nearly transparent sheet of vinyl.

"I don't need crystal to sense lust," she called. "The feeling is reciprocal, so let's stay far, far away from each other after this, okay?"

Reciprocal? Kurt didn't need to be told twice. He pried off his shoes and unfastened his jeans as the water came on.

EIGHT

"Who knew you hid all that under suits and ties?" Teddy said, stunned by the taut abs and firm pecs of her landlord as Kurt joined her in the tub, already half-aroused. *Truth serum*, indeed, this blasted pixie dust had a lot to account for.

She wasn't shocked that he'd taken up her half-assed offer. She'd known she was taunting a tiger. Her feelings were too complex to sort. She simply reacted as any sane woman would when confronted with gorgeous muscled male animal. She stepped into his arms and enjoyed the power of her femininity as he growled in appreciation and his erection lengthened against her belly.

He gripped her buttocks and lifted her so their mouths meshed while the water cascaded over their skin. Kurt Kennedy was no weak desk jockey. The man must work out his frustration in a heavy duty gym. And his mouth searing hers was akin to heaven and seemed the most normal, reassuring experience she'd had in weeks.

Teddy dug her fingers into Kurt's thick hair and gave up thinking. His kiss heated her to the core, stripped her of doubt, built desire into a bonfire no amount of water could douse.

He pushed her up against the tile wall so he could cup her breasts. His groan of pleasure was sufficiently satisfying for her to lift her leg and circle his back. She had to bite her lip to keep from shrieking when he snagged the grab bar and leaned over to suck her nipple.

"Truth," he muttered, just before sliding his hand between her legs and driving her out of her mind.

It had been so damned long. . . Kurt covered her screams with his mouth as release rocked her soul. Before the final ripples slowed, he drove into her.

Madness, sheer beautiful insanity. If this was the result of pixie dust, bring it on! She wrapped her fingers around his on the bar while he sent her up and over the top again. With their mouths meshed, her leg around his back, and all that. . . studliness. . . filling her, she understood the cliché of feeling as if they were one. She couldn't remember ever experiencing such an intense sensation.

Teddy bit Kurt's lip when he started to shout his release. With the water pouring over them, he yanked out, laughing and groaning. He crushed her breasts in his hand as he exploded as wildly as she had.

They'd barely had time to recover their breath before Walker pounded the door and shouted over the roar of heavy duty machinery. "Hurry it up in there. We could turn purple while you're using up all the hot water."

"Oh darn sugar heck," Teddy muttered into a broad, naked, wet shoulder.

"Darn sugar?" he asked, not releasing her.

"My mother's teaching. She wouldn't curse in front of us. With the kids around, I'm practicing." She lowered her legs. "It keeps my creativity employed."

"They're not around now, thankfully, but darn sugar heck sounds about right." He rubbed her nipple into arousal.

"We can't do this again. It will kill me," she warned.

Without releasing her, Kurt kicked off the water faucet. They hadn't used shampoo but their hair dripped into their eyes. Shoving hers out of her face, Teddy could feel him assessing her, but she'd shut down her Inner Monitor as well as her brains apparently. Gratefully, she accepted the clean towel he handed her.

"Pixie dust," he said with more cynicism than question.

"Truth serum, whatever. We're never going to get this stuff out of here. It's all over the floor." She rubbed at her hair and surreptitiously watched Kurt do the same. Damn, but he must spend time at the beach. Or on a yacht. He was brown *almost* all over.

"Bring mops," Kurt shouted back at Walker. "We can't get out of the tub without contamination."

That put the others off long enough for them to dress in the clothes from the laundry bag. They were ready except for shoes by the time the others knocked again.

"Don't touch anything," Walker warned as soon as he opened the door, wielding a mop. "The crew has to wash all the clothes and linen stored up here."

Outside the door, people wearing face masks and gloves scrubbed at the floors and walls. A roll of industrial carpet had been thrown over the hall and down the stairs, presumably to catch any stray dust.

"How much is this going to cost me?" Teddy muttered after the floor was mopped and they were allowed to ease past people extending long hoses into the attic and others scrubbing the walls of the stairwell.

"Insurance," Kurt suggested. "Although I'm not sure a policy covers asbestos much less pixie dust."

"Quit calling it that. You make it sound harmless." She lowered her voice to a whisper. "Do you think we would have done what we just did without it?"

"Absolutely," he said with assurance, placing a proprietary hand at her back as they reached the crowd waiting at the bottom.

Teddy didn't know how to take that, so she didn't punch him for pushing her around.

"You can't bring the children back here until Walker tells us the dust isn't toxic," Cassandra said the instant they entered the shop.

The regal older woman appeared to be the local authority on all things weird. Teddy's nature was to rebel, but she couldn't subject her sister's kids to risk.

"You can stay with me," Cass continued. "Sam is moving out of the studio, if you prefer your privacy."

"Teddy and the kids are going to the lodge tonight," Kurt replied firmly. "We have internet and cable and they'll be safer."

"Surrounded by evil?" Cass scoffed.

As much as she wanted to be anywhere but around Kurt, he had a point, and *evil* was a subjective topic. Before the argument could escalate, Teddy intervened. "One more night at the lodge won't hurt. The kids are at least familiar with it. I can't keep disrupting their lives."

"Keep his mother away from them," Cass warned.

Kurt practically shoved Teddy out the front door.

SAMANTHA

JUNE 26: AFTERNOON

"Pixie dust." Black braid swinging, Mariah slid into the booth across from Walker and Sam after the dinner rush. "Clarify. Whatever you did, the ghosts are congregating again, even after I've cleaned the town." She nodded at one of her beaded nets in the corner of the café's ceiling.

Sam studied the shivering net with scientific interest. "I feel no wind or earth movement, and I see nothing ghostly clinging to your strings either." But she'd been working here daily and had never seen the nets move before.

"It could take the lab weeks to determine the origin of the purple dust." Ever the proper police officer, Walker intelligently stuck to the practical while eyeing the swaying nets. "Weights hung on invisible threads might cause that motion."

"And so could loose ectoplasm," Mariah countered, before biting into her cinnamon roll. The feathers threaded into her braid seemed to have a life of their own—like her nets.

"We can't argue over an unprovable subject, unless someone wants to develop a test for ectoplasm. The more relevant question is whether or not purple dust has caused any testable effects," Sam said, revealing the direction of her thoughts these last hours.

"Such as?" Mariah raised her eyebrows.

Sam blushed. She wasn't about to mention that inhaling dust had raised their lust quotient into the stratosphere. "We would have to test to see if the adrenaline rush of the accident or the dust were factors in any unusual behavior."

"It isn't unusual for Kurt to be bossy or Teddy to think of the kids first. And you two looking pie-eyed at each other has nothing to do with adrenaline," Mariah stated, wiping crumbs from her mouth. "The two workmen were carted off before the dust hit. So basically, I see no effect except in my ghost catchers."

Sam chewed at her thumbnail. "Teddy sent me a cryptic message about truth serum. Maybe we should talk to her."

Walker frowned at his coffee cup. "Sodium pentothal is a barbiturate that causes people to lose inhibitions, but there's no guarantee that what is said is actually the truth. And it doesn't come in crystal sparkles."

Mariah ignored his scientific analysis. "I'll call the lodge, see if Teddy is available. She's fire to Sam's earth and my wind. Together, we might work this out." She slid from the booth and headed for Dinah's office.

"Fire? Earth?" Walker asked, holding Sam's hand beneath the table.

"More superstition, like the number thirteen and tarot cards," Sam explained.

"I'm worried about that truth serum business," he admitted. "Being with you in the shower felt honest and right, better than it's ever been for me. It was like some part of my gut finally opened up and allowed you in," he said, almost reluctantly.

Knowing the death of his wife and child hung heavy on his heart, Sam rejoiced, understanding and loving the large leap of faith he'd just made. "Pixie dust makes us face our innermost fears? Feelings? It scared me half to death," she confessed. "I had this sudden wild desire to make babies, even knowing you're not ready and having suffered the consequence of my father's illegitimacy."

"Earth mother." He laughed and kissed her hand, dismissing the woo-woo connection.

Sam wasn't as certain that psychic influences didn't exist. But for now, she'd have to bury the certainty that she wanted children. Walker wasn't ready, and she shouldn't be.

NINE

STEPPING OVER THE SNORING PRINCE HAIRY, TEDDY CHECKED ON HER sleeping Goths. Mia was adorable in her pink princess nightgown and Jeb in his blue superhero pajamas. Teddy thought they ought to mix it up occasionally and let Jeb wear the pink and Mia the blue, but she was fractured like that. Sydony wouldn't appreciate it.

Kurt had provided her with a suite this time—payment for services rendered? Or hope that she'd welcome him for another round? She shouldn't be so cynical, but she'd earned her pessimism the hard way. Men always wanted more than she was willing to give and occasionally figured she was a lightweight and tried to take what she didn't offer.

Desperate to find an emotional connection, she'd denied her Inner Monitor for years. She'd kept it shut down through way too many failed relationships. That had been a massive mistake she couldn't afford to repeat. No matter how lonely she was or how painful honesty might be, she wasn't falling blindly into any more affairs.

She'd put the kids in the bedroom. As much as she enjoyed sex, she'd learned the hard way that she preferred emotional stability. She was taking the couch.

That worked out well after she took Mariah's call. Company would be welcome. Maybe talking about what had happened would clear her head so she could sleep.

Teddy had room service bring up wine and munchies. Sam and Mariah arrived bearing cheese, grapes, and sangria. Walker followed with a six pack. The room was barely big enough to hold everyone. She hoped Hairy wouldn't decide to wake and bark. She was pretty certain the lodge didn't normally accept pet guests, but she wanted the kids to have their furry security blanket.

By the time she'd set up a table and poured drinks, her landlords, Monty and Kurt, knocked on the door.

Teddy leaned against the jamb and didn't let them in. "Need something?" she asked rudely. She couldn't help it. They were rich studs and men like that either wanted something or took control.

"She's a Lucy," Kurt explained to his brother. "I warned you."

"Mariah and Sam are Lucys. I can talk to them." Their surfer dude mayor shoved open the door. "We *have* to talk to them if we don't want this town divided right down the middle."

Deciding that almost sounded reasonable, Teddy let him pass.

"Lucy?" She met Kurt's eyes. "Are you calling me nuts?"

"Just weird," Sam called from inside the room. "Get used to it. Call them Nulls. Stereotypes work."

"Stereotypes divide," Kurt corrected, shoving past Teddy as his brother had done. "I am nothing like Monty or my mother. If anything, I'm more like my Uncle Lance."

Everyone in the room stared. Teddy closed the door and waited for an explanation.

"Lance is an absent-minded artist," Mariah said, helping herself to the grapes. "There couldn't be two more different people in town."

Kurt poured wine and swirled it, apparently comfortable with being called a liar. Teddy had to admire his aplomb. Mariah was something of a loose cannon.

"Kurt is an architect," Monty explained, perusing the spread on the table and then taking in the paucity of chairs. "He just didn't fry his brain on drugs the way our uncle did. Lance was an architect once too. He and Kurt were supposed to go into business together."

Without comment, Kurt picked up the phone and ordered his staff to bring more chairs. Teddy shivered. Even with her inner sense turned off, the concentration of strong power and temperament pushed the room to the brink of implosion. That's when she noticed the ghost-catchers swinging on the ceiling above the lamplight.

Conversation died as her guests followed her gaze. The crystals shimmered, the beads clacked, and the string drew taut.

"That's why we're here," Mariah said, popping another grape. "You've apparently unleashed evil that I thought we'd expunged from the town."

Mariah climbed up on a chair and ran her fingers over the ghost-catcher in a corner of the room. "I can see the shredded bits of ecto-plasm on here," she informed them. "My granny taught me how to absorb the sorry remains of life and send it on to whatever waits beyond."

Teddy tried to see what she was doing but could only tell that the net hung straighter now and no longer moved.

"The lodge is built on evil," Mariah continued matter-of-factly, climbing down. "The pixie dust is causing some kind of reaction that I don't understand."

"I thought it was the cemetery that held ghosts," Sam said. "Isn't that what you told me?"

"No, the cemetery is old, but it's a consecrated burial ground, not evil. Of course there are ghosts there. The whole valley contains the spiritual impressions we call ghosts from the time man first walked it. But the *lodge* was built on ancient evil that we don't understand, and the spirits here are real and not just impressions. This is where the original ranch was built, until it burned and the spiritualists told the ranchers to move into town. This land should be left *empty*." Mariah grabbed more grapes and her glass of sangria and sat cross-legged on the floor, ignoring the empty chair that had been delivered within instants of Kurt's call.

"Those are all old folk tales," Kurt insisted. "People have been making up stories about the town since its inception, drumming up business for their gypsy trade. I am not closing a profitable business because you make strings jiggle."

"Sam, when is your art dealer coming up to have a look around?" Mariah asked, deliberately averting the argument.

Teddy recognized that she directed the conversation to a subject the Kennedy brothers would appreciate.

Sam brightened. "Elaine said she'd be up tomorrow. I'm hoping she can tell us if Lucinda Malcolm painted the mural in the cafe. Do you think she can tell us about the crystals ground into the Ingersson paintings?"

Teddy held up her hand. "Explanations, please."

"Apparently the artists who used to live up the mountain ground crystals into their paints—maybe like the dust you saw today?" Mariah gestured for Sam to do the honor. "Sam was raised by artists. She knows the lingo."

Sam sipped her sweet drink. "Some of the oils haves been turning red—but only in the eyes, as far as we've noticed. Daisy keeps them in a hidden cache, but I saw one of a man I recognized, one who owned a real estate company. The portrait had red eyes, and it turned out that he was about as evil as a man can get."

Mariah continued without expression, "But another man whose eyes *had* been red in his portrait, gave up drugs and turned in the evil guy to the authorities. After that, the eyes in his painting returned to normal. So we think there's something weird going on with the artwork around town."

"OK, red eyes are beyond my scope, but what about Lucinda Malcolm?" Teddy asked. "Isn't she a famous painter? Was she one of the hippie artists?"

"Not that we know." Sam picked up the conversational thread. "We heard she had visited in the glory days, when the artist colony was famous. But that was the 70s, and she was quite old by then. The hippie lifestyle wouldn't have suited her. Still, we're hoping we'll find examples of her art to see if she used the crystals the others did."

"The spirit in the séance said to *find the art*." Teddy said, looking thoughtful. "I don't know anything about art, but I know crystals. Do you know what kind or where they got them? 'Crystal' can mean anything from diamonds to agates. I wouldn't think too many would occur naturally in these mountains, but I'm no geologist."

Teddy avoided mentioning the *power* of crystals, but that's what this session was really about. The Nulls wouldn't appreciate that kind of talk though.

"My background is environmental," Sam acknowledged. "I know a little about the geology of the area, and you're right, there's nothing particularly exciting or unusual about the crystals normally found here. There might be geodes of common quartz, surrounded by agate stone, maybe an occasional amethyst. That's the most to be expected."

"Because scientists don't understand evil," Mariah insisted. "You boys might as well leave for the bar now, because you definitely won't understand."

Monty crossed his arms and didn't move. Kurt poured more wine and laid a possessive arm over Teddy's chair back. She pried it off.

"Indulge us," Deputy Walker ordered, crossing his ankle over his thigh. He massaged the weak thigh muscle that caused his limp, but the position also tilted him closer to Sam on the couch.

"His mother believes in *chi* energy," Sam explained. "He doesn't believe, but he doesn't laugh either."

"I don't like theory," Mariah stated flatly. "I know evil exists because I can feel it. Sam feels it, too, although she calls it negativity. We feel it most on lodge lands, but it's on the Ingersson farm as well. It's not theory that I can see the ectoplasm of the dead. But what I see does not *prove* evil is centered at the lodge."

"I felt the *evil* in the pixie dust," Teddy offered. "I'm not entirely sure how or why. I work with crystal all the time, but I never noticed that negativity before now. The dust just felt. . . toxic. I think I noticed it the same way I notice how people feel. It's intuitive."

"Then I advise you not to spend much time on lodge land," Maria said. "There are spots that aren't polluted, and places more polluted than others, but it's not a healthy experience. We're afraid those of us with extra senses who spend too much time around the resort could eventually go mad, rather like Lance and the artists in the commune."

"That was drugs," Kurt said dismissively. "Snort enough cocaine, mix it with LSD and mushrooms, and anyone would be polluted to the brink of insanity."

"Crystal meth," Sam said thoughtfully. "Did they have that back then? Or could it be some variant? I'll need to look up the formula."

Walker patted her on the head. "You lead such a sheltered life. The basic ingredients for meth can be bought at the drugstore."

"Drugstore chemicals can be dangerous," Teddy argued. "Even salt is a crystal. The world is full of pollutants that can be made toxic. I just want whatever is in my attic to leave. Will your art dealer help with that? If not, then like Mariah, I'm not into a lot of theory. I want action. I want that ghost gone."

Mariah lifted her glass in salute. "Compadre," she said in satisfaction.

The room phone rang, and Teddy leaned over to grab it. She listened, then handed the receiver to Monty. He listened, growled, and got up.

"Valdis is back. She's howling at Teddy's house."

Mariah sighed." The Death Goddess has never been wrong yet."

TEN

TEDDY WOKE UP THE NEXT MORNING TO A HANGOVER AND THE GOTHS bickering in the bedroom. Groaning, she rubbed her eyes and verified she was decent and that she really had thrown out Hunky Kurt last night. After the others had departed to check on the *Death Goddess*— maybe Hillvale was just a little nuttier than she remembered—Kurt had lingered. But faced with too much stress and induced by too much alcohol, she'd performed her best Tempest Teddy meltdown, she remembered. He'd left her to it and escaped. Men didn't like dealing with emotional women, and Kurt in particular would have an aversion, she sensed.

Oh well, she didn't need another man complicating her life anyway. Although she might be far less hysterical after another round of the spectacular sex he'd offered—or maybe that had only been a fluke brought on by pixie dust.

She got up, tripped over Prince Hairy in the bedroom, and threw herself onto the big king-sized bed where Mia and Jeb were battering each other with pillows. They battered her instead. She was good with that. They needed to be kids and not worried about their mother.

"Can we talk to Mama again?" Mia demanded. "I want to tell her what I dreamed."

Well, so much for that theory. She'd managed to catch Syd for a brief Skype session last night, but they didn't dare spend much time online. They weren't techies and had no idea of what resources Butthead might have in play.

"This morning, we eat a *huge* breakfast, and then you're going for pony riding lessons," she said in her best good-aunt voice. She'd learned about the riding school from the receptionist at the desk, not taciturn Kurt, who probably had no idea what kids liked.

They looked rightfully dubious about these plans, but she got them dressed, found ragged jeans and a shirt she wouldn't mind throwing out after a morning in the filth of her attic, and took Prince Hairy for a walk before breakfast. She was in debt for the gems her ex had stolen after their break-up, but she still had enough money to pay for meals. That had been an expensive lesson in why she needed her Inner Monitor, but she didn't need charity yet.

She needed to contact her office, though, give them some instructions.

Add that to her enormous to-do list, along with chasing ghosts from her attic and death goddesses from her doorstep. She'd wanted to change her life—she should have been more specific.

With the kids bouncing on a sugary crepe-and-cereal high, Teddy marched them to the resort's children's center. At the height of tourist season, it was packed with children of all ages. Worried about last night's discussion of evil, she briefly opened her senses, but she detected nothing except anticipation, the usual childish worries, and really focused young guides. Not a hint of pain—or evil—anywhere. Maybe she could only detect crystal evil?

Or maybe living here was a total mistake, and she was losing her mind to even think such a crazy thing.

After dropping off Mia and Jeb, Teddy helped Prince Hairy into the van and drove into town. She'd been told that Valdis, the so-called Death Goddess, was Sam's aunt, who acted as the town banshee when spirits rose—usually from the dead and dying but occasionally from long-dead corpses. That didn't sound in the least promising if a banshee was haunting her shop.

And didn't that sound like a ridiculous way to start the day? She almost hummed in anticipation. Life had been grim lately. Banshees seemed an entertaining alternative.

As Teddy parked the van in the parking lot, a stream of Lucys emerged from the café. They'd obviously been watching for her since they headed straight for her place. Teddy started re-thinking her fond memories of small town living where everyone looked out for one another. She'd forgotten that was just another form of busybody nosiness.

The tall woman in flowing dark veil and skirts had to be Valdis. She paced up and down the board sidewalk while the others chattered. As Teddy approached with Prince Hairy on his leash, the death goddess halted and announced, "Finally," in a stage voice that would have carried any good theater. "That poor soul is waiting on us."

"That poor soul may have been dead a hundred years," Teddy countered, unlocking the door. "Hi, I'm Teddy, and this is my home. You're welcome to enter but please be kind to the ghosts."

Mariah snickered. Sam introduced her aunt, who nodded in tight disapproval but managed not to announce to every tourist in town that dead people resided here.

Someday, Teddy's Treasure Trove would need customers. Or maybe she ought to call it the Crystal Cavern.

While Teddy pondered shop names and held the door, Cassandra led the way inside, followed by several other Lucys. Orange-haired Amber crouched down and rubbed Hairy's head. He sniffed her be-ringed fingers, then headed straight for the kitchen and his sunspot, obviously unconcerned with spirits or pixie dust. Teddy figured the male dog was a Null.

"Walker hasn't heard anything from the lab about the chemicals in the dust," Sam said as they settled around the big table in the front room. "He said not to go upstairs until he gets back from Baskerville."

Teddy looked at the other women. "I'm not in favor of waiting. If the dust has been all sucked out, I want to get down to business. Anyone have a reason why I shouldn't go up there yet?"

"She needs release," Valdis intoned. "If she has a message she must share before she goes, we must be open to it."

"She's already told us to find the art," Mariah reminded everyone. "We need to know what art."

"Daisy's hoard is immense. Can there be even more hidden elsewhere?" Sam asked.

"Like in the attic?" Teddy suggested with only a shade of sarcasm as she headed for the stairs. "Maybe you can talk to her better up there. I'm going up if no one sees any objection other than male caution."

"Sometimes male caution makes sense," Sam said, although she followed right behind Mariah, who was on Teddy's heels.

Earth, wind, and fire, Teddy remembered. Sam's tall golden goddess along with Mariah's sturdy darkness, and Teddy, her fiery auburn disguised. How did they get *wind* out of someone as solid-looking as Mariah? The woman was a mystery.

"We'll open ourselves to the spirit world down here," Cass told the remaining Lucys in the shop. "Let the younger ones explore."

"Amber isn't much older than I am," Teddy muttered as they climbed the stairs. "Why do they treat her like an old lady?"

"Her weight holds her back," Mariah said prosaically, examining the ceiling. "I think it gives her knee trouble."

"We need magical healers. That would be a lot more useful than whatever it is we do." Teddy studied the attic door. "Why did they have to close the damned thing up?"

"To keep us out." Sam checked the bedrooms and emerged with a stepladder.

"That'll do it," Teddy said in satisfaction. "They left the bungee cord on. Now, if only the door hinges don't collapse on us again. . . Better stay back."

"And wear hazmat suits?" Mariah said. "I'm sorry I missed that yesterday."

She and Sam backed into the bedroom doorway furthest from the stairs as Teddy climbed up and gripped the end of the bungee cord. It was only meant to hold down cargo, so it wasn't too elastic, just enough for her to tug while she backed down the stepladder. She'd rather not crack her head open if the stairs fell down again.

The attic door slowly swung open as if on well-oiled hinges. "Someone fixed the sucker?" Teddy asked, staring at the perfectly ordinary wooden treads, almost disappointed at the lack of purple dust.

"Not that I'm aware of, but anything is possible," Mariah said. "Just seeing Kurt eating in the café yesterday was a first, so maybe the vampire hasn't completely consumed his soul, and he actually accomplished something useful."

Teddy let that comment pass by. Ghosts, yes, vampires, no way.

Mariah studied the open ceiling. "You first. I have ghost-catchers I can put up there if it's safe." She waved the leather bag she'd been carrying.

"Kurt was actually pretty handy yesterday. I'd like to hear his story someday." Teddy rattled the stairs. They seemed solid.

"It's nothing interesting." Sam peered up the ladder. "His father died when Kurt and Monty were still kids. His mother had to take over running the resort. There was a huge scandal about his father's bank and mortgages and whatnot, lots of lawsuits. She held things together while Kurt and Monty finished college, but by then, Lance's architectural firm had gone under. Kurt had been helping out at the lodge as best as he could while taking classes, so instead of using his new architecture degree, he just took over from his mother."

"What was the crack about his mother yesterday?" Teddy asked, stepping on the ladder and bouncing to test it with her weight.

"She's an emotional vampire," Mariah said without inflection. "She sucks the souls from anyone she comes in contact with. She's drained Lance as much as the drugs have. She'll do the same to Kurt and Monty if they don't find some way of getting rid of her."

Well that explained the earlier vampire crack. "I never know whether you're being literal or metaphorical," Teddy complained, climbing higher.

"Carmel Kennedy is pretty darned scary," Sam admitted. "It's been much more peaceful around here since they sent her to Hawaii to recuperate after the fire. Even Lance is emerging from his shell."

Teddy climbed high enough to stick her head into the dark attic. "I need a flashlight. I can't see a switch or lightbulb or anything else up here. There should be one on the dresser in the room on the left of the stairs."

Sam called "Got it!" and Mariah came up the stairs after Teddy, carrying the small light.

Mariah switched on the beam as she reached the top and whispered, "Holy crap, she's sitting right there. That's one damned strong ghost."

Below, Valdis began to howl. Prince Hairy took up the tune.

Warned by his brother that the Lucys were gathering in Teddy's shop, Kurt parked in the town lot and strode up the boardwalk. An operatic howl reverberated from the two-story building at the end of the walk—*Valdis*. Even though he knew she was only a crazy, he had to fight a shudder at the mournful wail. Or was that the dog?

He stopped to greet one of his regular guests emerging from the café.

"You have a little theater group going over there?" A Hollywood director, he had good reason to make that assumption.

Kurt tried not to roll his eyes or scare off the paying customers. "Opera, actually. I have no idea what they're performing."

Apparently not an opera fan, the director grimaced and strode on to his Escalade. Kurt hurried across the street.

How had he been reduced to keeper of an insane asylum? He was supposed to be transforming San Francisco's deteriorating historical buildings into models of modern energy-saving beauty. Instead, he was shutting up maniacs to prevent tourists from fleeing the resort in droves. They'd lost enough business with the fire. The whole town would be unemployed and bankrupt if they had to close the resort.

Responsibility for the town his father had destroyed weighed heavy on his shoulders and ground his molars to dust. If he could just get the rehab project off the ground and ease out from under the restrictions of the resort his mother controlled. . . soon. The financing was almost in place. He'd drive the first bulldozer over Teddy's shop himself.

Kurt entered to find the older Lucys gathered around the old oak table, hands connected while the dog howled. Valdis droned in an odd voice about killing and crystals and art. *Yeah, right.*

Without offering a greeting, Kurt took the stairs up to the second floor, knowing that's where he'd find Teddy. At least she wasn't one of the crazies.

Standing at the bottom of the attic ladder, Samantha whistled a warning to her partner in crime. Teddy's head appeared in the ceiling opening.

Kurt scowled up at her. "You're supposed to wait for Walker."

"Walker can't talk to ghosts. Hush. Let's see if Mariah can."

So much for thinking she wasn't one of the crazies. Kurt rolled his eyes but kept quiet and waited at the bottom of the stairs in case anyone flew down them. The two women overhead murmured, but he couldn't make out their words.

Below, Valdis wailed, "It's here! It's right here! Can't you see? It's proof that he killed me!"

"The apparition is gone," Mariah called down. "She could be circling Valdis."

Right, circling ghosts talking to a wailing banshee made total sense. "I'm coming up." Kurt glanced at Samantha. "You joining them?"

She looked torn but finally shook her head. "I probably ought to check on my aunt and Cass. They may be slightly off-balance, but they're all the family I have, besides you and Monty."

He hadn't really given much thought to Sam's orphaned state except for how her arrival had affected his plans for development. He really was a self-centered prick, but that's how he survived. "Family holidays ought to be entertaining," he acknowledged drily.

His niece actually brightened. "I can just imagine Thanksgiving up here!"

"I was thinking Halloween at Cass's place, Thanksgiving at ours. Walker will want football." That was about all the small talk he could manage. He headed up the ladder to the tune of Sam's laughter. If they had to adopt a stray relative, Sam wasn't a bad one to take in. He could just hope she didn't go looking for her birth mother, who was bound to be another Lucy.

Mariah was sitting cross-legged at the top of the stairs, shining the flashlight around the eaves while Teddy crawled about in the path of the light. Kurt had a good glimpse of her rounded posterior in well-worn jeans before she sat back and waved at him.

Yesterday's bathtub sex wasn't a scene he would forget anytime soon, but he respected her refusal to indulge again. Regretted, yes, but he didn't want to sue the woman he was sleeping with.

"So far, nothing but squirrel nests and ancient insulation. Take a look at that rafter though." Teddy pointed up and Mariah obediently turned the light to the overhead beam. "Looks like one of the original logs, doesn't it?"

Fascinated despite himself, Kurt stood up to examine the blackened center rafter. He had to bend his head to keep from conking it. "Possibly. They may have salvaged material from the original structure when they built this one. It's probably an old redwood log. Wood like that won't deteriorate in the weather conditions up here. This attic is little more than a tent with a roof."

"In other words, it will be hot as Hades up here in another hour," Mariah said. "I'm hanging my nets, then scooting. Your ghost or pixie dust has raised poltergeists all over town. I'm needed elsewhere."

"Thanks for braving the elements and resident spook," Teddy told Mariah as Kurt took the flashlight. "If this all wasn't so improbable, I'd wait for Walker to search for a skeleton under the floorboards. I can't believe you actually *see* her."

"It's unusual, granted," Mariah acknowledged, fixing a ghost-catcher near a vent. "I'm thinking your pixie dust has permeated this place and created unusual circumstances."

"Ground crystal," Teddy corrected. "Crystals have power. I just haven't encountered any that produces apparitions before."

Kurt searched for signs of the weird dust from yesterday, but the team had sucked up every trace as far as he could tell. He began testing the old planks underfoot while holding the light on Mariah so she could finish her netting.

Teddy continued poking into the narrow spaces along the eaves, but Kurt couldn't follow her and help Mariah at the same time. He was relieved when the ghostcatchers were hung and feather-headed waitress departed.

He swung the light back to Teddy and all those luscious curves he'd dreamed about all night. He understood why she hadn't let him share her bed, despite their mutual hunger. Women were simply less logical about basic needs. A man would stick a hunk of meat over a fire and call it a meal. Women wanted spices, recipes, roasting pans, and a roof to protect the fire before they'd start cooking. Sex—got even more complicated.

"The walls could conceal more of the original house," Teddy said, dragging him from his reveries. "Tearing down an historic structure like this would be criminal."

"There is nothing historic about rotting lathe and shingle siding. A good wind could shake this place apart, and it's not fire or earthquake protected." Of course, the building had stood here for decades. . .

She was twisting his head around. Kurt turned the flashlight on the far corners of the attic, looking for insect or animal damage. The floorboards were old, too, also salvaged from an earlier structure. Damn. Redwood was nearly indestructible and too costly these days to replace.

"The planks are loose over here," Teddy called, still crawling around in the far corners.

Quelling his libido, Kurt swung the beam to where she crouched. "That looks more like plywood. Back off before it crumbles."

She backed away but continued prying at it.

Below, Walker called up, "Couldn't wait for me, could you? I hope you aren't destroying any evidence."

"Of what?" Kurt called back, moving out of the way so the deputy could climb up. "You sucked up any footsteps with the pixie dust."

"Along with all the cobwebs and spiders," Teddy added cheerfully.

"Have you tested that stuff yet?" Kurt demanded. He didn't want to consider that he and Teddy had fallen into lust because of magic stones. That was too Disney to believe.

"Sheriff's department could take weeks if they know you're not all dropping dead up here. I sent some to my company's lab. Should have something in a day or two if it's not too exotic." Walker was out of uniform and in jeans today. He sat on the edge of the attic opening and watched as Kurt crouched beside Teddy and jimmied at the loose plywood with his pocket knife. "You need a pry bar."

"We need a hardware store," Kurt said. "I'll have to send up to the lodge for tools."

"Screwdriver, gentlemen." Teddy sat back. "I don't want to damage that wood. There's something weird about it."

"Screwdriver, I can do." Walker disappeared down the stairs again.

"Define *weird*." Kurt examined the four by eight sheet nailed to the rafters. "Someone just used cheap plywood to cover the rafters instead of the old planking. It may cover the wires to your father's stereo system." Reminded of that, he ran the light over the ceiling, locating wires along the front of the house. They dangled uselessly—with no sound system attached.

Teddy wrinkled her pert nose. "I guess weird means not right, peculiar, out of place, odd. . . But in this case, I'm feeling *crystal* energy. Want to run and hide now?" She glared at him defiantly.

"No, I want crystal energy defined. Crystals are rocks. Unless they're magnetic or radioactive or something, they're not particularly energetic." He crouched and ran the beam over the plywood, looking for missing nails.

"Do you feel gravity?" she demanded. "Can you dig down and find the forces that control gravity?"

He grimaced, grasping her point. "But scientists have proved the existence of gravity. There is no visible evidence that rocks have any supernatural power."

Walker reappeared before they could continue the argument. Kurt sat back, fighting the urge to put a protective arm in front of Teddy as the deputy pried at the odd board. Dauntless, she bent forward to see better. He knew she wasn't helpless, but she seemed so small and breakable that instinct drove him to shield her with his body. He didn't know what he expected to happen, but after yesterday's adventures, he was prepared to shove her out of danger.

Walker handed him a second screwdriver. Supplied with a right to do so, Kurt gave Teddy the flashlight. Then he eased in front of her to pry at one side of the board while Walker took the other.

"Be careful," Teddy warned. "That plywood could be important."

Neither of them replied but continued jimmying the old nails. Kurt derived satisfaction in the physical labor of thrusting, shoving, and pounding, but it still didn't distract him from Teddy's jasmine-scented presence. He ought to leave before she messed with his head any more, but now his curiosity had been aroused.

And he couldn't quit thinking in sexual terms.

With a sigh of relief, he removed the last nail from the side he'd taken while Walker edged up the final corner. With care, they lifted the old board and set it to one side.

"Oh crap," Teddy muttered.

Kurt thought a much harsher word.

The light beam caught the sparkle of crystal and the dull gray of bones.

ELEVEN

"I'll have to call the sheriff and bring up the homicide team." Walker reached for the plywood.

Teddy stared at the skeleton in dismay. There were a number of solid crystals between those rafters, but none of the ground ones they'd encountered yesterday. She needed a better look, but she was too horrified to go closer.

Sydony could end up like that someday. Sick to her stomach, she sat down and tried to jar that horrid thought out of her head. She had to hope and pray that her sister was smarter than whoever this was in her attic.

When Kurt and Walker lifted the plywood, she had to look away. In doing so, she caught a glimpse of colors and shapes on the backside of the panel. She grabbed Kurt's arm, grateful for any reason not to look at the remains. "No, wait a minute. Lift that plywood and shine the light on it."

Walker released the panel so Kurt could hold it up. Teddy flashed the light over it. "It's a painting, not oil but not watercolor either," she said as they gaped at the faded colors and figures.

"It's evidence," Walker warned. "We need to leave it up here."

"It has our fingerprints all over it. We've already smudged it beyond repair. The Lucys really need to see the artwork. It could be what the ghost is trying to tell us about." Teddy leaned over the attic opening and called down. "Anyone know where we can get a roll of packing wrap?"

"Aaron will have something," Sam shouted back up. "What did you find?"

"I'll get the wrap," Walker said in resignation. "Lay that thing down and don't touch it until I return. Not that I expect anyone to listen to me," he finished with sarcasm.

"I'll keep out the curious and sit on Teddy," Kurt suggested.

"For pity's sake, it's a piece of plywood and not about to talk to either of you." Not wanting to generate too much excitement by mentioning a skeleton, Teddy diverted her attention and the Lucys. "Have someone fetch enough wrap to cover two sides of a four by eight piece of plywood, please. I make no promises, but we may have a clue."

Walker sighed. Kurt groaned. Teddy ignored them and returned the light beam to the plywood. Below, the Lucys began tramping upward —the reason for Walker and Kurt's complaint.

"The spirit insists she was murdered," Cass called. "We can't get anything more forthcoming. She's too furious to be sensible."

"Her ectoplasmic energy is bound in emotion," Mariah called from a distance. "I'll be back with the packing wrap."

When Teddy left the stairway to examine the plywood, Walker planted himself in her place, blocking any access from below. She was fine with that. Whoever lay in that dry grave deserved a little more respect than becoming a spectator sport.

Rather than focus on who might have died in her attic, she tried to grasp the details of the paint on the plywood, but it was old and faded and the light was poor. If this was all the evidence they had, they were in a world of hurt.

"Shine the light along the edge there." She pointed to a dull red that stood out more than the rest—she hoped it wasn't blood. "Doesn't it look as if that's part of a skirt? Where is the rest of it? And look, above it, that's only part of a building. I don't think we have it all."

"The spirit mentioned a triptych," Sam called up, apparently listening in. "Can you see any similar pieces up there?"

"Not a one," Kurt replied in a masculine growl that raised all the hairs on the back of Teddy's neck. The man was seriously unhappy. "This looks like a center piece from a mural of the town. I recognize the café, but it's apparently before the lettering went on the window."

Teddy's eyes widened as she detected familiar structures behind the people. Her house would be approximately where the painter stood—on the missing left panel with the rest of the red skirt. The town hall would be on a right panel.

"Dinah added the gold lettering to the window a few years after she moved here, maybe eight or nine years ago," Cass said from below, also listening in.

Teddy tried to shake her cold chills with rationality. "So this means the panel could have been painted while my parents lived here? We moved out over twenty years ago."

Kurt beamed the light on the wiring running over the rafters. "Those brown cords are the old knob-and-tube wiring that would have been the originals used before the sixties." He ran the beam to white cables. "There are the new insulated power lines your father probably installed for his sound system. They're running through these rafters." He indicated the skeleton. "And I'm guessing this is where he installed the hardware for the system. It was bulky before Wi-Fi and Bluetooth."

"She was put there *after* the cable lines were run and my father removed the hardware," Teddy concluded, not exactly feeling relief. Her mother's cousin had moved in twenty years ago. She couldn't remember the date on the letter saying she was moving out. "It's just, the paint and the plywood look so old! Would my father have used plywood to cover his sound system?"

"Not to cover it. The system probably rested on top of the plywood so the wires could run beneath. The whole mess might have crashed through the plaster into the bedrooms otherwise." Kurt diverted the beam back to the artwork and away from their gruesome discovery.

"Can't you bring the painting down here?" Cass asked impatiently. "We can see it better in daylight."

"Evidence," Walker barked from his seat at the top of the stairs.

He'd been quiet while they talked. Teddy suspected that's what the lawman did—listened and built up a case inside his head.

"Mariah's running up the street with a roll of the packing wrap Aaron uses when he ships his antiques," Sam called from somewhere below. "But we won't be able to see anything once it's wrapped! And look, I think that's Elaine climbing out of the Mercedes that just arrived. I need to greet her. She'd be the one to judge whether it's part of a triptych."

"The art dealer Sam called about the mural," Walker explained at Kurt and Teddy's questioning silence.

"How much evidence can you get from an old piece of wood? We really need to see the details." Teddy crouched over the unusual piece, trying to make out faces, but the paint was just too old.

Mariah climbed the bottom steps and pushed the long roll of wrap up for Walker to take. "Someone owes Aaron for this. It's not me."

"I think I can swing the cost," Kurt said dryly. "After all, it's my attic." He shot Teddy a taunting look.

Did she really want a house with a skeleton in it? You bet your baby booties, she did. She glared and helped Walker unroll the wrap. "You can just do one sheet, can't you? So the art dealer can see it? After we have some pictures or whatever, then you can wrap it up to your heart's content."

"You could hurt the paint," Cass said worriedly from below. "Don't do anything until Sam returns. We should have a professional opinion."

"Now she tells us. We're not going to get this thing down unwrapped, are we?" Walker asked with a sigh.

"Gloves," Kurt shouted. "Find me some gloves, and I'll just cart the piece down."

"What, you have me running all over town for nothing when I could be working?" Mariah asked in a huff. "Someone else can hunt the damned gloves."

"In the trunk of my car," Walker ordered. "In one more minute, I'm moving back to LA if you don't all back off and let me do my job."

Eventually, they wrangled the awkward piece to the second floor. Kurt set it up against the wall. Walker raised the attic stairs and stood guard beneath them.

Sam arrived with a delicate woman in her mid-forties, immaculately garbed in a slim designer dress, carrying a Gucci handbag, and wearing one of Teddy's crystal bracelets. *Interesting.* Sam introduced her as Elaine Lee, the owner of the gallery that sold her late parents' work.

Elaine looked Walker over first and nodded approvingly. "Samantha says you are from LA and know nothing of Ling Fai, that you are not one of us. That is good."

Teddy processed that weird statement through her knowledge of San Francisco, widened her eyes, and kept her mouth shut. All Chinese in California were not related to each other, she told herself. Just because both Elaine Lee and Chen Ling Walker had Chinese ancestry did not mean they were related to the Ling Fai she knew, who also happened to have come from China—and possessed weird abilities like hers.

Teddy knew that because Ling Fai had been the one to point out the powers of her crystal before she knew it herself. People with weird gifts found each other, one way or another. Did Elaine Lee suggest that she had powers by the use of the word *us*? Interesting.

With the impatience of a practical lawman, Walker went straight for the facts and gestured at the piece of plywood leaning against the wall. "I need to take this into forensics. Before I do, if you could just look at it and make these ladies happy. . ."

Elaine lifted her painted eyebrows and turned to examine the filthy piece of wood. Her face stiffened. Her hand went to her mouth. She crouched and pulled a white glove from her Gucci bag so she could touch—caress—the aging wood.

Teddy's stomach tightened. She had a really bad feeling about—the art dealer? She opened her Inner Monitor and picked up only joy and fear and shock from Elaine.

"It can't be," the dealer whispered. "Lucinda died in the 70s. She was in her 90s then and hadn't had the strength to paint anything large for years. So this has to be *over half a century old*. But look at the detail! That car—that's not a 1960s car."

Beside her, Kurt whispered a curse. "That's my mother's Cadillac DTS. They didn't start selling them until around 2006, which is about when she bought it, I think. I don't remember how long she kept it."

"You're saying this could be by *Lucinda Malcolm?*" Sam asked in excitement.

Even Teddy knew who Lucinda Malcolm was. Apparently, so did everyone else—except maybe Kurt, who was focused on the details of the painting.

"Those aren't her bones up there, are they?" Teddy asked in horror.

Kurt squeezed her arm and shook his head. Right. The famous artist had died in the 1970s, and the skeleton in the attic had only been left there after her parents moved out.

Elaine looked up, her eyes glazed with shock. "Where is the rest of the triptych? This could be worth a fortune. It's one of her fortune-telling masterpieces!"

WHILE THE LUCYS EXCLAIMED AND TOOK PHOTOS OF THE PLYWOOD painting, and Walker stewed and threatened them with plastic, Kurt wandered over to the bedroom overlooking the main street. He tried to remember the years his mother had owned the Cadillac sedan. Dragged from the city, he'd been in a black humor back then, saddled with the resort business, and denied the career he'd chosen. He had no idea who'd lived in town at the time and hadn't cared.

He only knew for certain that it hadn't been Lucinda Malcolm because she'd died before he was born. The art dealer had to be wrong about the painting's origin. *So who had painted his mother's car and why?* His uncle Lance was an artist. . . But Lance only drew portraits, nothing as elaborate as this.

Futuristic paintings were one step into weird he couldn't take.

Standing in one of the upstairs windows, he saw two ponies shuffling down the road. The only ponies around here belonged to the resort stable. What the damnation were they doing in town?

Below, the dog began to howl, and his memory kicked in—Teddy's Goth kids, Thing One and Thing Two. Wasn't that what she called them?

They couldn't even be old enough for school! He marched out of the bedroom, grabbed Teddy by the elbow, and led her toward the stairs down. "Your Baby Goths have escaped their cages."

"Mia and Jeb? They're outside?" Looking alarmed, she raced down.

Taking one last, puzzled glance at the triptych piece, Kurt followed her. He really needed to be at the office, harassing lawyers into proving his ownership of this house.

But somehow, he couldn't force himself to get in his car and leave. He despised unanswered questions. Outside, he cast a glance back at the second story of the empty shop, but no spooks lingered in the window. He wondered if the ghost was happy now and would leave Teddy alone—and couldn't believe he was thinking like that.

The sheriff's car pulled into the parking lot, so Kurt guessed if a phantom wasn't occupying the shop, the police would be.

"What are you doing here?" Teddy asked the kids while attempting to lift the younger one from the saddle.

Jeb was a sturdy brat. Kurt grabbed the reins of both ponies and tied them to one of the boardwalk posts. It might be a tossup as to which had the least strength—the ponies or the post. He reached past Teddy, pulled the boy off, and handed him over. Then he turned to the girl, who wore a mutinous pout.

"Stealing ponies is a hanging offense," he told her.

The bottom lip stuck out even further. Oh well, might as well get kicked and charged with child molestation or something equally entertaining. He grabbed the girl by the waist and hauled her down. She collapsed in a heap on the boardwalk.

"I want to go home," she announced.

"I'm not cut out to be a mother," Teddy said in dismay, holding the heavy boy. "I just wanted to make jewelry in peace."

"This is Hillvale. Give up any notion of peace right now." Kurt held out his hand to the girl. "Hamburger or milkshake?"

She frowned as if she was thinking about it. "Cake," she decided. "Chocolate."

"Not unless I get a very good explanation of why you left the stable!" Teddy contradicted him.

The girl took his hand and glared at her aunt. "They don't like us there."

That earned Kurt a glare from Teddy. Oh well, this day had gone to hell anyway. "C'mon, chocolate cake and you can tell us all about it."

"Encouraging bad behavior is not a bright idea," Teddy informed him, dropping Jeb to the walk and dragging him along in their wake.

"They're not my kids," he retorted, maliciously living up to his reputation. "I just want to know why my staff is mean to them."

"Maybe they're infected with evil, just like you," she snapped. "I should leave them with you when they're all hyper and bouncing off walls."

"You just want to see what's going on back at the shop. The way I see it, taking care of kids should come first." How had they gone from arguing over rental contracts to raising kids?

Figuring he deserved gold medals for this, Kurt led them into Dinah's and seated them in a booth—making sure he sat next to Teddy. He was pretty certain their sniping was a byproduct of sexual frustration. He might as well push the boundaries.

Dinah herself popped out to wait on them, since her waitresses, Mariah and Sam, were apparently otherwise occupied with the art dealer and ghosts. As far as Kurt could ascertain, she was a *he* dressed in a shirtwaist dress from the fifties and wearing red lipstick bright enough for a movie star. But Monty swore by Dinah's food, so Kurt didn't much care what she/he wore.

"I promised them chocolate cake. Is that doable?" Kurt asked.

Dinah beamed. "I've got better, plus hot chocolate. Coffee for you two?"

Teddy nodded, and as the cook hurried off, she turned to the child who'd complained. "Who was mean to you and why?"

The girl glared balefully from beneath the black fringe. "Everybody."

"That's a lie." Teddy turned to Jeb. "Was anyone mean to you?"

He sucked his thumb and squirmed. His eyes were identical to his sister's, a light blue bordering on turquoise. Kurt almost sympathized with the poor kid.

"What if you just tell us what happened?" he suggested. He'd been managing people for years. Kids couldn't be a whole lot different.

"They laughed because we got no boots," the girl said with a pout. "And because we couldn't get on ourselves. I can ride! I'm just not big."

Teddy rubbed her forehead. "The staff didn't laugh, did they? You mean the other children?"

Both their little heads bobbed. Dinah arrived in the nick of time with steaming cups of hot chocolate and a coffee carafe.

The morning fog had lifted and the day was already warming up, but the children eagerly sipped the chocolate.

"Boots aren't needed for ponies," Teddy pointed out. "And you rode all the way into town by yourselves, so I know you can ride. You need to stick your tongue out at the bullies and keep doing what you like to do."

Which is probably what she'd done most of her life, Kurt figured. Teddy was tough. She hadn't screamed when confronted with a skeleton or gone into hysterics when he'd fallen down the stairs. A ghost didn't daunt her. She'd obviously taken on her sister's children without a clue of how to raise them, but she was soldiering on just as if she were their mother. If he'd ever given it any thought, she was probably the exact opposite of what he'd imagine a high-fashion jewelry designer to be.

Teddy wouldn't be a clingy neurotic once the lust wore off and they went their separate ways—he stopped to consider that. She'd had a dramatic meltdown last night, but he was pretty certain that had been stress and exhaustion. If she really got angry, she'd cut off his balls. Something to consider once she lost any lawsuit over the house.

"Mama says it's not polite to stick out our tongues," the girl said primly as Dinah slid a plate of chocolate-frosted chocolate donuts in front of them.

Even Kurt's mouth watered, and he didn't eat sweets. He waited for the children to dig in. Teddy helped herself, and he lost interest in the donuts while watching her savor them.

He needed to be watching what the sheriff was doing, but he couldn't see Teddy's house from here—just the sheriff's vans pulling into the lot and spilling men with equipment.

When he spotted Walker, Sam, and the gallery owner striding down the boardwalk in this direction, Kurt interrupted the etiquette discussion to elbow Teddy and nod out the window. "We'll have the whole town here in about two minutes. Want me to take the kids back to the play center when I send someone to fetch the ponies?"

She bit at her luscious bottom lip, and he almost forgot the question. Obviously, he'd been working too hard and hadn't had enough sex this past year since Kylie had dumped him.

"I really need to be working, but the sheriff won't let me in the shop, will he?" The question was apparently rhetorical. She continued without waiting for an answer. "I'll go back with you, talk to the stable staff, then take advantage of your internet. I'll have to hope they'll let us back home tonight."

Damn, that's not what he wanted. He wanted her right there at the lodge where he could find her.

Crazy Daisy putted into the parking lot in her golf cart, looking like a wild woman in her red feathered cape and flowing gray hair. With a sigh, Kurt slid out of the booth and held out his hand to help Teddy. "The circus is about to begin. Run now or regret it forever after."

Teddy sent a longing look toward the people spilling into the café, then glanced back at the children. "Syd is gonna owe me for this," she muttered, accepting his hand.

Sid? Boyfriend, brother, husband. . . ? Kurt's gut clenched. He didn't have time for this. While Teddy gathered the children, he held open the door for the parade of people streaming through. Teeth gritted , he nodded greetings. The Lucys ignored him as they collected around the counter to study the café's mural. Fine. He didn't like being social anyway. He shoved Teddy and the children out in the first break of the stream.

"The mural is not Lucinda's work," he heard the gallery owner state as they fled outside. "That's an Ingersson. Granted, the tempera is unusual for his style, but that's a solid block wall he's painted on. He was probably imitating medieval churches in a statement of irony. It looks as if someone has tried to repair it with an acrylic mix and varnish."

"If you don't turn Hillvale into spook hollow, you should turn it into an art gallery," Teddy said, shooing the children to her own van instead of his car. "The place is packed with potential, and the unique buildings are part of the charm." She added that dig as the kids reminded her of the dog, and she jogged back for the animal.

Kurt followed her swaying hips down the street of dilapidated structures bravely decorated with colorful planters and flowers. Teddy was worth watching. The graying wood and crumbling stucco was not. During the fire, he'd almost hoped the dump would go up in flame so he could use the insurance to rebuild.

But maybe not if there were priceless pieces of art hidden in the damned attics. *Shit.*

WALKER

USING HIS AUTHORITY AS POLICE CHIEF, WALKER CLOSED UP TEDDY'S empty shop after the coroner departed with the skeleton. The plywood artwork had left with the sheriff's forensic team, but he had some good photographs to work with.

He studied the town as he strode down the boardwalk to the café. If, in fact, the artwork had been painted ten years ago—and not half a century ago as the art dealer claimed—Hillvale hadn't changed a great deal. The painting had mostly been depicting people, with the eccentric array of buildings in the background. There had been tourists in shorts, with cameras hanging around their necks. The car lot had only been half full. What had caught his attention had been a man in a long coat and boots struggling to put a wrapped package into the back of an old woodie wagon.

If the artist was good at proportion, the package would have been about the size of a four-by-eight panel.

There had been a few familiar figures in the painting, some carrying packages, and no reason to believe any of them had anything to do with the skeleton. So much for talking to ghosts.

He shoved open the café door and was engulfed in a cool air-conditioned breeze and the aroma of fresh coffee. The place was standing room only, but Sam waved at him and lifted the carafe to indicate coffee was on the way. Just her smile boosted his day. Before he'd met Sam, he couldn't remember when he'd last felt happiness. His late wife's battle with mental illness had dragged them both into a dark place for too long. Sam was sunshine and roses in comparison.

The room gradually grew quiet as people noticed his entrance. He'd have to get used to that. In LA, he'd mostly been a faceless entity, sitting in an office and directing others to do the field work. Here, he was part of the community's fabric. In a diverse crowd like this, he blended in. Which meant if people didn't like him, it was probably because of his job, not his facial features or skin color.

He kissed Sam on the cheek when she delivered a mug of coffee. "They know I can't tell them anything, right?"

"They're reading your vibrations, your cards, and your chart," she whispered with a laugh. "Give them something. They want to help."

Finessing an entire eccentric community rather than a corporate board meeting was a challenge he'd have to learn to meet if he wanted to stay here with Sam. He shrugged and sipped his coffee. He'd learned to play the inscrutable card from the best—his mother.

They wanted to help? Fine. He could work with that.

"Forensics will have to determine date of death," he announced to the room at large. "We'll have to research who lived here and had motive and opportunity once we have that information. We'll have to hope those factors help us identify the victim, unless someone wants to confess."

The goateed antique dealer lifted a board from behind a bench and propped it up on the counter. "We enlarged the photographs Miss Lee took. We've identified several of the people in the painting."

Damn, but they worked fast.

"We think if we hang it in the café, people can identify themselves or others who lived here ten years ago. It's just a photograph, so we're writing on it." Tullah from the thrift shop pointed at a tall dark figure on the boardwalk. "That's me in my turban phase. My features aren't distinct, but everything else is pretty close."

Impressed, Walker made his way over to the counter to study the tidy writing. "This panel just depicts the middle of town, so your store and Aaron's aren't here. But Dinah's is always the center of attention. I wouldn't have recognized half these people." He took out his phone and captured a shot, then jotted down the names they'd already scribbled on it. "We still have no reason to believe this is evidence."

"There had to be a reason Lucinda painted this day in a future she would never see," Samantha insisted.

"A lot of these people don't live here anymore," Harvey pointed out. The lanky, black-haired musician leaned against the counter, helping Aaron hold up the photograph poster. "And people like me and Val weren't here at the time. Hillvale gets a lot of changeover."

"But there's Lance." Bracelets jangling, orange-haired Amber pointed at a tall familiar figure crossing the parking lot. The Kennedys' uncle had been graying even then. "And Cass. The artist captured a lot of familiar faces who might have lived in town when she painted this, whether it was 1960 or 1990."

Walker zeroed in on the guy with the woodie. Someone had written "Thompson" over his head. "And this guy?" He pointed him out. The name rang familiar.

Sam appeared at his side and murmured in a low voice, "Cass said he and his wife lived in Teddy's shop for roughly ten years and left about ten years ago, which confirms the date of the painting as between ten and twenty years ago. And Xavier says Thompson is the one who sold the shop to the Kennedys."

Bingo, Suspect Numero Uno.

TWELVE

"I'm moving back to the shop in the morning," Teddy announced defiantly to the table of people waiting for her in the lodge's restaurant. "I can't keep leaving the kids with babysitters. I'll just have to live with ghosts."

Kurt pulled out a chair so she could take a seat. She recognized Sam and Elaine Lee, but the older gentleman with the graying ponytail and rugged cheekbones resembling the Kennedy brothers was a stranger to her.

"Theodosia Baker, my uncle, Lance Brooks," Kurt gestured at the older man he'd seated next to the gallery owner. "He's known the art community as long as Cass has."

Lance shrugged his bony shoulders. "I can't claim to know them well. I grew up in the city, not here. But I did meet Lucinda Malcolm when she visited San Francisco. Lovely lady, very frail at the time."

"He's being modest," Sam said. "He's an excellent portrait artist and has captured the images of almost everyone who has ever crossed his path."

"Is that why Deputy Walker isn't here?" Teddy asked, glancing at the menu. "He's matching portraits to the photograph?"

Sam beamed. "Precisely. You sized him up quickly."

"And he's *Chief* Walker now," Kurt added. "I think the town has completed some formal arrangement with the county. We'll still have to call on the county for backup, but Walker will have his own office at the town hall, once we do some work on the upstairs."

"He hates the bureaucratic red tape of the sheriff's office," Sam explained. "Walker owns a firm of investigators he can order about as needed, although I don't think we've worked out how the town pays him if he has to use his private services. It's conflict of interest and complicated."

"So you invited me to this confab why?" Teddy asked, pointing at a chardonnay on the menu for the waiter leaning over her shoulder. "I don't know anyone."

"Because you are living in a building where a priceless piece of art was discovered," Elaine Lee said. "I understand ownership of the building is contested, which means ownership of the art is also contested."

"Oh. I hadn't given that any thought. You think my father may have originally owned the triptych? I can't imagine him treating it so carelessly. He worked with metals and crystals and not paint, but he respected the work of others." Teddy was more aware of Kurt taking the chair beside her than the absurdity of this conversation. If her father had ever owned anything priceless, he would have donated it to Greenpeace or something equally unprofitable.

"The only art *I've* ever bought is through a commercial dealer for prints in colors that match the lodge's décor," Kurt said dryly. "I'm quite certain we've never bought priceless museum pieces."

"Your father used to take art in exchange for services. Town did too, once upon a time," Lance said, sipping what appeared to be mineral water. "The mural at the café was probably painted to pay a meal tab. The Ingerssons didn't have much cash at the start."

"The Ingerssons were quite prolific in their time." Elaine sipped her wine and studied the artwork on the restaurant walls. "They eventually faded into obscurity, much the way many Expressionists were replaced by Pop Artists of the period. Some of their more famous work can still command a good price, but the market has moved on. Still, the pieces in your town hall could bring a good price if we bring collectors up here. But *Lucinda's* work is timeless, prized not just for the artistry but for the mystery behind the seemingly innocuous scenery."

Sam opened a digital notebook and passed a photo gallery across the table. "These are some of her fortune-telling pieces."

"Fortune-telling?" Teddy studied the images. She'd taken business and marketing classes in college, not art, but she knew good design when she saw it. These paintings would look spectacular on any wall. They varied from what appeared to be intimate wedding portraits to intriguing scenes similar to the one on the triptych panel.

Elaine took the notebook and scrolled to one of the portraits of a distinguished couple in a church. The slender blond lady wore a wedding gown in a mid-century style. The mustached older gentleman wore a chest full of medals.

"My grandmother started our gallery. She sold this Lucinda Malcolm piece back in 1940. I still have the invoice in my files. It's merely labeled *Royal Wedding*." Elaine pressed the screen and another image appeared. "If you'll look, you can see the resemblance to Grace Kelly and Prince Ranier in these photos of the royal wedding in 1956."

Teddy studied the two images. They weren't identical. In the painting, the bride was more radiant, the groom more *authoritative* than in the aging photograph. But the details of the gown and the medals were close enough to look like a copy of a photograph of the couple in a slightly different position. "An invoice doesn't mean this is the same painting as the one sold in 1940," she argued. "It's impossible for someone to paint a wedding nearly twenty years before it happened!"

Elaine shrugged and took the notebook back. "This is the only *Royal Wedding* portrait she's ever done, and it's just one of the more dramatic examples. Most are like the triptych. In her youth, people considered her a fantasy painter, drawing absurd cars and too-sexy clothes on people with odd hairstyles. Eventually, she stopped painting the futuristic and satisfied herself with fantasy sketches. She limited her more expensive oils to ordinary landscapes of flowers that don't change over the years, theoretically. But even her garden portraits contain plants that weren't imported or developed until years later. Only gardeners notice, however, so they sold well. She was extremely talented."

Kurt took the notebook to study the images. "Even if you convince us, and I'm not easily convinced, that Lucinda Malcolm could paint the future, you'll never convince a judge and jury if we find evidence in the painting that one of the people on the panel is a killer just because a ghost says so."

"Most likely not," Elaine agreed with equanimity. "You need to accept though, that the painting was not done in the period that it depicts. We believe she painted images of powerful emotional moments that are in some way connected with her rather extensive family. The Malcolms are related to some of the wealthiest, most titled families in the world. It was no coincidence that Lucinda painted Grace Kelly—the Kellys are a direct descendant of one of the distant branches of Malcolms. Lucinda's name wasn't actually Malcolm, however. That was a pseudonym."

Teddy gratefully sipped the wine the waiter set in front of her. "None of this makes sense," she admitted. "Why did she use a pseudonym?"

"According to the notes in our files, her name was actually Lucy Kelly Wainwright, but she claimed her ancestry was a Scots/English family of Malcolms who were descendants of Druids and often called witches. One of those witches was rumored to have painted works that later came true—although the original Lady Lucinda Malcolm's paintings were apparently more closely connected in time, so people recognized almost immediately what she'd done. Lucy Wainwright took that artist's name to keep her notoriety from affecting her wealthy socialite family."

"Lady Lucy/Lucinda," Sam exclaimed in delight. "Lovely irony and maybe the reason the artists here call themselves Lucys, not just because of the Lucent Ladies?"

"Lucent Ladies?" Teddy asked. "Oh, Hillvale's heroic spiritualist ancestors? Cute."

"So this Lucy/Lucinda painted a triptych of Hillvale," Kurt said with a layer of skepticism. "Since she died in the 1970s, she probably created it earlier, depicting a futuristic town and people based on those she saw around her, like Cass and Lance?"

"If she quit painting futuristic earlier in her career, then she probably painted this one in the 50s or earlier, before Cass and Lance were even born," Sam corrected.

Teddy was fascinated knowing there were people with even weirder talents than hers, but she was more interested in the reaction of the man beside her. Kurt was rubbing his temple and appeared in imminent danger of explosion. She kept her Monitor turned off for fear of cracking if he blew.

He took a large gulp of his seltzer before admitting, "Cass's mother, my father's first wife, was a Wainwright. She owned most of Hillvale. My father inherited half of it from her."

Mouths gaped around the table. Lucinda Malcolm/Lucy Wainwright's family had owned Hillvale? Kurt didn't look particularly happy about his admission, rightfully so. The Lucys would be all over it.

"*Ouch.*" Teddy sat back and thought about that. "So Lucinda Malcolm was actually painting her *family* when she included Cass in the triptych, and the painting may have reflected her version of infant Cass's future."

"I'm not believing any of this," Kurt declared, setting down his glass. "Just tell us what to do with the painting after Walker's crew is done with it."

"It will need restoration, of course," Elaine suggested. "You could donate it to a museum. Selling it without the rest of the panels would be awkward, but if you had the rest of the panels, it would be worth too much for any one buyer to acquire."

"Art gallery," both Sam and Teddy said together, casting each other laughing looks as Kurt groaned.

"It makes sense," Lance said stiffly. "The town is full of artwork. It would be a draw for the kind of wealthy tourists you keep saying we need."

"Not many towns can boast a genuine Lucinda Malcolm," Elaine agreed. "Unclutter the Ingersson mural in the café, reframe and properly display the artists currently hanging in your town hall, create a gallery of the 1970's era artwork scattered around the lodge, and the entire town becomes a fascinating museum of twentieth century art."

"And that doesn't even touch on the pieces hidden in Daisy's stash," Sam added in satisfaction. "Or Daisy's own pieces. Those planters are spectacular if anyone ever noticed."

"My parents have a storage rental crammed with ceramics," Teddy added with mischief, watching Kurt sliding down in his seat. She really shouldn't be so mean to him, but he was wrong to want to tear down her shop. "I could display them."

"The kiln at the Ingersson commune was famous in its time," Elaine said with interest. "Ceramics are not my specialty, but if you have any good examples from that era, you could draw many enthusiasts."

Newly-assigned Chief Walker sauntered up to the table as Teddy was trying to find images on her phone of some of the pieces her parents had collected.

"Ceramics, like pottery?" he asked, peering over her shoulder. "They make pottery up here? Is there a kiln nearby?"

The chatter halted and even Kurt turned to look at him with suspicion.

"I don't think the kiln is there anymore," Sam said. "I've not seen it. We could ask Valdis and Daisy. They practically live on the farm. Why do you ask?"

Walker grimaced, then shrugged. "Word will spread soon enough. Try to keep this under your hat until the coroner makes an announcement. The skeleton shows the body had been submitted to a high intensity heat before being interred in the attic—that's the reason there was no smell or evidence of decay."

THIRTEEN

June 28: early morning

Teddy kept her tablet's volume low so the kids wouldn't hope every beep meant their mother was messaging. It beeped now, before the sun was even up. She groped on the table beside the couch she was using as bed. No one but Syd would message at this hour. She listened for the kids as she pressed the Skype button. They were still asleep.

"Teddy," Syd whispered. She wasn't using her camera, just the audio. "Your message said urgent? Are Mia and Jeb all right?"

"They're fine, but do you want them living in a shop where a woman was murdered?" she asked sleepily. She'd had nightmares all night about a woman shoved screaming into the heat of a kiln.

Syd went silent. That was a strong statement from her extroverted sister.

"Sorry. I'm new to acting like a mother," Teddy said. "I should be able to make these decisions, but I panicked. There's an actual ghost there, and we found her corpse."

Syd made a gagging sound but blessedly didn't question ghosts. "All right, I'm tired of running, and I miss the kids. I should come up there. Does anyone know who we are?"

Teddy leaned against the pillow and tried to balance her desire to have her sister here against the danger involved. She wasn't used to playing cops and robbers and couldn't make up her mind.

"Yeah, the lodge owner recognized my name," she admitted. "He's not said anything though. The question is, will Buttass know your maiden name and be able to trace our parents?"

"It might be in my credit report, but how would he know to check their property records from twenty years ago?"

Teddy brightened. "Kurt says the property is listed in his corporation now! We'll need a lawyer to pry it out of his hands, but for the moment, that's cool. Buttass will have no reason to suspect we're here."

"His name is Ashbuth," Syd said tiredly. "He's still out on bail, and they've continued the court date until August. I'll never be able to stop running."

"He held you hostage!" Teddy tried not to shout but the memory of those fearful hours were emblazoned on her memory. "He beat and raped you! How can they let the monster roam free for that long?"

"They called it domestic violence, and remember, he's a cop. They just think it's a family argument, and I'm a conniving bitch who pressed charges. And now it's all my fault that he's on desk duty and stalking me. I've been tried and convicted by a jury of his peers."

Teddy rubbed her hair and tried to stay focused on the present. "Do you have any idea if he's on your trail?"

"No idea but I'm running out of cash," she admitted. "The moment I use a credit card, he'll have me."

"Okay, then get yourself up here. I can wire you more, if you need it, but this place seems safe. It's isolated and the only officialdom is a good guy. He'll listen to you, if necessary. But we can just lay low and play it cool until Dumbass does something stupid and gets picked up."

"And where will we stay, with the ghost?" she asked dryly.

"You have a better idea?"

"No," Syd said with a sigh. "We'll make a place for her at the table. Us battered women need to stick together."

And chances were very good that's what had happened to the ghost in the attic, Teddy recognized as she hung up. Some man had beat her up, killed her, and thrown her in the kiln to get rid of the evidence. If it was a shared kiln. . . he couldn't leave her remains in there.

She Googled kiln heat and cremation heat. Apparently, kilns could get hotter than crematories, but if this had happened ten years ago and there was no evidence of a kiln today. . . what were the chances it had disintegrated before the body was consumed? Or that it couldn't reach the necessary levels of heat?

She scowled at the horror story she was creating in her head. She needed to find a way to placate a ghost because she had to move into the shop if Syd was joining her.

～

JUNE 28: MIDMORNING

"THAT'S IT!" TEDDY CRIED CHEERFULLY. "SCOOT AROUND ON YOUR TAILS until those towels are dirtier than the floor."

She watched Jeb and Mia wriggle their butts around the oak planks of the shop as if dusting filthy floors was the best game ever.

While they played, she opened one of her jewelry cases. She'd cleaned the glass display case. She hadn't been carrying much inventory when she'd gone to see Syd in the hospital in Sacramento. That's when they'd concocted an escape plan which hadn't included going back to San Francisco for any of her work materials. The display case was all she could fill at the moment.

As soon as the dust settled—maybe literally—she'd have her office ship the rest. Her new life plans included experimenting with crystals, but Syd's crisis had interfered. She wished Walker hadn't carried off the ones in the attic.

The large shop window was great for watching cars entering town and people heading her way. Customers would be nice, but unlikely—she needed a sign. First, she needed a store name. Crystal Cave? Treasure Trove? Oh well, until she had customers, the window at least gave her warning of visitors.

The one approaching bearing bags from the café was more than welcome. "All hail Samantha," she called as the lithe, lion-maned waitress entered.

She knew Sam was more than a waitress, but that was her current function in Hillvale, just as Teddy's was kid-watcher and shopkeeper. *Almost* shopkeeper. Everyone needed a backup career.

"I thought you might be getting hungry. Dinah got a bit carried away testing donut recipes in her new fryer. Is that coffee I smell?" Sam set the greasy bags on the round oak table they'd used for their séances.

"It is. Tullah had a great coffeemaker just begging me to take it home. Do you mind pouring yourself a cup? I want to see how much empty space I need to fill before I send for inventory."

Jeb and Mia quit wiggling and jumped up to examine the bags.

"The ghost lady says we're doing a good job and deserve a donut," Mia said matter-of-factly, digging into the gift.

Teddy froze. Sam did the same. With a sigh, Teddy opened her Monitor, but she sensed emotional energy. She didn't hear words.

"She's still here, although not as angry," Teddy said in a low voice, as if that would prevent the phantom from hearing.

"I should have taken up ectoplasmic studies instead of environmental science." Shaking her head in disbelief, Sam left for the kitchen and returned with two mugs. "I don't see or feel anything *different*. Not even negative energy, although I left my walking stick over at the diner. Maybe I should fetch it, but I didn't feel anything earlier either."

"Walking stick?" Teddy asked.

Sam waved a hand. "Harvey carves them. The weird among us can feel various forms of energy through them, although the Nulls like to call them magic wands."

Teddy snorted. "Right. That's what I need, a wand to make everything better. If your gift is for plants, then it's Mariah who should have taken up ectoplasmic studies. I wonder if there is a university of the weird?" Teddy sipped her coffee. Sam knew how she liked it from her orders at the café.

As if she'd heard her name, Mariah crossed the street from the direction of the grocery—or maybe the town hall. Teddy saluted her as the black-braided ghost-hunter entered. "We're liking our ghost today. Leave her ectoplasm alone."

Mariah checked the swinging nets on the ceiling, then glanced at the children scarfing up donuts. "She likes donuts or kids?"

Teddy shrugged. "Both? What's the word on the commune's kiln?"

Sam leaned over the counter to admire the assortment of crystals Teddy had set out. "Daisy said—and this is Crazy Daisy now, not a historian—that the pottery was defunct at the end of the 90's. Several potters lingered in the area and continued to use the kiln."

Mariah helped herself to a donut. "I was a bad girl and borrowed Monty's computer. Records say the kiln exploded over nine years ago. They surmised one of the rogue potters overheated what was already a cracked and deteriorating system. The county newspaper screamed about the possibility of fire spreading through the brush since Hillvale has no fire department and demanded that it be dismantled. The town started volunteer fire training after that, but as far as I can tell, the kiln was never rebuilt. The remains may be buried under the mudslide that hit the bluff some years back. They weren't visible even before Gump blew up Boulder Rock."

"This sounds like a deranged and dangerous community," Teddy protested. Picking up the ghost's distress, she shook her head and put a finger to her lips to stop the discussion of how the ghost's remains had been disposed of.

"*Evil* is the word you want. I poked around a little more on the computer while I was there." Mariah settled on the floor to better examine the counter contents. "The analysis of the pixie dust merely shows ground quartz and glass. Can you make glass in kilns?"

"How did you get into the police lab records?" Sam demanded.

Mariah shrugged. "Magic?"

Teddy pondered the question rather than Mariah's magical computer abilities. "A lab can't test for magic or evil toxicity in the dust," she concluded.

"For all that matters, we can't determine if *evil* means intent or something actually toxic in the dust," Sam added.

"Let's not get metaphysical." Teddy lifted the last piece of rock quartz she was placing in the display case. "This is just basic Brazilian purple amethyst. Any good rock collector would disdain it. A laboratory would find nothing unusual. But I can grind it and add it to glass or carve it into a charm, and its healing properties are legendary. It blocks negative energies and exudes soothing ones."

Sam sat down beside Mariah to study the case. "Really? I'm not feeling what I felt with the dust. I don't feel any vibrations. It just sparkles pretty."

Mia and Jeb joined them on the floor, sitting on their dust towels and wriggling happily. "The ghost lady says *too ma lean*," Mia announced.

Mia really was talking to ghosts? Wait until Syd heard that.

Jeb wrapped his arm around Prince Hairy, who was licking the donut crumbs off his face. Teddy knew she was an awful mother, but if the dog wanted to be a washcloth—

"Tourmaline?" Teddy translated. "What did she say about it?" She couldn't believe she just asked that.

Even impassive Mariah was studying the six-year-old with interest.

Mia shrugged and spun around as if talking to invisible entities was perfectly normal. "It hides evil?" she asked, as if repeating what she heard. "And eggs," she added, happy to recognize a word.

"Cass and Valdis couldn't get this much out of your ghostly presence," Sam said in wonder.

"Cass and Valdis interpret through adult minds." Mariah finished her donut. "I doubt *tourmaline* and *eggs* came through clearly when they were asking for killers."

Teddy frowned and pulled out one of her research books. "I can't be certain, but I have this niggling feeling that tourmaline. . ." She pointed at a page. "Red tourmaline can be radioactive."

"Pixie dust," Sam said, looking alarmed. "But the lab didn't detect radioactivity."

"The dust was actually red and *blue* and turned purple when mixed." Teddy flipped through her quartz index. "There are dozens of crystals that contain anything from asbestos to uranium. They can be mixed in potter's clay or paint for any variety of reasons. Or it could all just be superstition and the killer dumped everything he had in the attic and hoped it would hide his evil deeds." Teddy shoved the book back on the shelf behind her. "And translating *eggs* is beyond my scope, except crystals often are found in geodes, which resemble eggs."

"Our gifts are limited, or we'd take over the world," Sam said thoughtfully.

"I don't suppose anyone has a gift for making the cable company hook up my internet?" Teddy asked, not liking to continue this talk with spooks and kids listening. "Or for hunting up the property records to prove this place is mine?"

"Oh, I did that." Mariah stood and dusted off her jeans. "This place is listed as owned by the Kennedy Corp, sorry. You'll need lawyers to fight a fraudulent deed."

Sam stood as well. "And does your magic computer cover my farm?"

"Don't poke fun." Mariah pointed a finger at her. "I'm not just good at ectoplasm. And yes, the last recorded deed is listed as owned by the Ingersson Trust. I didn't have time to look for where trust documents are filed. Your fancy lawyer can find out easily enough. The farm is yours, and the Kennedys can't build anything there."

Teddy heard the note of triumph, but the farm land wasn't the only property the Kennedys owned. They could still raze the entire town—Syd's only safe haven and her own hope for the future.

She'd have to hire a lawyer.

FOURTEEN

FOREWARNED ABOUT TEDDY'S ACTIVITIES, KURT ARRIVED IN TOWN wearing jeans, t-shirt, and an old Ralph Lauren denim shirt with buttons missing. He'd had to hunt in the bottom of boxes he'd brought back from college to find them—which made him feel old. When was the last time he hadn't put on a suit when he got up in the morning? He'd never planned on turning into his father.

Which was why he was here now, watching Teddy on her knees, bent over to add final touches to the exterior door she was painting. She reminded him that he wasn't dead yet. He'd apparently just been dating the wrong women. His task was to convince this skittish female that sex was good for their mutual health. He excelled at challenges.

Of course, she was happily repairing the building he meant to tear down.

Teddy met his gaze defiantly when he stepped up on the board-walk. "I think it's a rather dashing periwinkle blue, don't you?"

Like he was going to tell her she was wrong when he wanted in her bed? Right. He might lack social finesse, but he wasn't stupid. A coat of paint wouldn't stop a bulldozer. The door looked purple to him, but what did he know? "Did you sand the door first? The sun will peel the paint right off."

He removed his old Nikes from her reach when she feigned painting them in retaliation.

"I am not a complete idiot. I used a heavy-duty primer." She nodded at the window frame. "Like over there."

He examined the aging wood she'd coated in thick gray primer and nodded. "That will hold for a few months. These old windows are miserable in winter though. I trust you'll be moving on before then?"

Okay, so he was stupid. She glared and moved over to the window with her brush.

"I hadn't planned on staying for the winter with the kids, no, but if you're working on a ski resort, I'll have to think about replacing the old windows. I've set my parents' lawyer on the fraudulent deed and e-mailed them about their cousin. I don't expect an immediate reply. My parents have no internet until they go into town for supplies. But I *will* get this house back."

He'd damned well personally checked on the deed to this building. It was *his*, along with most of the rest of the town. This building was the cornerstone to the new construction that would create the prosperous town he envisioned in his dreams—and get him the hell out of the resort.

Kurt picked up a smaller brush she'd left lying on the porch and started the tricky job of painting along the window glass she'd taped. "Walker couldn't find a match for your Thompson cousin or her spouse in Lance's portrait gallery. Lance says they're probably in Daisy's stash of evil. Do you have any idea what he's talking about?"

"Why didn't you ask Lance? I haven't even met Daisy." She started on the wider part of the frame.

Kurt could hear the kids shouting and the dog barking in the newly re-fenced backyard. If he allowed her to keep this up, she'd turn the place into a decent rental—if the ghost was gone. He ought to smack himself in the face with the paintbrush to think like that.

"My uncle is vague on a good day. It's something to do with red eyes and crystal paint. The evil part is never clear, and anything to do with Crazy Daisy is a mystery." His frustration began to fade as he worked beside Teddy, actually performing a task with visible results.

He missed the days he'd worked on construction to learn the business from the inside out. Paperwork and glad-handing simply weren't the same.

"Sam will know. You could ask her. Apparently, all I do is feel angry entities. I don't even rate a magic wand." She didn't sound too concerned.

"You claimed you hexed your jewelry," he reminded her. The Lucys' claim to weirdness didn't faze him. He'd grown up in San Francisco in the center of weird. He just didn't want their fantasies inflicted on him or his goals. He drew the line at *ghosts* in the attic however. The structure wasn't stable and needed to be dismantled before it fell down of its own accord.

She shrugged and climbed on a stepladder to reach the top part of the frame, giving him an eye-level view of her well-rounded posterior in worn denim. His brain quit functioning.

"I don't do anything in particular," she asserted. "I choose crystals that fit the image in my head, carve them to fit the design, put the piece together, and sell it. I don't have Samantha's scientific background and haven't tested for cause and effect. I'm just working from verbal reports of what happens when its worn." She smacked the paint a little harder than necessary. "Gossip has spread that the bracelets are jinxed, so business is down. A stone that produces honesty isn't exactly a popular gift."

"Ouch. That's a marketing nightmare. Any plans on how to deal with it?" He knew about marketing nightmares. The blackened hillside had reduced his getaway vacationers to a trickle. Everything he wanted to do up here required huge loans, which meant showing a steadily increasing profit. He'd been gnashing his teeth this past week since the fire, looking for ways to compensate. Even an art gallery sounded good at this point.

Having mutual interests made it difficult to keep seeing Teddy as his opponent. He'd simply have to wear her down and sway her to his way of thinking.

"Online sales are strong outside of the city," she said. "Rumor hasn't spread too far. I'm thinking of developing a crystal-based business where people actually *want* stones with power."

"And how will you convince them your stones have power?" he asked skeptically.

"That's for marketing," she said in amusement. "Vegas is built on people who believe in the magic of luck. If you'll agree to an art gallery theme in town, I'll happily stock up on basic crystals as well as my jewelry—which are considered art pieces, mind you. And I'll send someone to sort through my parents' pottery. I can't sell their things unless they give me permission, but they'll be a nice display of local artistry."

Kurt slapped paint on the frame. "You want to support a town that will blow away in the next strong wind. We need earthquake-proof buildings, structures with decent heat and air conditioning, places where modern consumers will feel comfortable. This heap of junk and logs isn't worth marketing."

"Try it, what have you got to lose? If we fail, we fail, and you get what you want. Are you planning on razing the town in the middle of tourist season?"

"Of course not, but agreeing to a marketing campaign raises hopes and will cause hard feelings when we're ready to rebuild. You have no idea of the battles we've fought with locals before. They're likely to torch the lodge and not just the hillside next time." As Teddy climbed down to paint the lower portion of the frame under him, he inhaled her floral soap. Why in hell was he arguing with her? She'd be gone by summer's end. He should just agree with everything she said.

"The locals set fire to the mountain?" she asked in incredulity.

"Magic," he said grimly. "These things happen here. Don't ask me to explain. No one *meant* to set the fire, except the villain who was robbing us all, and he didn't actually light the match. If I were arguing with logical people, I might make my case, but no one here wants rational. They want what they want and aren't interested in changing their minds."

She laughed. "You say that as if you're any different."

He wasn't explaining life-long dreams and payroll expenses to a laughing pixie with bad hair color. "We'll agree to disagree. Set up your art galleries. Pretend I don't exist and keep me out of it. I think art would fare far better if it were displayed in a picturesque setting like

Santa Fe, but if you want the work with little return, go for it. I just wanted to ask if you'd like to bring the kids up to the lodge this evening where Serena can babysit them while we have dinner together."

Her look of excitement over the art galleries faded to one of disappointment at his dinner offer. "I hate to say no after your generous offer, if you really mean you'll support art galleries, but I'm hoping my sister will arrive this evening. I need to be here if she does."

"I don't say things I don't mean. Gather your Lucys and paint the town red if it makes you happy. Your sister is coming to pick up her children?" That would be a bonus—if Teddy remained behind.

"No, she's coming to stay. She has boyfriend troubles." Teddy stopped painting to study him. "I wish I knew how much to trust you."

"That's a rotten thing to say!" Kurt flung his brush at the bucket and glared at her. "Have I done anything to make you mistrust me?"

"You're male," she said with a shrug. "We haven't had a lot of positive reinforcement with the gender. Although Syd's first husband was decent, I suppose. But he was husband material, ready for commitment, so reasonably trustworthy. Most men aren't."

Sid. Her sister, not a significant other. He ought to practice remembering names if he meant to establish any kind of working relationship with the town. Kurt shoved his hair out of his face and tried to figure out how to respond to her bluntness. "I was ready for commitment until your jewelry got in the way," he retorted.

"Yeah, so you say, but I'm guessing she wouldn't have left if you'd been really committed. You just wanted a convenience, and she suited your image. But this isn't about sex. This is about *trust.* Men tend to believe each other more than they believe women, and in Syd's case, that's lethal."

"Around here, it's easier to believe men because they don't talk about negative energy and the lodge being *evil,*" he countered. "If you're saying your sister is breaking the law, then I probably can't help, and we should stop talking right now. Is that honest enough for you?" Kurt was already rethinking his offer. This woman could potentially be more trouble than an entire town of Lucys.

But the mind-bending sex had been more than worth it. He needed to be convinced that one episode wasn't a result of purple dust.

"Syd's not breaking any laws. Her ex is, but he's a cop and the cops don't believe her. So if he shows up here—and we hope he won't know about Hillvale—chances are good you'll believe the cop and not us. So you may as well go away now, sorry."

Crap on a stick, that wasn't what he wanted. "Walker is the man who will handle that, not me. If your sister isn't charged with any crime, then I don't see the problem."

"You will," she said with a sigh. "C'mon in. I need to make sure the kids haven't pushed Prince Hairy over the fence so he can chase squirrels. I'll fix coffee."

Kurt applied the last touch of paint and left his brush in the cleaner she provided. He stepped back to examine the effect of periwinkle purple against fading gray. Cheerful but eccentric, he decided, before following Teddy inside, hoping this meant she trusted him.

WALKER

WALKER FINALLY SAW CRAZY DAISY'S GOLF CART PUTT UP THE TRAIL TO the Ingersson Farm. The lawyers might still be wrangling over the deeds to the farm, but as far as he was concerned, that land belonged to a trust which had appointed Samantha and her Aunt Valerie as executors. Daisy didn't own it. She simply acted as guardian to what Sam claimed was a stash of artwork from the original commune.

His business partners would roll on the floor laughing if they knew he was up here looking for a painting that predicted the future. Walker justified it in his own head by considering the value of priceless art. Well, and curiosity—he'd seen the stash briefly and really wanted to investigate more.

He climbed out of the sheriff's official car—the mayor was still dickering with the county over its purchase—and jogged down the dusty dirt trail to Daisy's hiding place. The old farmhouse had burned long ago. An aging manzanita hedge hid the foundations. Daisy's foot-high row of rock and stick mannequins guarded her territory.

"Hey, Daisy, got a minute?" he called, to give her warning that he approached. She'd left the golf cart in a thicket of weeds but the sun glinted off the metal, so he knew she was here. "I'd like to talk with you."

Her wrinkled arm waved her walking stick from above the hedge—her usual signal that she was available. She didn't waste words unless she was time-traveling, as the Lucys called it. A psychiatrist would call it a manic episode or schizophrenia, but Daisy had never been dangerous. In any other community, she would have been homeless, but the Lucys took care of her.

Walker climbed through the scrub and found Daisy perched on her usual stone, wrapping wire around her stone sculptures. Today, she was wearing her bright red western shirt and denims, covered in her feathered cloak. The wind was chilly, he supposed. He didn't know how old Daisy was, but she apparently felt the chill more than most. As usual, her graying hair flew in a crinkled nimbus around her head.

"Are there some rules about who can see your stash of artwork?" he asked bluntly. "I'm trying to track down evidence of a murder from ten years ago, and several people think the pieces might be up here."

"Thalia," she replied enigmatically. "Not Gifted. She should have left him."

Walker had checked census records and knew the people who had lived in Teddy's house for ten years were named Thalia and Lonnie Thompson. He had one of his men hunting for the original deed and any other transfer before the one between the Kennedy Corporation and the Thompsons, but so far, they'd located nothing. Since this wasn't billable time, his people weren't devoting a lot of effort to it.

"Do you have any examples of Thalia's work in your stash?" he asked. "Portraits of the Thompsons? Any large plywood pieces?"

Daisy wrapped a small crystal stone onto the figurine she was creating. "Best to keep evil underground, where it belongs."

"Thalia's work is evil?" he asked, trying to make sense of insanity.

She shadowed her eyes with her hand as she looked up at him. "Not the work. The people. The evil is in their eyes. That's how she knew about his girlfriend."

He should have brought Sam with him to translate. Damn. He tried to think like Sam when he worded his reply. "So, when Thalia's spirit says to look at the artwork for evidence that she was murdered, we should look at what you stored away—because it shows evil?"

She nodded in satisfaction and returned to wrapping wire.

"If I could see the pieces, I might be able to determine how or why she was killed." He really didn't want to get a warrant to search for magical artwork. He'd be laughed out of the state. Maybe he could persuade Sam to talk to Val, and between them, they could persuade Daisy to let him in.

She narrowed her eyes in suspicion. "No one knows it's there. Better that way."

She could be right about that. A treasure trove depicting every criminal who ever walked through Hillvale could be highly entertaining—and totally useless. Most of the work had been painted fifty years ago, he figured. The subjects would be in retirement homes or dead by now.

Alan Gump—killer, thief, and arsonist—hadn't been. Could Lonnie Thompson have been one of Gump's fraudulent real estate pals?

"Thalia's spirit wants us to uncover it," he said, trying not to feel like an idiot. "Could I just see her work?"

"She fixed the mural," Daisy said, picking up another rock. "Lucinda gave her the secret. Tell Thalia I'll look."

Figuring that was the best he could hope for, Walker thanked her and jogged back to his SUV. It might be easier to see what name Lonnie Thompson was living under now than to wait for Daisy to produce magic. He sure as hell couldn't get a search warrant to open an invisible cave in search of haunted evidence.

FIFTEEN

TEDDY HAD GIVEN THE KIDS BATHS IN THEIR NEW TEMPORARY HOME AND sent them to bed. Mia claimed she didn't hear the ghost, and Teddy didn't feel any attitude smacking her sensitivity, so she guessed the ghost had downtimes. It might be interesting to converse about the hereafter, but from what she'd sensed so far, she didn't think ectoplasm worked on more than an emotional storm.

Anxious about Syd, she had to keep occupied. It wouldn't hurt to trim the interior frames of the display window with the leftover periwinkle. She would paint the walls a silvery-gray next, then paint the shelving white. The floors. . . she looked at the scuffed, worn oak. It needed sanding and refinishing, maybe in a dark stain?

Adding the finishing touches to the window frame, she noted headlights passing on the road to the parking lot. It was dark and had to be past ten. She crossed her fingers and sent a prayer to the universe.

The car let someone out. The driver unloaded the trunk. Cash was exchanged. . . It had to be Syd.

She wished she had a welcoming light to flip on outside. The overheads would glare and wake half the town. Inspired, she grabbed the candle left from one of the séances, lit it, and held it in the window. The new arrival instantly turned in her direction.

Teddy felt relief flow through her as she recognized Syd's determined stride. She hadn't realized how tense she'd been until this moment, when her sister appeared alive and unharmed. These past months had been hell.

Teddy held the door open and blew out the candle when Syd reached the shop. Setting the wax aside, she hugged her sister the instant the door closed.

"Thank goodness, let me look at you! I've been so worried!" Teddy pushed her older sister back a bit so she could run her fingers over Syd's once-battered face.

"It would be easier to see with a light," Syd said with a laugh. "Are we reduced to living with candles?"

"Only when the ghost is mad. But I didn't want to alert the town that you were here by turning on the circus lights. Let's take your stuff upstairs. We're sharing a bedroom. I've squeezed in another bed, but it doesn't leave much dresser space." Teddy grabbed the large suitcase and Syd carried up a box.

"We'll manage," Syd said confidently. "I want to see my babies. I'll get my strength back once I have them in my arms again."

While Syd carried the box to the children's room, Teddy got the suitcase into her small bedroom and turned on the bedside lamp. Syd was a fantastic mother and had probably filled the box with things the kids missed. She just prayed her sister hadn't been crazy enough to go back to their home to fetch them.

Syd hugged her again when she returned. Teddy could feel the tears running down her cheeks.

"Thank you so much for looking after them," she whispered. "But their hair looks awful! And so does yours. Do you think it's safe to let it grow out again?"

"It should wash out pretty quickly," Teddy said. "I have no idea about safety though. So I guess it depends on what Asshat is doing now."

Syd collapsed on the end of the bed. "I really made a mess of things, didn't I?"

Teddy sat on the end of the other bed. "No, you were just looking for what you had with Damien. You wanted the kids to have a father. No one can blame you for that. You were smart enough to get out the first time he hit you. That's more than many women do."

Syd rubbed the cheekbone he'd fractured—after he'd stalked her and got his revenge for reporting him to the police. "I have no good understanding of character. I had no idea he could be so vindictive or I'd never have got mixed up with him in the first place."

"Well, unless you're a mind reader, that's not possible." Teddy thought diversion from these gloomy thoughts might be necessary. "But I'm delighted to tell you that your daughter can hear ghosts, so let's not murder Asshat and pollute the shop, okay?"

Syd stared at her. "You're kidding, right? You think this ghost stuff is real?"

As if in answer, an invisible force knocked over Syd's large tote bag —spilling out a small handgun.

~

JUNE 29: MORNING

"YOU MEAN IT?" SAM ASKED IN GLEE, POURING THEIR COFFEE. "YOU talked Kurt into turning Hillvale into an art gallery?"

Teddy shrugged. "Actually, I suggested a year-around Halloween spook house. You're the one who suggested art displays."

The big black-and-white photograph of the triptych panel still hung on the café's wall. More names had been scribbled on it in Sharpie ink. Someone had added pink sticky notes of possible names, apparently doubting their memory. A more creative soul had crayoned periwinkle blue onto Teddy's shop door.

She didn't see any way that the triptych would find a killer, but it was bringing people in to check it out and opening community conversations, which was all good.

Dinah came over bearing a plate of donuts. "That Elaine got me the name of someone who might clean up the mural, but where will I put my stuff?" She gestured at the small appliances and cabinets needed for her business.

"Dinah, let me introduce my sister, Syd." Teddy gestured to the bench opposite her where her sister dealt with two excited children. Syd waved and plopped Jeb on her lap.

They'd decided last night there wasn't much point in disguising themselves any longer. Eventually, one of the older residents would put two and two together, especially with the triptych painting stirring memories.

"Pleased to meet you, Syd. Those two are the spitting image of you. You like your pancakes sweet the way they do?"

Syd ran her hand over her dyed brown curls and grimaced. "I'm good with toast, thanks. You could probably lower that back counter so your small appliances are beneath the painting. See where the coffee pots are painted into the picture? You could put the carafes right there and everything works together. And real cabinets could hang over the painted ones."

"Brilliant." Still hovering with the coffee pot, Samantha stepped back to study the painting of long-ago customers sitting at the café's counter, as if they were reflections in a mirror on that wall. "There's even a place for the juicer. It looks as if it might have been originally designed for just that purpose, but over the years, the appliances changed, and accumulated, and people forgot."

Mariah arrived with glasses of milk in time to hear this last. "How did you see that when no one else has?"

"Syd's an interior designer with an emphasis on spatial concepts," Teddy answered while Syd rescued a glass of milk and tucked a napkin into Jeb's collar. "She's helping me work out the shop's space."

Mariah and Sam had to return to waiting on customers, but Dinah lingered. "I have some cash set aside. Can you help me make that mural work?"

The tarot lady with the bracelets and amber rings—*Amber*—Teddy recalled, wandered over to join them while Dinah and Syd discussed re-designing the café. "Sam says we're starting art walks. How can I contribute?"

This was what Syd needed—a community to make her feel safe. Teddy had freaked over the gun last night and demanded that the cartridge be removed. The ghostly incident had shaken Syd into agreeing, but Teddy wouldn't be happy until the weapon was in safe hands.

She'd like to shake the client who had sold the gun to her sister. Syd had absolutely zero training in the use of weapons. She was simply living in a state of panic, for good reason, admittedly.

By the time the kids had finished their breakfast, a committee had formed. They trailed down the street after Teddy and Syd, ready to set plans for the art walk in motion.

Kurt waited at the shop door, leaning one shoulder against the newly painted panel. He wasn't wearing jeans today, Teddy noted in disappointment. Yesterday, he'd looked three kinds of sexy in faded denim. Not that he looked half bad today sans tie and coat. She could admire the bronzed column of his throat emerging from the open-necked shirt and hope for a glimpse of chest hair.

She was forced to admit that she had really wanted to take him up on that dinner invite. Working beside him yesterday had been a turn-on of epic proportions. Sex between frenemies, maybe? Except her lawyer had said consorting with Kurt while filing a lawsuit was a no-no. *Ugly*.

"Is this another uprising to which I'm not invited?" he asked as he straightened. His chiseled features displayed just a hint of uncertainty.

That was a good look on him, Teddy decided—no false arrogance. "We're planning an art walk. Since the lodge has the largest collection, you should join us." That wouldn't be consorting, would it?

"It's a throwback to our frontier roots," the sardonic musician who'd been introduced as Harvey said solemnly. "We'll have a barn-raising and picnic after."

Teddy noticed that—despite Harvey's heavy irony—the excited crowd grew tense with Kurt's appearance. That was a shame. She sensed Kurt's reluctant interest and desire to help. How often had he been excluded from the town's activities because of who he was? She had a clear memory of the little boy standing alone in his fancified suit behind a table full of expensive gifts, while his birthday guests played and laughed without him.

She'd been too young to think beyond her own excitement, but she'd known he was sad. At the time, she hadn't realized not everyone sensed what she did.

To hell with it. Kurt needed the art walk as much as the town did. Personal differences shouldn't intervene.

She caught Kurt's arm and dragged him inside. "I assume you know everyone? I just met Harvey. Since his walking sticks contain crystals, I thought I could display them in here. You said you studied architecture, didn't you? Meet my sister, Syd, the interior designer. We're talking about how we can fix up the city hall displays. Can you help with that?"

She waited for their resident ghost to protest Kurt's entrance, but Thalia—Teddy was thinking of her as her mother's cousin—seemed content to leave them alone today. For now. After the gun incident last night, Teddy worried about displaying anything breakable—like her parents' pottery.

Kurt seemed tense too as the conversation played out around him. He let Mia drag him out to see her tree house—Teddy realized her niece still missed her dad and was seeking a father figure. He came back in carrying Jeb, who was gnawing on a banana. Her nephew comforted himself with food. He needed stability. Maybe having Syd back would help.

Teddy kind of liked seeing the stiff executive deal unquestioningly with childish demands. She wished Kurt would be mean and yell at them, or even ignore them, so she'd get over this damned crush that couldn't go anywhere. But he actually made an effort where many men wouldn't.

Jeb went into his mother's arms, leaving Kurt empty-handed. Teddy wanted to ease his discomfort, but he'd started it by isolating himself from his neighbors for so long.

He was starting to loosen up and help Harvey re-arrange the hooks beneath her shelves when Cassandra Tolliver entered.

Kurt's tall, professorial, silver-haired half-aunt had a way of taking command with just her presence. The moment she entered, the others turned to her with explanations, questions, and requests.

Kurt eased up beside Teddy. "I'd better get back to my desk. Dinner tonight?"

Teddy shot him a look of disapproval. "As I understand it, Cass's mother owned this valley before your father turned it into his medieval fiefdom. She deserves a little respect."

"There's more to the history than that," Kurt countered. "Give me credit for being polite and allowing her to reign free of my presence."

"Discussion to follow," she replied sternly. "Tonight, over a good bottle of wine."

He not only looked relieved, but she thought she detected approval and a strong surge of lust seeping through his barriers. He squeezed her hand, said his farewells, and departed under Cass's regal glare.

The dead speaker wires cackled.

Shouldn't the damned ghost have left along with her bones?

SAMANTHA

JUNE 29: LATE AFTERNOON

SAM ADDED WATER TO THE NEW BEGONIA SHE'D DISCOVERED IN HER GHOST garden and added a top layer of compost. "Thank you, Gladys," she whispered to the spirit she'd once met in the yard. "Your garden makes a fabulous nursery."

Hearing Walker coming up the flagstone path, she stood and stretched the kink out of her back. She stretched a little more at his appreciative look, so the buttons of her shirt strained over her breasts. The man had a way of feeding her feminine power.

"You'll have to add this yard to the art walk." He kissed her thoroughly, then turned to admire the bed of blossoms that had practically sprung up overnight. "Art should be about expressions of beauty and life, shouldn't it?"

"For a man who spends his time digging through dusty files and dealing with black-hearted villains, that is an amazing understanding. You get extra bonus points tonight." Sam took his arm as they climbed the stairs of the cottage they'd just moved into. She liked the way he tightened his arm against his side to hold her hand in place. The man had muscles beneath his unprepossessing uniform.

"You may thank my mother for my sensitivity training. She'll be coming in for the art walk." Walker kissed her hair and wouldn't let go when Sam tried to yank away.

"You know perfectly well it isn't the art she's coming to see," she said nervously. "She won't like me. I'm too white, too non-domestic, too tall, too. . ."

He kissed her into silence, then led her toward the kitchen. "My five-foot Chinese harridan of a mother married a six-foot Irish cop. She has no grounds for complaint. And I promised her a memorial now that we have dad's remains to cremate. So it's not all about you."

"Okay, excuse my moment of panic. I was just getting used to a community that accepts me, and you threw me a ringer. I know how much you respect your mother."

Sam released him to open the refrigerator and remove their carry-out dinner. "Dinah was experimenting with sushi today, in preparation for the art walk. The lunch crowd wasn't appreciative. She has high expectations of a more sophisticated clientele once we bring in art lovers. I'll have to start paying to work there if she keeps sending gourmet meals home with me."

"Sushi is dangerous. Dinah could end up poisoning the crowd if she doesn't know what she's doing." Walker examined the neat, colorful bites revealed when he opened the carton.

"She says she had training in New Orleans. She's coming out of her shell a little now that she knows you won't arrest her for being who she is. Or maybe she's starting to believe her mixed gender really isn't against the law anymore." Sam set out plates and reached for wine glasses, making some attempt to pretend they weren't eating out of boxes. Domestic goddess, she was not.

"Or maybe Kurt actually deigning to eat in the café gave her courage," Walker said through a mouthful of sushi roll.

She poured the wine, frowned, and thought about that. "He's not a bad man. Having him around seems to be changing the town dynamic. If he's working with us, then there's less of the *us against them* mentality."

"And maybe common sense and peace will reign again?" he asked with obvious sarcasm.

Sam shrugged and moved on. "Have you had any word on the

identity of those bones? Teddy says her spirit is still hanging around, probably waiting for justice."

"Or revenge." Walker leaned his rangy frame against the counter instead of taking a seat at the tiny kitchen table that had come with the cottage. "It's not easy to collect DNA from burned bones. The kiln baked them pretty good, and the coroner isn't sure if these have been contaminated after enduring that level of heat. Even if they find something, we have nothing to match it against."

"Teddy won't be happy to hear that. She's hoping the ghost will pass over once she knows her killer has been caught."

"I think the lot of you are just guilting me into working my employees for free with this talk of dangerous ghosts. This police chief gig doesn't even pay our rent, so my guys need to work on the paying cases. But if it helps at all, they can't find any trace of Thompson after he left here. We don't have a social security number to work on and the world is full of Thompsons."

"Who needs money when we have free food, don't need a car, and my trust fund pays what your salary doesn't?" she stretched to kiss his cheek to show she was teasing. He smelled of expensive aftershave so she knew he'd stopped to clean up before coming home.

Home. It was lovely to have a home again. And someone she loved to come home to.

"In that case, shall I have them start hunting for your birth mother? No charge." He lifted a quizzical eyebrow.

That was a bit of a sore point. Her mother had taken her from Hillvale and her only family, given her up for adoption to a couple who deliberately moved to Utah to keep her from knowing her origins. Sam wasn't at all certain that she had any right to interrupt the life of a woman who had fled Hillvale for undefined reasons.

She shook her head without explanation. "I submitted more grant requests today," she told him, changing the topic. "I'd love to explore the quake fault in relation to the crystals my grandparents found up there. But it's not as if there's an easy application to real world uses."

"No one knows until you dig into it—that's what research is about. I'd miss Dinah's food if you started working a real job," he added with a chuckle. "This sushi is top notch."

"I can always have Dinah teach me to cook," she said blithely, "But

I'd rather grow food than cook it. What progress have you made with Daisy? Do I need to hunt Valdis down and talk to her?"

"Daisy promised to look for Thalia's pieces. Of the two, Daisy is probably more easily persuaded. Your aunt is rational enough to argue against touching the art she deems evil. Will she be helping with the art walk?"

"Put her on a stage and let her sing opera? I've been looking up Val's career. She mostly sang in California theaters, but she also performed in Chicago and New York. So far, I've not uncovered what sent her around the bend."

"It's her business and not ours. I think the Kennedys will give up the fight for the farm once they're convinced Gump lied about ownership. I'm starting to believe this legend about Hillvale attracting evil though. How can one tiny town have so much fraud *plus* two killers?"

"That you know of," she murmured wickedly. "Who knows what evil lurks in the hearts of men?"

An owl screeched in the tree outside. Her Aunt Val would call it an omen.

SIXTEEN

TEDDY CURLED UP AGAINST THE SIDE OF WARM, NAKED MALE AND SIGHED with pleasure. "So it wasn't just purple pixie dust."

Kurt chuckled, a sexy masculine note that shivered her in a good way. "We could blame a bottle of wine."

"I can handle two glasses just fine," she protested, snuggling into the bend of his shoulder and muscled arm. "This was just us."

Well, it had been a little more than that, if she was willing to admit it, but she wasn't ready to give him full view of her soul. Despite the lawyer's warning and their basic differences, she'd opened her senses over dinner. Probably a big mistake, but she just wasn't cut out to be cold and calculating, and this quiet, intense man interested her far more than he should. Normally, he cut himself off, but tonight, his desire and admiration had hit her like rain on a thirsty desert, and his lust had fed her own.

At least she'd tested him, which was more than she'd done with Ray. So, she was learning.

But Kurt kept himself so closed off, it made her extra sense a nice sexual stimulant and not a lot more. She really needed to be wary, or he'd steal her house like Ray had stolen her gems.

"*Just us* is pretty damned good." Kurt murmured, stroking her breast. "The distraction of wanting you every time I look at you may make getting any work done problematic."

"Horn dog." With a sigh, she extricated herself from the *distraction*. "I need to go back to the shop, though. Syd is still pretty fragile. I don't want her panicking if Thalia the Spook decides to shake things up."

She didn't want Syd shooting up the shop and herself, but she thought it best not to mention what was undoubtedly an illegal weapon.

He sat up, letting the sheet fall to his hips. Executives weren't supposed to have six-packs. The man obviously worked out—and baked himself on yachts, if his bronze was any indication. Teddy had to fight with her better self to keep from crawling back into bed with him.

"I was hoping you might consider staying up here now that your sister has moved in." He leaned back against the headboard. "My cottage is private. I could give you a key."

They were in one of the luxury cottages set back in the woods—out of sight of kids and family and tourists. Picking up her clothes in the enormous master bath, Teddy sent the steamy tiled shower a longing look. Even her nice apartment back in San Francisco had nothing this lavish.

"I'm pretty sure the Lucys will call this sleeping with the enemy," she said lightly, covering her neurosis about lying, cheating, conniving men. Ray had stolen from her. Assbutt had beat up on Syd. Prior boyfriends had used her connections to better themselves. . . And Kurt wanted her home. If only she could learn to separate sex from emotion —she'd probably be a basket case. "And we still don't know how safe Syd and the kids are. I think it's better if she has extra protection."

"I need to be on call here," he admitted grumpily. "Once my mother returns, I can hand the reins over to her and Monty, but neither of them alone can handle every situation that comes along."

"You need to hire a trainee manager. Don't you ever take vacations?" She shimmied into the dress she'd worn for dinner.

He rubbed his bristled jaw and thought about it. "I go into the city at least once a week when I know I have backup. Does that count? You'll have to meet my mother before you'll understand why a trainee never lasts."

"You ever thought of quitting?" Teddy knew she was overstepping boundaries, but she *liked* this uptight innkeeper. He deserved better.

"Every minute of every day," he admitted. "The condo project was to be my escape, until that fell through. All I have left is Hillvale. Once the new shops and apartments are profitable, the town won't have to rely on the lodge's income, and I'll be free. My mother can run the place into the ground, if she likes."

Amazed that he'd let her this far inside his head, Teddy didn't immediately reply. She understood his dream. She just didn't agree with it. But she didn't know all the history here. She leaned over and kissed his bristly jaw. "I'll send Thalia the Friendly Spook up here to help you."

He snorted, pulled her down for a better kiss, and let her go. He climbed out of bed to walk her to the door. "I should have sent a driver for you so you couldn't escape."

"Which is why I drove myself, thank you very much." She smiled at his masculine growl, kissed him again, and fled before she changed her mind.

The drive back to town only took a few minutes. She could see the nightlight she'd set up in the shop through the front window. Entering, she stopped to open her senses in the quiet. Everyone appeared to be asleep. It was peaceful here in the half-light, with no one nattering at her. She wasn't the heavy-duty extrovert that Syd was. She needed moments like this to fill her creative well. She hadn't designed a piece of jewelry in weeks, but the hours with Kurt had inspired her. She needed to get back to work.

The crystals in her display case gave off their own lambent light. Harvey had hung the straps of a few of his walking sticks on hooks along the front wall. The crystals he'd used in them weren't particularly powerful and provided no illumination. She suspected they were tourist souvenirs, not his real pieces. She'd admired the carved handles of the staffs several of the Lucys carried. If she stayed here, she should probably ask Harvey to make her one.

If she stayed here.

Her heart pounded a little faster at the possibility. That was probably a bad sign—especially if she sued the guy who owned the town, the one she'd just *slept* with. Would she ever learn?

She ran her finger over the newly-cleaned shelves ready for inventory. Syd had painted a board white and used calligraphy and purple paint to write *Teddy's Treasure Trove* on it—decision made.

She wasn't quite ready for her lonely bed—with her sister in the same room, just as if they hadn't left twenty years ago. Life was passing them by. They needed to move forward.

She sat at the oak table and opened her laptop to test if the internet had been installed as promised. Smiling with satisfaction when the connection worked with the password the cable company had given her, she checked her e-mail. She had the standard responses from her office staff, but the one that caught her eye was from DCD-Baker—David and Cynthia Devine-Baker, their parents. Her timing must have been close to perfect to reach them this quickly.

To Teddy's shock, they gave her Thalia Thompson's e-mail address and said last they'd heard, she was living in Monterey. *Thalia was alive?* Then who had been hidden in the rafters? The one thing the coroner had been certain about was the body was female. Thalia was the last female who'd lived here.

She e-mailed the information to Walker so he could check on it in the morning.

Her parents verified they'd never sold the building, that Kurt's rental agent, Xavier Black, had been handling maintenance and rentals while the Thompsons lived there, and they'd lost track after that. Mail to Malaysia didn't happen and their business affairs went to a banker, who apparently knew nothing about the rental. That was typical of them to not even inquire.

But they were enthusiastic about showing the pottery and asked that any sales go to the nonprofit they were currently working with, of course. Teddy was fine with that. Pricing the pottery might be a little tougher. She e-mailed and asked for suggestions for people who might help with that, although she didn't have a lot of hope for a response.

She flipped through the office messages. Most were routine. A few were voice mail text, mostly from customers. She needed to respond to them soon. One was a message from an unknown number asking if this was the number to reach Teddy Baker.

No, it was her office number, for Theodosia Devine. How many people knew they were the same person? Not many, and those few knew her personal number. She shivered and lost her satisfaction in finishing up her routine.

For a moment, she debated e-mailing her mother's cousin, but instinct balked. "Hey Thalia, is that you?" she whispered at the still air.

An owl hooted in reply.

She'd ask Walker in the morning what she should do.

JUNE 30: MORNING

KURT PRIED ANOTHER FILTHY PAINTING OFF THE WALL OF THE TOWN HALL and added it to the stack. He'd hated this uninspired montage of bad art for a long time, but Monty had been the one who had to look at it. Given permission to clean it up, Kurt was happy to do so. The physical exercise beat another mindless work-out in the gym.

"Some of those pieces give me the creeps," Monty admitted, working on the other side of the hall. "Is that gallery person coming back to tell us which ones we can relegate to the trash can?"

"Hell if I know. You'd think one of the Lucys would know about art." Kurt studied the bare—filthy—wall and figured a good coat of white paint would work wonders.

He'd rather demolish the whole place, but even he had to admit that this building had been here since the late 1800s and probably still had redwood logs in the walls. It would make a quaint tourist attraction if restored.

He'd spent his teen summers working on San Francisco's historic housing under Lance's tutelage. Not one of them had been log structures. He'd have to do some research.

"Daisy may know art, but she just comes by and steals pieces when they start corroding," Monty said. "I'm pretty sure the Elaine person pointed out the more valuable pieces. Sam probably kept a list."

They both looked at the disorganized stack of frames. "We should have asked her before we took it down." Kurt scowled. He'd been more interested in stripping down to bare walls.

"We were probably supposed to wait for Teddy's sister to decide which pieces she needed for decorating." Monty went to his office and returned with bottles of water. "Not that it's any of my business, but are you sure you want to get involved with Teddy? Those two are Lucys if I ever saw them."

"*Lucy* in the existential sense of interfering females, or are you attributing them with superpowers?" Kurt drank his water and scanned the barren front room of the town hall, looking for more things to tear down. If he couldn't bulldoze the entire town yet, ripping off ugly would make a good start. Not wanting to hear his brother's answer, he continued, "I'm not a eunuch. Unless you have someone to replace me at the lodge, I need a life. Teddy will be back in the city by fall, winter at the latest. Works for me."

"Don't be too sure of that. I thought for certain Walker would leave the instant he found out what happened to his father, but he gave up his fancy LA place to live here. Samantha ought to be working with a university, but she's settling in. I think the crazies are coming home to roost."

"Walker isn't crazy. He lost a son and wife in LA and had reason to leave." Kurt swigged from his water, then set it down on the counter to tackle a wall of ugly pamphlet holders. "Teddy and Sam aren't particularly crazy. They just talk the same language as the Lucys. That's a female thing."

Monty snorted. "Right, you keep on living with your head in the sand, and you're going to get your ass kicked. You think they made up that ghost?"

"You think Mariah's really keeping them from haunting the lodge?" Kurt countered. He applied the back of his hammer to yanking the old plywood off the wall.

"Hell if I know." Monty parroted Kurt's earlier reply. "But she looks good while she's doing it, and we have no more howls and rattles, so I'm happy."

They pried the pamphlet holder off the wall just as Teddy and Syd arrived, followed by Goth One and Goth Two, although Kurt noticed their hair wasn't as black as before. And the kids wore normal jeans and colorful shirts instead of black. He was sure that was a statement of some sort, but he was more interested in Teddy. She'd washed out the worst of the black, leaving her mane of curls lighter with a definite sparkle of red.

He smiled his approval, then leaned over the counter to investigate the stuffed creature the youngest was showing him. "An octopus? Where did you find an octopus?"

The kid shoved his thumb in his mouth. His sister answered for him. "Momma got us presents at the aquarium. We went there before. It's neat."

"The aquarium is a lot of fun," he agreed. "Will you be drawing fish for the art show?"

Mia beamed. "Could we? I got colors."

"You planning on turning the walls into canvas for the kids to work on?" Syd asked, looking around at the bare walls and filthy paint.

"We could paint on this," Mia suggested, pointing at the plywood they'd just removed. "It's already got stuff on it."

Kurt froze. The panel was the same size as the triptych panel. Teddy sent him a glance and skirted around her sister and the kids to where he balanced the old wood with his hand. "No, it couldn't be," she whispered in shock, crouching down to look closer.

Kurt peered over the top. There were definitely colors on it.

Monty and Syd looked over Teddy's shoulder.

"That's the town hall," Monty said, pointing at one of the squares. "That's the bluff stairs that go up behind here. Don't know who that is walking down them."

"Orange curls," Teddy said, sounding a little sad. "She looks a lot like our mother."

"Are you saying this is a piece of the *priceless* triptych we almost mangled off the wall?" Monty asked. He lifted it a lot more carefully then he had earlier and carried it over to the window where the light could hit it.

Kurt got down on the floor to examine it closer once Monty propped it against the wall. "Yup. Looks just like the other one, dull cracked colors and all." He glanced up to see Mariah standing outside and Sam crossing the street. "The posse is arriving."

"How do they *do* that?" Monty asked as Teddy and Syd went to the door to flag them down. "Maybe we should advertise Spook Art and send the women into the streets for the tourists to figure out."

Teddy turned and winked. *Halloween Hillvale,* she'd suggested. Kurt wasn't ready to give up his dream of luxury living. Art walks were good for city dwellers. Spooks. . . not so much.

He rummaged under the counter, found some old flyers and colored markers and handed them to the kids. "Practice drawing fish on here until we decide where to put them, okay?"

Entering and recognizing what they were looking at, Mariah stripped off her café apron. With care, she used it to dust off the decades of filth and cobwebs. "Which idiot Null thought priceless art made a good pamphlet stand? They've put staples right through it!"

"If this is Lucinda's, then it's at least half a century old." Teddy sat down where Kurt had been to examine the images now that they were less dusty. "Any number of blind idiots could have repurposed it. The better question might be why she painted on plywood."

"Tempera," Sam explained. "Lucinda was experimenting with medieval tempera for some reason and needed a hard surface. No one wanted a mural on their walls, I'm guessing. A town hall would be the ideal place to display a large piece like this, but Hillvale had no mayor or public building fifty years ago. This was probably someone's home and shop, like yours."

"But there's city hall in the picture," Teddy pointed out. "She painted a triptych to go on the walls of a building she *imagined*?"

"So if I'm understanding this legend," Syd said in disbelief, "half a century ago this famous artist drew a painting of places that didn't exist and of our mother's cousin walking down the bluff before she was born?"

"Well, Thalia might have been an infant at the commune fifty years ago. That's where our parents grew up. I don't think Thalia was a lot younger than Mom." Teddy leaned over to examine the details. "If this is supposed to be an image of ten years ago like the other, the kiln was still working. She's carrying a fired clay pot."

"I don't suppose that's the two of you standing on the corner with glum looks?" Sam asked, glancing back at Kurt and Monty.

Monty leaned in to see what Kurt had already found. He whistled.

"Are you sure this couldn't be someone imitating Lucinda's work? Someone who was standing on the roof of Teddy's shop ten years ago? Because this sure looks like the day we came to town to decide what the hell we were going to do with the mess we'd inherited."

"The day you turned twenty-one and came into your shares of the corporation," Kurt said, remembering their despair. "Mom told us we were nearly bankrupt and if we didn't do something, the town would disappear and the resort with it."

"And you said good riddance," Monty said with a laugh. "You haven't worn those cowboy boots since."

"That's your football jersey you're wearing. You said you'd accept the NFL offer and send money home to help, as if we were on welfare." Kurt wondered if he'd made a mistake discouraging his younger brother from following a sports career.

"Yeah, because I really needed one more concussion," Monty said with sarcasm, reminding him of why they'd chosen the path they had. Monty had just got out of the hospital after a particularly bad tackle. Making the lodge profitable had seemed the safer course.

"So, this is a specific moment in time." Arms crossed, Mariah stood back to study the faded colors. "Aaron wasn't in his shop then. It looks abandoned."

"Most of the town looked abandoned back then." Kurt glanced out the window at the town today, with its colorful planters spilling with blooms along the boardwalk. Tourists roamed the streets, stopping to admire the displays in shops like Aaron's. He had the window crammed with glittering jewelry, chandeliers and the kind of antiques that city dwellers coveted. Tullah's Thrift Shop was equally eye-catching. Ten years ago, it had been a dusty pawn shop at best. The town wasn't thriving, but it had improved under their guardianship.

"A few boutiques, a ski shop, and you've built a profit center," Teddy murmured.

"That isn't exactly what I want to hear," he muttered for her ears alone. "High end dealers won't want these shabby structures."

"I'm high end," she retorted. "I love my shabby chic shop."

"With eccentric electricity and ghosts instead of insulation. Right. Tell me that come winter." He turned back to the painting. "So, where do we store priceless art?"

"The lodge vault?" Monty suggested. "Until it can be cleaned, valued, and insured at least."

The women objected, then began taking photos to blow up and hang with the one in the café.

Teddy strolled off without a word, and Kurt's gut sank. Surely she couldn't be serious about wanting to keep that useless building when she could have an all new, luxury villa? What was *wrong* with women?

SEVENTEEN

JUNE 30: AFTERNOON

STILL IRKED BY KURT'S DISMISSAL OF HILLVALE AND HIS OWN DAMNED history, Teddy opened the box her office had express shipped. "Do you think we should just stick with showing the crystals for now, or should I set out some of the less expensive jewelry?"

"Jewelry," Syd said decisively, removing crystals from the floor display case to add to the shelves she'd been decorating. "Show them how the crystals can be used, encourage them to wear pieces that accentuate their powers."

"But maybe not the aquamarine pieces," Teddy said dryly, removing a jewel case from the box. "No point driving off the customers with honesty."

Syd leaned over to admire the pieces in the box. "I *love* the aquamarine. Maybe it affects different people different ways? How much experimenting have you done?"

"Not much. Things kind of started falling apart about the time I learned the crystals might affect more than just me. I was thinking if I could scale back expenses by living up here for a while, I might have more time to explore." Teddy sat back on her heels to admire the sparkle of one of her more elaborate necklace designs.

"That's a miniature chandelier. You need someone with size Ds to wear that. Did you design it for yourself?" Syd asked, picking through and finding daintier pieces to drape on her more slender frame.

Teddy laughed. "Probably. I don't really give it much thought when I start wiring up the sparkly bits. They just kind of call out to each other and I listen. So it's my id doing the talking?"

"Or responding," Syd said with a shrug. "We didn't come with instruction books. We learn by doing." She checked on Mia and Jeb busily scribbling fish on construction paper. "I wish I could teach them better than we were taught."

"I don't think you can teach kids the correct way of hearing ghosts. Just accepting that Mia can should be enough for now. It's not that any of our extra gifts are of much use, but we shouldn't have to pretend we don't have them."

Although she had done that most of her life. From harsh experience as a child, she'd discovered that knowing things others didn't had made her *different*. And when her Inner Monitor had hurt her one too many times, she'd figured out how to shut it down. After a while, it had been easier to just leave it off. Only after learning her crystals actually affected others had she gained the courage to explore her odd ability. If she'd been brought up in an environment that encouraged her oddity, she might be further along the path to enlightenment.

"Hiding Mia's gift would be like hiding a wart on her face," Syd said in exasperation. "She really will have to control it when she's older or risk being ostracized. Our gifts are a little easier. People just think we're intelligent or creative." Syd pinned a red fish on the wall.

Teddy laughed. "And still despise us for being different, unless we hide our light under a barrel as women have done for centuries. I think I'll enjoy being scary." She set the glass display case on a low counter beneath the plate glass window where the light would refract through the gems. "Here comes Sam with Chief Walker. Do you think they've found Thalia?"

Syd arranged a crystal vase of flowers from Samantha's garden. "As long as they're not coming to tell me that Ash is on the way, I'm good."

"Did you even tell Walker so he'll know to be on the lookout?"

Syd shrugged again. "I don't like asking for trouble."

"You are such a crab, and I mean that in an entirely astrological way." Teddy opened the door for their visitors. "Tell me good news first."

Sam laughed. "Walker's brilliant crew has created posters of our triptych pics, and we now have another one hanging at Dinah's. Should we hang the spare pics on the walls in here just to fill them?"

"What, Harvey's staffs aren't enough? Wouldn't it be better to leave space for any art leftover from the Kennedys' destruction of everything in Town Hall? Can we get you anything? Coffee only takes a minute." Teddy gestured at the kitchen.

"Why don't we leave Sam here to help the kids with their paintings while we go back to the kitchen?" Looking official even wearing jeans, Walker gestured for them to precede him to the back.

"Not sounding good," Teddy said in a low voice. She hurried to the back to set the coffeemaker on.

"Just not anything we want spread around yet. Kids hear a lot more than we know." The newly installed police chief leaned against the counter while Teddy added coffee to the machine. He accepted the bottle of water Syd handed him.

"You tracked down Thalia's address?" Syd asked.

"We did. No Thompsons live there. Neighbors have no recollection of her. It's a rental, so she may have lived there years ago, and no one would remember. The more important point is that we have the rental agency records. A Donnie Thomas rented it ten years ago."

"Lonnie Thompson, Donnie Thomas—if mail was addressed to either one, the mailman would just think it was an error and deliver it." Teddy got down mugs from the newly-scrubbed cabinets. "So even though Mom had an address, that didn't necessarily mean Thalia lived there."

"Exactly. And after Thompson moved, if he left a forwarding address, her cards would have continued being delivered for another year. And you said she stopped sending paper cards some years back, so she may never have had them returned to her." Walker helped himself to a spoonful of sugar from the bowl. "Since this is a murder case, the sheriff's department is handling it. They're running credit bureau and DMV checks under that address and both names."

"But Thalia's e-mail address is still good? I was afraid to send anything, but Mom likes electronic cards now. She sends them out on birthdays and holidays, scheduling them when she has internet access. She apparently thinks that address works."

"She sets up the cards so she knows if someone doesn't open them," Syd added.

"That's what we need to talk about." Walker sipped the coffee Teddy poured for him. "E-mail addresses can float out there into eternity if no one closes them. If the cards are being opened, Thompson could be checking regularly or just around holidays. We'd have to get a court order to go into the account. We have almost no basis to go to a judge and ask for an invasion of privacy. I'd like to experiment and send a test e-mail."

Teddy raised inquiring eyebrows.

Walker explained. "One, we'd like to draw a response from him so we can find his ISP. Two, if we can come up with just the right message, we might draw him out of hiding, or at least, get information from him—provided he opens it. This could be a long-term maneuver if we have to wait for a birthday."

Syd poked around on her phone. "I have a copy of Mom's on-line calendar. Thalia's birthday is early July."

Walker shrugged. "Worth trying."

"Saying she's won the lottery won't do it, will it? No one believes that." Teddy sipped her coffee. "But bait draws cockroaches."

"It would help if we knew what he was doing now," Syd added. "If he's still working with pottery, free clay or discounted tools might draw him out. Otherwise, it almost has to be cash."

"But we don't have *his* e-mail. If this is Thalia's address. . . Is there some way of mocking my mother's e-mail address and telling Thalia about a new art gallery for displaying her work?" Teddy wasn't fond of the idea of sleuthing or even e-mailing a possible murderer, but if Thompson had sold their house. . . She wanted him nailed.

"We can set up the e-mail account to use your mother's name and run it through a different website," Walker explained. "Most people don't look to see more than the name, or they assume the correspondent changed providers. But Thompson won't be interested in an art gallery— unless he's still doing pottery, and we mention the gallery accepts all kinds of art. He needs to see something in it for himself."

Teddy grimaced at Walker's sensible words. "We'd just about have to invite him up here— 'Grand homecoming of Hillvale Commune and Art Walk.' Then mention Kurt plans on razing all the houses after the get-together. Wonder if that would frighten him into looking for bones?"

"If he's a potential killer, it's too dangerous," Walker decided. "If we sent an e-mail requesting a correct address so your mother could send a package, we might frighten him off. Maybe we can say the Ingerssons left a legacy for all members of the commune, and Thalia has to go to a certain bank to pick it up. He might assume he qualifies too."

"Good one," Teddy said admiringly. "No time frame in case he doesn't check soon. It could be forever before he shows up, though. How will you manage the bank end?"

"Bank of Walker," he said with a decided twinkle. "It's a basic mail-drop set-up. We do it frequently. If I have your permission to pretend to be your mother, I'll get to work on it."

"We probably ought to have Mom's permission, but start work anyway. I don't want to worry her if Thalia really is alive, and we're jousting at windmills." Teddy led the way back to the front room where Sam was hanging the kids' wall art in the empty spaces.

"She wants kids," Walker said, admiring his significant other, but giving what sounded like an unhappy sigh.

"She can have Syd's." Teddy refrained from opening her Inner Monitor to what was a private issue between the chief and his girl-friend. Sometimes, her gift was too much like spying.

He laughed, breaking the tension so Mia and Jeb had no reason to suspect anything was wrong.

"Ummm, were you expecting package delivery by golf cart?" Syd asked, glancing out the front window to the street.

The golf cart stopped in front of the store, on the narrow potholed road instead of in the parking lot. A woman with a wild head of gray hair and wearing a feathered cape lumbered out—Crazy Daisy. After their discussion of differences, Teddy would have to quit using the Null epithet for her.

"I asked Daisy if she'd bring me some of Thalia's artwork," Walker said, watching with surprise. "I don't know how she knows where I am though." He jogged out to help with the awkward canvases stacked in the back of the cart.

"Prepare yourselves for a trip beyond known boundaries," Sam whispered. "I'll go help. Daisy is sane enough most days, but her head isn't always in this time frame."

Teddy exchanged glances with Syd. "Do we need to take the kids outside?"

Syd held up her finger, then crouched down to admire their artwork. "Those are really good, but we'll need the walls for a little bit. Why don't you take your drawings upstairs and watch one of those new DVDs I brought for you?"

"*Finding Dory*," Mia said in satisfaction. "C'mon, Jeb, you like fishes."

"You're raising sea creatures?" Teddy asked as the kids trudged off with their colors and papers.

"When we had the apartment with the swimming pool, Jeb practically lived in the water. And we visited the marina right before I got mixed up with Ash. That's a happy memory I encourage." Syd held open the door so the others could enter with a trio of different-sized paintings.

Teddy had them line the canvases along the back wall where the light from the window would catch them best. The oils didn't seem very striking or interesting.

Daisy fluttered nervously, glancing at Harvey's walking sticks and the crystals in the floor display. "I brought you guardians," she said. "You will need them."

Sam headed back for the door. "Daisy's guardians may have stopped an avalanche, so do not scorn the offering."

Walker went out to help carry in the boxes that had been hidden under the canvas.

Better than the paintings, the stone-and-wire figurines had character. Teddy sorted through them in admiration, sensing their power.

"These are fabulous! Look at this one—she looks like she's holding a crystal sword! They'll be perfect in here."

"Do you want them to remain as guardians, or is it all right for Teddy to sell them?" Sam asked as Daisy started distributing the statuettes around the room.

"I'll only take a small commission for handling," Teddy explained, worried that Daisy appeared confused. "Your pieces will draw in customers to buy my stuff."

"They will be needed soon," Daisy said, nodding. "The art is safe, but you are not. Spread the army around."

Teddy hated opening her Monitor where there were so many people and mixed emotions, but she didn't want to take advantage of Daisy's lack of business knowledge.

The instant she opened up, a tornado of fury and anguish struck. The canvases flew across the room. Prince Hairy howled.

And Mia screamed.

EIGHTEEN

KURT STEPPED OUT OF HIS CAR IN THE TOWN PARKING LOT, ANNOYED WITH himself for doing so. Why did Monty think he ought to check on Daisy's arrival with a cartful of canvases? He had bankers breathing down his neck and the lawyer to call back and—

The howling dog and a child's scream drove all practical thought from his head. He ran for Teddy's shop. That damned building was cursed and needed to come down—*now*.

Half the town poured toward this end of the boardwalk. Kurt waved them back. "Someone go around back and check on the dog," he shouted over the animal's howls. "We don't want to frighten the children more by everyone crowding in. Wait here."

To his amazement, they did, although he was barraged with warnings about negative energy and suggestions for warding off evil as he shoved open the door.

Before he could roll his eyes at the insanity, a hurricane wind nearly blasted him off his feet. He hung on, got inside, shoved the door closed, and the wind reduced to a nasty breeze. *Damn,* that felt just like the pressure that had knocked him flying off the stairs. There was a bad wind funnel in here somewhere. But no one was lying flat on the floor this time. He studied the front room warily.

Syd was holding her excited daughter—undoubtedly the issuer of screams. Mia was safe, so he relaxed a fraction.

With narrowed eyes like some stone-faced cop on a TV show, Chief Walker stood protectively in front of Sam while he surveyed the circus. Paper and *stone statues* flew. Harvey's sticks rattled in the weird breeze. No one seemed overly concerned —because of the woman holding their attention.

Kurt had been avoiding looking directly at Teddy. He didn't want to acknowledge that she might be the instigator of whipping breezes and flying figurines. Gritting his molars, he shifted his gaze to watch Teddy using both fists to hold up two of Daisy's stone sculptures as if they were victory trophies. Sunlight played in a few fiery red strands of her hair as her compact body swirled. Her eyes were shining that weird gold he'd occasionally noticed. She winked at him and continued circling.

"She's saying *look at the pictures*," Mia said from the safety of her mother's arms. "I think she's crying."

What the hell?

Deciding they could all go crazy as long as they were safe, Kurt looked for Jeb but didn't see him. He edged around the perimeter of the shop, in the direction of the kitchen.

Crazy Daisy sat against the back wall, mending one of the figurines apparently damaged in the storm or whirlwind or whatever it was. The high-end businesses he envisioned for Hillvale wouldn't allow a bag lady like Daisy across the threshold, much less let her play with the merchandise. Where would Daisy go if he tore down the town? Should he care? His head started to pound, and he slipped past to the back of the house.

Jeb sat on the back step with a box of cereal in his lap. The dog had stopped howling—apparently because Jeb was feeding the creature cereal. One of the women—Amber?—waved to indicate she was keeping an eye on the kid. Reassured that some form of normal existed, Kurt returned to the spectacle in the front room.

"I think she's wearing down," Teddy called, gingerly setting the figurines on the floor instead of a shelf, evidently to prevent further flying objects.

The breeze did seem to be dying. Kurt leaned against the door jamb, crossed his arms, and observed these seemingly intelligent people going ga-ga over a little wind. These mountains were windy. The cursed house apparently funneled it. Flying stone statues. . . that was a bit much, admittedly. Maybe they weren't really stone.

"Should I fetch Tullah?" Sam asked, stepping out from behind Walker and studying the shop's damage.

Since there hadn't been a lot of merchandise to begin with, the debris mostly consisted of fallen rock sculptures and the canvases Daisy had brought to town. Even Harvey's sticks hadn't come off their hooks. Kurt didn't see where his aid was needed, but he lingered anyway.

"I don't think our resident spook is likely to be any more coherent with Tullah present." Teddy lifted one of the smaller canvases. "Mia is translating pretty well."

Mia was clinging to her mother's neck, looking proud of herself. More at ease with mundane tasks than the supernatural, Kurt joined Teddy in righting the artwork.

"I don't suppose there's any sensible explanation for this?" he asked, with no hope that they were practicing a scene from *The Exorcist*.

"Depends on whether one believes in ghosts. Otherwise, a stray wind blew from out of nowhere, and Mia is hearing voices in her head." Teddy sat back to study the canvases. "But just in case, I wouldn't comment aloud on the quality of the work."

"Primitive style?" Kurt suggested, studying a painting that appeared to depict several crudely drawn tents and campers. A camp-fire burned in the foreground, and sturdy, faceless, almost square figures frolicked around it. Several had red stripes where the eyes should be.

"Cubist," Sam said, displaying another work consisting mostly of colorful rectangles.

The whirlwind circled in agitation, but nothing went flying. Kurt refused to believe a ghost was pacing the floor.

Walker turned the largest canvas so everyone could see it. "This one is more realistic, but it's corroding."

"Evil," Daisy said succinctly from the far corner, by the counter.

"Those are the red eyes Lance says are caused by the decaying crystal in the oils used by the artists in the commune." Sam sat beside Walker to examine the third canvas which appeared to depict a night time scene of hell—or a kiln. "Daisy calls them evil, and she may have a point. Kurt, did you ever see that painting of Alan Gump? His eyes were red like this."

Reminded of the real estate mogul who had destroyed his dreams of a condo resort, Kurt studied this more realistic piece. Teddy took his arm, steadying his earlier unease at her swirling ritual. Together, they studied the hellish scene. The painted figures working on various stages of pottery gave him the creeps. He didn't think it was just their red eyes but something in the intensity of their posture, but he wasn't about to admit that aloud. "I tend to agree with Lance. He's been experimenting with that crystal paint for decades. The oils are corroding. How old are these pieces?"

Knowing Teddy hadn't come to any harm let him relax a little. He generally wasn't comfortable in informal social situations, but these people didn't seem to mind his reticence. He just needed a moment to recover from a near heart attack at hearing screams emanating from her shop.

"If it's Thalia's work, then it's probably only twenty or thirty years old at most. She wants us to look at the art, but I'm not seeing anything useful," Teddy complained.

"Thalia?" Kurt asked warily, seeing no stranger in the room.

"That's what I'm calling our resident ghost since my mother's cousin seems to have been the last woman to live here," Teddy explained.

Resident ghost, right. Maybe he should mosey back to the car and return those calls.

Teddy pointed at the pottery painting. "Look, this guy with the corroded eyeballs resembles the one stuffing a panel into his truck in the triptych. We can guess it's Thompson. But all he's doing here is carving clay."

"She dated the paintings." Walker picked up the small primitive piece. "This is just signed *Thalia*, but if I'm reading the numbers right, it's from about twenty years ago."

Teddy beat her fist in the air. "Got it in one! And that sounds right. My parents and their various cousins were children of the commune. Their parents settled here in Hillvale, and my parents were still living here when they married," Teddy said. "I can vaguely remember dinner parties with colorful laughing people who got louder as the night progressed."

"Mom would come up, and if we weren't asleep, she'd turn on the sound system to our room," Syd said. "But I don't remember visitors during the day, when the shop was open."

"That's because you went to school in the valley with Mom, who worked all day, while I stayed with Dad," Teddy reminded her. She turned a defiant look to Kurt. "We weren't rich."

He glared right back. "Neither were we. My father was in debt over his head. So stuff it, Theodosia."

She grinned in a way that spun his head on its axis.

"The lady keeps saying *look*," Mia piped up.

"What are the other dates?" Kurt asked, needing to return logic to this discussion before his libido overruled common sense. "Let's develop a timeline."

"The primitive is the oldest, maybe from the time Teddy is remembering over twenty years ago. According to this date, Thalia's cubist period was roughly five years after that," Sam reported from her position on the floor. "Signature is the same. This dark nightmarish one with the kiln furnace and the evil eyes is the most recent, from ten years ago."

"The crystal corrodes after only ten years?" Kurt asked, but everyone shrugged. Okay, he got it—no one had done scientific research on crystal paint.

"We can assume at least the last two were painted in the years Thalia was living in this house," Teddy said, sitting down next to Sam. "The primitive could be a depiction of the tent city the Thompsons were living in before they moved in here. The realistic one was presumably painted before the furnace blew up, right before they left Hillvale. Still not seeing any clues."

Teddy turned the oldest canvas around to examine the back.

"Maybe she left notes on the paper or hid clues behind the backing? Some artists paint over old works or re-stretch the canvas, blank side out, if they're short of funds."

Sam held out her palm to Walker. "Pen knife, please."

Kurt produced his own, carefully slitting the brown paper backing on the nightmare painting. Walker did the same with the primitive one, then handed the pen knife to Sam to do the cubist.

Mia started to whimper and cling more tightly to her mother's neck. As if disturbed by the forces, Jeb and the dog wandered in. Harvey's walking sticks clattered, but Kurt didn't notice any more air disturbances. He crouched down beside Teddy, who examined the frame and back of the nightmare canvas.

"Nothing," she said in disappointment.

Seeing squiggly trails across the stiff brown paper backing, afraid it might contain spiders or worse, Kurt lifted it away from her knees.

Teddy snatched it before he could carry it off. "Wait a minute. Those look like pencil marks." Standing, she took it over to the window.

Which was when Kurt realized half the town still hung around outside, looking in. "Do I send for wine and cheese?" he asked dryly. "Or just Dinah's donuts?"

Sam uttered an expletive and handed her paper backing to him. "I need to get over to the café and help Dinah. I didn't mean to linger. Let me know what you learn."

Carrying her walking stick, she strode out, talked to the crowd, and led them away like the pied piper.

"How does she do that?" Teddy whispered, gesturing at Sam and her parade.

"Magic," Walker said in a low growl. "Which means we'll have Cass or Val or one of the old witches here soon. What have you found?"

Kurt grimaced at this prediction as much as at the filthy offering Sam had shoved at him. But curiosity ruled, and he studied what did indeed seem to be pencil scribbling. "I think we may need experts in hieroglyphics to decipher this," he concluded. "The pencil has faded to almost nothing."

"Yeah, same here." Walker turned his small piece back and forth to catch the light. "It looks like handwriting, but it's pretty bad."

"This one is the most recent," Teddy said with excitement. "I can make out words. There are dates, like in a diary. Maybe they're journals of the time she painted these?"

"Or they're recipes," Syd said dryly. "Take them out in the sunlight and see if that draws your entity out of here. I want to take the kids down the street, in case there are any revelations that cause Daisy's guardians to go flying again."

At hearing her name, Daisy hauled herself off the floor and lumbered over, speaking more lucidly than Kurt had ever heard her.

"We're having a farewell party at the camp after Lucinda finishes her painting. We're gathering crystals to send with her. Do you have any left?"

Kurt had no idea how to react to crazy talk. Even Teddy froze. And then she threw a glance at Walker, who was scowling. Kurt couldn't blame him there.

"Is the sheriff done with the crystals we found with Thalia?" Teddy asked.

"They could be evidence. He'll hold them until we solve this case."

"Lucinda doesn't like the red ones," Daisy said with a shrug. "She says the blue are purer, but I'm all out. I'll see if I can find more."

With that weird statement, she wandered out. Kurt watched as she climbed into the golf cart. Dressed in her usual black veil, Sam's aunt, Valdis, floated down the street to join her.

"The lady likes Daisy," Mia said from her mother's arms. "Can we go and play now?"

"Please tell me ghosts and crazies are safer than the real world," Syd pleaded before taking Jeb by the hand and heading for the back door, Prince Hairy in tow.

Kurt didn't have time to wonder what real world was more dangerous than ghosts and crazies before he spotted his half-aunt, Cassandra, striding down the street. The day was about to go from hell to worse.

∾

Teddy had partially opened to the bombardment of emotions in the front room, trying to monitor an absurdity so far beyond her experience that she didn't know up from down. Flying figurines and Mia's screams had terrified her, until she'd learned to catch the wind—or steady Thalia's incoherent rage—by spinning in circles.

Kurt was the one solid factor in the whole scenario. Not believing in the supernatural, he apparently analyzed the impossible rather than succumb to fear. His calmness in the face of the emotional tempest had been wonderfully steadying.

The arrival of Cass shut him down to the point of knocking Teddy off balance, as if she'd actually been leaning on him.

Wow. He had a mental and emotional super-blocker even better than her own. *Why?* Most people had no need to block what they didn't know existed.

Had he learned to protect himself against *Cass?*

Kurt's half-aunt certainly knew how to protect herself. Teddy could barely sense her opening the door. Their resident ghost evaporated the moment Cass crossed the threshold.

"I'll have to take this paper down to the sheriff. It could be evidence," Walker said, starting to roll up the piece he held.

"You'll do no such thing," Cass responded curtly, without greeting any of them. "Those paintings belong to the community, as does all the artwork Daisy keeps stored. We will restore them and allow you to peruse them as needed."

"Possession being nine-tenths of the law," Kurt contradicted his aunt's imperious pronouncement, "I'd say the paintings belong to Sam and Valdis since, as I understand it, they're stored on the Ingersson farm. At the very least, these three belong to Teddy's family, since the artist is her relation."

Teddy stepped in between Cass and Kurt before an argument could ensue. "Do we have people in Hillvale who can restore and preserve the paper backing? The oils aren't difficult. The sheriff doesn't need those, and Syd and I can handle cleaning. But the paper could contain valuable evidence."

Her Inner Monitor picked up nothing from either Kurt or Cass, forcing her to read their body language. Cass held her thin frame stiffly. Kurt rolled his fists belligerently. But she couldn't read if hostility was the cause or simple unwillingness to give in to each other. Kurt had explained the old grudges between Lucys and Nulls. Maybe he was right to be wary, but he needed to accept that Cass held a very large key to the town population.

The old woman shot her an unreadable look, almost as if she knew Teddy was testing her. Teddy held out the dusty backing, and Cass ran her long bony finger over it.

"Cleaning, fixative, and bright light, all of them available in my studio," she stated flatly. "Bring them along, Chief Walker. You can make copies when we're done."

She walked out again, as if expecting everyone to follow.

Teddy felt Kurt stiffen and knew he was about to reject Cass's offer. She grabbed his arm and forced him to lean down to hear her whisper. "I won't let her turn you into a frog. Come along, let's make sure she doesn't magically burn anything. Maybe we'll find out if a ghost can name a killer."

He gave her a chocolate-brown glare. She beamed. And physical awareness drove them out into the light of day after the others.

SAMANTHA

SAM CAST A GLANCE AT THE SHIMMERING GHOST-CATCHER IN THE FRONT corner of the café, frowned and checked out the front window. "Cass just arrived. And Kurt must still be over at Teddy's."

Mariah untied her apron.

"Where are you going?" Sam poured water for the last of the lunch rush. "We need to help Dinah clean up."

"Teddy has no idea what she's getting into if she stands between Super-Null and Cass. We need her to stay in Hillvale, not run screaming for civilization." Mariah leaned through the kitchen doorway and called to Dinah. "I'm heading up the hill. I'll come back later and finish up. You put your feet up for a while and listen for explosions."

Samantha worriedly reached for her own apron ties. "Walker's over there. He's a Null. I don't want him running back to civilization either."

"You anchor him, and he doesn't have an emotional vampire for a mother as far as I'm aware. Kurt and Monty. . . Well, let's just say they've had to develop super-abilities to stay alive. Cass doesn't respect boundaries." Mariah grabbed her staff and headed for the door.

"You're worried about *my uncle*?" Sam threw off her apron and grabbed her walking stick.

"Cass lived inside your head for how many days? What do you think?" Mariah hurried down the boardwalk. Daisy and Val sped by in their cart. Intentionally or otherwise, they always left trouble in their wake.

When the small party left Teddy's carrying rolls of brown paper, headed in the direction of the cemetery, Sam broke into a run. "Kurt's head will explode if he goes inside Cass's place."

"Damn, what is Cass thinking? We have to turn him back." Mariah dashed after her.

NINETEEN

June 30: early afternoon

"Hey, Kurt, Monty is trying to reach you!"

Kurt turned to see Sam and Mariah racing after the party marching up the hill to Cass's place. Why did this picture not compute?

Because Sam and Mariah seldom spoke to Kurt if it could be avoided.

He halted, scowling. "I'm not letting your coven take off with evidence. Walker doesn't know what he's getting into."

"I resent that," Walker called back without inflection from the lead of their little procession. "I just see no reason to take these papers to the state lab if Cass can process them in a more timely manner."

Kurt would have preferred the state solution if it meant keeping Cass's weird madness out of it, but he wasn't trespassing on Walker's territory just because he didn't trust his damned half-aunt. He was here because of Teddy, right? Because he wanted in her bed—not because he was worried about her, because he had no reason to worry about a woman who would move on in a few months. Right?

And maybe he was a little curious about the illegible writing.

Cass continued up the hill, head high, disregarding the argument.

She didn't deign to carry any of the backing papers but had left them in Walker and Teddy's charge.

Teddy stopped to wait for Mariah and Sam. "Coven?" she asked when they caught up.

"That's what the Nulls call us when they're being nasty," Mariah explained, giving Kurt the evil eye. "We're not witches. We're not even Wiccans. And Walker and Teddy are perfectly capable of keeping an eye on whatever you think you've found. But if you don't want to talk to Monty —" She shrugged and started up the hill after Cass.

Teddy placed a hand on Kurt's arm. Her touch oddly steadied him. "If it's important, would you like us to wait until you've talked to your brother?" she asked.

"Nothing is as important as discovering why there were bones in your attic," Kurt responded dismissively. "Sam, if you're worried, tell Monty where I am. He can come find me."

His niece bit her bottom lip and looked uncertainly from him to Walker. That blew it. Kurt started marching up the hill. "Whatever Mariah told you is just the usual Lucy nonsense. You're a scientist, Sam. Work it out."

"Will someone please explain what's happening?" Teddy insisted, running after him. "Sam and Mariah are really worried. And even though you repress everything, I can tell you're not happy. If Cass has the equipment we need, why is everyone on edge?"

"I repress *everything*?" Kurt lifted his eyebrows. "Really?"

She smacked his arm. "Emotion, then. Lust is not emotion. It's a physical reaction."

"Damned right. I am not a Lucy and have no need to express hysteria." He didn't think Sam was inclined to it either, but she was clinging worriedly to Walker's arm as they continued up the hill in the direction of the graveyard and Cass's home.

He'd never been inside his aunt's house. His mother would have another nervous breakdown if she knew he was even headed in this direction.

"Cass has this crazy garden shed that looks like it ought to fall over any minute," Walker said, speaking over his shoulder. "But inside, it looks like every modern gardener's dream. She caters to illusion, so be wary."

"I'm feeling a weird energy up here," Teddy called up to them. "Is this where the vortex is? My parents never let us play in the cemetery."

Kurt wanted to growl at this inanity about an invisible hole in the ground, but he kept his mouth shut and his eye on Cass and the evidence. *He* wouldn't be sucked in by illusion.

Sam gestured to the left. "The vortex is in a natural amphitheater on the other side of that hill. I can't feel the energy unless I have my walking stick with me." She held up a wooden staff with a crystal gleaming in the handle. "Maybe you have a natural energy sensitivity because you were born up here?"

"I haven't given any thought to where I was born. I just figured in a hospital, of which Hillvale has none, I now realize," Teddy said dryly. "Where were you born?"

"My birth certificate says San Francisco. I'm adopted, but my birth parents are from here."

His niece had been born to a half-brother Kurt had never known, a brother Cass had raised as her own—another thing his parents had neglected to tell him. He should stay in his office where he belonged. He didn't need the family's dysfunctional history discussed by one and all. Some things were meant to be *private*.

Teddy tilted her head to look up at Kurt. "Can you feel the vortex energy? Or were you born in San Francisco too?"

"This is a ridiculous topic. I grew up in the city. That's where my family is from. So is Cass's. Hillvale was just wasteland my grandmother's family owned and was never more than a summer retreat when we were kids." Kurt studied the tall Victorian house they approached. "My grandfather built a hunting lodge back in the fifties and invited his friends up here. There was probably a gas station and a lot of deserted buildings."

"A ghost town," she said in satisfaction. "Cool."

Kurt snorted. "That's one way of looking at it. Life would have been simpler if he'd just stayed in the city, where we belong." He nodded at Cass's house. "That's a bad imitation of the house Cass's family lived in back on Nob Hill. She stayed with her mother's family after her mother died and my grandfather remarried."

Mariah and Cass waited on the wrap-around porch. Kurt despised the shadowy pine-lined drive that blocked out sun and air, hid half the house from view, and created the kind of ominous atmosphere Cass cultivated.

It didn't seem to bother anyone else. They eagerly picked up the pace.

Cass's gaze focused coldly on him. "My studio is around the side. We'll go in there."

"She doesn't trust you," Teddy whispered as they walked around to the side of the house. "Why?"

"How do you know that? I barely know the woman." Kurt hung back as Cass unlocked a side door and sailed inside, leaving them to follow.

"Maybe because you don't know her, and you live all of three miles away! Honestly, I'll never understand families." She dragged him along after the others.

Kurt wondered if good sex was worth whatever calamity was in store for him when word got out that he'd actually crossed Cass's portal.

~

TEDDY THOUGHT THE HOUSE SHIVERED AROUND THEM AS THEY ENTERED. She glanced to Sam and Mariah for confirmation, but they were busy studying the studio. Suspicious, she considered the room they entered. High-ceilinged and spacious, filled with natural light, it was a perfect studio. The white-painted walls wore countless works of art that would fascinate any museum. She wanted to gravitate toward the paintings and fall into the beauty, but Kurt's tension kept her at his side.

"Unless this is the entire ground floor, the house isn't large enough to hold all this," he muttered, stopping just inside the door.

Ignoring her guests, Cass switched on a strong light over a work desk and began removing tools from a drawer. "Lay the paper out here, please."

While Walker spread out the smaller paper on the desk, Teddy wished Syd were here to explain what Kurt saw. Depth perception wasn't her specialty, and she hadn't really looked at the house as they'd walked up the drive—part of the illusion, perhaps. A studio this size would be an unusual addition to a Victorian, but if Cass had removed the walls of a few parlors and a dining room and extended the house out back, it seemed feasible.

But then where would the front door be? Not in here, unless it was hidden by paintings. She understood why Walker warned about the house's illusion. How did Cass do it?

She realized she'd instinctively shut down her Monitor when they'd entered. Did she dare open it up?

Sam and Mariah were still acting unusually watchful. Hadn't they been here before? But not in this room, they'd said. What were they expecting to happen?

Sam hovered over the desk, watching Walker work. He was pinning the paper down with weights while keeping a close eye on everything their hostess did. Good for him.

Kurt remained tense, studying the interior, probably with the eye of an architect. Biting her lip, Teddy opened up enough to sense if there was any danger.

Overwhelmed, she quickly shut down again. *How was it possible. . .* ? She glanced at Cass, who had looked up and was now regarding her with interest.

The house was packed with. . . *souls*. Not ghosts, per se. It was if they'd crossed a veil into another dimension where the living and the dead mixed. Maybe here, *she* was the ghost. It wasn't logical, but she could sense the interest and emotions of so many different. . . whatevers. . . that she couldn't breathe unless she shut down.

This had been a property owned by Lucinda Malcolm's family—the same Lucinda Malcolm who painted the future.

Here was the center of Hillvale's weirdness—not the vortex or cemetery. But studying the perfectly ordinary studio, Teddy couldn't figure out exactly how it was all wrong.

Kurt covered her hand where she'd dug her fingers into his arm. "Okay? Want to go closer?"

She wanted to run. No way in hell could she explain that. She nodded, hoping this might be a quick process so she could take her papers and leave.

Did no one else notice all these presences? Kurt and Walker obviously didn't. They were intent on watching as Cass turned back to the desk and began dusting off decades of dust and old spiders with a light brush.

Teddy released Kurt's arm and inched closer to Mariah, the person who claimed to see ectoplasm and catch ghosts. There were no ghost catchers on the ceiling of this room. "What in hell is this place?" she murmured, trying not to disturb the others at the desk.

"No clue," Mariah said. "I haven't seen this part before. I think Cass invents what she needs as she goes."

"Different dimensions?" Teddy asked sarcastically. "Or are we sitting on a giant graveyard and walking through illusion?"

"Or all of the above," Mariah said with a shrug. "You shouldn't have brought Kurt here. He's damaged already. I can't think this place is healthy for him, although he's handling it better than I expected."

"That's because he's shut off everything inside him with a giant wall," Teddy retorted. "He's not really here."

Mariah raised heavy dark eyebrows in interest. "You can tell that? Is there any Kurt left to be here then?"

"Does this conversation make any sense in the real world?"

"I live inside a computer, so yes, in my real world, it makes perfect sense. In your reality, probably not."

"Oh, damn, we're living in a virtual reality! Hillvale really isn't on the normal plane, is it?" Teddy covered her eyes, shut down her senses, and tried to adjust her thinking.

"Cass may be living in virtual reality, maybe the cemetery and vortex too, but I'm pretty sure the town is solid," Mariah whispered consolingly. "Well, most of it, anyway. Dinah's kitchen can get weird, but I figured that was Dinah."

Teddy never played computer games. The only technology she managed was e-mail and Skype. She even hated her computerized bookkeeping. So virtual reality was something from a bad sci-fi film and could mean almost anything. She just knew there were spirits here, and Kurt said the room dimensions didn't work. *Illusion*, she told herself. Cass had created a massive illusion—or a mass hallucination—for reasons only she understood.

Teddy watched Walker and Kurt hovering over Cass's desk, felt the tension rising, and asked Mariah in cynicism, "If this is virtual reality, who do you think controls the joystick?"

"I don't think they use—" Mariah's eyes widened as she followed the path of Teddy's thoughts: Lucys weren't inclined to use technology. "The *Nulls*?"

"It would follow," Teddy said with a mocking shrug. "Lucys are metaphysical, Nulls are as about as physical as it gets. They're the ones who control the town."

"I don't like this metaphor," Mariah concluded, turning back to watch the men at the desk with Cass. "I came up here to be free of male coercion. I will not be controlled again."

Teddy thought that sounded like a personal declaration of war. Did that mean Mariah understood Cass and what was happening in Hillvale? What happened in this weird house?

Could *Cass* be the reason for Thompson leaving and the body in the attic? Or the joy-stick-wielding Nulls?

TWENTY

"THE ARTIST WAS CERTAINLY NO WRITER," CASS SAID DRYLY AS SHE SERVED sangria on the front porch. "The use of the pronoun 'he' is less than illuminating."

The last tedious hours of attempting to read bad handwriting deserved alcoholic reward, Kurt decided. He wondered if Cass had once been an English teacher—and realized he knew next to nothing of her. He studied his iced drink and pondered whether it was safe to taste.

"She occasionally uses the initial 'L.'" Walker had taken photos of the newly cleaned backing from the paintings and was zooming up the results on his phone. "That would correspond with her husband's name of Lonnie."

"Or any of two dozen other people here ten years ago, including my uncle Lance," Kurt pointed out. "I haven't had time to dig out employee and rental records, but the commune—"

"Had shut down," Mariah said, declining a glass and starting down the stairs. "If your head hasn't exploded yet, I need to go back and help Dinah so she has time to prepare her dough for tomorrow."

Kurt scowled at the vague insult and figured she was heading back to report to her coven. Mariah just needed a pointy hat to look the part of witch. Or maybe, with those feathers in her braid, she was going for Native American shaman.

After waving farewell to Mariah, Sam continued where they'd left off. "The farm where the commune once operated should have been deserted before Teddy's cousin moved to town. My grandparents died, and the farmhouse burned almost twenty-five years ago."

"But we have the news reports showing that the kiln was there, and people were using it *ten* years ago," Teddy argued. "There could have been RVs or tents hidden up there."

"There were," Cass said dismissively, taking what Kurt thought of as the throne chair—wicker with an over-large rounded back and a stack of cushions. The rest of them sat on more mundane mesh chairs available from any big box store. "Hillvale has the homeless just as anywhere else. Only ours tend to be itinerant artists. The pottery produced in that kiln was once world famous. There are those who mourned its loss."

Kurt wanted to be skeptical, to question everything the old lady said, but he knew she was right. His father had collected some of those pieces. "Did you know the names of the potters? Did any of them start with L?" he asked.

Cass turned blue eyes eerily similar to Sam's in his direction. "The talented potters from the commune are well known—Peterson, Williams, Arthur. Your Thompson may have worked with them in his youth, but by ten years ago, they were long gone. Many of the children from the commune returned to stay here after their parents moved on, though. Your uncle Lance, Lars Ingersson, and Lucinda Malcolm are the only L's coming immediately to mind, and two of them were dead at the time."

"Or *Lucy*," Kurt said cynically. "Ten years ago, Lance was still drying out. I can't imagine him being involved with the Thompsons."

Teddy was still examining the photo of the illegible writing. She'd been buzzing with impatience all afternoon, even after they had conceded that Walker needed to take the papers in for further processing with better equipment. She pointed at one of the more recent, legible passages. "Thalia says 'his work is almost as good as

Peterson's, but it will never resemble a Williams. He hit me again when I told him so.'"

Kurt wanted to say her cousin was as looney as any Lucy, but he was willing to listen to other interpretations. He'd spent the better part of his life listening, after all. But this discussion made his skin crawl. "If her husband was hitting her, she should have left right then."

"Not all women are that strong—or have resources to escape." Sam finished her drink and stood up. "I need to get back to Dinah's, and I'm guessing Walker is eager to take these things to the sheriff."

Walker stood up with her, holding the carefully wrapped paper. "Do we need to start asking in town about people with L initials?"

"Very few of today's residents were living here ten years ago." Cass spoke up in a tone meant to be heeded.

Kurt watched with interest as the others halted and waited for further enlightenment. Apparently, Cass did not impart her knowledge often. Maybe not talking was a family trait inherited from his grandfather—Cass's father.

Walker took out the phone he used for notes. "Would you mind telling us who lived here? They might shine some light on Thalia's domestic situation."

"I lived here, of course," Cass said coldly. "And Kurt's mother, when she wasn't in the city. The lodge employees. A few people like Susan McQueen and Marta Josephine who bought cottages long ago. Tullah moved in a few years before Pasquale bought the old general store, so they were here. Mostly, people only came up on the weekends, so Kurt's rental records would be more accurate, although probably not helpful. Renters are usually short term and don't mix with the locals. And his records won't include those camping on the farm. I don't remember anyone operating the crystal shop after it closed decades ago, not even during the time you indicate Thalia lived there."

"So, my mother's cousin probably had few close friends," Teddy said quietly.

Kurt reached over to hold her hand. She squeezed back, and he appreciated her acknowledgment. She made him feel as if he were part of this conversation instead of just an observer. "I'll dig out the records, but most of my employees have always lived elsewhere and seldom mix with the locals. And you, Cass?" he asked daringly. "Do you know the locals?"

She sent him a look of scorn. "More than you or your family do. But I didn't know Thalia. There were always young people in that house. If they exhibited no traits to disturb the energy, I had no reason to seek them out. Perhaps that was a mistake on my part," she conceded.

Kurt left the *energy* comment hanging. Walker was preparing to leave with Sam and just frowned. Teddy was the one to leap on it.

"How does a person disturb energy?" she demanded. "Did my parents disturb it? If my cousin was being abused by a vicious killer, shouldn't that energy register?"

"Your parents were a positive disturbance, entirely content within their circle of family. They had no need of me. And if your mother's cousin was a Null, then I'd not notice her," Cass said, standing in dismissal. "I'm guessing Thalia did not inherit the family traits."

That left a conversational gap wide enough to run a river through. Kurt stood and dragged Teddy up with him. He wasn't about to linger when the others were leaving.

"Family traits?" Teddy resisted his tug so she could face Cass down. "My family is related to yours? To Sam's? To Mariah's?"

"Yes, at some distant point perhaps. But like recognizes like. That's why Hillvale exists, why it has always existed. Do not ask me for the genealogy. I don't have it. There are answers elsewhere for those who seek them, I've been told. I had more than I could handle as it was and didn't need more." She began gathering empty glasses on a tray.

Kurt tugged Teddy down the steps after the others. "Family tree another time. I have to go back to work and you have a sister wondering if you're lost."

She stomped after him in her ridiculous high-heeled boots. "You don't think it's weird that the cousin I *know* I'm related to isn't part of the weird *energy* that relates me to complete strangers?"

"I think everything about Cass and this town is past weird and well into crazy," Kurt said. "It's time we tore it down and started over."

Oops, wrong thing to say. Teddy shot him an incredulous look and hurried to catch up with Sam and Walker, leaving him in her dust.

～

IRRITATED AND FRUSTRATED, TEDDY STOMPED INTO THE SHOP TO DISCOVER Syd had covered all the bare space on the walls with artwork she'd collected from all over town. Teddy swung around to study the magnificent colors sprouting on her boring bare walls. "Wow. Now we need lighting."

"Thalia has been helping." Syd nodded at Mia, who sat playing with a doll on an oval braided rug that hadn't been there before.

Jeb was busily stirring sand and water in bowls in an uncarpeted corner of the floor, while Prince Hairy slept beside him.

"Thalia's telling you how to hang the art?" Teddy walked up and down the shop, looking for red eyes. She located Thalia's three pieces in strategic locations, where light from the big window fell on them. But those were the only pieces with red where eyes might be depicted. The cubist would take some study, but there were red stripes there too.

"The lady said there was paintings in the attic," Mia said prosaically, braiding her doll's hair. "We got ice cream."

Teddy raised her eyebrows questioningly. Syd nodded confirmation. "The attic of town hall and one of the abandoned buildings across from the ice cream parlor. This town is littered with art."

"I wonder how many murals got buried behind boring beige?" Teddy studied the old paint on her walls. "I've always wanted murals on my walls."

Mia tilted her head. "She says at the art store."

"All right, this is just a bit scary. Murals in the art store? We'll have to figure out which old building was an art store." Teddy sat down on the new rug. "Where did the rug come from?"

"Tullah's." Syd continued working with the picture hanger she'd attached in one of the few blank spaces left. "She had some kid clothes come in today, and I bought those and the rug. But I'll have to start looking for a job soon. I want to save Damien's life insurance money for the kids' college, and I've about exhausted my savings."

Teddy knew Damien, the children's late father, had left the family a substantial insurance policy, as well as a retirement fund. Combined with her own income as an interior designer, Syd had been reasonably well off until now.

Teddy wanted to talk to Mia about ghostly voices, but Syd was in a tough place, one Thalia couldn't solve.

"I don't suppose you can ask the lady what happened to her?" Teddy asked, just in case.

Mia shook her head rapidly and pouted her bottom lip.

"I tried that," Syd admitted. "Mia got hysterical. The voice volunteers information that doesn't touch on emotional subjects, but ask anything direct and things fly."

"A ghost in denial." Teddy sighed and stood up again. "I don't think you'll find a lot of use for your decorating talent up here, unless Kurt wants to redo the lodge. I have a feeling that's a firm no. We can set up a printer, create business cards, but the café seems to be the place where the town passes on information. Leaving word there probably works best."

"I take it you didn't learn much from the backing?" Syd straightened the oil she'd just hung.

"We learned that Thalia had the world's worst handwriting, and pencil scribbling smears and fades. They seem to be journals of a sort. Walker's taking them into Baskerville for more examination. He e-mailed his photos to my account, if you want to take a try at them."

"I'll look later. I hired a truck and movers to go to the storage unit to pick up the parental ceramics. Since it's all boxed, I just told them to bring all the boxes. Aaron at the antique store says he rents one of the vacant buildings for inventory, and we can store them there until we see what we have."

"You made arrangements with the storage unit management to let the movers in?" At Syd's nod, Teddy dug her wallet out from behind the counter. "Then let us repair to the café and begin inquiries into jobs, art stores, and people who know something about pottery."

"Aaron says he does. He's eager to look at ours. I told him if we sold anything, the proceeds would go to charity. That didn't scare him off." Syd helped Jeb up and led him to the kitchen to wash.

"Man, you've been crazy busy! I don't think we should display breakables here," Teddy called after her. "Thalia is likely to destroy the collection. Daisy's stones are safer."

"The town has half a dozen vacant buildings," Syd called from the kitchen. "You need to talk Kurt into letting us use them for galleries. They're not residential, like this place. They're just empty storefronts. Maybe we can offer to paint the walls or add shelving or something."

"I've hired a lawyer to sue him." Teddy checked in display mirror to see if her hair needed attention. "I'm not sure I should be the one asking."

Mia came over to peer into the counter with the crystals. "Can I touch this?"

She picked one of the most boring stones in the case, a dull blue rectangle of anhydrite from Peru that gemologists had named Angelite. Teddy displayed it because she sensed its power, but it was not a stone most children would choose. "Why that one, sweetheart?" she asked, using a square of felt to lift it from the shelf and hold it out for Mia to touch.

"It has voices," Mia said, reverentially stroking the stone.

Voices! Teddy vowed to look up the powers of Angelite. She was aware the stone was claimed to enhance psychic abilities and communication beyond the veil, but Mia couldn't have known that.

"I'll make it into a pendant for you, if your mama says it's okay," Teddy promised. "But you must be careful to only listen to those voices when you can tell others what they're saying, okay?"

And now that she'd said that, she was terrified to let the child have the stone. Had bringing Mia here enhanced her previously unknown psychic abilities?

Syd returned to hear the last part of their conversation. She frowned in worry. "Can you tell which crystals are safe?"

Teddy shook her head. "I need to start researching and experimenting. I've never thought about why I choose the crystals and gems I use. Intellectually, I know their purpose, because I use it in marketing. But I didn't realize I was adding power to them. Maybe exposure to the energy in Hillvale also adds power?"

Mia carefully laid the stone back in the case. "There are too many voices at once," she said pragmatically. "But it's like singing and I like it."

"Then it's yours. We can decide if you want it to look just like that or if it needs a prettier shape. Think about it, and let's go find food for now." Teddy took her niece's hand, opening herself to Mia's trust and happiness.

It suddenly hit her that with a little practice, she *could* be a good parent someday. At least, she would always know how a child felt.

What the hell had made her think of that now? Having Kurt around, helping her as if they were a real couple?

That scared the crap out of her. Children needed two full-time parents, and she barely had her act together while learning to cope with her weird Inner Monitor. She'd never been good at dealing with full-grown men when she'd thought she was *normal*.

And then there was Kurt, who was a complete mystery to her Monitor—and a man she was suing, for pity's sake. If her thoughts turned to kids when he was around, she'd better stay miles away from him, if she knew what was good for her.

When had her impulsive instincts known what was good for her?

TWENTY-ONE

JUNE 30: EVENING

"THAT WOMAN IS CLEARLY INSANE, AND HER PROPERTY RIGHTFULLY belonged to your father." Carmel's icy tones radiated from the speaker phone the bartender had set on the bar in front of Kurt and Monty. Her spies had obviously warned her of Kurt's visit to Cass. "But if you think you can get on her good side—she has no other heirs. Just don't make it a habit."

Their mother cut off the communication before either of them could reply.

Beside him, Monty whistled and said nothing. Kurt swigged his Perrier, wishing it were beer. The bar had some fine local craft brew he'd been meaning to try—

"I think that went over well," Monty said, quaffing his beer without compunction. "I've been waiting for the roof to blow off."

"There are days when I hope it will," Kurt admitted. "Maybe she'll let go and agree to sell the land then."

"Not happening, bro," Monty advised. "She's obsessed. Speaking of which, Lance wants us to let him have one of the vacant storefronts for another gallery. The whole damned town will be full of them soon. Why does Lance's give me a bad feeling?"

"Because he's never displayed his work before? Because criticism sends him in a downward spiral? Because he's a fine architect but only a competent portraitist?" Kurt nodded acknowledgment of the appetizers the bartender slid in front of them.

He didn't want to think about why their uncle had gone weird. He'd had enough weird for one day.

"Because Aaron also asked for extra gallery space for the pottery?" Monty added. "And Mariah is both gloating and gloomily predicting the end of the world?"

"An ill wind that blows nobody any good," Kurt quoted, then added his own gloom. "Our lawyer says there are inconsistencies in the property filings on the Thompson-Baker house. He's looking into that and the others. Maybe we should give up and find real jobs."

Monty slugged back his beer. "I think it's too late for me to join the NFL. Know any other towns that can use my poli-sci major?"

"Don't be an ass. All you need to do is schmooze a little, watch for an opening, and pounce on some city manager position." Kurt gestured his approval of the appetizers and ordered a steak. "But if I walk, who takes my place?"

Monty scarfed the last of the shrimp and grinned at the mirror behind the bar. "The Lucys."

Kurt glanced over his shoulder, saw Teddy arriving, and his spirits inexplicably rose. But she was trailing Sam, which could not be a good thing. They only needed Mariah to complete the triumvirate of fair, dark, and fiery. Teddy's hair was reverting to the true auburn he remembered. Her tight jeans swayed lusciously with every booted step, and she'd left her spangled cowboy shirt partially unbuttoned at the throat. He had to bite his tongue to prevent it from hanging out. She was so totally *not* the chic city woman he usually dated. Obviously, the lack of company in this town was messing with his head. And other parts south.

"Hello, boys," Teddy purred, stepping up to the bar and signaling the bartender, ordering her own glass of wine without waiting on them.

He'd learned that Sam had been raised in Mormon territory and didn't like wine. She consulted with the bartender over syrupy umbrella drinks.

"Aaron and Lance already hit us up for gallery space," Monty said, oblivious to Teddy's sexy purrs and focused on his own agenda. "Those buildings are valuable property. If we find businesses actually prepared to pay rent and cover liability insurance, the galleries have to close."

"You thought we only came here for business?" Teddy asked with a little pout. "Shame on you. We were promised karaoke."

Kurt flashed a mental image of Teddy swinging those hips in front of a bar full of his male guests, and he covered his eyes. They wouldn't even hear her voice for watching her boobs in that sexy shirt. "No karaoke, *ever*. Where's Walker?"

At his bark, Sam glanced at him in puzzlement. Tasting her green frothy drink, she swung the barstool in a circle, not overly concerned with his mood. "Still in Baskerville. I wanted to ask if Monty could park his car somewhere else so I can turn that vacant lot at city hall into a park. People need a place to sit and eat their ice cream."

"The last time I parked my car in the public lot, it got egged. You promising that won't happen again?" Monty asked.

"We promise to clean it if it happens," Teddy agreed with a bright smile that Kurt knew meant trouble.

"And that's all you want?" he asked.

"Well, money for plants and gravel, a fountain and benches would be good," Sam added. "But I can find plants here and about."

"You'll have half the lodge's shrubbery transplanted in town," Kurt grumbled.

Monty chuckled, but Kurt focused on Teddy. She wasn't here about plants. She settled on the stool beside him and sedately sipped her chardonnay. He remembered where that pouty mouth had been last night and fried a few brain cells.

"Mariah's tired of stepping on my car roof to climb the bluff stairs," Monty guessed. "And Val simply wants me out of her way."

"Oh, sure, and that too," Sam agreed guilelessly.

Their niece was new to Hillvale and didn't participate in the town antipathies, but the Lucys were apparently finding her a useful communication tool. Kurt wondered how long that would last. He knew how long Teddy's patience would last—until he took her to court over the house. Would she come after him then with a pitchfork or a chainsaw?

"The town doesn't have money for a park," Monty said, digging into the salmon a waitress delivered. "If they want a park, they'll have to raise funds for it."

"Fair enough. Teddy?" Sam leaned around Kurt and Monty to see what Teddy was up to.

Teddy's subtle jasmine perfume was driving Kurt crazy, but he pretended not to notice as he dug into his steak without asking the women if they'd eaten.

Teddy leaned over the bar to see Sam, displaying her ample cleavage in that half-buttoned shirt. "You, Aaron, and Syd price what we need, and I'll see how much fits my budget. I need to get the shop functional soon though, if I'm to provide funding for a park. My credit only stretches so far."

"You could have called Monty and done this in the morning," Kurt complained, trying not to grit his molars. His dentist bill would be astronomical at this rate. "What is it you really want?"

"Your presence, of course," Teddy said, widening her eyes in surprise. "And we don't like plotting behind your back. Sam is instigating a new policy of openness. I'm just along for the ride. And info, maybe. Do either of you know which store was once an art shop?"

That caught him off guard. Kurt quit cutting his steak to figure out where that question had come from.

Teddy answered without his asking. "Thalia tells us there's a mural in the art store. If we could uncover it, it might be valuable."

Kurt glared at her. "Your dead cousin's *ghost*? Or did you interpret more of the backing?"

"Ghosts talk?" Monty asked, always curious.

"They talk to Mia." Teddy cast them a wicked smile. "We think she's either affected by my crystals or Hillvale, or both."

"They're indoctrinating children now," Kurt said with a sigh. Maybe he'd give up the no-drinking-on-the-job policy. He really wanted that beer. How could he be enthralled with a woman who was so foolish as to believe in ghosts?

Maybe this was just her way of messing with his mind. He could deal with that.

"Did you ask Xavier about the art shop? He's been here longer than we have," Monty suggested, skipping ghosts and heading for pragmatic—the reason he was mayor material and not Kurt. "I don't remember one."

"Lance would," Kurt admitted. "He's been coming up here every summer since he was a kid. He probably lived at the commune at some point. If there was an art shop, he'll know."

"Does he have a phone or should we go over and visit?" Sam asked. "He tends to ramble a lot, and I wanted to get home before Walker comes looking for me."

"You go home," Kurt said, his lower brain devising a strategy on the spot. If he could keep this all about sex, he might survive pitchforks and chainsaws. "I'll take Teddy over. If Lance plans on having a gallery, she'll have to introduce him to her sister. He knows damn all about hanging art."

"Is that okay, Teddy? Kurt can give you a ride home." Sam slurped the last of her drink and stood.

Teddy, trapped up here without her getaway vehicle—Kurt liked that thought real fine.

～

TEDDY KNEW MANIPULATION WHEN SHE HEARD IT. SHE SIPPED HER WINE and thought about whether she'd let Kurt win this one. She really wanted to talk to Lance. She could do so tomorrow, she supposed, but she had a store that needed opening and jewelry that wouldn't make itself.

This was where impulse overruled common sense. She cast a glance at the steely set of Kurt's jaw and opened her senses just a hair.

The man was practically emanating frustration. *Cool.* Something was breaking through his tough barriers! She hoped it was her. That offered a modicum of validation for her impulsiveness.

"My lawyer says I shouldn't discuss our impending litigation," she said, just to raise his hackles a little more and remind him that she wasn't a pushover.

"My lawyer says screw yours." He finished chewing his steak, took a gulp of water, and stood up. "Go on, Sam. I'll take Teddy home."

"I'll just sit here and think about karaoke," Monty said.

Teddy sensed his amusement, even if she didn't understand the cause. She finished her wine and patted Monty's thick, stylishly mussed hair. "I'm happy one of you has sense. This place looks like a baby boomer museum. Your guest roster will die on the vine unless you market to younger people."

"Says the marketing genius hiding from her customers," Kurt said, catching her arm and dragging her away.

"Are you sure you want to go with Kurt?" Sam called after them. "I can talk to Lance tomorrow."

Teddy waved her on. "Don't worry about me and Kurt. I eat nasty boys for lunch."

She almost laughed when Kurt's lust spiked. That didn't take any mind reading.

She untangled her arm from his grip and took his in retaliation. He was still wearing his suit coat. "It's evening," she told him. "Aren't you allowed happy hour at the very least? Shrug out of the coat, put on jeans, a nice tight t-shirt. . ." She let her voice trail off suggestively.

His tension ratcheted another notch. "You don't want to hear the guest complaints I've addressed these past few hours. The only way to deal with executives on vacation is to put myself into a position of authority and talk to them on a level they understand. If I'm in a suit and they're in shorts, I already have the upper hand."

She sighed loudly. "You are so wasted on this job. Hire a retired army officer."

She thought she sensed a hint of amusement, but he kept himself too tightly controlled to know for certain.

"He wouldn't last, but I'd like to watch a general handle adult temper tantrums, howling dogs, and screaming tots, while juggling a drunken sous chef, a housekeeping thief, and a report to investors on why our ROI isn't what it should be." He led her out a side door and around the lodge toward the back, where the forest darkness loomed over the parking lot. The scent of ash still hung in the air. The fire line had come dangerously close to this portion of the resort.

"He'd need an army to command," she replied in the same tone.

"You could dress your staff in khaki shorts and safari hats and let him give marching orders."

That almost elicited a chuckle. Teddy patted herself on the back for reducing his irritation levels. There was a highly intelligent, perceptive man underneath that uptight grouch. She'd really rather work with him than against him, if that was possible.

He nodded at the well-lit timber cottage ahead. "My uncle did drugs too long, lost his architectural firm and most of his mind. His art has been all that's kept him occupied these last years. He never displays it. He can't take criticism. But when he's coherent, he has a useful memory. He's been coherent a lot more lately."

"Scientists really don't understand brain chemistry," she said thoughtfully, studying the cottage. "His brain may be repairing itself with the artwork. Or the artwork could be the source of his memories. I know I have almost no understanding of how and why I create what I do."

He didn't reply but led her up the stairs to his uncle's studio. He rapped but the door was already partially open. He pushed it aside and led her into what must once have been a large living-dining area. The white walls were nearly bare. The dark plank floors were covered in stacks of canvases stacked from end to end.

"Are these all the paintings you're displaying?" Kurt asked his uncle in obvious incredulity. "Do we have a vacant shop big enough?"

The tall, graying-blond man studying a canvas in his big hands looked up. His uncle was bony where Kurt was muscled, but Teddy could see some resemblance in the rugged cheekbones and wide shoulders.

"I need to either oil out or paint over that pile there." Lance nodded at a long line of stacked canvas on the far wall, then gestured at a smaller, closer batch. "These are the ones I want to display. I figure the old church should do it. It has windows that will provide natural light."

The canvas backs were all turned to the door so Teddy couldn't see the artwork. She didn't know whether she should ask to see them or let Kurt take the lead. Judging by his pallor and lack of weight, his uncle didn't appear to be entirely a well man, but he seemed purposeful.

"Church? How can we own a church? I didn't think the town's hedonists allowed one." Kurt crouched beside the stack of canvas Teddy wanted to see.

"Well, that's what we used to call it. It has a bell tower, but I'm not sure it was ever used as a church. Meeting house, maybe? I think a dollar-store type of place was in there last." Lance added the canvas in his hands to the reject pile.

Since Lance didn't seem to object to Kurt examining his work, Teddy crouched down beside him. The subject of the first piece appeared to be a lovely woman in a costume from some old musical —*Hello Dolly*, maybe?—huge fluffy hat, sweeping gown, flinging her hand dramatically toward a badly sketched setting in the background.

"I remember the cheap-goods store, there at the end next to Aaron's and across from city hall. The tower has roof rats. It will take some work to clean up that place." Kurt flipped to the next oil—the same woman, this time in petticoats and a skirt from the fifties.

"Sam said she'd help. And it has shelves for pottery. Someone was going to display that, right?"

"That would be me," Teddy said. "My parents collected from local potters. We're having it shipped up here for the art walk. Why does the woman in these paintings look vaguely familiar?"

Lance looked pleased at her recognition. "That's Valerie, when she was much younger. Her voice was even better than her looks. We should have musical evenings so she might let us hear it again."

"Valdis of the black veils," Kurt said in an undertone. "These had to be painted thirty years ago."

Which reminded Teddy of why they were here. "Do you know if there was ever an art shop in town? One with a mural on the walls?"

Lance waved a dismissive hand. "Back in the 80s, the commune tried to operate one for a while. Mostly, we just came in and painted the walls while we got high. It started with a psychedelic rainbow with a VW van traveling over it—not very original. Then Lars added his own face driving the van, so his wife added hers in the passenger seat."

"Lars?" Teddy asked, immediately interested in an L name.

"Ingersson, Sam's grandfather. He owned the farm and the commune. That was before Geoff started buying up the town.

Whoever owned the building didn't object when we all started drawing ourselves on the rainbow. We added unicorns and dragons and hell if I remember what all. If you want to call that a mural, then sure, it's behind the ice cream counter. When the family corporation bought the building, it got painted over in mint green. The crappy painter used acrylic over the oils."

Mia had known about a mural and an art shop that hadn't been in existence since before she was born! Her niece really was speaking to a *presence*. Teddy didn't know if she should be excited or terrified.

She kept Lance talking while she pondered that knowledge. "Even I know better than to paint acrylic over oil. Guess the ice cream parlor covered up the peeling mess with their big chalkboard. Do you think the acrylic can be removed without harming the oil?"

Lance polished a pair of reading glasses and studied her. "Why would you want to see that old thing? There wasn't a speck of artistry to it. Graffiti would be a polite name for it."

"I'm not sure," she admitted. Well, it was now or never—Kurt either believed or he didn't. "My resident ghost said there was a mural in the art store. I guess I wanted to know if my niece was making up stories in her head or if the ghost really was talking through her."

Both men stared.

Oh well, now they thought she was just plain crazy, like all the other Lucys.

Teddy glared defiantly at Kurt. "You've seen Mia talking to Thalia. Call us liars and you'll never see my naked ass again."

TWENTY-TWO

LANCE LAUGHED.

Totally caught off-guard by Teddy's defiant declaration, and his uncle's unusual display of humor, Kurt couldn't help flashing a grin too. So, she amused him, go figure.

"What happens if I call you gullible?" He stood up, caught her arm, and led her toward the door. He called back to his uncle, "I'll have maintenance take a look at the old church, although let's call it a meeting house. I'd rather not have any religious group haunting us along with the ghosts."

Lance saluted and returned to his work and his usual taciturn self. Still, hearing his uncle cogent and erudite as he'd once been improved Kurt's mood.

"I am the furthest thing from gullible as you can imagine," Teddy informed him as they stepped into the chilly night air. "I've already considered that someone has been feeding Mia information that she's simply repeating, but that's even more far-fetched than ghosts. I can *feel* our resident ghost and see and hear her tantrums. That house is not wired for special effects—you've seen it yourself. You're the one who is naïve for not believing there are more things in heaven and earth, than dreamt of in your philosophy, Horatio."

"You don't know Mariah well, do you?" he asked drily, steering her toward his cottage, refusing to acknowledge her statement about *feeling* ghosts. "Or Cass."

She shrugged. "They have no reason to manipulate a six-year old. You are supposed to be taking me home, not back to your place. The lawyers call that fraternizing with the enemy. I refuse to let you steal my house from me. That's worse than Ray stealing my gems!"

"I am *not* stealing your house," he said. "Your family abandoned it for ten years and my family has been paying the expense of upkeep. It's a legal issue the lawyers will settle. Quit comparing me to an outright thief."

He should be outraged, but he understood Teddy in ways that he didn't understand many others. They had both been burned and were fighting physical attraction. Maybe a little of the conflict had to do with pixie dust and what had brought them together, but he wouldn't let Lucy talk deny him the best sex he'd ever had.

She dropped his arm to drag her hand through her hair. "Anyway, we have absolutely nothing in common. I just don't have space in my head for compartmentalizing sex right now."

He grimaced at her bluntness. "Why do women do that? Why can't sex just be pleasurable? Why does it have to come with attachments?"

"Because we're not all animals," she said in scorn, glaring at him in the moonlight. "And I'm no longer a bored teen. Just because it's possible to have sex without children these days, doesn't mean women aren't still wired for relationships. I can't turn off that part of who I am. So I'll be the grown-up here and walk home if that's all you have on your mind." She started walking toward the parking lot.

She left a cold spot where she had been. He was tired of being cold —and alone. And apparently the only way of gaining her company was to give her a piece of him. Kurt wanted to resist, but it had been a really long day. He had denied himself the beer, but he couldn't deny himself the comfort Teddy offered, in any form she preferred. It didn't even have to be sex, he had to admit.

"That's not *all* I have in mind," he called after her. "I really did want to show you something."

He really hadn't, not until this minute. But now that he'd said it, he figured it had come from his subconscious. He wanted her to know who he was.

She made him vulnerable in a way he hadn't been since childhood.

She turned and eyed him skeptically. "What?"

Impatiently, he jammed his hands in his pockets. "I'm not announcing it to the world. Either trust me or not." And there he went, building walls and undermining himself again.

In the dim outside light, he could see her do that weird thing where her eyes turned gold, and she kind of drifted inside herself. She hesitated, then returned to the moment with a nod. "I don't have reason to trust men," she said. "But in the interest of open communication, I'll try."

He didn't dare question why she'd changed her mind. It felt too much like defeating his purpose, which was to keep her with him for as long as he could.

They didn't touch as they strode up the mulch path to his place. As much as he wanted Teddy in his bed, he also wanted—*needed*—her to understand where he was coming from. No one else really did, except in a money-making sort of way.

He flipped the overhead light switch as they entered. He'd had bright LEDs installed a few years back so he could use the front room as his office and studio. He certainly never entertained there. He shoved back the portable divider to open it up.

"I didn't see any of this last night." Teddy studied the lay-out with interest. "You literally kept me in the dark."

He shrugged. "I don't share much."

She snorted at his understatement and wandered over to his old-fashioned drafting desk. He'd rescued it from his uncle's office before the contents had been auctioned off. Kurt waited as she studied the large-scale drawing pinned to it.

"This is how you envision Hillvale?" she asked, concealing her opinion behind neutrality as he usually did.

He stood behind her to observe his work as she was seeing it. "I added Sam's flowers and the mosaic planters recently. They're nice touches. If everyone wants to promote the artwork theme, I could add outdoor sculptures. But it's the architectural effect that I want to see carried out."

She traced the outline of the building that would stand where her home did. "Three stories and balconies? How come it doesn't have stucco like these others?"

"I was trying to keep the different architectural styles already established. I know it's not historically accurate. That would be impossible if we want wiring and windows. But the town is a mash-up of timber, stone, adobe, and brick. I wanted to reflect that. Your house is currently wood siding, but wood is prone to rot and termites and has to be stained every few years. I'd use synthetic material that insulates and is far more durable but looks just as good."

He wished he could see her expression, but he was trying not to push. He wanted her to *understand*.

"It's a creative dream," she said thoughtfully. "This is a beautiful fantasy town, like building castles in the air. Real towns don't look like this. They only dream of looking like this."

"Planned communities look like this," he insisted.

"Planned communities are not real towns," she argued, but with more curiosity than anger as she continued to examine his *dream*. "They're profit centers. That could be where our disagreement lies. I like flaws and character and real life. This. . ." She gestured at his drawing. "This is the product of a man who likes control of his environment. But real towns and real people are *messy*."

He didn't know how to respond to that. Of course he wanted control of his environment! Who wouldn't? Wasn't that the whole point of owning a town?

"You've created an idyllic retreat for the rich without any thought to the personalities who live and work here, just like the lodge. I admire your imagination, but it won't suit me or Cass or Aaron or Dinah. . ." Before he could follow the ramifications of her argument, Teddy swung around, stood on her toes, and kissed him. "You need to lighten up," she whispered against his lips. "Lose a little of that control."

He knew how to respond to that well enough. And yeah, maybe he lost a little control as he grabbed her ass and yanked her up against him until her kiss seared his mouth and boiled his blood.

"Does this mean you trust me?" he asked when they came up for air.

"Too much negativity around here to say for certain," she muttered back, running her kisses down his neck. "But I *want* to trust that you'll see your dreams aren't necessarily what's best for all."

Dismissing the negativity remark, he pulled her up against him again and returned the kiss, using his body to ask what his mouth didn't. She responded *positively*.

Just as Kurt lifted Teddy to carry her to the bedroom, his front door crashed open.

TOTALLY SUCKED INTO THE HAZE OF HEAT KURT GENERATED, TEDDY CLUNG to his neck and kiss a moment longer than she should have.

"Kurtis Dominic Kennedy!" an outraged female voice shrieked. "What are you doing with that tart?"

Shrieking drama queens meant a little more than crashing doors, but not enough to take them seriously. Teddy reluctantly pulled back a little to stare over Kurt's shoulder at the virago letting in the chilly night air. Too old to be an outraged lover, she concluded, before Kurt muttered, "My mother."

He carefully set Teddy down. She felt the chill of his departure and hugged his lingering warmth to herself as he blocked her view of his mother and vice versa with his broad build. "I had a lock installed on that door for a reason, Mother."

"And maintenance keeps copies of the key for a reason," she mocked in the same tone. "I saw the lights and assumed you were working. I just wanted to let you know I was home."

Between Kurt's icy withdrawal and the announcement that this shrieking shrew was his mother, Teddy was wary enough to open her Monitor. *Negativity* blasted icily through the room. In this case, she'd almost believe in evil. This was how Thalia had felt when she'd knocked Kurt down—only worse, because this was a living, breathing, thinking ball of fury, hate, and anxiety.

Teddy stepped from behind Kurt to contradict the outright lie she sensed in his mother's volatile emotions. "No, you did not. You interfered on purpose, just to see what Kurt was doing."

She studied the tall, wide-shouldered female version of Lance. Kurt's mother looked considerably healthier than her brother, almost ruddy-faced in anger under that full head of coiffed blond hair. "You were furious before you even stole the key to unlock the door. Did someone report Kurt was with me? Or did you just want to see why he isn't at the lodge? Now I understand why your son needs to control his environment."

"Teddy," Kurt said warningly, before resorting to etiquette. "This is my mother, Carmel Kennedy."

Before he could finish the introduction, Carmel shrieked like a peacock. "Where did you find this creature? She can't possibly be one of our guests! Are you consorting with *Cass's minions* now?" she asked in tones of horror.

"She's not really real, is she?" Teddy asked, only in half-jest, waiting for the harpy to foam at the mouth. Her ability to sense Carmel's distress beneath her volatility lessened the impact of this ludicrous scene.

"Don't," Kurt murmured. "We'll talk later." To his mother, he said, "This is Theodosia Baker, one of our tenants. I'll take her home after you give me that key." He held out his hand.

His mother glared at Teddy and defiantly flung the key behind her, into the heavy shrubbery surrounding the cottage. "This is my home, and I'll not have it defiled by your philandering ways, Kurtis. I spoke to Kylie. She's willing to take you back. All she needs is a little courtship. She's the class of woman you need to help move your plans forward."

Teddy raised her eyebrows and stayed out of that one. This was where that *trust* thing fell apart.

Carmel sent her a triumphant glare, as if confident she'd won this round. Teddy really wanted to smack that smirk off her face, but she and Kurt didn't have anything remotely resembling a relationship. He'd once been engaged to Kylie—his ball to roll.

"I don't need a woman, or Kylie's father, to move my plans forward, Mother," he said, tugging Teddy toward the door. "I already have my own plans in place. If you'll remove yourself, we'll be going.

Another attack like this, and I'll return to the city and leave you to run the resort on your own."

That staggered the woman enough that they could push past without any more shrieks. Even though she'd shut down her extra sense to avoid the collision of her usual pain and confusion with Carmel's hungry need, Teddy still felt the lie in Kurt's retort as well as Carmel's disorientation. There was too much going on to sort it all out.

Carmel Kennedy had to be the *emotional vampire* the Lucys had declared her. The consequences of living with that kind of psychic drainage—wow. She wasn't much of a deep thinker, but even she could grasp some of the parameters.

"I've heard of people like that, but never met one," she muttered in awe.

Without comment, Kurt hauled her down the lane to the parking lot. Teddy hurried to keep up with him. Thank heavens she wore boots and not real heels.

"Well, now I understand why you keep everything bottled up," she said brashly as he flung open the door of his Mercedes. "That was practically Shakespearian."

"She studied drama," he said drily, before closing the door after her.

"With Valdis?" she asked when he climbed in the other side.

"They hate each other's guts, so probably." He turned the ignition and roared the motor.

Teddy pondered that for all of half a second. "Lance has been painting Valdis for thirty years. He's about to throw Val in her face, isn't he? Lance said he used to visit the commune, and if I'm understanding the history here, Val's parents owned the commune that your father bankrupted. Romeo and Juliet?"

Kurt remained silent as they cruised down the resort road toward town. Not until they hit the parking lot did he answer. "I never thought about the romantic relationships involved, but you could very well be right. We'll have to send Mother back to the city before Lance hangs those pieces, or she'll have another breakdown."

What kind of man protected a virago from herself? One who knew how to love despite all reason. Teddy couldn't decide if that was deeply impressive or deeply insane, but it softened her belief that Kurt was just another stiff suit.

"And here I thought I was settling in where Syd would be safe, and I could work in tranquility. Instead, Hillvale is just one giant soap opera. Who needs TV?" When Kurt turned off the car in town, she climbed out without his aid and glanced automatically to her own home. The shop was still lit.

"If you mention *negativity* and *emotional vampires*, I'll let you walk yourself home," he said, unamused.

"You know, I might have a crystal to help." She walked down the boardwalk a little faster than she'd planned. Kurt's soap opera would have to wait. Why would Syd still be in the shop at this hour? "I buy crystals because they call to me, even though I don't know why until I recognize a need. Would you like a ring?"

"Through my mother's nose?" he asked, still without humor.

"Well, if you could persuade her to wear it all the time, I could come up with a pendant for your mother that might neutralize her to some extent. I've never really tested my abilities, though. I don't know what I can do. That's why I'm here—to find out." She stopped outside her door and peered through the glass.

Syd was pacing up and down, the wireless landline in her hand, although she didn't seem to be speaking into it.

"Let's talk about this in the morning," Kurt said, rubbing his hand through his hair. "I'm just not in the mood to be polite tonight. What is your sister doing?"

"That's what I'm wondering. Come in a second, will you? Syd has problems, and she needs to understand that the whole world isn't out to get her."

Kurt rested his hand on her shoulder before she opened the door. "Look, I'm sorry about the scene back there, and I'm sorry for being a dick. Maybe we can go into the city and do this properly, with dinner and theater and normal?"

Teddy hadn't realized she'd been wound tight ever since Carmel Kennedy's intrusion. At his apology, the tension loosened and she leaned into him, relieved. "It's okay. We haven't had any good reason to discuss family. But that's what this package is about. I've already told you that I can't just do sex and walk out. Do you get that?"

He squeezed her shoulder and kissed her hair. "I'm trying. Give me time. If we're learning family, let's see what's wrong with your sister."

Reaching for her pocket, Syd swung around as Teddy turned the key in the lock. She looked both relieved and guilty when she recognized them. "You were gone so long, I worried."

Teddy didn't need to open her Monitor to know that Syd was more than worried. "I'm sorry. We had a lot of plans to discuss. What happened?"

Syd cast Kurt a look of doubt. "Nothing. We can talk later."

"Shall I leave?" he asked, his chiseled face revealing nothing.

But Teddy sensed his concern. She actually *felt* him for a change, without need of her Monitor. This was almost as good as sex. Better, actually. It meant he trusted her enough to lower his barrier!

Or that the evening had worn it down. Still, she kissed his cheek, then strode toward the kitchen. "Stay," she told him. "Syd, speak. I'm fixing coffee. Whatever it is, we'll work it out."

"Does she always treat friends and families like Prince Hairy?" Kurt asked.

"She doesn't fix coffee for the prince," Syd replied.

Teddy hoped that meant the two of them were willing to talk to each other, because she couldn't take much more soap opera. She yanked out the coffee beans and the grinder and filled the kitchen with the kind of noise that expressed how her brain was feeling right now.

"You want your iPod?" Syd asked over the noise. "Or is coffee enough to take the edge off?"

"You do not want to know." Teddy glanced up, saw Kurt looking for mugs and Syd setting out cream and sugar. That worked. She concentrated on calming her rattled nerves while she poured grounds into the magic machine. What would it be like to have a man around the house again?

Now wasn't the time to find out. "Okay, I'm ready. Tell me what happened."

"Nothing, really," Syd said. "It's me being paranoid."

"And sometimes, people really are out to get you," Teddy countered. "So let us decide."

"I was using your computer to set up the shop books. You never think of things like that. I e-mailed your office asking if they had a system I could work with." Syd filled the pot with water and handed it to Teddy.

"Thank you, I think." Syd was right. She preferred working with crystals to computers. "Is there something wrong at the office?"

"They forwarded your voice mail messages. You haven't been answering them." Syd didn't sound as if she were scolding.

"They're usually from customers with special orders and I haven't had time. I need to think about expanding and hiring help." The coffee started perking and perfuming the air.

"I recognized one of the numbers."

Syd said that in such a way that even oblivious Kurt stared.

"It was the number Ash uses from his office."

Assbutt, the abusive cop—calling *her office*? "He got into your laptop, didn't he?" Teddy asked in horror.

He could be on his way to Hillvale, right now.

SAMANTHA

JULY 1: MORNING

SAM STUDIED THE PHOTOS HANGING ON DINAH'S WALL. THE enlargement1s of the two panels of Lucinda Malcolm's triptych had developed a life of their own. "I like the colored Sharpies," she said, admiring the newly emerging colors. "Dinah, is this the color you want your door painted?"

Dinah wiped her hands on her apron and peered near-sightedly at the photo people had been coloring on. "Does turquoise go with the gold letters on the window? I like my gold."

"Purple might go better," Mariah called from behind the counter.

Dinah grabbed a marker from the mug on the counter and began re-coloring her window frame. "Yes, that's better!"

"I'll take the turquoise for my windows," Aaron called from his seat at the counter. "Navy blue on the door."

"Color your own, lazy man," Pasquale from the grocery store said as he carried in a load of napkins Dinah had ordered.

Pasquale never came through the front door. He always trundled his boxes on a dolly to the back. Since he aimed directly for the photos, Sam assumed they were his goal. She got out of the way and returned to waiting on the breakfast crowd. She watched in amusement as the diminutive, graying Italian examined the increasingly colorful photographs. Word had been spreading.

"Are we labeling people we know?" Pasquale asked, squinting at the names scribbled beside the people depicted. "Not many of dem still 'round."

Sam glanced at Walker. He didn't turn to watch but she could tell Pasquale had his attention. Interference from officialdom tended to squelch conversation, so Walker seldom said much. In this case, she knew how to speak for him. "Were you here back then? We think the original painting depicts a day about ten years ago."

"Sure, dat's me hanging da sign before I open da store. I couldn't afford a big one back den. When it got blown off, I replace it with da big one dat's dare now." He added his name to a figure with a full head of black hair with his back to the artist. "Ten years about right. It will be ten years in August dat I open da store. Dare's Lonnie Thompson packing up his car to take his wife's work to some gallery. He use to sell pottery down in Monterey."

"Did you know them?" Sam poured orange juice and tried to sound casual. "I think his wife is related to Teddy and her sister."

Pasquale chose red for his store colors, but he painted the wood siding instead of the window frames. "I knew him from Monterey. He told me about Hillvale. I tink his wife was upset 'bout leaving here. I taught it was 'cause she didn't want to leave her friends."

Dinah put down her coloring pen and peered at the cramped writing. "That inkblot is Lonnie Thompson? He was a philandering prick who yelled at his wife all the time. A'course, she yelled back a lot."

Sam glanced at Walker. He was frowning, listening, sipping his coffee—and waiting for her to draw out Dinah. She rolled her eyes at him. He winked in return.

"I didn't know you were here back then, Dinah," Sam said, although now that she thought about it, Cass had said she'd arrived before Pasquale. "You've been here ten years already? Or longer? Do we need to have an anniversary party?"

"Goin' on about twelve years." Dinah stepped back to admire her handiwork, then glanced over at the panel depicting the town hall. "That's Thalia Thompson coming down the bluff. He made her carry his stuff down until one day, she flung a bowl at him. Maybe that's the day. They had a huge blow up in the street and left pretty soon after."

In August then—according to the newspapers, the kiln had burned that month.

"You know for certain they left together?" Walker finally asked.

Dinah turned and glared at him. "I don't snitch on customers," she informed him. "I told you all I know." She marched back to the kitchen, her short figure ramrod straight in her engulfing white apron.

Pasquale watched her leave with a puzzled expression. "What dat about?"

The café grew quiet. Pasquale seldom ate here or participated in the gossip. Sam was pretty sure that Walker would have questioned the grocer about Thalia though. She didn't know what to say.

It was Aaron, the urbane antique dealer, who spoke up. "Walker thinks Lonnie killed Thalia and left her bones in Teddy's attic. Dinah presumably doesn't agree."

"No, Dinah just doesn't talk to the police," Walker said, rising and leaving his payment on the counter. "I respect that. But if anyone else knows if Thalia left with Lonnie, I'd appreciate hearing about it."

Walker had had no response to the e-mail temptation he'd sent to Thalia's mailbox. Whoever was picking up the mail, if anyone, didn't do so regularly.

Pasquale finished coloring his building. "Dey were not a happy couple, but it's hard to tink of eider of dem as killers. Dey took care of friends. Lisa woulda starved when she broke her arm."

"It could have been accidental," Walker said. "Do you know this Lisa? Does she have a last name?"

Pasquale shrugged. "None of dem did. Lisa helped paint pots, lived on da farm, and left with da rest."

Tracking a homeless tribe from ten years ago was hopeless, Sam figured. "Do you recognize anyone else in that photo who hasn't already been identified?"

"Dare's Orval before he grew his beard." Pasquale inked in the name.

Sam knew Orval Bledsetter as a retired veterinarian who wore a scraggly gray beard, ponytail, and overalls. He didn't come in often, and he'd been obnoxious the few times she'd met him. Walker had probably already talked to him, but he leaned over Pasquale's shoulder to look anyway.

"I don't remember dem using a moving truck," Pasquale said, standing back. "Dey didn't have much. Dare's Tullah, did you ask her?"

"She said pretty much the same," Walker admitted. "She thought they left in the dead of night. She thinks that was before the kiln burned."

Pasquale scratched his head. "Da kiln blew up a few weeks after I open da store. I remember worrying if my insurance covered fire. I check and made sure it did as soon as da fire trucks left. I'm pretty sure da Thompsons were gone before den or Lonnie would have been right in dare wit dem. He was da last of da potters using it."

They could very easily be looking at a painting of the day of Thalia's death.

"You ought to be asking the Nulls." Harvey, the long-haired musician found a seat at the end of the counter near the photos. "Carmel just flew into town last night."

Mariah arrived through the kitchen door, tying on her apron. "On her broom, you mean? If she wanted to take someone out, she'd hire a hitman and be in Hawaii when it happened."

"I doubt if Mrs. Kennedy knew the Thompsons any more than Cass did," Sam said, delivering water to Harvey and a few new customers. "Unless she collects pottery and bad artwork, that is. Has anyone asked Daisy about Thalia?"

"I tried. No forward progress yet." Walker kissed Sam's cheek. "I'm heading over to Teddy's to recommend security. Mariah's ghost traps aren't strong enough."

Sam laughed, but she'd heard him talking to Teddy on the phone last night. The ghost was the least of her worries. They needed human traps.

TWENTY-THREE

"CAN'T WE HAVE HER INSTITUTIONALIZED?" KURT ASKED, PACING UP AND down Monty's office in the building they used as their city hall. "I can't work with her interference anymore."

"Mom's not crazy," Monty pointed out. "She just needs handling with care, and you're the only one who knows how. If you go, the lodge goes, and the whole town with it. The only other solution is to buy her out, and I'm not sure even that works. She probably still wouldn't leave."

Kurt ran his hand through his hair, unwilling to discuss the scene Teddy had been subjected to last night. She'd been brilliantly understanding, but she probably thought he'd meant it when he threatened to walk out. Monty brought him down off that cloud.

He was either chained to the lodge or played the coward and left everyone to hang. Right now, he seriously leaned toward the latter. "Mom owns half the corporation. We'd have to mortgage our personal assets to the hilt and still probably come out lacking."

He needed a window to look out, to see what was happening out there.

Last night, he'd left Teddy agreeing to call Walker, but Syd had been reluctant. One dead body in the attic was more than he could accept. Fearing for Teddy and her family had set his mind off kilter. He couldn't focus on the argument.

"Marry Mom off," Monty suggested facetiously.

Kurt thought about what the Lucys called their mother—an emotional vampire. She'd been a nag and a bitch before their father died. With the financial wreck he'd left behind dumped on her, she'd pulled out all the stops. So in a way, the Lucys were right, although it had nothing to do with the supernatural and everything to do with her desperate need to control everything in her universe.

He winced as he remembered Teddy nailing that about him. And that was the reason he wasn't calling Walker himself and demanding more security—even though he was wearing a hole in the floor to prevent picking up the phone.

They had *children* over there.

He paced more.

"If Kylie's father is still interested in the town condo project," Monty said with hesitation, "Would it hurt to talk to him about a loan to buy Mom out?"

Kurt rubbed his head, hearing Teddy's voice calling his dream no more than a *profit center*. He needed profit to buy his mother out of the lodge. Was that so wrong?

He came from a long line of male philanderers. He could marry Kylie, have Teddy on the side. . . Even *thinking* that gave him a headache. Teddy had been pretty damned clear she didn't fly that way. And he didn't blame her. She deserved honesty.

"I can ask, but I think Kylie and her father are a package deal, and it may include Mom," Kurt admitted. "Kylie's father is just her sort."

"He's married," Monty said with a grimace.

"When has that stopped her? She's always needed a man in her life." Restless, unable to accept any of his alternatives, Kurt strode out of Monty's windowless office to check the street from the front window. Someone had started painting the walls of the lobby a stark white, which contrasted badly with the battered dark floors.

Monty followed, if only to check the cloudy sky. "It's not supposed to rain in July."

"Pray it isn't heavy. Half that mountain is likely to slide onto our doorstep—another reason we need money *now*." The other side of the equation was that if there was no rain, the remaining half of the mountain could easily catch fire in the dry heat of summer. "Remind me why we stay here?"

"I'm starting to wonder as well. I vote we leave Hillvale to the Lucys and become beach bums."

Kurt followed the path of Monty's thoughts—police chief Walker was headed this way. "If we build a real town out here, we'll need real city services to fight fire and flood and crime. We'll have to tax the hell out of ourselves."

Monty laughed. "That's one way of looking at it. Or we tax the tourists."

Walker entered, looking less enigmatic than usual, more in the direction of grim. "The lab found enough DNA on Thalia's canvases to positively identify the bones as someone who had their hands all over those paintings. That may be as conclusive as we get."

"I thought the labs were backed up and it would take months for an analysis." Kurt began pacing the floorboards, testing for rot in the old wood.

"*My* lab," Walker said with a shrug. "If there's a killer lose in Hillvale, I want to know about it now, not next winter. Consider my company's services in lieu of taxes, like the artists used to do."

"You're renting. You don't pay taxes," Monty reminded him. "We'll give you artwork in exchange for your services."

That almost made the expressionless officer smile, Kurt noted. "What about Teddy's sister?" he demanded. "Did she call you?"

"I just came from there. That's next on the agenda. We need security cameras in the parking lot and at the entrance to town."

Kurt tried to feel relief that the women had been sensible, but Walker was only one man. He couldn't eliminate all danger.

The police chief pulled out his phone and called up a website with the equipment he apparently had in mind.

"If you want cameras, you'll have to pay for them," Monty said, glancing at the images. "I don't think the website will take paintings in trade. Or crystals," he added in an attempt at humor. "Why do we need cameras?"

"We need protocol for how much I can reveal and to whom." Walker punched at his phone.

Kurt figured he and Monty were about to receive links to the cameras. Coming from a wealthy, non-police background, Walker wasn't inclined to wait for what he wanted.

"I already know about Syd's domestic situation," Kurt told him. "You won't be revealing anything new."

"City mayor ought to have access to police information," Monty said, jotting notes in his own phone. "I'll add protocol to the council agenda."

"We have a town council?" Walker asked in interest. "When does it meet?"

"Whenever the Lucys get a bee in their bonnet and start raising hell." Monty shoved his phone back in his pocket. "What's Syd's situation and why do we need cameras?"

"Abusive cop boyfriend," Kurt said, keeping Walker from fighting with his conscience over confidentiality. "He put Syd in the hospital when she tried to break up with him. He broke into her house while she was laid up, stole her laptop and is sending threatening messages pinpointing her location. So she's hiding up here and living on cash. He's out on bond and still has access to all official investigative resources. The women didn't think he knew how to find Teddy, but he recently tried to reach her through her office."

Walker added, "Teddy's office is shipping her inventory here. If this creep wields his credentials, one of her people might believe they have to give him the address. Since he appears to consider himself above the law, he might even have hackers breaking into her website. We have to consider her hiding place has been compromised."

Kurt winced. "Crap. Did you get a chance to check out Syd's story?"

"I verified the details this morning. Ashbuth has been written up before for heavy-handedness, but no one has pressed charges until Syd. I have no proof he's a bad cop, but my gut says Syd and Teddy aren't lying. They're vulnerable out there with those kids at the end of town." Walker glared out the window to the street where a few early tourists roamed the boardwalk, along with the usual regulars. "Cameras on the parking lot and on the road coming in would let us know when people come and go."

"*After* the fact," Kurt said, gripping his hands into fists in frustration. "We can't monitor them constantly, watching for the bastard, even if we knew what he looked like."

"I sent Sam over to the shop," Walker admitted. "The Lucys have their own weird system of protecting their own. I try not to ask, but it seems to involve those sticks they carry."

"Magic wands?" Monty asked in amusement. "That's taking the superstition a step too far, isn't it?"

"Probably, but you weren't there when the avalanche halted at Daisy's guardians. Sam and Valdis could have been buried alive in that bomb shelter they pretend we don't know about, but the Lucys chanted and pointed their sticks and the rocks stopped. The whole scene was spooky weird." Hands behind his back, Walker continued to study the street.

"Rock guardians and walking sticks don't stop guns," Kurt said. "If this bad cop is working a desk job, why can't we just have him followed? Stick a monitor on his car or something."

"Same problem as the camera—we need someone monitoring the GPS. And he has access to more than one vehicle, so we'd have to follow multiple cars. If I had a camera right there at the corner where he'd have to enter town. . ." Walker glowered. "It would have to beep every time a car passed. There are no good solutions."

"Looks like Sam is performing her pied piper act," Monty said from the window. "There goes Harvey, carrying sticks to our new residents. Hell if I know what Aaron is taking over there, but it doesn't look like cookies."

"What do you mean, *pied piper*?" Kurt looked past his brother. He didn't see their niece, but there did seem to be quite a bit of purposeful movement in the direction of the opposite end of town—and Teddy's shop.

"For whatever reason, people just naturally follow Sam's direction," Walker said, as if he merely announced his girlfriend was serving supper. "She never *says* much. It just happens."

"I don't need to hear more weird," Kurt said in frustration. He thought his head might explode as it was. "I want to hear what action we can take. And if we can't take action, I'll just bulldoze the damned house and send the women to the lodge—where we *do* have security cameras and monitors."

He stalked out, knowing Teddy's defiant response to that. She'd already given him her opinion last night.

∿

TEDDY POLISHED THE MAHOGANY-COLORED OBSIDIAN, DECIDING THE STONE reminded her of Kurt's eyes and worrying about the reddish overtones. Still, the stone emanated a fierce protective aura and a gentle grounding that would serve him well once she chipped it into pieces and fitted them into a silver ring.

She only wished she could feel equally confident about the protections she'd given Syd and the kids. If only she'd realized earlier that there might be more to her jewelry than she knew, she could have experimented and known if they'd help.

She worked and watched as the Lucys gathered in the shop. Harvey had presented her and Syd with his beautifully carved walking sticks. Teddy's was made of a fabulous redwood with a raw fuchsite crystal stained with ruby corundum. The crystal was astoundingly rare, beautiful, and *powerful*. When she'd asked Harvey where he'd found it, he'd shrugged and said it was inherited.

Like hers. There was history here, should anyone look into it. She'd paid him well, even knowing he hadn't a clue of the value.

Tullah was apparently channeling an African goddess today by wearing a colorful dashiki and spreading dried herbs along the walls. Amber, the sociable tarot reader, had chosen to paint protective sigils in places that weren't covered by artwork. Daisy's stone guardians seemed to be multiplying. Teddy had found one on her coffeepot this morning.

She just wished that she could believe hocus-pocus would help against human interference better than it had against Thalia. Syd had refused to even participate. She was upstairs with the kids, playing computer teaching games—although she'd gripped the walking stick fiercely and carried it with her, like a weapon.

"Thalia feels agitated," Teddy said, just to remind her company that she existed. "I'm not sure protection is what she wants."

"She's vengeful," Tullah said. "She's looking for trouble. How does Harvey's staff feel to you?"

Setting down the stone she was rubbing, Teddy lifted the gorgeous staff. "I feel the crystal's power. I don't think Harvey recognizes the dangerous energy of this particular stone. I think he was just matching the color with the wood. If I could learn more about how crystals work, I could probably summon lightning with this thing."

That would be preferable to the gun Syd had in her sweater pocket last night. She'd promised to unload and put it away. . . But Syd was seriously frightened, and Teddy couldn't blame her.

"Try not to set fires," Sam said wryly from the corner where she was labeling one of the artworks Syd had hung. "Do you feel the power as vibrations? I only feel it when I'm outside, near nature."

Aaron plugged in the small stone fountain he'd brought over. He'd set it on one of Teddy's shelves, moving some of the guardians to make room for it. "If we conclude staffs resonate with our varied gifts, then mine is probably reacting to strong emotions."

The antique dealer had the slightest accent that Teddy couldn't place. He intrigued her. Why couldn't she be drawn to him or Harvey, men who understood weirdness?

"My staff is pretty neutral in nature, unless it's in a battlefield," Aaron continued. "But it vibrates almost convulsively in here. Thalia has left her mark."

"*Thalia* vibrates almost convulsively," Tullah said. "She must have been truly volatile in person. I don't know how you're staying here, Teddy. You really should look into one of those rental cottages."

"I can't rent both the shop *and* the cottage. My finances are in precarious shape right now. What does that fountain represent, Aaron?"

"*Chi* energy, mostly. I've been studying it since I found this thing. The previous owner left a strong positive mark on it, as if he might have been one of us. The fountain itself radiates a powerful force." He flipped a switch, and the water he'd added began to trickle, making a pleasant splashing noise. "It isn't the ocean, but it should help soothe restless spirits. I'm hoping it will be stronger than that, but it's untested."

Like her. Teddy wanted a teacher who knew what she and the others could accomplish. They needed psychic journals and websites to educate themselves.

"Isn't it odd that most of us have peaceful gifts, not violent ones?" She returned to sorting through her treasured box of inherited crystals. Her stupid ex had taken the jewelry with the monetarily valuable gems, without touching the worn box with the powerful stones her parents had given her. She tried to be grateful for ignorance and a narrow escape, but the loss of all that work and the extra cash needed to buy more had set back her efforts to help Syd.

Apparently no one else found non-violence odd, so Teddy continued, trying to find more pleasant subjects than worrying about Assbutt, "Do you think we could incorporate *chi* energy in the town park if we added a fountain?"

"We'll ask Walker's mother," Sam said, finishing her label work. "She's coming for the art walk, and he says she's a feng shui expert. I'm terrified about meeting her, and that will give me a topic to talk about. I need to find a book or website and study up."

"I have some reference material." Satisfied that the fountain was running properly, Aaron headed for the door. "But a lot depends on the fountain itself and the placement. Stop by anytime and borrow whatever you need."

Once Aaron had left, Amber rubbed her ample hip and crossed the room to study the stone fountain. "It does seem to exude powerful energy. I wonder if it will soothe Thalia."

Teddy put down her work to join her. "I can see and feel that it contains complex crystals. Whoever built this had a sensitivity to the power of stone. But I don't think it can stop guns, or even fists, and those are my main concerns."

"Here comes Walker. He's not looking happy." Preparing to leave, Sam had her stick in hand.

"How can you tell?" Tullah asked, looking over her shoulder. "Even with those big green eyes, he works that Asian inscrutability well."

Sam chuckled. "That's his mother's training. Just wait until you see him angry, then he's all Irish fury, I assume like his father."

"Stereotypes, ladies," Teddy scolded. "Kurt is just as stoic as Walker, and his family probably came over on the Mayflower. And Syd and I test nearly half Irish, and we don't drink or lose our tempers."

"But you have to admit, it's a convenient label," Amber argued. "Redheads are supposed to be thin-skinned."

"Thin-skinned in that I have circles under my eyes and puncture easily, yes, but it takes a lot to make me angry. What I lack is impulse control." Teddy shut up as the police chief entered and looked warily around. His eyes warmed when he saw Sam, so he wasn't all enigmatic.

"The town has no money for security cameras," he said into their silence. "And I've received a few reports on the writing on Thalia's paintings."

"And?" Teddy prompted when he didn't continue.

"And, she added more crystals to her paints every time her husband hit her. She seemed to think it would reveal his evil. The journal entries indicate when she upped the formula and why." Walker waited expectantly.

They all turned to look at Thalia's paintings prominently displayed on the back wall. Each one had red eyes or red stripes where eyes might be depicted.

"That only reveals bad paint technique, not evil," Sam argued doubtfully. "And evil tells us nothing. We already knew they didn't get along."

"She started adding what she called almandine to his clay to see if it would make his hands turn red," Walker continued. "His pots started selling for a lot more, if we're translating her notes correctly."

"Almandine is a common form of garnet." Teddy reached for her books. "It can run as deep as purple but is usually a dark shade of red —like the stones we found in the attic. One of its uses is to eliminate inhibitions."

That would explain a *lot*. Remembering the Shower of Love, Teddy buried her head in the book to hide her pink cheeks and look for anything she'd forgotten. "For the Nulls among us, almandine is a type of ferrous silicate and can contain aluminum, but it's not inherently poisonous. I've never seen it turn anything red though."

Sam was the first to connect the dots. "My grandparents' paintings started selling for small fortunes after they added crystals. That could be because the crystals in some way removed their inhibitions, allowing them to more freely access the creative parts of their brains, like alcohol or pot."

"But with inhibitions removed," Teddy said, following the path of her thoughts, "they may have developed tastes for bigger, better, more. . ."

"And learned greed," Tullah said sadly. "If those crystals are in our mountain, they've been bleeding greed into the ground for millennia."

TWENTY-FOUR

JULY 1: AFTERNOON

"KURTIS DOMINIC, WHAT ARE YOU *DOING* UP THERE?"

There was no need to turn around to recognize the speaker. Kurt continued chipping away at a strip of peeling paint behind the ice cream parlor counter and dabbed at the next stretch. "Remembering the good old days," he retorted.

That hadn't been the point when he'd first removed the chalkboard covering the wall, but he'd enjoyed this past hour of working with his hands. He'd already stripped enough paint to recognize the rainbow painting Lance had described. He even vaguely remembered it from his youth, although he didn't recall much of the art shop.

"You need to be updating our financials," his mother complained. "Where is the profit in uncovering obscene graffiti?"

"Have you never done anything for the pure pleasure of accomplishment?" His mother was an unhappy woman. Kurt was fairly certain she had never done anything just for fun. "Studies show nonessential acts are more satisfying than essential."

On the other end of the counter, the parlor owner had stripped enough paint to reveal the VW bus. Midweek on a gloomy day was slow for business, and he'd happily joined the project. Rainbow walls brightened the gray light.

Kurt's question apparently perplexed his mother. He'd never known her wealthy socialite parents well—they'd always been too busy to visit with their grandchildren. He assumed his mother and Lance had been raised by nannies until they were old enough to contribute to the household. His mother never talked about their childhood. He should ask Lance—if his uncle stayed coherent.

"It's graffiti," she repeated. "You could at least paint City Hall so Monty doesn't die of mold poisoning."

"In case you haven't noticed, we did that first. Anyone can paint walls. Uncovering art is more delicate. Hire an accountant if you need the financials immediately."

It felt good to say that. He despised accounting. Come to think of it, he despised glad-handing guests. There was very little about his job that he enjoyed except the chance to rebuild and create the village he envisioned. Ugly rainbows hadn't been on his restoration agenda, but it was a cheap improvement not requiring bank loans—which was what his mother was after.

"You know we can't afford accountants," she protested, keeping her voice down.

Kurt thought about that as he peeled off another strip of acrylic. Of course they could afford accountants. Basically, his *mother* couldn't afford them to take a close look at the books she'd cooked for years. Probably best not to make that argument in public.

A damp wind fluttered a poster as a customer entered. Kurt didn't turn to see who it was until Teddy spoke. "That's pretty damned impressive graffiti. Good day, Mrs. Kennedy. I didn't figure you for the ice cream type. What's your favorite? I like the toffee."

This conversation could have gone so many different ways—Kurt climbed down from the ladder prepared to act as shield. Even though he knew Teddy was being facetious, she didn't deserve to be hit with his mother's foul humor.

Carmel didn't deign to answer the question. She merely glared at Kurt. "I'll need those financials by this evening. Kylie and her father will be dining with us."

"Have a nice dinner," he said with malicious intent. Bringing Kylie back into his life was one step too far, even for his mother. "I'll be eating at Dinah's. Teddy, would you and your family care to join me?"

The black dye had been eradicated from Teddy's hair, leaving a rich sheen of waving copper. She wore it tied back in a green ribbon, but stray curls brushed her cheeks and framed her topaz eyes—which were currently dancing with mischief. She was enjoying the confrontation.

He breathed a deep sigh of relief that she was warped enough to have forgiven him for last night's humiliating scene. When had he developed a taste for weird women?

"I can't answer for Syd," she replied, "but I'd love to. It's good to get out of the house, occasionally, you know?"

Hooking her thumbs in her faded jeans—had she come here to help him?—she turned back to his mother, who was dressed as if she were heading for Rodeo Drive. "You must have been here when my cousin Thalia and her husband sold my house to your company. Do you remember the transaction?"

Wham, bang, right upside the head. No one had ever dared tackle Carmel Kennedy front and center on her potential thievery. Kurt's first instinct was to step in and shield—who? His mother? Teddy? Both of them? Or maybe himself from the backlash, because there would be a horrendous blow-up later, in private, usually ending in tears and hysteria.

Maybe it was time he stepped back and let his mother flame out.

"I do not deal with business," Carmel said coldly. "I pay people to handle it for me."

"Oh, then Xavier Black had power of attorney to purchase the house?" Teddy screwed her face into a puzzled pout. "I thought Mr. Black was. . ." She hesitated as if searching for a polite word. "He wasn't quite up to his legal self ten years ago, when the transfer was made. If he was in charge, the transaction could be questioned in court."

Kurt suffered a familiar squeeze in his gut—she'd said she'd hired a lawyer. She hadn't been kidding. He needed to remember that.

Xavier had been a drug addict for decades and not completely in his right mind for years—one of the reasons Kurt and Monty had to take over the family business. That had been right about the time the house was sold, except he didn't remember the purchase or Thalia or her husband, so Xavier probably had handled it—with their mother's consent.

Xavier was gradually recovering, but ten years ago he might have bought the Golden Gate Bridge had it been offered cheaply enough.

"You will have to discuss this with our attorney," Carmel said, before turning her glare on Kurt. "The financials, by this evening." She stalked out on her high heels.

Her chauffeured Escalade waited, engine running, in the parking lot. Kurt rocked back on his heels and watched his mother parade across the crumbling street in an outfit that would have fed a family of four for a year.

"The mural in here isn't important, you know," Teddy said softly, watching with him. "I was just curious to see if Mia really was talking to a ghost who knew things we didn't. Pity Thalia isn't more coherent about her death."

"If I believed in ghosts—which I don't," Kurt said in consideration, "I'd say Thalia suffered from the same delusions as my mother. In which case, her poor husband was probably expected to adhere to her demands, and when he didn't, she erupted like Vesuvius. And she's blocking that out by not telling you everything."

Teddy whistled at his insight. "You could be on to something. I wonder if your mother ever dabbled in crystals?"

"Not buying crystals either. See you at Dinah's at six." Roiling with anger and frustration, Kurt climbed back up the ladder and jammed his paint scraper into the peeling acrylic.

"No, I don't want to horn in on your date with Kurt. I want to go home, lock the doors, sit at the window with a shotgun, and watch the road." Syd angrily whacked a nail into a newly-painted City Hall wall. "I'm only out here now because I know that's not normal."

Syd had tucked her dyed-brown hair into a painter's cap and covered her slender frame in bulky overalls—and she still looked like Syd. She couldn't disguise herself if she tried. Teddy handed up the canvas her sister wanted to hang and wished she really did have a magic wand.

"It's not a date. He's furious with me. He thinks I'll roll over on giving up my house so he can rebuild Hillvale into his dream town. I can appreciate having a dream, but he'll have to take it elsewhere. There are a blue million pretty developments in this world, but only one Hillvale."

"Hillvale creaks," Syd reminded her. "It needs to be bulldozed. I don't want to be up here come winter."

"What if all Europe thought that way?" Teddy asked in horror. "We'd have nothing of history left!"

"So?" Syd climbed down to check how the painting hung.

"It's not as if we can rely on ghosts to transmit information on our pasts! If we don't know our history, we're doomed to repeat it." Teddy stepped back to admire the gallery effect Syd was creating on the white walls.

It needed more lighting, but the artwork stood out now. They'd cleaned up a few of the older pieces so the colors caught the light from the front window, adding a mosaic of brilliance to the otherwise boring room.

"If we didn't know about the commune and Lucinda Malcolm, we wouldn't have any understanding of what's happening here. We'd be wallowing around in superstitious ignorance," Teddy argued. "If only we had Lucinda's knowledge, we could educate each other, and we'd better understand our weirdnesses. If someone had taught me, I'd know how to *use* my crystals. Without history and a solid education, we'd all be living in caves."

"Some people prefer living in caves," Syd said cynically. "And my ability to visualize a welcoming room or a dignified showplace is *not* weird."

"You could do it before you went to school for formal training. I know you use objects that have power, because I've felt them. I bet if Aaron tested one of the rooms you've designed, he'd find objects with positive memories or chi energy or whatever. You're playing with dynamics you don't understand but react to instinctively. Think how much better you could work if you'd had training in the weird."

Syd snorted but didn't argue. Teddy took that for agreement that her sister felt something in the objects she chose for a room. They'd just never really questioned their abilities until they'd met Hillvale.

Seeing Mariah crossing the street carrying her satchel of ghost-catchers, Teddy and Syd waited before packing up. Teddy was convinced the black-braided waitress was far more than she appeared, but she and Syd weren't in a place to debate the need for disguise.

"A van is coming up the road," Mariah announced without any preliminaries as she entered. "Could be your pottery. Better have the mayor call our police chief down here, just in case." She glanced around at the artwork and nodded in unsmiling approval.

"Why do we need Monty and Walker to help unload pottery?" Syd asked, reasonably enough. "The van drivers will do it for us."

Mariah dragged the stepladder over to a corner and swept the ghost-catcher there with her fingers, performing a ritual Teddy had seen her do elsewhere, calling it ectoplasmic exorcism. "Because the ghosts are quivering and you have a stalker who may have followed the van or be driving it. Stranger danger applies here as well as anywhere."

Syd drew in a sharp breath, put down her tools, and hurried out. She'd left the kids with Amber. Teddy watched out the window as her sister half-ran to the tarot shop. "That was fear-mongering. Why do you do that?"

Mariah shrugged and climbed down. "Evil exists. We need to learn wariness."

Apparently drawn by Mariah's voice, Monty emerged from the rear of the hall. "Goodness exists as well. Why don't you look for that instead?" He turned to examine the work they'd accomplished this morning. "Your sister is talented. I didn't think those ugly old oils could look this good."

Teddy almost laughed at his pointed lesson. "Find the positive, I like it. We could fill the town with rainbows and unicorns and drive out the blackness."

Mariah wrinkled her nose in distaste. "And carry a big stick. This isn't Candyland."

Teddy shrugged and finished packing up Syd's tools. "Come over and help us unload the pottery my folks collected. They liked the colorful and unusual. I think if evil exists, it does so in darkness and ignorance and only creeps in where it's welcomed. If we fill the town with color, cheer, and positivity, we create barriers against depression and paranoia."

"Jobs and money help," Monty said dryly, holding the door for her.

"Well, they certainly add to the good cheer, granted. Are you coming with us?" Teddy asked over her shoulder as she carried out the box of hammers and nails Syd had gathered from all over town.

"Do I need to lock up now that we're displaying valuable artwork?" Monty followed them out but hesitated at the door.

"Those locks could be picked by an infant. Just kiss them with good cheer, and I'm sure no evil will enter," Mariah said flippantly.

"Or better yet, cast a spell on them," Monty countered, taking the box from Teddy. "And if that van is full of steaks for the lodge instead of pottery, you owe me one for dragging me away from my desk."

"I'll owe you one anyway, after you get finished hauling boxes. It was a huge storage unit."

The plain box van rumbled over the potholed road and hesitated at the corner of Teddy's shop. Intelligently assessing the danger of stopping on the narrow highway, the driver pulled into one of the many empty parking spots. On a weekday, the town had few customers.

Kurt emerged from the ice cream shop. Lance popped out of the gallery/meeting house across from City Hall. Aaron locked up his antique shop and strolled down the boardwalk as if heading for an early dinner at Dinah's.

And the Lucys began arriving, carrying their walking staffs. Teddy prayed there were only boxes to unload and no evil for this eccentric army to fight.

TWENTY-FIVE

JULY 1: LATE AFTERNOON

KURT LEANED BACK IN DINAH'S BOOTH AND STUDIED THE CUTS AND blisters on his previously manicured hands. Aaron had opened his storage area for the ceramics delivery. Hauling dozens of wooden cartons had worked up their appetites. "Maybe financial statements are better than life as a mover."

"Define *better.*" Teddy dug into Dinah's shrimp risotto and sighed with what he took as delight.

Kurt enjoyed watching her savor her food with the same sensuality she brought to the bedroom. He'd never look at another salad-picking woman again. And she wasn't afraid of hard work either. Her manicure looked as bad as his.

"Moving boxes is honest labor with very few ethical considerations involved," she continued. "Financial statements are a boondoggle that would corrupt a saint."

She put her finger on a nerve with that one, if she only knew. Another good reason they shouldn't pursue a serious relationship. Teddy would have a dim opinion of his parents' ability to manipulate financials.

"All right then, accounting is easier on the hands and back," he corrected. "I think your parents must have bought the entire pottery, wheels, clay and all."

"And maybe a portable kiln or two," she acknowledged. "Since my father occasionally worked with clay as well as stone and metal, there might be some of his stuff in there. We won't know until we pry it all open. I'm just relieved no one followed the truck."

"If your sister's stalker is still actively employed, he wouldn't have time to stake out a storage unit just in case someone used it, even if he knew the location." Kurt savored the basic chicken pot pie Dinah had served him, despite his order for a chef salad.

"If he knows the location, he could threaten desperate junkies to watch it," Teddy said pessimistically. "Assbutt is a real work of art."

"Let's hope that's a long shot. I'm more worried about him pinning your jewelry company to you and your sister. Computerized stalking is simpler." Digging into the pie, Kurt wondered how his staff would react if he hired Dinah. The town would probably kill him though. And his guests might object to meals the cook thought they ought to eat instead of what they ordered.

Teddy poked at her food. "Yeah, I'm pretty sure my cover is blown if Assbutt is reading Syd's computer and is smart enough to follow a bunny trail. I never met the man, and no one ever calls me Theodosia, so I had some hope he wouldn't put two and two together. But once he has Syd's maiden name, the Devine is a bit of a giveaway. My mother couldn't resist keeping her name and calling us Devine-Bakers, even though none of us has ever baked so much as a biscuit in our lives."

Kurt swallowed bile along with his food. He wanted to send them all far, far away or build a road block into town, but he knew his protests were futile.

Before he could react, Teddy reached into her leather shoulder bag and produced a small square box. "I need you to help me experiment."

Kurt warily took the box she shoved across the table. "Experiment with what?"

"I'm trying to learn the power of my stones. There's only so much I can learn from books. This is mahogany obsidian, not a particularly rare stone, but this particular piece resonates with me the same way you do. Don't ask me to explain, but according to my research, it should protect the heart, especially if worn over an artery or vein that will carry the power to the heart."

Resonates with her? Was he supposed to understand that? "I thought mahogany was wood."

"It describes the color. Quit stalling." She shoved the box at him.

Kurt warily opened it to reveal a ring studded with reddish-brown stones. He wasn't a jewelry expert, but he recognized originality and expertise. This was very definitely a Theodosia Devine design—but masculine in the entirety. Even his Rolex didn't appeal to him as much as this ring. "I can't accept this. It's a remarkable creation. You could sell it for a wicked price."

She waved away his protest. "We'll work it out once the lawyers decide the fate of my house. In the meantime, I'm willing to absorb the cost of an expensive experiment. Would you mind wearing it?"

"Is this where you expect me to reveal my true nature and steal everything you own?" he asked, sliding it over the ring finger on his right hand.

"Right now, the house is my biggest asset, and you're already stealing it," she pointed out.

"Not stealing," he insisted, without resentment as he examined the ring. He supposed she had reason to hope magic would reveal a man's nature. "It's a damned fine piece and fits perfectly."

She looked pleased, and he didn't have the heart to take it off. He did intend to fight for that damned shed she called a house. He hoped she was reasonable enough to accept facts, because he actually cared about how she felt. Friendship didn't happen often in his life. If friendship was all he could have of Teddy, he wanted her to be happy. If superstition helped, then fine.

"These aren't the honesty stones, although I'm starting to think I ought to add a chip of those to every design." She glanced out the window. "Does our police chief never take a break? Sam went home half an hour ago to have dinner with him."

Kurt had a sudden desire to go back to the days when they didn't need their own police force, peaceful days when all he had to do was pacify angry customers and read financial statements. But if he meant to turn Hillvale into a real town. . . crime came with it.

He cast a look at the two black-and-white photographs of the triptych pieces still hanging on the walls. From here, it looked as if the creatives had begun coloring the town to their tastes. Even Sam's bright patches of colorful flowers had been inked in. How did he adjust his plans to match that of a town full of unbridled eccentrics? A can of paint wouldn't cure what ailed these buildings.

Standing behind the counter, Dinah filled a coffee pot and worriedly watched Walker's approach. Mariah appeared from the kitchen bearing clean mugs. By the time the police chief entered, they had fresh coffee prepared. Walker gratefully accepted the mug and carried it over to the booth.

"Got a bite," he said conversationally.

Teddy shifted to one side of her bench and invited him to take a seat. Kurt wished Dinah had a liquor license but signaled for more coffee.

"A bite?" he asked as Dinah poured. He knew she listened. That's what the town did.

"I sent an e-mail to that address Teddy provided for Thalia. My assistant made it up all pretty, looking like a legal notice to all former Hillvale residents telling them to provide proof of their residence here during the past forty years so they can be added as part of a class action lawsuit compensating them for damages."

"Damages?" Teddy asked.

Her tone conveyed amusement, but Kurt saw concern wrinkling the corner of her eyes. Here was one more danger added to her growing list—not just Syd's stalker but Thalia's possible killer.

"Yeah, well, my assistant got creative. The point is, we got a reply. The e-mail address is still active. The person using it filled out the form and attached an old bill for a phone at your address, but they only gave a post office box and no current phone number."

"It's not easy to trace an e-mail address, is it?" Teddy left her coffee growing cold.

"We've got the IP address. My team will track the ISP it belongs to and ask for information, but they can't force anyone to provide it, and most generally, they won't. I'd rather not indulge in illegal hacking, so I'm suggesting a second e-mail asking for specifics and hinting at a large settlement."

Kurt covered Teddy's hand and squeezed. "We really don't need this Lonnie clown showing up here. I'd like to catch him sooner than later, but we can't justify doing anything illegal."

"Appoint me as the mayor' secretary," Mariah said from the counter. "Send the e-mail to Monty's computer. I'll take care of it."

Everyone turned to stare at her. She looked grim but undaunted.

Only Walker didn't look puzzled at the feathered waitress's suggestion, Kurt noted.

"I'm pretty damned sure Monty would not approve," the chief said without inflection. "Thank you for the offer, and we may revisit it if this doesn't work."

Mariah glared but nodded. "Lives are important." She retreated to the kitchen.

"What was that about?" Teddy asked in surprise.

"Confidential information," Walker responded in his usual unruffled manner. "Keep her away from computers at all costs. So, do I have your permission to continue?" He finished his coffee and stood up.

"Yes, please," Teddy agreed, looking lost. "I'd only hoped to track the bastard who stole my house, but if it turns out that he killed his wife, do whatever you need to do."

"It became an official case when the bones turned up, so don't worry about the bill. I'll take my expenses out of the town in artwork," Walker said dryly, before striding out.

Teddy chuckled. Kurt didn't. Still holding her hand, he leaned back in his seat and watched Walker take the path up to his cozy cottage where Sam waited. How did the chief tolerate responsibility for an entire town filled with whackos?

"I don't suppose you'd be interested in returning to my place tonight," he said. At the squeeze of her fingers and shake of her head, he nodded acceptance. She needed to be near her sister. "Want to use up our excess energy tearing open boxes?"

TEDDY WATCHED IN RELIEF AS SYD TORE INTO THE CRATES AFTER KURT pried them open. Kurt's suggestion to start on them tonight was just the energy booster everyone needed. The kids played in the layers of packing material while Syd exclaimed happily over the creative contents.

Uninvited, Aaron joined them, spreading his long fingers over crates to decide which ones had the most promising vibrations. "I'm hoping you'll find a few Arthurs or Simmons in here. They were the most famous potters from the Ingersson era, although that would have been before your parents' time."

Teddy held up an evil-looking ebony vase carved with red figurines. "Can you tell us what to look for?"

The antique dealer took the vase she offered. "Arthur favored cat figures in one form or another, often creating grotesque cats that stretched into peculiar angles. He occasionally carved cats into practical pieces like pitchers. Simmons was pretty much the opposite, forming practical pieces into odd shapes, often heavily adorned with flowers and leaves. He favored blues in his work, whereas Arthur favored grays and browns, all popular colors today."

"Blue flowers and brown cats, got it." Teddy dug around in her box but found mostly entertaining pitchers with noses, along with salt and pepper cellars in pop-art designs. "These potters must have been as high as the painters."

"Or your parents only collected the weird ones," Kurt added snarkily, pulling out a plate that was half avocado green and half orange, with red and yellow butterflies painted on.

"That's actually a *Peterson*," Aaron said in excitement, putting down the pitcher to take the plate. "I hadn't hoped for museum pieces! We'll need to invite collectors, create a catalog, if there are many more like this."

"We're talking a lot of money?" Teddy sat back on her heels, not touching the ugly—possibly valuable—plate.

"I wouldn't want to quote numbers until I did some research. Ceramics aren't my specialty, but the non-profits your parents specified will be very happy."

"Watch out," Syd called from her box. "Teddy's wheels are turning. We're all about to be deluged with two tons of work."

"I'm just thinking that we could form our own non-profit to support artists in some kind of learning environment here in Hillvale. . ." She let her voice trail off as she tried to form the idea in her mind.

"And ask dad to contribute the sale profits to something not third-world?" Syd asked with a large measure of doubt. "Or are you planning on calling Hillvale uncivilized?"

Kurt and Aaron both made grunting sounds of what she assumed was agreement. Teddy narrowed her eyes and ignored their cynicism. "It wouldn't hurt to ask," she said defensively. "The town needs money. Establishing a reputation as an art community takes galleries and catalogs and marketing. Bringing in teachers and putting them up. . ." She turned to Kurt. "You could design an artists' village!"

"Not happening," he said. "Buildings require more money than a few pots will bring in. Banks like cash and land as collateral, not artists and dishes."

"We'll exchange artwork for interest on the loans," Syd said with a snicker. "The bankers can decorate their walls."

She was sounding happier and more confident than she had since she'd arrived, so Teddy figured her suggestion at least served a purpose, even if it was pie in the sky.

Aaron dug into another box Kurt had opened. "You've got a problem here." He removed what appeared to be a teapot in sage green with molten brown dribbling down the sides. He flipped it over. "It says R. Williams, but the vibrations are. . ." He hesitated, turning the pot and studying it with his long fingers. "Greed, cynicism, envy—in other words, evil. This pot is a fraud."

In the ensuing silence, Syd stood and gathered up the children. "Time for bed, kids. We have a busy day tomorrow." She hustled them out without explanation or farewell.

"Syd doesn't take well to fraud," Teddy said, moving to the box Aaron was rooting through. "A friend of hers lost her career after being charged with art fraud and theft. Syd sticks with commercial art these days. I wonder if our parents paid a lot for that piece?"

"If they believed it to be a genuine Williams, then it wasn't cheap. Do they have bills of sale for any of this?" Aaron dug through the box, discarding similar pieces, apparently hunting for more *vibrations*.

Kurt examined the ugly teapot. "I'm guessing you have to buy from a legitimate gallery owner to have anything as practical as a bill of sale."

Teddy pulled out a charming brown-and-gray cat, curled up with his tail over his nose. "And even if my parents were inclined to buy from galleries, which I'm pretty sure they couldn't afford, they would never keep pieces of paper. It's not their style. My guess is that like everything in Hillvale, they took a lot of these pieces in trade, simply because they liked them. They're not collectors looking for profit."

Aaron nodded appreciation of this. "That would make sense. There's a lot of amateur work here. The cups and dinner plates are more useful than artistic. They grew up in Hillvale, didn't they? So this could be handed down from their own parents?"

"Along with the attitude," Teddy agreed. "I remember Grandmother Devine had a cabinet full of clay creatures, porcelain plates, colorful dinnerware. They had an estate sale after she died, but my parents kept bits and pieces and used them while we were growing up." Teddy handed the cat to Aaron. "Is this the kind of work you were looking for?"

He took the cat, ran his fingers over it, and nodded. "This one's genuine, a very nice find. We need to lock these doors tonight."

"What about this piece you say reflects evil? Not that I believe in evil, but fraud is criminal." Kurt lifted the teapot to look inside it.

"There are more pieces with the same vibrations in there. I have no way of knowing who created them, but that one is a replica of a rather famous piece." Aaron rummaged in the box and pulled out a pot of a similar color, flipping it over to show the signature. "This is a weed pot made by the same hand. Whoever did this planned to sell it as a genuine R. Williams. I read up on the Hillvale potters and know Williams died in the 80s, but I'd say from the feel of this that it was made much more recently. I'd have to do some research to see who owns the original."

Teddy looked at Kurt, who was studying her with concern. "Do you think. . . ?"

"Cousin Thalia's potter husband?" he finished for her. "We have no way of knowing, do we?"

"That takes some of the fun out of this, doesn't it?" The risotto wasn't sitting so well as she studied the fraudulent pieces her parents may have received from Lonnie for something of value. The family home? Surely not. "I think I better check on Syd."

Kurt helped her stand. "Aaron, you have the keys? Want to lock up?"

The antique dealer eyed him warily. "You're trusting me to a warehouse full of valuable ceramics with no inventory list or invoice backup?"

Teddy took Kurt's arm. "Trust is more important than material things. If we can't trust each other, where would we turn?"

"That's how you get tricked by criminals like Lonnie and your ex," Kurt said with a hint of grimness. "But if Walker is letting Aaron walk around free, I'm guessing he has nothing on him." He turned back to Aaron. "These belong to Teddy, not me. She gets final say."

Teddy stood on her toes and kissed his cheek. "Thank you. I'll work on providing honesty stones for everyone in town, okay?"

He chuckled, nodded at Aaron, and led her into the moonlit night.

Not until they arrived at the shop and saw the front door wide open did she have reason to feel fear.

TWENTY-SIX

July 1: evening

THE DOG'S SHARP BARKS RAISED THE HAIRS ON THE BACK OF KURT'S NECK. In his experience, lazy Prince Hairy only barked with that much energy when seriously disturbed. Kurt gripped Teddy's arm to prevent her from entering the shop's open door.

The terrified shouts of the kids halted any illusion of holding her back. She tore from his hands and ran into the shop, grabbing the wooden walking stick by the door.

She wasn't bigger than a feather, and she thought she could beat a brute with a tree branch?

"Teddy, no!" Keeping his voice low, Kurt caught up with her and hauled her from her feet. "Call Walker first."

While she wiggled and squirmed in his arms, he headed for the landline on the counter. Above, the dog yipped and the kids screamed frantically. Syd's silence was ominous.

Swinging her stick until his grip loosened, Teddy wriggled out of his grasp and headed straight for the stairs. "My sister and her kids are up there. I have every right—"

An unfamiliar male voice rang out from above. "Who's there?

Don't come any closer. This is a police matter." The voice sounded more drunk than authoritative.

"Assbutt," Teddy spit out in a whisper. "I'm going to *kill* him."

"Not if he kills you first." Giving up on the phone for the moment, Kurt covered her mouth with his hand and shouted back. "I'm the landlord here. I have a right to protect my property."

Teddy bit him but he ignored the pain.

"He hurt mama," Mia cried with a broken sob that nearly had *him* running up the stairs.

He ground his molars and stifled the urge. He didn't need the psychopath killing both sisters. He had to keep Teddy safe.

"She's armed and dangerous. Back off, let me handle this." Ashbuth's words slurred but he still spoke with officiousness.

Yeah, right, like that was happening. "Call Walker," Kurt repeated in a whisper, pushing Teddy toward the phone.

She jammed her elbow into his solar plexus and raised her stick again. He was about to grab a thicker staff when a wind whirled through the room. Teddy froze.

"Thalia, and she's furious," she whispered in terror. "Warn Syd to stay low."

Syd could be dead or unconscious, but Kurt was relieved that she understood the desperate drunk above would respond more readily to a male voice.

"Mrs. Bennet," he called, trying to sound like a landlord, "If you can hear me, explain to your visitor about the dangerous staircase. The wind is picking up, and you need to take cover." That was the best warning he could improvise without saying *watch for ghosts* and losing all credibility.

Teddy glared but kept quiet. She picked up the phone and punched in an apparently pre-programmed number for Walker. 911 was useless for swift action this far up the mountain.

Feeling entirely out of his league facing an armed cop with nothing but a wooden stick, Kurt aimed for the whistling staircase. At least this time he was prepared for the blow that had knocked him down earlier. He refused to call it a ghost.

"What's wrong with the stairs?" the cop called down.

"Wind pushes the treads," Kurt said—a ridiculous explanation, but the cop had presumably worked up his courage with alcohol and didn't question. "Is Mrs. Bennet under arrest? We don't have social services up here. Someone needs to take the children."

Gripping the thick staff on both ends, he eased up the stairway with his back to the wall. The kids wept. The dog yipped, then growled ferociously.

"*Get off me*, you mangy mutt," Ashbuth shouted.

Go Prince, Kurt thought as he edged into the whirling wind. He could easily understand why Teddy called the ghost angry. This was one damned violent breeze. "Got a problem?" he called up, trying to sound sympathetic and not frighten the brute. It was almost like placating an angry guest. "I'll come up and get the hound. He's not supposed to be in here."

A shot fired. The children wailed. The dog howled in pain. Like a furious fairy, Teddy materialized, wielding her staff again. The crystal in it gleamed like a beacon, and she practically threw off sparks in the darkness.

Kurt could almost believe she caused the whirlwind.

A large male staggered to the top of the stairs, shaking his leg and trying to aim at the animal gripping his trousers without blowing off his own foot with his unsteady hand. "Get this damned hound off me!"

"Go Prince," Teddy whispered, echoing Kurt's earlier thought as she edged up behind him.

Kurt reached back to hold her in place—and felt her freeze.

"Downstairs," she murmured urgently. "Now!" She caught his hand and yanked him back.

Stumbling, Kurt did as told. At the top of the stairs, the cop cursed and tried to aim his gun at the dog again. The intense air pressure in the stairwell multiplied. Just as Kurt nearly fell on top of Teddy in the shop, the wind howled maniacally.

The uniformed cop abruptly flew face-first down the stairs, shrieking all the way. Kurt winced as Ashbuth slammed into the floor at their feet. That had to be good for a busted nose, at the least. From the bent angle of the cop's knee, he'd say Ashbuth wouldn't be up and running soon.

"Yay, Thalia!" Teddy cried, no longer hiding her presence. "Syd, Syd, can you hear me?"

She slammed her toe into the groaning cop's ribs and held her stick ready. "Break any bones, Assbutt? How does it feel?"

Apparently too drunk to notice bones, the cop shook his shaved head and attempted to turn over. That's when Kurt noticed the gun still in his hand.

He flung Teddy behind him, toward the front door. "Get Walker, *now.*"

Before Teddy could go anywhere, Syd materialized at the top of the stairs. The wind whipped up again, and she sounded hollow. "I'm here, and this time, *I'll kill him.*"

"That's Thalia speaking," Teddy murmured in horror. As Syd raised her arms, Teddy screamed, "Syd, no! Put the gun away!"

Drunk or not, the cop on the floor acted reflexively, flipping over with a groan and aiming his weapon.

Before Kurt could react, Teddy screamed "Freeze!" and held up her stick like a magic wand. The red crystal glowed eerily.

A bright light abruptly flashed like a meteor across a moon-dark sky, and—*the cop froze.*

Syd didn't. She stepped down the stairs like one possessed, raising her small pistol in a firing position.

Too shocked to do more than react, Kurt dashed up the stairs and yanked Syd's gun arm up so the bullet harmlessly hit the ceiling. He ripped the weapon out of her limp fist.

Realizing that the wind had blessedly frozen with Teddy's command—or Syd's possession?—Kurt turned and aimed at the man on the floor. At least the gun was solid and real, unlike whatever else in hell was happening here. "I'm considered an expert marksman. I'd recommend that you lower your weapon."

The cop gazed stupidly at his raised gun but didn't move. Maybe he was concussed. That didn't explain Syd's behavior. How in hell did he logically act in an illogical situation?

Maybe concussions caused delusions and hallucinations, and *Kurt* was suffering from his earlier one. Whatever the hell was happening, he couldn't just stupidly stand here while Teddy waved a wand at an armed cop. Kurt stepped down and with one hand, yanked the cop's gun away as one would take a toy from a toddler.

With the danger gone, Teddy seemed to melt into herself, collapsing on the floor with her no-longer glowing staff.

He wanted to rush to help her, but he had two maniacs and apparently a ghost on his hands. At the bottom of the stairs, Ashbuth attempted to sit up but grabbed his leg and cursed. Weaponless, Syd tried to shove past Kurt, presumably to kill her ex with nothing more than fury. Kurt stood between them with a pistol in one hand and a Glock in the other, desperate to go to Teddy but unable to let down his guard.

The wind picked up energy again.

To his relief, Walker entered the open shop door with his weapon raised. At sight of Kurt's two-handed weaponry, the chief raised his eyebrows. "Landlord, huh? Raised in the wild, wild west?"

"Shut up and cuff the bastard," Kurt replied with a growl of impatience.

"Syd?" Teddy called carefully. "Syd, you okay?"

And just like that, the wind stopped, and Syd sat down and cried.

GRATEFULLY, TEDDY TOOK KURT'S HAND AND LET HIM HELP HER OFF THE floor. She could barely stand.

Had she really frozen Assbutt or dreamed it?

She tried to wrestle to keep her staff, but she was too weak to resist his manhandling. She let him set the staff aside, while she gripped his arm to steady herself.

Syd. She needed to go to Syd. But her sister was no longer on the stairs. How had that happened?

Teddy frantically gazed around, finding Syd on the other side of a groaning Assbutt. Walker was backing her sister into the kitchen, away from the handcuffed prisoner on the floor. When had he been handcuffed?

"You need to see to the Goths," Kurt murmured, holding her up while she wobbled. "Walker has to question your sister."

That got her going. Stumbling, Teddy caught the wall of the stairwell and stepped over a moaning, Assbutt. His leg, at the very least, looked broken. Pity it hadn't been his neck.

"I'd assumed Thalia died being pushed downstairs," she mused, trying to steady her spinning head before she climbed up. "This is where her rage is centered. But neither you nor Asshole broke your necks."

"I wasn't very far up. And Syd's ex was too drunk to do more than flop. It's the reason drunks always walk away from accidents." Kurt held her steady.

Glancing up the stairwell, Teddy decided Thalia had settled down. Shaking off Kurt, she made her way up the stairs to Syd's kids. Mia and Jeb fell into her arms, nearly knocking her over again.

Kneeling, she rocked them while they wept, vowing to find protective stones to hang around their necks so they never had to suffer such a scene ever, *ever* again.

After some bearded man she didn't know climbed the stairs to carry a bleeding Prince out, she helped the kids downstairs to reassure them that Syd was all right.

"Lock him up this time," Syd was screaming hysterically as they came downstairs. *"Why didn't they keep him locked up?"*

Walker looked uncomfortable at the hysteria. "He probably told the judge it was justified, that you were waving a gun at him, like this time. It's no excuse for what he did, but it happens."

"I didn't own a gun then," she cried. *"Nothing* justifies what he did to me. He put me in the hospital!"

Teddy wanted to take the kids back out again, but they ran to their mother. Becoming aware of their presence, Syd instantly wiped her eyes to hug them.

"No, ma'am," Walker said grimly. "Nothing justifies anything he's done, I agree. But his fellows know him, and they don't know you and unfortunately, it happens. It won't this time. Nothing excuses him stalking you. He'll go away for a long time. I'll personally see to that."

"Why the hell don't men just walk away when we say no?" Teddy demanded, recovering from her odd weakness. "When will they realize they don't get to tell us what we think or do?"

"All men aren't bullies," Kurt protested from where he leaned against the door jamb, landline phone in hand as he poked numbers into it from memory.

Rationality didn't satisfy her rage, even though she knew he was right. Kurt had stepped back every time she'd told him no. Shutting up, Teddy heated milk for the kids as half the town began streaming in. Samantha arrived and set herself as guard at the door, allowing in only those she judged worthy in no logical order Teddy could discern.

The wiry older woman she remembered as a nurse arrived to look after Syd's injuries. From the report Syd was giving Walker, Teddy gathered Ashbuth had knocked her sister around, then punched her unconscious. The nurse checked her for concussion, promised there were no broken bones, and let the children continue to cling to their mother.

Cass arrived, of course, as did Mayor Surfer Dude. Teddy lost track as the Lucys began talking about another exorcism. She hoped Thalia had got enough revenge and would just go away.

Through all the commotion and hysteria, Teddy was aware of Kurt standing guard over the prisoner, making calls, talking to Walker and Monty, seeing that everyone had what they needed. He had been her rock when she needed one, but now he was distancing himself. He managed the scene just as if this were his resort, and he was dealing with recalcitrant guests—leaving her to the emotional drama of the children and her sister.

She wanted to fall into his arms and weep, feel his strong arms holding her up, his reassuring voice steadying her. She wanted him to explain what had just happened here. She wanted him to *accept* what had just happened. But he was blatantly rejecting the drama, the mystery, the emotion—and her—in favor of dealing with logistics.

She understood his reaction, she really did. She didn't grasp what had just happened entirely herself. Kurt was her hero—wielding two guns and keeping Syd safe.

But when Monty and Walker followed the medics out to the ambulance with the prisoner, leaving only the Lucys behind, Kurt went with them.

Not a reassuring hug, a brief kiss, a promising word—he just left.

She really should have put an honesty stone in his ring. At least then she might know what he was really thinking.

"Can the exorcism wait?" Teddy wearily asked Sam. "The kids need to be in bed and Syd probably needs a good hot toddy more than ghostly wails."

Samantha nodded sympathetically and began the task of rounding up the overeager Lucys. With Cass's aid, she ushered them out after they'd liberally distributed protective herbs in every corner.

"I'd rather have my gun," Syd muttered under her breath as the last candle was blown out.

Teddy handed her a walking stick. "Try this. It works miracles." And maybe Thalia couldn't inhabit sticks, but she didn't know if Syd remembered being possessed. Her sister would run screaming down the mountain if she did.

Syd had almost killed a man.

Teddy had done something weird with a glowing walking stick that had frozen a violent drunk.

They'd held their ground, fought back, and defeated Ashbuth. They'd accomplished what they hadn't been able to do before they arrived in Hillvale.

She hugged Syd and whispered reassuringly, "We can do anything, with a little help from our friends."

TWENTY-SEVEN

KURT SIGNED THE LAST CHECK, INITIALED THE FINANCIAL STATEMENT HIS secretary had prepared, and checked the time. His mother was blessedly not speaking to him after he'd blown off Kylie last night. His restaurant staff reported his former fiancée and her father had left after dinner instead of staying. All good. After last night's Horror in Hillvale performance, he might have pulled a gun on them and ordered them out—and his mother too.

He felt as if ants were crawling under his skin. He couldn't sit still. He'd barely slept. He tried to tell himself it was because he wasn't accustomed to violence and the kind of behavior one expected from uncivilized scum.

But he knew what his father had done to the people of Hillvale. Civilized violence was quieter but equally cruel.

Which left him wallowing in uncertainty—which he definitely wasn't used to. Allowing Teddy to get close had cracked the safe walls he'd built these past years—walls that had confined him as much as shielded him.

He wanted to know how the art galleries progressed. He wanted to finish stripping the rainbow mural. He'd found Lance's painted image riding one of the unicorns yesterday. Who else might be under that green acrylic?

He wanted to know if Teddy and her sister were all right, to see how they were handling last night's episode, to help them with the pottery. . . He wanted to know what the hell had happened last night.

He wanted to see Teddy.

That was the thought holding him back. He'd left her to the madness last night, walked out on her in an effort of self-preservation, to protect the civilized, rational man he'd thought himself.

Right now, he wasn't certain that man, the man who wanted to rebuild the town to escape his mother, was worth preserving.

The man who had accepted the madness of ghosts, possession, and magic wands had saved two women, two children, and a dog.

Did he want to be the kind of man who accepted lunacy over practicality?

He studied the ring Teddy had given him. It suited him in ways he couldn't explain—natural elements, elegant, with a touch of gold for promise. Is that how she saw him? Did he have any future as anything except a money-making automaton?

With that uncomfortable thought, he returned to his cabin, changed into jeans, and drove into town to set up in the ice cream parlor. Working with his hands returned him to a time when he'd been happy. Scraping paint didn't involve emotional drama, or any talking at all. He almost whistled as he worked.

He finished uncovering his Uncle Lance's face, then worked on the area surrounding it. His uncle had painted himself as a white knight, sitting on a pink unicorn—with a woman at his back, clinging to his waist.

The woman had long blond hair blowing in the wind and a vague resemblance to the now black-haired death goddess—Valdis.

Shit. So much for no emotional drama. Teddy had been right. Lance and Valdis had a history, one that showed them happier than they were today. *History.* Maybe he really needed to know more about the town's past, about the Lucys and the Nulls, and the reason they were at odds.

Putting down his scraper, he walked over to the café for coffee. The

place was packed, standing room only, and he belatedly realized it was
the lunch hour. Samantha handed him a mug of coffee, shrugged, and
returned to taking a customer's money at the register.

The other customers pretended he didn't exist. He liked it that way,
didn't he? He lifted the cup to indicate he'd return it and walked out.

Carefully avoiding Teddy's crystal shop at the town entrance, Kurt
walked in the opposite direction, toward the old meeting house where
Lance was setting up his gallery. Maybe he ought to talk to his uncle
for a little background of the town.

One of the lodge's electricians was installing lighting on the tall
ceiling of the old hall. Kurt didn't remember giving permission for
that, but he supposed the lodge could donate the time toward a cause
that would increase tourism. *There* was the practical Kurt he knew.

Syd was directing the hanging of Lance's artwork and the direction
of the lighting. Deciding not to interrupt, Kurt backed out past a
couple of tourists peering inside.

He crossed the street to City Hall to see what Monty was doing.
The front office was a thousand percent improved, with the bright
white walls now lined with colorful oils and the newly cleaned
windows allowing in enough light to gleam on recently waxed floors.
From the back, he could hear his brother yelling at someone.
Oh well. . .

He could go back to the rainbow mural, but perversely, he strolled
around to the warehouse behind Aaron's antique shop.

He didn't know if it was in relief or disappointment that he found
only Aaron and Walker inside. They both looked up and waved
him over.

"I've been researching these fraudulent pots," Aaron said without
preliminaries, making Kurt feel right at home. He liked a man who
stuck to business. "I've contacted a few experts in the field. They agree
there have been a few excellent reproductions that have seeped into
the market. I have someone knowledgeable coming in to examine the
Baker cache."

"Teddy e-mailed her parents to ask about the expensive pieces and
the fakes," Walker said, handing Kurt one of the ugly orange and green
plates.

"If these things are old, the perpetrator could be dead by now,"

Kurt pointed out, examining the signature on the back. "Is there any reason we need to be concerned?"

"If we inadvertently sold fraudulent pieces, yes," Aaron said. "Reputation is everything in this business. I can't always tell the age of these pieces. I've sorted out the ones I've judged as *wrong*, but that doesn't mean they're fake. Maybe when he created that thing you're holding, Peterson thought of himself as an evil criminal for foisting ugliness on an ignorant public. I could be reading the vibrations wrong, and he really did make these."

Okay, that wasn't quite as sensible as Kurt had hoped. "He ought to at least have been ashamed for creating *this*." Kurt stayed away from the *wrongness* issue and handed back the orange and green plate. "Are there any pieces we need to start displaying? The long holiday weekend would be a great time for a soft open, but that's only a couple of days away."

"If we just display and don't sell, we could whet a lot of interest," Aaron agreed. He turned to Walker. "Is Syd okay? Should I talk to her about where things should go?"

"She's with Lance, hanging lights," Kurt informed them, happy to have something useful to contribute.

"Ashbuth is behind bars and screaming for his lawyer," Walker added. "I've talked to the D.A. He's not letting the bastard out. Not sure Syd entirely believes it after her last experience. It will take time before she trusts again, but it's good to know she feels safe enough to stay."

Aaron nodded sympathetically. "We'll need to keep her busy, make her feel safe again. The expert I'm bringing in might interest her if she has strong opinions about fraud."

Walker turned back to Kurt. "Thanks for your help last night. The way you slung those guns around, I could make you a deputy."

Kurt shrugged uncomfortably. "We learned guns from our father, played on the rifle team for a while. Living out here where there was no law, it was necessary."

Walker nodded. "As long as you're licensed. Syd's gun wasn't. That's going to take a little finessing. She had no business handling that thing. She could have shot the kids."

Which flung Kurt right back to the impossible scene he was trying to forget and felt like a fool bringing up. Gritting his teeth, he looked for the politically correct way to say Syd appeared to have been possessed by a ghost. He was an expert at diplomacy these days. "I'm not sure she was herself last night. For all we know, their ghost had the gun hidden away."

Aaron looked intrigued.

Walker frowned. "The sheriff won't buy ghosts, but he might buy that the gun had been there, left by a previous tenant. Good thinking. Explaining Hillvale to a jury just isn't worth the effort. I'm glad you're on board." Amazingly perceptive for a cop, Walker left for his rounds.

"I'm *surprised* you're on board," Aaron said. "Teddy getting to you?"

Kurt ran his hand through his hair, realized he hadn't gone to the city recently for a cut, and tried to sort out an answer he didn't have. "If I'd been Syd, I'd have shot Ashbuth on sight. She didn't. Let's just say she ought to get credit for that."

"There's still a dangerous entity in that house," Aaron reminded him. "And a possible murderer still out there. Are you sure you don't want to head back to the lodge and stay out of this?"

"Take your pot and stuff it." Kurt walked out, berating himself for getting involved in Lucy business. But Aaron was right, and he couldn't leave Teddy and the kids in that psycho house any longer, regardless of whether he believed in ghosts or not.

Teddy admired her periwinkle door and the Teddy's Treasure Trove sign swinging over it. Syd had lined the purple letters with a sparkly silver that caught the sun. The rain had never arrived, and the day promised to be beautiful, so she left the door open. She was ready for business.

Well, she wasn't really, but it had seemed to make sense when they'd discussed it this morning. They had to move forward. They had work to do. Syd wanted to go home, to put the kids in their own beds, but they'd felt safer waiting together to see what happened with Ashbuth.

Teddy was glad of the reprieve. She didn't know how she would handle living here all alone, with Kurt ignoring her. She'd tried calling him several times this morning, but he'd never returned the calls. She could scarcely blame him after all the craziness last night. If she were a Null, she'd run far and fast in the wake of that insanity.

She had to admire a man who could handle the horrid situation with such assurance and pragmatism, but damn, it had hurt when he'd walked out, leaving her bleeding from the soul. A shadow crossed the open door way and she looked up.

Speak of the devil. . .

Damn but he was a good-looking devil. As Kurt stopped in the open doorway, the sun caught on his dark hair, highlighting the streaks of mahogany that matched his eyes. She dropped her gaze to his ring. He was still wearing it. He *wasn't* wearing his suit, which made her foolish heart pound a little harder. She liked the jeans on him—they made him more human. A devil in blue jeans?

Still, he'd hurt her pretty badly when he'd abandoned her. Given her luck with men, she needed to pay more attention to how they treated her. She continued polishing the stone she was working on and waited for him to speak.

"I saw your sister helping Lance," he said hesitantly. "How is she holding up?"

"She'd be better if she could have shot off the bastard's dick. She'll never be completely all right. Neither will the kids. Before he put her in the hospital, he *raped* her. These things sink deep into the psyche and cause nightmares for a lifetime. But she's strong. She'll keep going. It just makes me angry that women have to suffer like that in this day and age." Teddy strung the stone bead on the fine chain she'd been working on.

"This house is as dangerous as your rogue cop." He entered and studied Thalia's oils on the wall.

"Did you notice that the eyes on Daisy's guardians were gleaming last night? I'd blocked that until this morning, when I saw one blinking out." She threw that into the universe to keep him off balance, to build up the defensive shield she needed against whatever weapon he meant to turn against her.

"The crystal in your stick glowed red," he countered. He shrugged and moved on to examine the other paintings Syd had chosen for their walls. "That doesn't make this place any less dangerous. Did the Lucys smoke out any ghosts this morning?"

"They tried. Mia told them the lady was sorry. I think that means Thalia is still here, although I'm a little unclear as to what she's sorry about—knocking Ashbuth down or not killing him when she did." She was trying to adapt to the notion of a six-year-old medium, but it didn't sit well. Syd might be right to take the kids home. But she refused to give him additional ammunition for that *dangerous house* business.

Kurt didn't call her on the ghostly aspect but continued as if they were discussing dinner plans. "How's Prince Hairy? Orval's a retired vet. We use him sometimes at the stable."

"The bearded mountain man? Cool. He says Hairy just has a flesh wound, but he wanted to make certain it didn't get infected. Who knew the old dog had it in him?" She'd told Tullah to look for a warm doggie bed fit for a prince. She'd have to start respecting the lazy lump.

Kurt brushed off the dog topic to stay focused on what he'd come in here for. "You shouldn't be here if Lonnie decides to take a quick visit to the old hometown," he warned, studying the paintings and not her. "In fact, I think we need to raze this whole building so he runs as far in the other direction as he can."

"Don't be absurd." Teddy's stomach roiled—because she almost agreed with him as much as she wanted to argue. "My lawyer says I have a strong case. You can't just pull the house down around my ears. We have a contract."

They'd had stunning sex in that upstairs bathroom. It should be immortalized, not dismantled. But Kurt lacked a soul, she decided. Maybe that was the problem with Nulls.

He ran his hand through his hair and finally turned to look at her through haunted eyes. "I just don't know if I can *do* this. I've spent years trying to salvage some small part of me. . ." Obviously uncomfortable, he picked up one of Harvey's walking sticks and toyed with it. "I think I've built walls inside when I couldn't build them outside."

Even if he didn't accept that the bond between them had opened a door in his wall, she could still read him as clearly as if he wrote a letter in the air. "You've built a barricade against emotion to prevent your mother from sucking you dry. I get that. I really do. And me and my family and our ghosts are whirlwinds of emotion." She stopped and thought about that. "Well, I've seen worse families. This is just a bad month for us."

He laughed curtly. "Got that. But you deserve someone who can offer. . . what I don't seem to have."

Teddy relaxed infinitesimally. "Oh, you have it, all right. It's just bottled up all tight. One of these days, you'll explode if you don't find some way of letting off steam." Thinking of their night together, she hid a grin. "You do steam just fine."

That boldness was rewarded with a smoldering glare. "Even I know sex isn't emotion."

"It's passion. It's a start. You were definitely not just going through the mechanics. You're not a robot, and you need to start figuring out how to tear down the emotional wall, instead of physical ones. If you need to build houses to do so, then build houses. Just don't start with mine." She rubbed the stone a little too hard and it leaped from her hand to roll across the floor.

He captured it and brought it over to her. "Is this another magic stone?"

"I have no idea if stones are magic, mind you. I'm experimenting. But the crystal in my staff damned well did something weird last night." She waited expectantly. She'd wanted to talk about this all morning.

"It glowed red and he froze," Kurt said flatly, understanding her need for confirmation. "Ashbuth froze as if paralyzed simply because you told him to do so. I don't understand the psychology. Or the physics, if it comes to that."

She nodded. "That's okay. I just wanted to make sure I didn't imagine it. I kind of got fuzzy after that."

"You were out of it," he said, the harshness of his tone reflecting his fear. "I was afraid you'd fried your brain, but we had to deal with Ashbuth and your sister, and I was terrified that you'd be gone before I could reach you."

"You terrified yourself," she nodded, feeling his fear as he spoke. "Logically, you knew I was fine, and you should just go about your business. Emotion isn't logical. You freaked."

He considered that. "Yeah, I freaked big time all around. And that's supposed to be a good thing?"

"Considering how little experience you have in dealing with freaking, you handled yourself pretty well. And then you froze up like a Popsicle. It's the Popsicle I worry about. The freak is cool. Is the café packed? I'm about to starve."

She had to forgive him. A proud man like Kurt would never grovel, but he had come close enough to suit her for the moment. Just his wearing jeans instead of a suit and tie spoke volumes. She looked up at him expectantly. They were either on the same page or had to go their separate ways. She felt a painful twinge at the thought of the latter, but at least she hadn't lost a boxful of gems this time.

"The freak is cool?" he asked in wonder, before holding out his hand. "Are you willing to have lunch with a freak who might turn into a Popsicle?"

She gifted him with a blazing smile. "We might be able to work with this new self-awareness."

Just to prove he was the same old Kurt, he asked, "Will your inventory be safe if we go out?"

She set aside her work and laughed at his soul-deep Nullness. "The gems are in the safe. If anyone steals my magic rocks, they'll be really sorry. What do you think Dinah has on the menu today?"

"I suspect if she had roasted toads, we'd eat them. The whole town is ensorcelled, isn't it?" He took her hand and helped her down from her stool.

His hand was firm and his grip was strong, and Teddy had a feeling she never wanted to let go. She leaned in and kissed his cheek. "You can be the sleeping prince and your mother the wicked witch. Let's go find the poison apple."

He swung her into his arms and covered her mouth with his, and she forgot about witches and apples and just let him sweep her up in all that lovely whirling emotion he kept so repressed.

She'd worry about ghosts and murderers another day.

SAMANTHA

SAMANTHA'S EYES WIDENED AS WALKER ENTERED IN THE COMPANY OF A diminutive older woman wearing a skirt, jacket, and heels that reflected discreet wealth. Chin lifted in hauteur, her lovely moon-shaped face and hooded eyes in perfect enigmatic composure, black hair streaked with an imperial silver, she could only be Walker's mother.

Sam swallowed hard and attempted a welcoming smile. She wasn't certain she was successful. From the tales Walker had told, Jia Walker was a force of nature and a holy terror. She'd raised him as a single mother after his father had disappeared. She had to have a backbone like steel to turn her son's suppressed anger down productive paths.

The café was still filled to overflowing. Sam couldn't just pull off her apron and hide. Poking Mariah and indicating the newcomer, she handed over the coffeepot and abandoned the counter to kiss Walker. There, let's see what his mother thought about a tall, skinny wild-haired blond woman kissing her gorgeous son.

Walker wrapped a possessive arm around Sam's waist. "Mom, this is Sam, the scientist I told you about."

Sam hid a snigger. She had a master's degree, all right, but that *scientist* bit was just score one in gamesmanship. The best she'd managed in her short career was teacher.

"Sam, I'd like you to meet my mother, Jia Walker. She's come for the art show."

"A scientist is smarter than that, my thick-headed son. She knows I have come to meet the woman who has called you away from your home and your work." Jia looked Sam up and down. "You can do better than this."

Walker's embrace tightened and Sam nearly choked on words that wouldn't come out. Before either of them could speak, his mother gestured disparagingly at the *café*.

She was saying *Sam* could do better than the café, not that Walker can do better than her? That Jia Walker had immediately set to changing *her* life spun Sam's thoughts around.

"I can, and I will do better," Sam said, as long as they were being blunt. "But right now, feeling part of the community is what I need. When I know what the community needs, I will give back."

"And you will hold my son here, away from his ghosts?"

Sam didn't even try to puzzle whether that was a good or bad direction from Jia's perspective—it was the *correct* interpretation, for now. "Walker knows what he wants and will do what he needs to do. Life is a puzzle we work one day at a time."

Jia's straight lips bowed upward. "You were raised properly, as my son says. You will make him understand *chi*?"

A booth opened up and Sam led them toward it. "I am still learning myself. We could use a good teacher up here. The energy is very strong."

"I will send someone," Jia said with a firm nod. "I know people."

Walker rolled his eyes, but he kissed Sam before he let her go and slid into the booth across from his mother. "Bring us whatever Dinah recommends today."

Sam beamed. "Good choice."

Kurt and Teddy entered, looking rumpled and satisfied. For half a second, Sam considered sitting them down with Walker and his mother, but lovers needed space to find themselves. The impetuous, magical jeweler and the stiff-necked Null made an odd pair, but they radiated positive energy, which should be encouraged. Another booth opened, and she gestured them toward it.

Cass had other ideas. Tall and regal, she followed the couple and took a seat beside Teddy, across from her nephew, without asking.

Uh-oh. Sam hurried back to the counter to warn Dinah of impending explosions.

TWENTY-EIGHT

STILL LIGHT-HEADED FROM SHOWING TEDDY HOW MUCH PASSION—OR steam—he possessed, Kurt had to snap his mouth closed when Cass joined them in the diner booth.

Teddy, too, seemed unusually speechless. After their earlier make-out session, her tousled auburn hair curled in wisps around her face. He longed to push that red silk behind her ears.

Cass's presence froze them almost as well as Teddy's wand had frozen Ashbuth.

Looking like a prim professor with her silver hair pinned close to her head, Cass swung the first blow. "If you continue leaving yourself open like this, Carmel will suck you dry just as she did Lance and Geoffrey. You'll need to leave town."

Kurt opened his mouth to defend his mother, but nothing came out. Cass was right, although she was probably talking in metaphysical terms, and Kurt didn't think the supernatural described his mother's temperament as well as a good psychologist could.

Teddy held up her hand, and he bit his tongue before speaking any part of that thought. She sent him a deprecating grin that kept his temper on simmer. Who knew he had a temper? It felt pretty satisfying to let himself feel the *steam*.

"If the lodge fails, the town fails," Teddy said sensibly. "Kurt has a duty to Hillvale."

Cass tapped her long bony fingers on the table. "Granted. But if he's letting down his barriers, he'll have to do it from a safer distance."

"Wait a minute." Kurt thought his head might gyrate off its axis. "After all these years, *you want to look after me*? I think I may be a little too old for that."

Cass gave him a condescending look. "In spiritual years, you're an infant. I do not interfere in Null business, and your family made it clear they didn't want me interfering in yours, but Teddy is one of us. If the two of you are a pair, then you become my concern."

"That's making a whopping lot of assumptions. Let's just skip past all that and go right to what you came to say," Teddy suggested.

He loved the way she cut to the chase in a very un-Lucy-like manner. Kurt had a feeling most people didn't talk to his aunt that way.

Cass looked miffed, but she stiffly soldiered on. "Once we remove Thalia from the shop, the energy there should be safer for you. It's closer to the vortex and further from the lodge's negativity. The evil at the resort drains resistance."

If he was translating Cass's meandering thoughts correctly—the aunt who had barely spoken to him since birth wanted him to move in with Teddy? Kurt would love to hold his tongue and let Teddy deal with Lucy weirdness, but he had a few things he'd like to make clear. "First of all, Teddy might have something to say about what happens to her shop. And if you mean I need to move out of the lodge, I'd prefer to keep the amenities to which I'm accustomed. That means I need to build new houses, not move in with Teddy."

Under the table, Teddy punched his thigh for the *new house* crack, but she maintained solidarity with his position by staying silent.

Cass frowned. Instead of arguing, she changed the subject. "I've enlarged the photos of Thalia's writing. If Walker's people can't translate it, someone has to."

That wasn't his bailiwick. Enjoying the freedom of handing the crazy to Teddy, Kurt let her pick up the thread. She was so enthralled by Cass that she didn't even notice when Sam put an over-sized bowl in front of them. Apparently, fresh tomatoes, mozzarella balls, and barbecued shrimp instead of ham and *bleu* cheese were Dinah's spin on a chef salad.

"Have you figured out more?" Teddy asked eagerly. "Do you know Thalia's story?"

"I enhanced the earlier, more faded piece," Cass said stiffly. "Your mother's cousin met Lucinda Malcolm, as did your parents, when Lucinda stayed with your grandparents on her Hillvale visit."

"*Lucinda Malcolm* stayed in my shop?" Teddy asked excitedly.

"That was what, fifty years ago?" Kurt had to interject. Not that he had a clue who or what Lucinda Malcolm was other than another artist. "Thalia and Teddy's parents had to have been children then."

"Senior citizens are not dinosaurs," Cass said in reprimand. "I was a teenager in the city, learning from professionals at the time. Thalia may have been younger, but she was certainly old enough to help Lucinda mix her paints. According to her unorthodox journal, Thalia knew Lucinda gave Teddy's grandparents a compendium on crystals that had belonged to her family. And Thalia was old enough to steal it. That confession was her first entry."

"A compendium?" Teddy's topaz eyes lit with that inner glow Kurt thought might be what she explained as *opening her Inner Monitor*. Was she studying Cass?

And did he believe she could actually read how others felt? That ought to scare the shit out of him. Oddly, it didn't. Empathy had a sound neurological and psychological basis.

"Thalia also confesses that she knew Lucinda had brought the triptych panels to present to Lars, as a gift to the community. He had been the one to identify Hillvale, even though Lucinda's work showed a twenty-first century version they could scarcely recognize back then. Thalia didn't understand their value as a child and hadn't known where the panels went until they were found in the building you had cleaned up for your City Hall."

"We decided to use that building the day we came to town, the one in the triptych," Kurt said in disbelief. "We hired locals to clean out the debris. Anyone could have hauled them off."

"So the panels belong to the town," Teddy exclaimed in excitement. "Surely Thalia's journal is enough proof?"

As the women launched into a discussion that could only be speculation, Kurt listened and stayed out of it—until Teddy abruptly flinched. She cast a glance over her shoulder as if struck by a cold breeze. Since it was sunny and warm, Kurt hadn't even noticed the door opening. He and Cass checked the entrance at the same time.

The lunch crowd had started to thin so it was easy to notice the stranger. His bronzed face was wrinkled from sun, and his long, grizzled mustache was stained from smoke. He wore his charcoal-gray hair pulled back with twine. He'd look the part of homeless vagrant if it weren't for the gold watch, and the designer jeans and sandals.

"*Evil*," whispered Teddy and Cass at the same time.

Kurt got cold chills from the way they said it. Ominously, the café's chatter lessened. Kurt glanced around, noticing only a few tourists remained. The majority of the customers seemed to be Lucys lingering over their coffee and Dinah's decadent desserts—or watching Cass. One by one, they turned to study the newcomer with alarm, as if he'd shouted *Fire*.

Apparently as Null as Kurt, the stranger didn't appear to notice. He started for the half-empty counter, then stopped at the enlarged photograph of the triptych's center panel. "Cool, man, where did this come from? That's my old woodie."

That was the panel that had covered the skeleton—the one showing Lonnie Thompson packing up and presumably leaving town—*in a woodie wagon*.

From the booth behind Kurt, Walker spoke up. "That's an awesome car. What did you do with it?"

Thank God there was another sensible head still here.

Walker was wearing casual clothes, not his cop uniform. No guns were likely to be brought to play if this stranger took a turn for *evil*. But Kurt looked around for weapons, just in case—and noticed the Lucys were all gripping their walking sticks.

"The old lady made me trade it in for a Beamer. Is that photo part of the art show I heard about?" The stranger took a stool at the counter and picked up a plastic menu Mariah pushed toward him.

His old lady? *Thalia*? Or was this not Lonnie?

"Hadn't thought of it that way," the waitress said in a deceptively pleasant voice. "Just old photos to celebrate our town history."

"Yeah, heard you folks had some history. The old lady said something about a lawsuit?"

Kurt held Teddy's hand against the table when she tried to ball it up. The only outsider who knew about the imaginary lawsuit was Lonnie Thompson. Kurt tried to find this grizzled old fellow in the painting that depicted the town ten years ago. Lonnie hadn't aged well, but the weak chin and rounded shoulders were the same.

Figuring Walker needed to play this close, Kurt got up to take the offensive position. He sat on the stool next to the fiend who may have burned his wife's body in a kiln, the criminal who had sold Teddy's house out from under her. "Who's your old lady? Did she live up here ten years ago?"

Lonnie squinted at him. "Yeah, bunch of us did. What's it to you?"

Hating having every eye on him, Kurt gritted his teeth and beamed his best resort-manager smile. "My father thought he owned the town. He robbed a lot of people. The courts didn't approve. Did you and your wife own property here?"

Lonnie rubbed his bristled jaw. "Might have. Thought I'd talk to my lawyer first." He considered a little longer, and his eyes narrowed. "That make you a Kennedy?"

"That makes me a Kennedy." He stuck out his hand. "Kurt, and you?"

"Lonnie. Don't remember you around here much back then." He ordered coffee and a donut and gave the menu back to Mariah. If anyone was capable of putting spells on people, Kurt would wager on the black-braided waitress. She was casting Lonnie looks that would fry woodwork. But she kept her mouth shut.

"You mentioned a wife?" Kurt said. "Did she own property too?"

"My wife did, that's why I'm poking around. She passed, but Lisa thought maybe the lawsuit applied to my wife's old house, since it asked for addresses." Donut crumbs stuck to his mustache as he spoke through the bite he'd taken.

"Lisa?" Teddy joined Kurt once the customer on his right abandoned his seat. "I think I remember a Lisa from when I was a kid."

"Lisa, my old lady. She used to live here back then too, up at the old commune. A pretty young thing like you couldn't have been old enough to know her though." Lonnie gave Teddy a lascivious look.

Kurt would have punched his lights out just for that, but Teddy put a restraining hand on his arm, and he remembered their purpose here.

Drifting up in her long black veil, bearing her walking stick like a scepter, Valdis, their resident death goddess, stopped behind them. "Your wife? Thalia? She passed? I hadn't heard. When?"

Even Kurt could hear the iciness in her tone but Lonnie shrugged her off.

"'Bout the time we moved. She and Lisa didn't get along too hot." He stopped what he was saying and looked uneasy, as if he hadn't meant to say it.

Teddy responded sympathetically. "I remember Lisa had a temper."

Lonnie nodded in relief. "Then you understand. Thalia did too. Man, that woman packed a wallop when she got mad."

"I'm sorry to hear about Thalia," Valdis said without an ounce of inflection. "She knew a lot about art, didn't she?"

Where the devil had that come from? Val hadn't returned here until some five years or so after Thalia died. Kurt hadn't thought his aunt had even noticed Thalia's miserable paintings.

"Thalia dabbled a bit. She helped Susannah pretty up that painting back there." Lonnie nodded at the mural behind Dinah's counter, the one Sam and the others had been working to open up and make visible. "Ingersson was a cheap SOB, made his own paints, but the eyes started bleeding red. Looked right evil before Thalia fixed it. She said Lucinda Malcolm told her how, and she taught Susannah."

Susannah—Sam's mother, Val's sister. Kurt couldn't see Cass or Walker, but even Null that he was, he noticed the air had electrified. As he understood it, no one had seen Susannah Ingersson Kennedy since she'd given up his niece for adoption.

"Dear Lucinda," Cass said sweetly from the booth he and Teddy had deserted. "Thalia must have been quite young when she met her."

His aunt had never had a sweet day in her life. It was all Kurt could do to keep from swinging around in disbelief—why the effing *hell* had he thought he could help this confusing array of people? But as he glanced from one grave face to the other around the room, he grasped what they were doing, almost.

The Lucys were *playing* Lonnie, just the way he had been. If the weird glow in their crystals was any indication, they were doing more than that.

He ought to get the hell out of here before his head—or Lonnie's— exploded. Teddy's hand on his arm kept him pinned to the seat.

Lonnie took a big bite of his donut and gagged it down, as if trying to keep from answering. Mariah came along and refilled his coffee cup. He followed the donut with a long drink and wiped his mouth with a paper napkin.

"Anyone who knows Lucinda Malcolm around here is a saint," Kurt said, taking an insane leap of faith and gesturing for Mariah to refill Lonnie's plate. "I'm buying. Tell us everything."

LONNIE'S TORTURED ANGER, GREED, AND FEAR PIERCED TEDDY'S BRAIN and twisted her into knots. *This* was why she'd never explored her abilities—they hurt too damned much. Leaving the door open forced her to suffer all the volatile energy spiking through the room, from Val's rage, Mariah's inexplicable need for vengeance, Walker's hunger for justice, to Sam's curiosity and sadness. And all that emotion demanded that she *act*, without the skills to cut through the confusion.

But she needed to know who the skeleton was in her attic and if Lonnie had anything to do with it. She had to stay open and concentrate.

"I don't know nothin'," Lonnie protested in answer to Kurt's question. "I just sell pots."

Teddy read his spike of anxiety. Underneath all the other Lucy reactions, she experienced an odd *energy* similar to the one surging through her last night when she'd ordered Assbutt to freeze. She wished she'd brought her walking stick with her. A good glowing red crystal would frighten the heck out of everyone, except the Lucys.

A couple of people slipped out the door. She immediately sensed Sam's absence, and possibly that of Walker's mother. Sending them away was probably a smart move on the chief's part. Sam would want to ask about her mother, and that would only distract from the essential investigation of Thalia's death. And Jia didn't need to be here to see the Crazy, if it happened.

"We're setting up a pottery display along with the artwork," Kurt said affably.

Teddy could tell he wasn't happy with questioning a potential murderer, but he was the perfect person to do it. Walker needed evidence before leaning on the weight of his authority. The rest of the Lucys were too biased and lacked the ability to dissemble. But Kurt was a Null, the kind of wealthy man who was beyond suspicion—and he had years of practice in diplomacy.

"I'll have to take a look," Lonnie mumbled. "You the one gotta pay out on the lawsuit?"

"Trust fund," Kurt said with a vague wave of his ringed hand.

The mahogany obsidian she'd woven into the gold glowed almost as nicely as the Lucy's crystals—except she'd carved it without facets. So what did that mean? The stone was supposed to protect his heart—against his mother's depredations. She'd hoped that opening himself up to her today showed that he trusted her with that protected heart. Did that mean he was trusting that she had his back now?

Crystal lessons were hard to learn.

"What the hell does *that* mean?" Lonnie asked, sounding a little more belligerent.

"The town has a trust fund," Teddy said brightly. "From old lawsuits, land sales, whatnot." She waved her hand in the same vague manner as Kurt had. "The lawyers handle it. We're restoring the mural, did you notice? Thalia did some really nice work. I wish she were here to tell us how she did it. An art dealer says it's a priceless asset."

"She did?" Lonnie finally looked interested. "You got a dealer up here to appraise things like them panels?" He pointed at the photographs.

Teddy could feel Kurt turn ruthless, and she shivered. Here was the Null businessman she really didn't want on her doorstep. She was glad he was after Lonnie and not her house right now.

"We had to put the panels in a safe. They're apparently rare examples of Lucinda Malcolm's work. If we only had the third panel, we could buy the entire mountain and turn it into Disneyland if we wanted."

Teddy hid her wince behind her coffee cup. Lonnie's greed soared straight through the roof. The Lucys. . . almost *vibrated*. If the Nulls wanted to sell those panels. . . mountains would crumble in the war that would ensue.

She really needed to shut down before she fried her brain. She resisted. She had to learn to *use* her gifts.

Harvey and Aaron slipped in through the front entrance. Teddy felt their arrival but didn't glance over to verify their energies. She was starting to wear a little thin staying open this long.

"Is there a finder's fee if someone uncovers the third panel?" Lonnie asked, studying the painting behind the counter—the one his wife had apparently worked on with Susannah.

His greed contained distinct threads of villainy. Did he think Kurt was a sucker who would buy a fake if he conjured one?

What if he wasn't manufacturing a fake? Teddy felt a cold chill down her spine.

"I'm sure a finder's fee could be arranged. We just never thought the panel could be found," Kurt said generously.

The door opened and another customer entered. Kurt turned to nod at his brother, the mayor. Had Sam warned him what was happening? Teddy couldn't *feel* Monty's presence, but he sauntered over to join Walker in his booth. He was as Null as Kurt and blocking like crazy.

Mariah carried over coffee without being told.

"Lisa kept that old panel," Lonnie said with satisfaction. "It showed her leaning against my wagon. We thought those old panels was just junk, so we took that one with us."

TWENTY-NINE

LONNIE HAD THE THIRD PANEL?

Kurt placed his arm over Teddy's shoulders before she could levitate off her stool. Even he felt as if he could hack the tension in the room with one of Dinah's butcher knives.

Glancing around, he noticed walking sticks tilted toward Lonnie, their crystal heads now glowing in varied colors. How the hell did they do that? Or better yet, *what* were they doing?

"Interesting," he said flatly in response to Lonnie's declaration. That the bastard actually possessed a valuable piece of art wasn't so important as what he'd just said was on it. "So Lisa was your girlfriend in the painting?"

"Yeah," Lonnie said uneasily. "We got tired of living up here and decided to take our work down to Monterey, where the money is."

Young Lisa leaning against the car as Lonnie packed up to leave—and old Thalia coming down the mountain lugging Lonnie's pottery like a slave, able to see it all. He and Monty choosing that moment in time to decide to claim their inheritance and set up a town hall, thereby releasing the artwork that had been lost. That was one hell of a painting Lucinda had dreamed up.

He might have to start believing in Lucy absurdities—once he had time to work through the logic of them. Now wasn't that time.

"I think I know your gallery," Aaron said conversationally from his seat at the end of the counter. "I've been researching Hillvale pottery. You have quite a few pieces, don't you?"

Lonnie spun around, apparently relieved by this direction. "I do. I've got Peterson, Williams, Arthur, all of them, if you know the names. I used to work with them up at the kiln, before it blew."

Cass held her teacup as if it were the queen's china and gazed haughtily over it. "Your wife was still living when you took the panel to Monterey with your girlfriend?"

Apparently his aunt had tired of the cat-and-mouse game. Kurt wanted to leap in, smooth the sharp jab over, but Teddy caught his arm and squeezed. What was she trying to tell him?

Lonnie turned a darker shade of red and his reply was even more belligerent. "That's the way things were done back then. You're old enough to know."

"That's the way things are still done," Teddy said lightly. "But if you divorced Thalia, then it's her heirs who inherit any moneys from the lawsuit."

Kurt blinked. He was pretty sure crystals gleamed hotter all over the room. He wanted to hide in the back with Dinah. There was a reason he stayed at the lodge and didn't participate in town activities —he had more than enough crazy in his life.

"I'm her heir," Lonnie said hotly. "I was all she had."

That was an outright lie if Teddy's mother was Thalia's cousin. There was probably more family as well.

"There you go," Kurt said, hiding a sigh and joining in. "With a will and a death certificate, you'll be fine as far as the lawsuit goes."

Lonnie obviously struggled to get his words out. Kurt tried not to study the way the thief's face twisted as if he was having difficulty moving his tongue. Kurt took some comfort in knowing that Teddy wasn't aiming her weird wand at anyone.

"I ain't got. . ." Lonnie shoved another donut in his mouth.

He didn't have what—a will or a death certificate? Not if that had been Thalia abandoned between the floorboards. Considering the deed selling Teddy's place to his corporation might have been falsified by this asshole, Kurt went all out and ratcheted the interview up another notch.

"Would your girlfriend be able to find the paperwork for you? She could bring it up here with the panel, let our experts verify the painting's authenticity." Kurt thought if he drank any more coffee, he'd start throttling the man for answers. He wanted this over and done.

Lonnie looked a little craftier as he considered the suggestion. "Sure, ain't often we get rich. You got cell service up here yet?" He took out his phone and glared at the lack of bars.

"Mountains block the towers," Monty said from Walker's booth. "Is she Lisa Thompson on Via Vista in Monterey?"

Looking panicked, Lonnie spun on his stool. "Who are you and how do you know that?"

Monty shrugged. "I'm the mayor. I'm the one who has to pay out the money. I have wi-fi. I can e-mail her if you give me her e-mail address."

Kurt figured Monty and Walker were in collusion on that one. Walker wore his best poker face, his heavy lids lowered and his mouth flat. But his thumbs were flying over his phone—as police chief, he had the password to the same wi-fi network as Monty. As owner of a major investigative firm, he had minions to hunt all the Lisas of a certain age, with prior addresses in Hillvale, currently living in Monterey. That she'd taken Lonnie's name even if they weren't married had made it simple. Throw in an arrest record or two. . .

"Nulls work in mysterious ways," Teddy leaned in to whisper, apparently discerning the same thing as he had.

"And what exactly are the Lucys doing?" he asked, probably churlishly.

"Don't know exactly, but it's making him talk when he doesn't want to. I can feel his panic rising but he seems stuck. Keep at him."

That was an impossible assertion, but Kurt had no problem acting on it. "We're opening the art walk this weekend," he said, looking for ways to encourage Lonnie to talk. Appealing to greed usually worked. "If we had that triptych complete, we'd be an overnight sensation.

Property values will soar. That will increase the funds the lawsuit can draw on."

Well, if they were creating fictional suits, they might as well have fictional parameters.

"I'm not just handing over that panel," Lonnie protested, apparently relieved to have a direction he understood. "If it's valuable, I need to have it appraised."

"No one can sell it without proper provenance," Cass said coldly from her booth. "Not even Hillvale, although our records show Lucinda gifted the panels to the town."

That was a lie too. All they had were Thalia's notes. Hillvale wasn't a proper town fifty years ago, just a gas station and a hippie commune and apparently, a lot of ghosts in vacant buildings.

"Lisa don't look at e-mail," Lonnie argued, a trifle weakly. "I have to call her."

Mariah returned from Dinah's office carrying a cordless landline receiver, but Teddy shook her head, and the waitress surreptitiously slipped it into her apron pocket.

When Teddy stood up, Kurt had the appalling notion that he was reading her mind. He slid off his stool and blocked her. She smiled and patted his chest, and he really thought throttling might relieve his *steam*.

"Don't you dare," he muttered.

"Trust us," she murmured, gesturing at the other Lucys rising around the café.

Trust manipulative Cass and the *Lucys*? He really was out of his friggin' mind. But if Teddy was a Lucy. . . And he wanted Teddy. . . A good psychologist might help, but to hell with it. This was more fun than he'd had in a long time. This time, he meant to join the party, if only to keep an eye on Teddy.

He'd loved watching her when she was just a red-haired, gap-toothed six-year-old sprite spinning around the room. Buoyed by this discovery of his hitherto unknown rebelliousness and unnerved by Teddy's intentions, Kurt draped a possessive arm over her shoulder as she tapped Lonnie on the shoulder and played him like a fish.

"Come along. I have a land line you can use. This is the most exciting thing this town has ever known. A Lucinda Malcolm panel! I can't wait to see all of them together. Do you think we'll need security guards?"

She was surrounded by Lucys with big sticks. Even Walker and Monty got up to guard her back. And Kurt's instincts still wanted to fling her over his shoulder and run. . .

Which was when he realized he *believed* that Thalia was really a ghost—and Teddy was leading Lonnie to slaughter.

She had him believing in ghosts! And things that went bump in the night.

Which meant he either had to believe Teddy—and the Lucys— knew what they were doing, or give it all up and retreat to the resort and his comfortable, quiet niche, undisturbed by the improbable. He could buy a few dissatisfied guests drinks, sign a few checks, talk to a few more bankers about developing the fire-scarred hill. . .

Kurt followed Teddy.

So did Lonnie.

~

TEDDY WANTED TO SHOUT AND LEAP WITH RELIEF WHEN KURT STAYED AT her back this time. She was scared out of her mind, but she had to do this. They hadn't been making any progress with Lonnie back there, despite all the forces they'd brought to bear. The time had come to up the ante—and the danger, admittedly. She could hope Thalia had worked off most of her energy last night, and that she'd just fling a few of Daisy's guardians around.

But just in case. . . She sacrificed her own safety net by whispering to Kurt. "Check that Syd and the kids are still out, please. And don't let them come in."

He glared, stepped aside from the crowd pouring from the café, and signaled his brother. They conferred, and Monty sauntered off to take an alley behind the shops. Kurt caught up with Teddy just as they reached the front door. He wouldn't abandon her, even in this insanity! Her heart opened wider to this normally dignified businessman she knew wanted to be anywhere else but here.

Feeling all his powerful *steam* at her side again, Teddy gathered the courage to unlock the shop. "Come on in, folks. The inventory is still sparse, so there's plenty of room."

Lonnie had frozen on the boardwalk, but the Lucys relentlessly crowded him forward. He stalled at the entrance, looking panicky, but bless Kurt, he grabbed Lonnie's upper arm and dragged the bastard inside the house he'd inhabited for ten years.

Everyone chatted about the panel, about Lucinda Malcolm, about the art walk, while Teddy headed for the counter.

She casually picked up the honesty necklace she'd been working on and thrust it at Lonnie. "Good vibes on this. Wear it, and we'll hope it brings luck."

He dropped the leather over his head without question and clutched the stone.

She hid the crystal handle of her staff under the shelf, just in case it started glowing. Locking her jaw, she kept her overworked senses open to danger. Lonnie was on the verge of panicking, but his greed was stronger than good judgment. She handed him the cordless land-line. "Here you go. Tell Lisa we all say hi."

"I didn't get your name," he said, surreptitiously glancing toward the stairs. His greed fought with his cowardice as he held the receiver.

She pointed at the sign outside the open door. "Teddy, as in Teddy's Treasure Trove."

Kurt stationed himself between Teddy and the entrance to the stair-well. She had opened her inner Monitor and sensed his anger and need for justice battling his concern for her, but oddly, the sensation wasn't as painful as usual. She could almost relax with Kurt's emotional barrier to shield her. Reaching under the counter and gripping the crystal staff, she learned that drained a little of her excess energy so she wasn't as hypersensitive.

The Lucys scattered about the small shop, holding Daisy's guardians, wielding their staffs. With her Monitor open, Teddy could sense that the crystals were deflecting their emotions, thanks to all that was holy. She needed more practice at this.

The energy level in the room escalated as it could not in Dinah's larger space. Another lesson learned, Teddy reflected—energy can be stored and magnified in crystal. As if in response, a howl formed over-head and whistled through the ceiling.

Lonnie didn't seem aware of it. He punched in Lisa's number. Teddy helpfully leaned over and punched the speaker button.

"We don't want any," the speaker said clearly, apparently reading caller ID.

"Hey, babe, it's me." Lonnie was trying for brash, but his gaze darted nervously from Teddy and Kurt to the other Lucys. He toyed with the honesty stone around his neck.

"Who's Teddy and what kind of treasures is he selling?" the woman on the other end asked suspiciously.

Sweet of Kurt to register the phone in her shop name. She lifted her eyebrow and he shrugged.

"It's a shop," Lonnie said in irritation. "I'm up here in Hillvale, and they still don't have cell reception. You still have that old plywood with you painted next to my wagon?"

Lisa didn't answer immediately. Upstairs, it sounded as if the wind was rattling the windows. A glance outside verified that no dust blew —the day was dead calm and sunny.

Apparently, even Lonnie heard the rattles. He glanced at the ceiling and edged toward the door. Aaron and Harvey leaned against the jamb, pretending nonchalance by mock-fighting with their sticks, while deliberately blocking the exit.

In the light from the front window, the dark crystals in Daisy's guardians began to glow white.

"Yeah, I've been using it out in the garage as a shelf, why?" Lisa finally replied.

"Well, it could be worth a lot. Think you can get it in the truck and bring it up here?"

Apparently greed won over cowardice, Teddy noted with interest. Did that mean the honesty stone worked? She really wanted to shut down her Monitor, but she needed to know what Thalia was doing. She leaned on the wall next to Kurt's reassuring presence, in direct line of Thalia's fire at the bottom of the stairwell.

Teddy was as aware of Kurt physically as emotionally. He was blocking the worst of his fear and fury, but he was a huge stew of conscientiousness under all that macho attitude. All these years of shouldering responsibility had probably left him thinking it was his duty to make this scene come out right.

She elbowed him. "Relax. What happens, happens. You can't control everything."

He shot her a grim glare that disagreed.

The speakerphone rattled off Lisa's irate response to Lonnie's request.

Walker sidled over to whisper, "I have men zeroing in on her house now. Keep him talking, if you can."

"Thalia's about to add her two cents," Teddy warned. "Be prepared to take cover."

He nodded and passed the warning on to Amber. Her bracelets clicked as she eased over and whispered to Cass. Kurt's aunt nodded and gestured regally at two Lucys to attend her. Gradually, as word spread around the room, walking sticks rose in defense. Their crystals gleamed in the sunlight from the front window.

Satisfied she'd done all she could to warn the others about Thalia, Teddy squeezed Kurt's arm for reassurance, then stepped up to Lonnie and the phone. "Hi, Lisa, it's me, Teddy Baker. You probably don't remember me, but maybe you remember my mother? She owned the house Lonnie and Thalia lived in here in Hillvale."

The wind abruptly shrieked. Harvey's harmless consignment staffs chattered. The Lucys murmured their chants under the howl, keeping their sticks in defensive positions.

Lonnie's expression reflected terror, not of Thalia, but of discovery —and he emitted a cyclone of guilt. *Good*, Teddy thought in grim satisfaction. But he couldn't be convicted for guilt. She needed evidence.

"Thalia?" Lisa asked warily on the other end of the line. "What's she got to do with the price of eggs?"

How unsurprising. Lonnie had *lied* about his girlfriend sending him up here looking for Thalia's share of the imaginary lawsuit. He'd meant to keep the money for himself. He was so easy to read.

Teddy studied him contemptuously as she replied to Lisa. "She's my mother's cousin. We've been sending her cards and hadn't realized she'd died."

In fear of his depredations being exposed, Lonnie backed toward the door, but he was glued to the phone receiver, where Lisa was demanding that he return home immediately.

In a sudden furious gust of wind, Teddy's books flew off the shelf.

Kurt caught her elbow and dragged her up against the wall with him. She held her staff in front of both of them. The red crystal pulsated with dangerous energy.

With everyone edging toward the walls, Lonnie was suddenly isolated in the center of the shop. Thalia took advantage. The display of rock crystals on the oak table flew at him. He ducked, wide-eyed in surprise.

"Look, babe, what else was I supposed to do?" He argued with Lisa as rocks whistled over his head. "How do you think I had the deposit for the shop?" He glared at Teddy.

He'd sold her mother's property for money to start his own business! He was so Null, so wrapped up in himself, that he couldn't even see the supernatural warning signs coming right at him.

"Have you already forged Thalia's death certificate?" Teddy asked, giving up on subtlety. "The way you forged the deed you sold to the Kennedys?"

Lonnie finally had the sense to look alarmed. "Look, babe, I'll call you back. I've got to go."

Lisa screamed, "You don't hang up on me now, you bastard! Tell me what you're doing. I swear, you don't have the brains of a mongoose. Why would you fuggin' go back to Hillvale? Are you out of your *mind*?"

Lonnie hunted for the speaker button, but a book flew at his head. He dodged under the table, then finally pried the phone out of his hand. Dropping it, he jumped up and ran for the door. Two large tree branches blocked him.

Teddy could almost see the leaves and sticks emerging from Harvey and Aaron's walking sticks, but she figured it was an illusion.

Lonnie staggered backward. "What the freaking hell?" He glanced around frantically while the phone still squawked.

Kurt helpfully spoke up. "Hey, Lisa, Lonnie is a little occupied right now. Want to tell us what happened to Thalia?"

The squawking shut up. In the silence, urgent knocking could be heard over the line.

"That's probably the cops," Kurt said helpfully. "You might want to tell them what you know. It will probably get you off easier."

"Lisa did it," Lonnie shouted, fear escalating over greed. "She and Thalia had a knock-down, eye-scratching cat fight!"

How could she know if the honesty stone had made him confess that? She couldn't. The wind shrieked, and Lonnie staggered to one side, as if unable to withstand a gale.

"*You* knocked her out, you bastard! *You* punched her, and she fell. I didn't push her, I swear! You'll fry in hell if you say anything different, Leonard Thompson!"

"*Kill him,*" the dead speaker in the ceiling cried in a hiss of electric sparks. Rocks and crystals flew, slamming into Lonnie. He covered his head and ducked under the table, but the guardian statues flew off the shelves in his direction, battering his back. "*Kill him!*"

"And whose idea was it to cremate Thalia in the kiln?" Kurt asked conversationally as Walker edged around the wall to pick up the phone. Not walking into a maelstrom of flying crystals and guardians was a wise idea.

"His, all his!" Lisa cried. "I was stoned and didn't know what I was doing. He said he needed to bury her in the cemetery and make a burial marker and everything. We didn't have no money, and that made sense, you know?"

Stoned—oh the irony, Teddy thought as Daisy's rock guardians picked themselves up and flung themselves repeatedly at the man huddled beneath the table, making himself as small a target as possible.

"So how did she end up in the attic?" Kurt asked conversationally.

Teddy aimed her staff at Lonnie. To her immense surprise, he answered.

"The ground was too damned hard. She'd been grinding all those rocks, jinxing us with them, so I dumped them on her when I stuck her in the kiln, tried to get rid of all of it, but the kiln cracked. We had to fix that upstairs wall where she hit it, so I just put the remains in the attic and used the plaster to cover it up. She would have *killed* us," Lonnie bleated. "What the hell is with these damned stones?"

"Thalia," Teddy said cheerfully. "She's still trying to kill you. How does it feel?"

Lonnie screamed as the guardians all gathered power at once and hit him from every direction.

"Do you have enough, Walker?" Cass asked wearily from her protected corner.

"Yes, ma'am, I do." He held up the phone, but Lisa apparently had just answered her door. An official voice emerged from the speaker, "You have the right to remain silent. . ."

As the cop on the other end of the line read Lisa her rights, Cass gave a signal Teddy didn't quite catch. The Lucys lifted their staffs and spoke their exorcism spell—again.

THIRTY

KURT ALMOST FELT SORRY FOR THE BASTARD BATTERED BY GHOSTLY FLYING sticks and stones and reduced to gibbering under a table, except Lonnie started whining excuses for all his foul deeds. Thalia needed to take a big stick to his fat head.

In disgust, Kurt pried Teddy off the wall and led her outside. She was practically shaking in her shoes, and he wanted to cradle her and haul her far, far away. Let the Lucys chant and Walker cuff the weeping culprit, he was taking care of Teddy—because he'd finally admitted that she was a gem he wanted to keep.

He didn't feel the least bit of anxiety in thinking that. Theodosia Devine-Baker was many, many things, so many it might take him a lifetime to understand, but she was also reliable, honest, and coura-geous, and that's what he craved. With her, he could be himself without fear. Even when the world around them was insane, he could relax his defenses knowing she would hand him the sword he needed, when he needed it.

"Stoned," she cried, almost hysterically. "They were all *stoned*. I'm never touching pot again. And I'm having second thoughts about alcohol."

Kurt would be amused if ten thousand unanswerable questions weren't spinning in his head. Were the Lucys creating the chaos back there with their weird wands? Or was Lonnie's dead wife really tearing his head off? He hoped it was the latter, but either was too far-fetched for logic.

"We need to get you and your sister somewhere safe from flying stone men," he said decisively—the only rational reply he could offer. "I'll have Xavier open one of the rentals if you don't want to stay at the lodge."

He hated saying that. He wanted her in *his* house—but after today's inexplicable events, he was willing to accept anything she told him about *evil*, or wicked, foul, and negative—whatever word they wanted to use. Lonnie Thomas was all of them and a murderous prick as well. So if she said the lodge was evil, he'd have to cope.

Teddy sank into his embrace. Kurt relished just holding her close, knowing this courageous, brilliant woman believed he could help. He simply held her, waiting until she regained control.

Abruptly, she straightened and spun around, looking up at the fire-scarred mountain, the towering redwoods, Sam's colorful planters—and the road out of town.

His heart sank.

"I can go anywhere," she announced. "Syd needs to get over her fear and go home. I can set up shop in any tiny tourist town while I experiment with crystals. Give me one good reason to stay here with looming evil, maggots crawling from the woodwork, and only one Null cop to stop them all."

"I'm applying for Dinah's liquor license," he answered nonsensically, because he was only a dull male and no matter how much he wanted to say the right thing, he didn't know what she expected him to say after a morning like this one.

To his amazement, she *laughed*.

"I get that," she said, turning to hug him. "You're overwhelmed, don't know what to say, and you need a drink to think about it. And you can't go up to the lodge and drink because you'll be on duty. Am I close?"

She *understood*. Gratefully, Kurt wrapped her in his arms, kissed her hungrily, then shoved her toward his car. "Thalia can have your damned shop. My mother can have the lodge. I want a place just for *us*."

"Can Dinah still have her liquor license?" she asked in amusement, following his lead.

"Restaurants should have liquor licenses," he agreed as he took his seat, having no idea how they'd settled on this topic with all the other things needing to be said. "Drunken Lucys could be our Friday night entertainment."

She nodded as if that made sense. "If Hillvale is going to have crystal art, it should have a crystal expert."

Kurt played around that notion as if it were a sore tooth, looking for the hole. As far as he was concerned, *she* was their crystal expert. He drove past the shop and down the main highway, turning up a driveway right below the Treasure Trove.

"Crystal art?" he asked cautiously. He didn't think she was having hysterics, but experience had taught him that drama often led to bombshells exploding in his face.

"We'll call it that," she said cheerfully, not sounding as if she would explode. "We'll play the crystals up as the magic behind the commune's success, get scientists to identify the elements in the compounds, psychics to extol the virtues. . . It will be fun." She peered through the windshield at the stone and wood cottage they approached.

Kurt gripped the steering wheel and studied the structure, but his thoughts weren't on the vacant rental. He wanted to be certain he was interpreting correctly. "You're staying?"

"Are you?" she asked a shade too brightly. "Because I'm pretty certain you or Monty will end up killing your mother if you hang around her too long."

"I can handle her," he said stiffly. "Someone has to keep her honest —" He bit his tongue on the implication.

She nodded as if in understanding—as she always understood. He didn't have to speak his fears to Teddy, *she knew them.*

He should beat his head against a wall and hope for logic to return, but he inexplicably felt lighter as he got out of the car, believing Teddy read the emotion he couldn't voice.

"I can't explain Hillvale either," she said, taking his hand and following him up the flagstone walk. "But there is something inherently *wrong* in the land around the lodge. And it affects those who stay too long. You know the history better than I do."

Even dismissing the legends of the early settlers being haunted and burned out of their ranch, Kurt knew the unhappy history from this past quarter century. His father had succumbed to greed. His mother was slowly descending into the same pit. Her chauffeur, the security manager, even poor Xavier had been corrupted. And then there had been the developer who'd tried to crush the Lucys. . . could all that venality in one tiny town be coincidental? Maybe it was something in the water.

"Thalia and Lonnie and Lisa?" he asked, unlocking the cottage door with his master key. "They didn't live or work at the lodge."

"They stayed at the commune most of their lives. From what I understand, the crystals they worked with carried pollution from the lodge up to the farm. But that's where Sam and I step in. We need to get Thalia's crystals back to study them and compare them to mine and Harvey's. Are they all bad? Can Harvey's sticks be carrying pollution? Daisy said Lucinda liked the blue ones—would the famed Lucinda Malcolm use corrupt crystals?"

Not giving him time to ponder any more insanity, she stepped inside the cottage and smiled at the sunlit room. "Gorgeous!"

"One of our better houses. We've just had it cleaned up after the last tenants left." He steered her past the granite and steel kitchen down a short hallway to the master. The cleaning service kept clean sheets on the beds, just like a hotel.

"Sam and you?" he asked, half-reluctantly, pondering her comments. Why did he have such difficulty translating?

"Sam's the scientist. She can help me design the experiments." She didn't seem to pay attention to what she was saying but examined the bland hotel headboard and high-end comforter with interest.

At least she wasn't running.

"This place has potential," he suggested, hope rising, as well as other parts south, as she dropped his hand to tug her tank top over her head. He'd had all the drama for one day that he could tolerate.

"You need to let off steam before you explode," she said with a teasing grin, nailing his problem.

"Steam potential, yes," he said solemnly, flinging his t-shirt toward the dresser. Her lacy bra barely covered her substantial assets, and steam would pour from his ears just looking at her. "There's a science to steam power. Want to help me explore it?"

"If you promise I won't get burned. That's a pretty big responsibility. Are you sure?" She wrapped her arms around his neck, all amusement gone.

Kurt closed his eyes and let bliss envelop him. The day's weirdness didn't seem so peculiar when he held her like this. Anything seemed possible. All he had to do to gain all this passion and pleasure was offer commitment.

He drank in her sensual jasmine scent, the press of soft flesh, and the honesty and understanding she offered. This wasn't as difficult as he'd feared.

He let down his walls and lifted her into him. "I'm in more danger from you than you are from me. I will never burn you or let you be burned. I want to give us a chance."

There, that only hurt in about a thousand different places. He carried her to the bed, praying fervently but expecting nothing.

She wrapped her legs around him and whispered, "So do I. A Null who believes in me is rare and valuable and I want to learn you from the inside out."

Filling with light and air and pride, Kurt laughed and covered her with his body. "Then I'll learn you from the outside in. We'll make beautiful bubbles together."

"Bubbles?" And then she laughed. "Steam bubbles!"

Which made as much sense as anything else that had happened that day.

∾

JULY 2: EVENING

Standing in front of her beautiful periwinkle door, admiring the purple petunias in the planter by her doorstep, Teddy drank in the wonder of this moment—one so different from her arrival barely a week ago. Hillvale had a way of accelerating and magnifying life so it could be examined from all angles at once.

The man with his hand at her back opened the door just as he had in their first encounter as adults. They'd just spent a blissful afternoon in bed, and she wasn't ready to let him go.

He was still protecting her, though, only in a different fashion. Instead of warning her away, he was checking to see if it was safe to enter.

And this time, Syd was with her kids in the van, where she belonged. Well, maybe her elegant designer sister didn't belong in a beat-up van, but she was with her children, and that's what counted.

"No wind?" Teddy asked, leaning on the jamb and peering inside as Kurt opened the door. "Look, they've picked up all the statuettes."

"No gleaming crystals?" Kurt asked warily.

"Not a one. Listen, music is playing through the speakers! Does that mean Thalia is happy?"

"No, it means Monty persuaded one of the electricians to fix the system and hooked up a player to test it." Holding out his arm to keep her from entering, he stepped inside.

"Such a Null thing to say." Teddy followed him, pressing a kiss to his bristly cheek. He hadn't been back to the lodge all day. In jeans and t-shirt, with dark bristles covering his jaw, Kurt was looking as disreputable as Harvey. She slid her arms around his waist from the back and glanced around at her beautiful shop. "I think the Lucys have even dusted."

"Do you want me to check upstairs before we let the kids back in?" He half-turned to kiss her before prying her off his back so he could endanger life and limb by climbing her haunted stairs.

"Your protectiveness will never change, will it?" She took his hand and headed for the stairs with him. "I need to learn to live with my very own security guard who looks after me and my shop and my sister and his hotel and this town and. . ."

"Want me to run for president and take over the country?" he asked mildly, forcing her to walk behind him as he eased up the stairs.

"No, but if you could clone yourself. . ."

"I could live in the city, at the lodge, in D.C., and you can have a mini-me everywhere you go," he concluded. Standing at the top of the stairs, he studied the attic door before preceding to check the bedrooms and open and shut the windows. "All appears normal."

Teddy laughed. "Good thing I've given up my traveling trunk show. I don't want you spread around the world." She danced into the room she shared with Syd and picked up a blue crystal on her pillow. "Where did this come from?"

"Probably Crazy Daisy," he said, unconcerned. "Or maybe the Lucys cleaned house and found it under the bed."

She carried it over to the window. Syd was stepping out of the car, looking up, and Teddy waved. Her sister nodded and opened the door for the kids. "Syd is feeling braver. She's heading this way." She held up the crude, unpolished crystal. "I could be wrong, but this looks like blue topaz. It's extremely rare. It fractures easily and doesn't refract enough to make a good gemstone, but I can practically feel it brimming with confidence."

"Confidence," Kurt said flatly.

"And peace," she added, teasing him with her knowledge. "It's perfect for Syd. I wonder if this is the stone Lucinda liked."

Mia and Jeb ran up the stairs calling "Aunt T, Aunt T" loud enough to wake any ghosts. "We got to ride the ponies *everywhere!*"

Teddy stooped down to hug them as they spilled over with the excitement of their day bonding with their mother. She glanced up at Syd, who looked a little less wary, a little more together than she had in a while, despite the nasty bruise on her jaw. "Hey, Sis, Thalia left us a gift." She hefted the crystal in Syd's direction.

Once a skilled softball player, Syd caught it easily. She looked at what appeared to be an ugly rock and set it on the dresser. "Just don't make pixie dust out of it."

"It will build your confidence," Teddy insisted. "I'll make a pendant for you. Do you think you'll be okay here alone tonight or shall I stay?"

Syd studied Kurt, who studied her back. Teddy didn't know what they were communicating over her head, but Syd was her older sister. She'd always looked out for Teddy when they were younger. So her two guardian angels were battling it out. Teddy took the kids to their room and found the iPod producing the boring instrumental music.

She punched a few buttons and blasted some reggae. Someone had eclectic taste.

Kurt found her a second later, spun her around in the smoothest dance move she'd ever experienced, and when she was properly enthralled, he aimed for the stairs. "Karaoke in the bar, really?"

Understanding exactly what he asked, she added, "Yoga in the atrium. Classes on art, crystals, and spiritual healing in the meeting room. Young people, creative people, not just rich old farts."

"Polluting them with evil?" he asked, leading the way down the narrow stairs.

"Black tourmaline and smoky quartz—add teardrop crystals to Mariah's ghostcatchers, sell the stones in the gift shop. They cleanse negative energy. Talk to Sam. She has theories about plants cleansing the air. Maybe all we have to do is find the right combination of materials to neutralize whatever's polluting the ground. It's all a learning process, like the honesty stone. It's really tough to say what works."

"You really mean to double-down on this crystal business, don't you?" Holding her hand, Kurt led her through the quiet, dark shop and into the fading light of day.

He was asking if she meant to stay weird—just as she'd teased him about his protectiveness. Relationships really were a learning process.

She studied the sharp angles of Kurt's face and the warm mahogany of his eyes. He wasn't laughing at her. He wasn't exuding negativity. He was just asking, and she smiled so wide that her suave businessman tripped. "I've been holding back all my life, skimming the surface of what I can do and what crystals can do, so yes, I'm doubling down. If we're going to be a thing, you have to accept weird."

Kurt cupped her face and ran his thumb on the underside of her chin. "Are we going to be a *thing*? I'm fascinated by anything you do, and don't think you're weird. *Inexplicable* simply means we haven't found an explanation yet."

Oh, lordie, she had it bad for this formidable man. Her heart performed a perfect triple axel and she was short of breath. "If I stay in Hillvale," she murmured, captivated by the intensity of his gaze, "my expenses will be small, and I can afford to dabble more and work less."

"Would you consider living with me? That will save you even more."

"Oooo, you sweet-talking lovely man."

They were standing in the middle of the street. She had to learn to curb her impulses if she meant to live in a small town. She caught his hand, kissed it, and tugged him toward the café before she embarrassed them both. "Could we live in that cozy cottage and not near your tiger shark mother?"

"We could live in a cave on the mountain, if you like, just as long as I have you in my bed each night." He leaned over to kiss her—and let down the barrier to his soul.

He inundated her with his love and his fear of loving and his happiness—and his fear that he didn't deserve any of it—the silly man.

She grabbed his hair, poured all her passion into returning his kiss, then gasping, backed away. "I'm afraid I don't deserve anyone as heroic as you. You're standing between an entire town and the monster who owns it. You've turned yourself into a robot to protect your heart. I'm here now to battle the monster with you, and my price is a place in your heart. How's that for a deal?"

He practically smoldered. All that flood of fear dissipated, and his delight practically sparkled with purple pixie dust.

"I'll take it. I still want to build condos and a ski run and rebuild your haunted house." He pushed her inside Dinah's, where the light was bright, the company cheerful, and the air smelled of roasting chicken.

"Remodel, not tear down," she countered. Pointing at the colorful mural adorning the café's backsplash, she added, "History counts. Someday, your image will be on these walls."

He chortled and pointed at the triptych photo of him and Monty standing on the corner looking flummoxed. "That's how I'll go down in history. It's what I do with each minute that matters, not a painting on a wall."

"Ha, share those minutes with me, and you're in for a wild ride."

Kurt laughed, he actually laughed, and Teddy beamed with delight. They would definitely make beautiful bubbles together.

EPILOGUE

JULY 4: LUNCHTIME

KURT CLIMBED OUT OF HIS MERCEDES IN THE PARKING LOT AND STUDIED the holiday crowd strolling the boardwalks. If he were Teddy, he'd say the air blossomed with joy. Or excitement? Fun? Okay, so he was clueless, but people seemed happier than usual. They smiled, eagerly pointing out a particularly showy planter or an interesting object in a shop window—and best yet, they carried shopping bags.

Walker joined him in admiring the happy bustle. "Think it can carry over to Christmas?"

"If you think you can persuade your buddies to release the rest of the triptych, maybe. Syd and Lance are designing an altar in the meeting house for it." Kurt headed for the café.

"An altar?" the chief asked in amusement, following. "As in Lucys worship Lucinda Malcolm?" At Kurt's shrug, he continued, unfazed. "The panels should be released any day, but they may need security guards. And Lonnie is screaming he's being robbed. Lawyers can't be too far off."

"We'll need money," Kurt agreed, curling his lip in distaste. "We'll have to charge admission to cover expenses or find grant funding. There isn't any chance Lonnie will be released on bond?"

"We have Lonnie and Lisa on so many charges of art fraud that we can hold them on those until the DA puts together the murder case on Thalia. And with you pressing charges on deed forgery—no worries there. They can't raise a red cent on bond with half their inventory labeled fraudulent." Walker shoved open the café door. "Have you and Teddy settled what will happen to the shop once her family is the clear owner again?"

Kurt winced at the direct hit to a sore point. "The lawyers have traced the shop deed straight back to one of the early Lucys from New England. It's been in Teddy's family ever since. With those original logs still in there, it could very well be considered for the National Historic Register if they requested, although I'm pretty certain that second floor was popped up from the original construction."

"Ouch, that complicates matters," Walker said in sympathy.

"Her parents are officially deeding it to both sisters, so any changes are a joint decision." Kurt was remarkably good with that these days. He had ideas percolating that hadn't been there before. "With proof that Lucinda Malcolm once stayed there, it might become a shrine. I'll just have to start work with another building until they decide what they want. Maybe I'll go back to historic reconstruction, which is Teddy's thing. What's happening with Ashbuth?"

"The sheriff is out to fry the bully's butt. He hates bad cops, and he's none too happy with the city's department for protecting him, so he's demanded all of Ass's files. He has a clear record of assault that should have had him locked up years ago. The DA thinks he has enough evidence to move Syd's original case out of domestic violence to half a dozen felonies. Add that to stalking and assault, this time with witnesses, and he's going down for a long time. Does make one wonder about Hillvale's ability to attract scuzzballs."

Kurt grimaced. "Or we can start believing in evil and negativity that attracts more of the same. Or Lucys inviting violence—people have been burned as witches for lesser reasons than flying stone men. I'm glad we have you up here now. I hope you're staying."

"As long as Sam does," Walker said without hesitation.

Kurt searched for Teddy in the café crowd. Once she waved at him from the nearly full counter, he relaxed enough to acknowledge a few familiar faces. He was starting to feel a little easier around the Hillvale inhabitants who'd always despised his family.

Samantha was pouring tea in Teddy's cup and talking to Aaron and a tall, broad stranger. They made room for the new arrivals.

Aaron gestured at the stranger. "Kurt, Walker, this is Keegan Ives, the ceramics expert who can authenticate the Baker collection."

With dark curly hair and brooding dark eyes, the newcomer towered over everyone in the room. He looked more like a massive NBA player than an art expert. Kurt offered his hand, and the expert caught it in a rough, callused grip.

"Hillvale is fortunate to have a generous benefactor like Miss Baker," Ives said in a distinctly British accent. "You have some museum quality pieces. Unfortunately, ceramics are underappreciated in the current market. Museums lack the necessary budget."

"We're just asking advice at this stage." Teddy stepped in, disarming Kurt's immediate defensive reaction to any slur on her family's collection. "We're enjoying the popularity of displaying quality work that celebrates our history."

"Liar," Kurt whispered against her ear. "History won't buy security guards."

She caressed his jaw, and he settled on the stool beside her to see how she played the crowd. That Teddy had some serious empathic abilities couldn't be denied. Whether that was *weird* or not wasn't for him to judge.

"We've only begun to touch our history," Sam said, delivering a fish taco to Kurt without his asking.

Dinah's uncanny culinary talent might also be weird, but he could get into it. The fish was better than anything the lodge was serving.

Sam gestured at the mural. "Those are the artists who made the pottery and paintings half a century ago. Can we even identify them now?"

"Better yet," Mariah intervened, refilling water glasses, "if corroded eyes indicate evil, and Thalia and Susannah had to blot out the corrosion on the mural, can we assume all the people in the mural turned evil since it was painted?"

"Watch out for septuagenarian villains?" Walker asked in amusement.

They all turned to study the painting of Lars Ingersson and his commune cronies. The people in the portrait were young, healthy, happy, and chowing down on hamburgers and fries. It would have been almost a mirror image of them as customers at the counter, except for the conceit of positioning them like DaVinci's Last Supper.

Walker slapped down his glass of tea, catching everyone's attention. "We can ask Susannah when she arrives."

Silence descended. At this mention of her long-lost mother, Sam gasped and covered her mouth.

From her favorite booth in back, Cass asked, "You've found Susannah, and she's actually agreed to come home?"

"She found us," Walker corrected. "She read about the art walk and called the number in the press release."

"Does she know I'm here?" Sam whispered.

Kurt wondered how he'd managed to live in Hillvale all these years and miss all this drama. Probably because his mother had provided more drama than he could endure, so he hadn't needed to seek more.

Teddy squeezed his hand, and he squeezed back, letting the tension go. She was the reason he could sit here and listen like this—she defused his steam.

"She knows nothing, and I thought it better that way," Walker offered. "She called herself Susannah Ingersson and said she had some pieces to contribute. I told her Hillvale would be honored and offered to put her up when she arrives. I have no reason to interrogate the lady."

"You didn't want to scare her off," Mariah said. "Good boy." She returned to the cash register.

"Another day, another soap opera," Kurt said, not unhappily. At Teddy's uplifted eyebrow, he gestured. "We get to see what happens when Sam finally meets her mother, maybe learn who the people are in the mural and if they're truly evil, what Thalia meant about the crystals. . ."

"And maybe by then, we'll have translated all Thalia's writing in her journal," Teddy added enthusiastically. "Answers to all our mysteries!"

Dinah emerged from the kitchen, wiping her hands on a towel and eyeing Keegan Ives warily. "Or maybe you ought to be asking *him*. If he's an art expert, maybe he knows more about your Lucinda and the crystal book Thalia says she stole."

The newcomer didn't have time to recover from his surprise before she slammed a chocolate malted down in front of Kurt. "And you, boy, this will sweeten you up so you can tell that nice girl that you love her so she'll hang around and paint more doors."

Surprised, Kurt couldn't immediately respond.

Teddy, seldom ever speechless, chortled. "The nice girl already knows. Buy the paint, Dinah, and I'll do your door next."

"I love you," he whispered in her ear. "Just in case you need to hear it."

She sent him a brilliant smile that nearly melted the malted. "Yeah, I kinda do. It gives me a warm schmaltzy feeling that can lead to better things for tonight. And how can I not love a man who doesn't run when I put an experiment on his finger?"

She loved him? Swallowing hard on the immensity of that declaration, Kurt admired the mahogany ring. Deliberately, he wiggled it off his right hand and slid it over his commitment finger. "Think your experiment is working?"

For a moment, she looked serious. "If it allows you to let down your walls and live again, yeah, I think it's doing something right."

With a satisfied sigh that he might have got something right, Kurt leaned back against the counter, sipping the thick syrupy ice cream. He studied the café's patrons returning to their private conversations. "Does this mean I'm not the Big Meanie anymore?"

Teddy leaned over and whispered, "I'll make us both swords and you can be villain to my heroine. Will that keep you in practice?"

He didn't have to think twice to answer that. "I still have my sword. Use your stick, and we'll go home and rewrite Robin Hood and Maid Marian."

She hugged his arm and stole a sip of his malted and for that one moment in time, Hillvale and its inhabitants were at peace.

ABOUT THE AUTHOR

With several million books in print and *New York Times* and *USA Today's* bestseller lists under her belt, former CPA Patricia Rice is one of romance's hottest authors. Her emotionally-charged contemporary and historical romances have won numerous awards, including the *RT Book Reviews* Reviewers Choice and Career Achievement Awards. Her books have been honored as Romance Writers of America RITA® finalists in the historical, regency and contemporary categories.

A firm believer in happily-ever-after, Patricia Rice is married to her high school sweetheart and has two children. A native of Kentucky and New York, a past resident of North Carolina and Missouri, she currently resides in Southern California, and now does accounting only for herself.

ALSO BY PATRICIA RICE

The World of Magic:

The Unexpected Magic Series

MAGIC IN THE STARS

WHISPER OF MAGIC

THEORY OF MAGIC

AURA OF MAGIC

CHEMISTRY OF MAGIC

NO PERFECT MAGIC

The Magical Malcolms Series

MERELY MAGIC

MUST BE MAGIC

THE TROUBLE WITH MAGIC

THIS MAGIC MOMENT

MUCH ADO ABOUT MAGIC

MAGIC MAN

The California Malcolms Series

THE LURE OF SONG AND MAGIC

TROUBLE WITH AIR AND MAGIC

THE RISK OF LOVE AND MAGIC

Crystal Magic

SAPPHIRE NIGHTS

TOPAZ DREAMS

Historical Romance:

American Dream Series

MOON DREAMS

REBEL DREAMS

The Rebellious Sons

WICKED WYCKERLY

DEVILISH MONTAGUE

NOTORIOUS ATHERTON

FORMIDABLE LORD QUENTIN

The Regency Nobles Series

THE GENUINE ARTICLE

THE MARQUESS

ENGLISH HEIRESS

IRISH DUCHESS

Regency Love and Laughter Series

CROSSED IN LOVE

MAD MARIA'S DAUGHTER

ARTFUL DECEPTIONS

ALL A WOMAN WANTS

Rogues & Desperadoes Series

LORD ROGUE

MOONLIGHT AND MEMORIES

SHELTER FROM THE STORM

WAYWARD ANGEL

DENIM AND LACE

CHEYENNES LADY

Too Hard to Handle

TEXAS LILY

TEXAS ROSE

TEXAS TIGER

TEXAS MOON

Mystic Isle Series

MYSTIC ISLE

MYSTIC GUARDIAN

MYSTIC RIDER

MYSTIC WARRIOR

Mysteries:

Family Genius Series

EVIL GENIUS

UNDERCOVER GENIUS

CYBER GENIUS

TWIN GENIUS

TWISTED GENIUS

Tales of Love and Mystery

BLUE CLOUDS

GARDEN OF DREAMS

NOBODY'S ANGEL

VOLCANO

CALIFORNIA GIRL

ABOUT BOOK VIEW CAFÉ

Book View Café Publishing Cooperative (BVC) is an author-owned cooperative of over fifty professional writers, publishing in a variety of genres including fantasy, romance, mystery, and science fiction. Since its debut in 2008, BVC has gained a reputation for producing high-quality ebooks. BVC's ebooks are DRM-free and are distributed around the world. The cooperative is now bringing that same quality to its print editions.

BVC authors include New York Times and USA Today bestsellers as well as winners and nominees of many prestigious awards, including:

Agatha Award

Campbell Award

Hugo Award

Lambda Award

Locus Award

Nebula Award

Nicholl Fellowship

PEN / Malamud Award

Philip K. Dick Award

RITA Award

World Fantasy Award

Writers of the Future Award

Made in the USA
Middletown, DE
11 May 2018